P9-CMW-182

ACCLAIM FOR IRMA JOUBERT

Advance Acclaim for *Child of the River*

"Irma Joubert is known to transport her readers to another world. In *Child of the River*, she masters her craft, weaving a page-turner that shapes our souls. With each scene, we learn something new, not only about the darker side of humanity, but also about the resilience of the human spirit. Filled with lessons of grace and love, forgiveness and fortitude, *Child of the River* is a story that reminds us all to hold steady through life's most fragile hours.

—JULIE CANTRELL, *NEW YORK TIMES* AND *USA TODAY*
BESTSELLING AUTHOR OF *INTO THE FREE, WHEN
MOUNTAINS MOVE,* AND *THE FEATHERED BONE*

The Girl From the Train

"Readers will adore intrepid Gretl and strong Jakób in this story of war, redemption, and love."

—*PUBLISHERS WEEKLY*

"Joubert reminds readers how love triumphed over the difficulties faced by WWII survivors as they navigated new boundaries, revised politics, and the old faith prejudices that defined post-war Europe."

—*CBA RETAILERS + RESOURCES*

"Right from the start, Joubert sets up a palpable, tension-filled atmosphere and visually striking landscape. Mixing factual events with fiction, Gretl and Jakob offer interesting viewpoints on the world around them."

—*RT BOOK REVIEWS*, 4 1/2 STARS

Child of
the River

ALSO BY IRMA JOUBERT

The Girl From the Train (Available in English)

CHILD OF THE RIVER

IRMA JOUBERT

THOMAS NELSON
Since 1798

Published in Nashville, Tennessee, by Thomas Nelson. Thomas Nelson is a registered trademark of HarperCollins Christian Publishing, Inc.

Thomas Nelson titles may be purchased in bulk for educational, business, fund-raising, or sales promotional use. For information, please e-mail SpecialMarkets@ThomasNelson.com.

Scripture quotations are from the King James Version.

Publisher's Note: This novel is a work of fiction. Names, characters, places, and incidents are either products of the author's imagination or used fictitiously. All characters are fictional, and any similarity to people living or dead is purely coincidental.

Translation: *Elsa Silke*

Library of Congress Cataloging-in-Publication Data

Names: Joubert, Irma, author. | Silke, Elsa, translator.
Title: Child of the river / Irma Joubert; [translation: Else Silke].
Other titles: P?ersomi. English
Description: Nashville, Tennessee: Thomas Nelson, 2016. | Includes glossary of terms used and definitions.
Identifiers: LCCN 2016019360 | ISBN 9780718083106 (paperback)
Subjects: LCSH: Young women—South Africa—Fiction. | Women, White—South
Africa—Fiction. | GSAFD: Bildungsromans.
Classification: LCC PT6593.2.O8314 P4713 2016 | DDC 839.3/636—dc23 LC record available at https://lccn.loc.gov/2016019360

Printed in the United States of America

16 17 18 19 20 21 RRD 7 6 5 4 3 2 1

To my son Wikus

GLOSSARY

biltong—lean meat, salted and dried in strips

bioscope—an early form of motion-picture projector, which came into use during the early twentieth century

Blacks—an ethnic label for dark-skinned people of pure African origin. One of the four main racial groups (Blacks, Coloureds, Indians, Whites) defined politically during the apartheid era. Used interchangeably with the term "native" during certain periods of South African history.

Boer—inhabitant of the Transvaal and the Free State in the time of the Anglo-Boer War; a white, Afrikaans-speaking person

Boer War/Anglo-Boer War—The Second Boer War was fought from October 11, 1899, to May 31, 1902, by the United Kingdom against the South African Republic (Transvaal Republic) and the Orange Free State. The war ended in victory for Britain and the annexation of both republics.

Brandwag, Die (The Sentinel)—a weekly Afrikaans magazine discontinued in 1965

bushveld—a subtropical woodland ecoregion of southern Africa that encompasses most of the Limpopo Province and a small part of the North West Province of South Africa

bywoner—sharecropper

Coloured—an ethnic label for people of mixed ethnic origin who possess ancestry from Europe, Asia, and various Khoisan and Bantu ethnic groups of southern Africa. Not all Coloured people share the same ethnic background. During the apartheid era, in order to keep divisions and maintain a race-focused society, the government used the term Coloured to describe one of the four main racial groups identified by law: Blacks, Whites, Coloureds, and Indians.

coolie—during the nineteenth and early twentieth centuries, a term for a locally sourced unskilled labourer, mainly from the Indian subcontinent or South China; used pejoratively in mid-century South Africa to describe inhabitants of Indian descent

dominee—reverend, clergyman; also a form of address

dung floor—a mixture of sand and soil, with cow dung added to make the mixture hard and smooth

Eyetie—a derogatory term for an Italian that came into use during World War II, when Italy joined forces with Germany

Khaki—British soldier; derisive term for any Englishman

kloof—a steep-sided wooded ravine or valley

kraal—an enclosure for cattle or other livestock surrounded by a stone wall or other fencing, roughly circular in form

longdrop—an outdoor nonflush toilet with a long shaft dug into the ground underneath to collect waste

lowveld—the name given to the area that lies at an elevation of between five hundred and two thousand feet in the South African provinces of Mpumalanga and KwaZulu-Natal

matric (matriculation)—the final year of high school and the qualification received on graduating from high school

mealie—maize

Nagmaal—Holy Communion

native—pre-apartheid term for dark-skinned people of pure African origin. The term was loosely defined in the 1903 Intercolonial Conference as "embracing the present and future status of all aboriginal natives of South Africa."

oom—uncle; also a form of address for any older man

ouma—grandmother

oupa—grandfather

phthisis—pulmonary tuberculosis or a similarly progressive systemic disease

Red Tabs—South Africans who volunteered to fight Hitler's African armies, so called because of the red strips of cloth attached to their uniforms

riempie—a thin strip of softened leather used for the backs and seats of chairs and benches, for shoelaces, and as string

rusk—a hard, dry biscuit

serenade—Young men from university in midcentury South Africa would often strum a guitar and sing below the girls' residences and serenade, usually for the benefit of their love interests, and the girls would perch in the windows and flicker their lights in appreciation. Later, this practice evolved into an annual competition between universities across South Africa.

tickey—On February 14, 1961, South Africa adopted a decimal currency, replacing the pound with the Rand. The term *tickey* is applied to both the 3d and 2½c coins.

Tommy—an ordinary soldier in the British army; any Englishman

Tukkies—informal name for the University of Pretoria or its students

Vaderland, Die (The Fatherland)—Johannesburg-based daily Afrikaans newspaper, 1936–1988

Van Riebeeck, Jan—Dutch colonial administrator and founder of Cape Town

veldskoen—a rough shoe of untanned hide

Voortrekkers—Dutch pioneers who journeyed to the Transvaal in the 1830s to escape British rule

Wits—The University of the Witwatersrand, Johannesburg, is the third-oldest South African university in continuous operation. Wits has its roots in the mining industry and was founded in 1896 as the South African School of Mines in Kimberley.

PART I

ONE

JULY 1938

ONE WINTER'S MORNING WHEN PÉRSOMI WAS ELEVEN, HER brother Gerbrand said out of the blue: "Ma, I'm going to Joburg. To find a job in the mines."

Pérsomi stood in the feeble winter sun just outside the back door, her back pressed to the wall, her bare toes burrowing into the gray sand. Gerbrand stood in the doorway. If she reached out her hand, she could touch him. But she didn't. Gerbrand didn't like being touched. She knew, because he and Piet shared a mattress, and if Piet happened to come too close, Gerbrand let fly with his fists. Piet was older, but Gerbrand was stronger.

"Heavens, Gerbrand, fetch some water and stop making up stories," said her ma. Baby was fussing and Gertjie had been coughing all night. Ma was exhausted and her patience was wearing thin.

Gerbrand turned without taking the bucket. In his hand was a bag, the kind Mr. Fourie used for the oranges. Through the mesh Pérsomi could see his flannel trousers, white shirt, and battered school shoes. She didn't see his sweater and feared he would get cold. But she didn't say anything, just followed Gerbrand on the rocky footpath down to the river.

Piet came walking up from the river. He stared at Gerbrand, challenging him with his gaze. Who would step aside first? Piet

3

was eating a tangerine, dropping the bright orange peel on the gray stones and the sparse grass as he walked.

They never went hungry in winter. There were plenty of oranges and tangerines in the groves. Not that they were allowed to pick any, but if you reached deep into the prickly inside of the tree, Mr. Fourie would never know.

Gerbrand went right up to Piet and looked him in the eye. "If you so much as lay a finger on Pérsomi while I'm away, I'll kill you when I get back," he said. Then he pushed past Piet and continued. Pérsomi gave Piet a wide berth.

Near the river, Gerbrand turned and looked at her. "If Pa wants to hit you, or touch you in any way at all, run for it. Even at night—just run. You can run fast, you'll have no problem getting away."

Pérsomi nodded. She wasn't afraid. "Ma can't run fast," she said.

Gerbrand shrugged. "I can't stay here any longer, please understand. But one day I'll come back to fetch you."

"When?" she asked.

"As soon as I've saved enough money. Go home now."

"When will you be back?"

But he didn't answer, just slung the bag over his shoulder and crossed the river, jumping from one stone to the next to keep his feet dry. She watched until his copper-colored head disappeared among the orange trees.

Pérsomi sat down on a flat rock and stretched out her legs. The sun struck bright sparks from the water at her feet. The rough body of the mountain, *her* mountain, came slowly to life in the early morning sun.

In Joburg men are swallowed by the mines, her uncle said. She hoped the mines wouldn't swallow Gerbrand.

After a while she picked two tangerines and walked up the mountain. Just below the baboon cliffs she sat down and peeled the first one. Her mouth filled with saliva as she anticipated the first sweet bite into the juicy, sun-ripe fruit.

Mr. Fourie's farm lay below her, between the toes of her mountain. To the left the mountain split open and she could see the river, the Pontenilo, winding like a thin ribbon through the trees, occasionally forming shallow pools between its sandy banks.

On the side where the sun went down lay the *brakrant*, a stony ridge, cleared and plowed years ago in an attempt to grow some kind of crop. But the soil was poor and rocky and faced west, and salty patches rose to the surface from deep below. "This soil is good for nothing, and everything burns to a crisp in the bloody afternoon sun," her pa always complained. "I work like a slave to try and make a living here."

Her ma would try to calm him. "Mr. Fourie treats us well. Where would we go if he told us to leave?"

But her ma had better watch out, or she'd get her face slapped. Or worse, she'd get the strap. Her pa took no nonsense from woman or child.

Against the brakrant was their home. It stood in the open veld with no trees to provide shelter, its two small windows staring blindly into the sun. The surrounding land was bare and stony, with not a sprig of grass in sight. To the right, the soil had been dug over, and the scorched earth lay with its insides exposed to the sun.

Pérsomi knew exactly how hard that soil was. At the end of winter the small field had to be tilled to plant mealies. Because he was the strongest, Gerbrand would stand on the plowshare, forcing it down into the earth. Pérsomi would walk ahead, tugging at Jeremiah's halter to coax him up and down the rows. Old Jeremiah was lazy and stubborn, as only a donkey can be.

Now that Gerbrand was gone, Sissie, who was fatter than anyone else, would have to stand on the plowshare.

To the right of a rocky outcrop she could see the winding road. In the distance, where the sun came up and the earth stopped, the road drowned itself in a big dam. Far beyond the shimmering expanse of water lay the town. Pérsomi had never been there.

When the sun moved in behind the mountain and an icy wind began to bite through her thin dress, she got up and went home.

Their house consisted of two rooms. In the middle of the front room stood a wooden table and four chairs. Against the back wall, next to the door, was a stove, and beside it a wagon chest. An upside-down tea chest in the corner held the Primus stove and an enamel basin for the dishes.

The children's mattresses were stacked under the table. Six of them slept in the front room: Piet and Gerbrand, Sissie and Gertjie, with Pérsomi and Hannapat on the third mattress.

"Why do I have to sleep with Gertjie? He coughs all night and he pees," Sissie would complain nearly every morning. Then their pa would slap the side of her head to shut her up.

Pérsomi's ma and pa slept on a proper bed with a mattress in the bedroom. Baby slept in a box next to the bed. A threadbare length of fabric separated the rooms.

The house was in permanent semidarkness. And the enamel basin was permanently stacked with unwashed dishes.

The one whose turn it was to do the dishes had to carry the basin to the river and wash the plates and mugs in a pool. The pots were the hardest. They had to be scrubbed with sand to get them clean.

"Sissie, go wash the dishes," her ma would say.

"Ma-a! Why must I always . . ."

When this happened, Pérsomi ran away before she could be given the job.

Pérsomi knew exactly who she was: the child of a *bywoner*, a sharecropper on Mr. Fourie's farm, the fourth and middle child of Lewies and Jemima Pieterse. She was tall and thin, with dark eyes and straight dark hair. She bore no resemblance to Sissie and Piet, who had inherited their pa's short, stout figure and small, watery eyes. Or to Gertjie and Baby, who had their ma's frizzy red hair. Hannapat was a good mixture of their parents, with her bulging tummy, thin legs, and curly ginger hair. Even Gerbrand's hair was red, like their ma's. Pérsomi looked different from the rest, presumably taking after her maternal grandma, who died a long time ago.

She attended the farm school on the boundary between Mr. Fourie's and Freddie le Roux's farms. Pérsomi, her cousin Faansie Els, and Irene Fourie were the only pupils in standard four. If there was one person in the world Pérsomi simply couldn't stand, it was Irene Fourie. She had no defense against Irene's sharp tongue.

"My ouma says Hannapat must knock on the back door when she comes begging for flour," Irene said loudly as she took her seat next to Pérsomi. "And my pa says if he catches any of you lot among the orange trees again, he'll chase you from the farm without blinking an eye. You *and* your miserable donkey."

Only three children in the school, including Irene, were *real* children. The rest of them were the children of bywoners.

❦

Sissie had the falling sickness. They all had to look out for her, Pérsomi's ma said, because you could see when Sissie was about to get a fit. Then you had to make her lie down. The most important thing to remember, their ma said, was to put something between her teeth, or she would bite right through her tongue, which would be a very bad thing.

Sometimes Sissie got the falling sickness at school. The first time it happened Pérsomi was in grade two. When Sissie began to jerk and kick like a rabid jackal, everyone ran away. Pérsomi noticed that her teachers were so flustered that they forgot to put something between Sissie's teeth. Pérsomi told them to roll Sissie onto her back and hold her down. She took Meester Lampbrecht's pointing stick and struggled to insert it between Sissie's locked jaws. All the while Sissie looked at her with froth bubbling from her lips and wild eyes, as if she didn't know Pérsomi at all.

"You're a very brave girl," Meester told Pérsomi the next day. After that she was never afraid again when Sissie got the falling sickness.

And Meester never ever raised his voice at her.

Gerbrand had been gone for more than six months when Piet also left for Joburg, and Sissie began to cry at night. But not because she missed her brother.

There was no one Pérsomi could talk to about it. "Heavens above, Pérsomi, sweep the front room and stop making up stories," her ma said, tucking her red hair behind her ears.

*cinderella slept on the floor in front of
the cold stove with the broken
oven door she took care to sleep close
to the back door so that she
could run away
at night when the wolf was on the prowl
the sister cried
and cinderella ran away
she came back at dawn the wolf was gone*

*she slept on the mattress with
hannapat as if she had never
been away*

The next day when she had finished her sums and was waiting for Meester to give the standard fives their next task, she remembered that there was no wolf in Cinderella's story.

Pérsomi made sure she slept close to the back door every night.

During the 1939 April school vacation, Gerbrand came home after an absence of nine long months. One evening after dark he appeared in the doorway. "I came with De Wet and Boelie," he said, "from Pretoria." That was where the Fourie boys were studying at the university.

Pérsomi stood against the wall next to the back door. She stood quite still. She couldn't stop looking at Gerbrand. She couldn't believe he was really there.

"You should have let us know," their pa said. "We would have kept you some supper."

She wished she could touch her brother. But she knew she couldn't.

Gerbrand lifted the lid of the cast-iron pot on the cold stove. Pérsomi knew there was just a little cold porridge inside. She wished there was some meat for Gerbrand.

"Nothing has changed, I see," said Gerbrand, annoyed. He took a spoon and scraped out the burnt remains. "What happens to the money I send every month?"

Pa takes it all, Pérsomi wanted to say. But she kept silent.

"I said you should have let us know you were coming," their pa said, frowning. "We're careful with the money, it doesn't grow on my back!"

Gerbrand turned to Pérsomi. "What did you have tonight?" he asked.

"Porridge," she answered.

"Thought so," he said. "Get off that chair, Hannapat, I want to sit. And that's my mattress, Sissie. Lift your fat behind."

"Ma-a," Sissie complained shrilly, "listen to Gerbrand! He says it's his mattress. When he left—"

"Shut up, Sissie," said their pa, pointing a finger at her. "Gerbrand sleeps on his mattress and that's the end of it. Stop moaning."

Tonight Pérsomi wouldn't have to sleep close to the door, because Gerbrand was there. Tonight she was going to put her mattress next to Gerbrand's and lie close to him all night.

❧

Friday morning Pérsomi heard Gerbrand get up at the crack of dawn. He left his mattress and blankets on the kitchen floor, stepped over her and the sleeping Hannapat, and went out through the rickety back door.

Pérsomi slipped out from under the rough blanket, taking care not to wake Hannapat, and followed him outside.

The sun wasn't up yet, but it was light enough. Gerbrand walked some way ahead of her on the footpath leading down to the river.

Maybe Gerbrand would take her along, she thought as she followed him. Maybe he would turn and say: "Pérsomi, would you like to come with me? You can look for honeycomb and I'll hunt a mountain tortoise."

Instead of going up the mountain, he crossed the Pontenilo

and followed the rutted track through the orange grove to Mr. Fourie's house, the Big House. He would fetch Mr. Fourie's sons, Boelie and De Wet, if he was going to hunt a tortoise. Pérsomi followed at a safe distance and sat down on a rocky ledge under a wild plum tree. This time of year the tree had none of its delicious sour fruit, which ripened around Christmas time.

From her seat she had a good view, but she could no longer see Gerbrand. Eventually a shiny black car stopped at the Big House. Christine, the daughter of Freddie and Anne le Roux of the neighboring farm, got out with a friend.

Oom Freddie was the nicest of all the real people, but his wife, Old Anne, was the unkindest. No bywoner's child was welcome on her property, ever. She wouldn't think twice about putting the dogs on you if you dared go there. But Christine was kind and really pretty. Sometimes she would give them some of her old clothes.

After a while the girls came back out of the Big House, along with Mr. Fourie's daughters, Klara and Irene, and they set off along the footpath in the direction of the kloof.

When she could no longer see them, Pérsomi got up. She knew every trail on her mountain, so she chose a roundabout route to follow the group. She knew where they were heading.

In a ravine higher up, the river formed a small waterfall. Under the waterfall was a pool—not very big, but so deep that you couldn't see the bottom. It was full to the brim this time of year.

She hurried around the back of the mountain and clambered down until she reached a spot where she had a good view of the pool below. She sat down, resting her back against a stone.

She could see Gerbrand playing in the water with the other young people. A large dead tortoise lay in the shade, waiting for Gerbrand to take it home.

Pérsomi leaned forward to get a better view. The girls were all in bathing suits. They were all pretty, especially the friend Christine had brought along. She had long dark hair and long legs and she wore big sunglasses.

Pérsomi heard Gerbrand laugh. The girls shrieked and splashed as they tried to get away from him and the other boys, Boelie and De Wet.

Gerbrand was playing with them as if he were a real person.

What if Gerbrand looked up and saw her? What if he laughed, the way he was laughing with the girls? What if he called out, "Pérsomi! Come and play with us!"

Klara looked up. Pérsomi sat quite still, but she was sure Klara had seen her. "Come and join us, Pérsomi!" Klara called out.

Pérsomi felt Irene's eyes on her. Slowly she slid backward. When she could no longer see the pool, she got to her feet and retraced her footsteps home.

That evening Gerbrand said, "Don't slink after me like a sly jackal. If you want to come along, come. If you want to stay, stay. You're a human being with a head on your shoulders, Pérsomi. It's not there just to keep your ears apart."

🌿

On Monday afternoon she found Gerbrand down at the river.

Gerbrand was holding a reed with a line attached to it. A cork bobbed in front of him in the wavelets churned up by the wind. She sat down quietly, a short distance away, so that she wouldn't touch him by accident.

"I ran away," she said after a while. "Many nights."

He nodded. "Good," he said, his eyes on the cork in the water. Then he turned to her. "Pérsomi, I'm going to tell you something. But you must never, ever repeat it to anyone."

"Okay." He had never told her a secret before.

"Swear."

She spat on her fingertips, crossed them, folded her hands over her heart and said, "Cross my heart and don't say."

He was quiet for so long that she thought he had changed his mind. Then he blurted out the words: "Pa isn't your real pa."

She turned her head and looked at him. His eyes remained fixed on the cork in the water.

She didn't understand, so she waited for an explanation.

He looked at her and said, "Lewies Pieterse is a pig. It's important for you to know he's not your pa."

The words stayed in her ears for a while, then slowly began to take on meaning.

That man in the house, that man who was her pa, was not her pa.

She wasn't sorry, neither was she glad. She felt kind of confused and almost . . . pleased.

"Is he *your* pa then?" she asked.

"No," he said, "my pa is dead. Piet and Sissie are Pa's children. Their ma died. You and I are Ma's children. Hannapat and Gertjie and Baby are Ma and Pa's children."

She thought for a while. "Do you and I have the same pa?" she asked.

"No," he said, "my pa is dead. He wasn't a pig."

She sat quietly, going over his words in her mind. Lewies Pieterse was not her pa. And her pa wasn't dead. "Do you know who my pa is?" she asked.

"No," he said.

After that she often wondered about her real pa. But she couldn't ask her ma, because she had made Gerbrand a cross-my-heart promise.

She never thought of Lewies Pieterse as her pa again.

Meester Lampbrecht went to the map of the world that was mounted on the wall above the standard fives' desks.

"Children, this is a date you must never forget: the first of September, 1939." Meester pointed with his stick. "Last Friday, Germany"—he placed his stick in the middle of Germany, then moved it over to Poland—"invaded Poland."

"That's stale news," Irene said. "It's been on the wireless all weekend. There's a war."

Pérsomi was shocked. War? Like when the British put the Boers' wives and children in concentration camps?

"Irene," Meester said wearily, "put up your hand if you have something to say." He tapped England with his stick. "England immediately served Germany with an ultimatum—"

"What's that?" Lettie Els asked, sniffing loudly.

"It's a message, a . . . warning, that if Germany didn't withdraw from Poland at once, England would enter into a state of war with Germany."

Pérsomi drew a deep breath. It sounded serious.

"By Sunday," said Meester, turning to face the class, "the Germans had not responded to England's ultimatum. The two great powers, England and Germany, are therefore now at war."

Irene flew out of her desk, her hand up, her fingers snapping. Before Meester could give her permission to speak, she shouted out the news: "And Smuts won the election against Hertzog and now the Union is smack in the middle of the war and my brother Boelie says—"

"Irene Fourie, sit down and be quiet!" said Meester, running his freckled hand over his sparse hair. "The Union of South Africa is at war, too, yes, but luckily it won't affect us here in the bushveld. Take out your arithmetic books."

"Aren't you going to tell us a Bible story today, Meester?" Irene asked.

That afternoon, Pérsomi tried to tell her ma about the war, but her ma just said: "Good heavens, Pérsomi, stop making up stories and fetch a bucket of water."

"Serves you right for making up lies," Sissie taunted as Pérsomi took the bucket.

It was dark by the time Lewies Pieterse came home. He nearly upset the candle on the table. Pérsomi looked up, startled.

"There's a war," he mumbled, his tongue thick with drink. "The Khakis are making war again. And it seems Smuts wants to join in, bloody Khaki-lover."

"Smuts?" her ma asked, baffled.

"The general and prime minister, you dumb cow," Lewies snapped. "Where's my food?"

Her ma scurried about in front of the stove. "But I thought Hertzog . . ." She stopped, too afraid to carry on.

"Yes, yes, you shouldn't be thinking at all. You're much too stupid."

"I'm not stupid!" her ma protested.

His open hand struck the side of Ma's head. "Shut your trap, woman."

Lewies began to dig in his pockets. "Sissie, my girlie, come see what Pa's got for you."

Pérsomi knew Lewies was giving Sissie sweets.

that night the three little pigs slept in the
cleverest piglet's house, made of stone
they lay snugly behind each other's backs

on the cleverest pig's mattress
the wolf huffed and puffed and growled and puffed
then sissie cried
then the fastest piglet ran away

Lewies Pieterse was a wolf. But she said nothing, because she wasn't sure exactly what had happened.

No, that wasn't true. Her mind knew, but the thought froze before she could turn it into words.

❧

When Pérsomi woke up one morning she knew at once that something was dreadfully wrong. She could see it plainly.

"Ma-a!" Sissie shouted shrilly. "Auntie Flo has come to visit Pérsomi!"

Pérsomi had no idea what Sissie was talking about.

"Sissie, show Pérsomi what to do. Heavens, it's hard to be a woman. And Pérsomi"—her ma gave her an earnest look—"from now on you stay away from boys and men. Completely. Understand?"

"Yes, Ma," said Pérsomi. She followed Sissie to the river.

❧

There was indeed a war. From the very first week, Pérsomi knew all about it. All the stories were in the papers. With photos.

She could hardly wait for Mondays, when she could fetch the previous week's papers from the Big House. Before tearing them into squares for the outhouse, Pérsomi sat down with them in the orange grove and arranged the papers according to their dates, so that the stories would be in the right order.

Then she began to read. A new world opened up to her.

On the tenth of April, when the leaves were turning yellow and red, Pérsomi read in the previous week's paper that Germany had invaded Denmark and Norway and issued an ultimatum, demanding that those two countries accept the protection of the German Reich without delay.

She knew an ultimatum was a message. She liked the phrase *issued an ultimatum*.

Hurriedly, she unfolded the next day's paper and read that Denmark had surrendered without striking a blow. Not a single shot had been fired. Nice words, *without striking a blow*, she thought. The reporter found the right words to describe the war. Norway had resisted, she read on, but their harbors, airports, government buildings, radio, and railway stations were now controlled by the Nazis.

She was not quite sure who the Nazis were.

She looked at the photos. One caption said: "Hitler's armored corps crawls west across the northern German plains like an army of caterpillars."

She folded the two sections containing the articles neatly and took them to school. She wanted to ask Meester about the Nazis and she wanted to show him how well the reporter wrote. When Irene saw her she muttered, "You like sucking up to Meester, don't you? Must be why you always get the highest grades in the school."

❧

Something was wrong with Sissie. Not the falling sickness, something else.

Pérsomi found her ma down at the river with the washing. She went down on her knees, grabbed the first piece of clothing within reach, and rubbed clean sand into Hannapat's blue dress. "There's a stain on the front you must try to get out," her ma said.

"Ma, what's wrong with Sissie?" she asked.

Her ma flinched. "Heavens, Pérsomi, there's nothing wrong with Sissie. Don't make up stories!"

Pérsomi rubbed and rubbed at the stain on Hannapat's blue dress. After a while she said: "Sissie is going to have a baby, I know."

Her ma's head jerked up again. "Goodness, Pérsomi, what kind of stories—"

"I'm not stupid, Ma, my head isn't just for keeping my ears apart," she said firmly. "I know what you looked like before Gertjie and Baby came."

Her ma sat back on her haunches. She closed her eyes. "Heavens, child," she said. "Have you told anybody?"

"No, Ma, I'm asking you now. Do you know Sissie is going to have a baby?"

Her ma lowered her head and pushed her wet fingers through her hair. "We mustn't say anything. If Mr. Fourie hears about it, he'll chase us from the farm. And where would we go?"

Pérsomi rubbed the collar of Hannapat's blue dress. "Why would Mr. Fourie chase us away?" Pérsomi asked.

"Heavens, child, don't talk about things you don't understand. Just keep quiet," said her ma and rubbed the shirt really hard against the stone. "Do you hear me?"

"Yes, Ma."

She lifted the blue dress out of the water. It looked reasonably clean.

"It's hard to be a woman, child." Her ma sighed and picked up one of Baby's nappies. "Hard, I'm telling you."

✿

Before the June chill began to creep across the bushveld, the Nazi caterpillars had rolled across the Netherlands and Belgium, all the way to the French border. One Monday Meester brought Pérsomi his own newspaper. British, French, and Belgian troops were trapped on the beaches at Dunkirk, she read. Hundreds of thousands of them. Stranded. Without supplies.

Two days later Meester told her that boats of all shapes and sizes had rescued a quarter of a million British soldiers in an almost superhuman operation. Some of the vessels that set out from the coast of England across the wide, stormy sea to France to rescue the stranded soldiers were nothing but fishing boats.

"It was brave, wasn't it, Meester?" Pérsomi asked.

"Yes," Meester replied. "No wonder they say Britannia rules the waves. But don't forget, Pérsomi, they're still the enemy."

"Why are they our enemy? I thought Prime Minister Smuts—"

"Is obligated to support the British, yes, thanks to the defense pact."

"But you don't like them."

"One cannot be pro-Afrikaner *and* pro-British, child. Hertzog understood this."

"Then why did he lose the election?"

Meester set his lips in a thin line and shook his head, then said, "Why certain citizens are so eager to rush to war, I'll never understand."

Two weeks later, she read in one of the papers that the first South African troops had left for Kenya in British East Africa. They were going to fight the Italians in Abyssinia.

The next day she looked for the places she had read about on the map on the classroom wall. "Are we at war now, Meester?" she asked, worried.

"Not *our* people, Pérsomi," Meester said calmly and ran his hand across his thinning hair. "Only the English and the Red Tabs."

"Who are the Red Tabs?" she asked, frowning.

"Smuts is not such a fool to force South Africans to enlist, or he'd have a civil war on his hands as well," he mumbled. "But he has called for volunteers to fight beyond our borders. Those who go wear red tabs on their shoulders, on their epaulettes," Meester explained. "But don't worry. *Our* people won't be affected."

❧

One morning during the second week of the July vacation, Lewies Pieterse said: "You women must plow the land today. I can't do everything around here. I have to check the fences all week."

Old Jeremiah lay buried in a shallow grave near the erosion gullies—lazy and stubborn to the end.

The patch of land they were expected to till was parched and rock-hard. They tried to plow with Pérsomi and Hannapat tugging at the front, while their ma tried to break the soil with the plowshare. But it was no good, so Pérsomi and her ma each struck the ground with a hoe, while Hannapat stood on the two-pronged fork, trying to force it into the unyielding soil.

If only Gerbrand were here. But he was in Joburg, working in the mines.

Sissie sat leaning against the back wall in the sun, her legs stretched in front of her, her feet wide apart. Sissie had been sitting like that for nearly a month. Her time was drawing near.

But no one mentioned it, because no one was supposed to know.

When the morning sun had moved into the afternoon, Pérsomi heard something at the front of the house. She put her hoe down and hurried around the corner, then froze.

Mr. Fourie's daughter Klara was at the front door. She was home from university for the holidays, she and Boelie and De Wet.

"Hello, Pérsomi, is your ma around the back?" asked Klara, making her way around the corner.

Slowly Pérsomi followed. She saw Klara's surprise when she noticed Sissie.

She saw her ma's fear.

Sissie didn't move.

She heard Klara say, "Good morning, Aunt Jemima."

"Yes, Klara," her ma said, not moving.

Klara looked uneasy. "It's nice to be home from varsity," she said.

"Yes," said Pérsomi's ma.

Silence. Then Klara said, "It's lovely here on the farm."

"Yes," said her ma.

A dove called loudly to its mate.

"I've brought a letter from Gerbrand," said Klara.

"Thanks," said her ma and held out her hand. She tucked the envelope into the front of her dress without opening it.

"He also sends a message," said Klara. She licked her lips, as if they were dry.

The dove kept calling.

"What does Gerbrand say?" asked Pérsomi. "Is he coming to visit?"

"Yes, but not soon," said Klara. "Gerbrand says he's doing well. He no longer works in the mines. It's good, because he didn't like working in the tunnels."

Her ma's hand flew to her mouth. "Did he lose his job?"

Klara turned to her. "He's enlisted . . . He's joined the army, the soldiers."

In her mind's eye Pérsomi saw the caterpillars in the newspaper photographs. She saw the soldiers crouch and run, rifle in hand, she saw their round steel helmets, she saw the bombs.

"He . . . what?" she blurted.

Klara turned to her ma. "He's in the army, Aunt Jemima. And . . . he's enjoying it, it's better than the mines. The money is also . . ."

Pérsomi's mouth was dry. In the army? With the . . . enemy? "Where is he now?" she asked.

"He said to tell you not to worry. And he sends his regards."

The dove was quiet now. Hannapat stood motionless beside the garden fork, her bare feet on the dry clods. Sissie sat leaning against the wall, her chapped toes stretched in front of her. Only Gertjie's hacking cough broke the silence.

"Where is he now?" her ma asked in a strangled voice.

"He asked me to tell you"—Klara drew a deep breath—"that he's boarding a ship for Kenya this coming week. With the troops."

The words struck Pérsomi like a blow to the head. They entered through her ears and reverberated through her body.

Gerbrand . . . Kenya . . .

She ran. Her feet flew across the turned clods, across the dry stubble and the loose stones and the thick sandy patches. She fled from her ma's fearful eyes and Hannapat's blank face and Sissie propped against the wall. She fled from the small house and Gertjie's coughing.

She fled from Klara's voice.

She ran until she reached her mountain. She dashed up the steep incline and across the rocky plateau. She skirted the baboon cliffs and ran past the wild fig desperately clinging to its precarious patch of soil and through the ravine where Gerbrand always found honey.

The sun blazed down on her bare arms, her chest was on fire, her parched tongue stuck to her dry palate, the sharp stones and thorns tore at the soles of her feet.

Klara's words burned and tunneled through her body, all the way to her heart.

When she reached the open cave, she sank to the ground. She couldn't go any farther.

The words turned into newspaper photos.

After a while she lay down on her back. The sun was on the decline but still blazed down on the earth and the rocks. The sky overhead was blue, and pale fleecy clouds drifted through the branches of the wild fig.

Klara's words and the photos in Meester's newspapers merged to form a single picture, with Gerbrand at its center.

Once, long ago, Gerbrand had comforted her. He stroked and stroked her hair and told her not to cry, because he had no idea how to treat a girl who was crying, he said. So she stopped, and he stroked her hair one more time. "Don't cry again, d'you hear?" he said, getting up.

"Fine," she said. "Will you stroke my hair again?"

"No," he said, "it's over now." Then he left.

Afterward, she had often felt like crying again, so that he would touch her. But she didn't, because she had promised she wouldn't.

He never touched her again.

Now he had gone to war.

When the sun was low, she went down to the fountain and drank some water. Then she picked up a flat stone and used it to dig a shallow hole in the warm sand of the cave.

She crawled into her mountain.

The picture shaped from the words and the photographs moved in front of the sun, darkened the blue sky, and hung in the branches of the tree like a broken moon.

With the darkness came the cold. There was nothing between her and the cold.

But not even the bitter cold just before sunrise could take the words away.

She saw the new day break. She heard the baboons wake up. When the sun was warm enough, sleep enfolded her like a blanket.

When she woke, she saw him sitting on a flat rock. Motionless. Mr. Fourie's eldest son. He had covered her with his jacket.

"Boelie?" she said softly.

He kept staring at the horizon. "Are you hungry?" he asked.

Hungry? She didn't know what it was not to be hungry.

"Yes," she said.

He put his hand into his pocket and produced two rusks. "Here," he said and extended his hand behind him.

The dry rusk stuck in her throat.

"Gerbrand joined the war," she said after a while.

"Yes," he said.

She looked at his back. It was broad, like Gerbrand's. His khaki shirt stretched across his shoulders.

"Meester says *our* people don't go to war," she said.

"Meester is right," he said.

She remained silent for a long while. Then she asked, "Then why did Gerbrand go, Boelie?"

He turned. For the first time he looked at her. His eyes were dark, like the water in the pools in late summer. "Weren't you cold during the night?" he asked.

The night was still inside her. "Klara says it's better than the mine tunnels?" she asked.

He turned his back on her again and looked into the distance below. "Bloody Khakis with their bloody war," he said after a while.

"Bloody Khakis," she said.

"Watch your language, you're a girl," he said, getting to his feet. "Are you coming home? Your ma is worried."

"In a while," she said.

"Okay," he said and set off down the mountainside.

He forgot to take his jacket. She curled up under it. The rough fabric was warm and comforting on her cold body.

TWO

AT THE END OF THE FIRST SCHOOL DAY AFTER THE JULY VACA-
tion, Pérsomi walked home slowly. She had wanted to tell Meester
about Gerbrand joining up, but she didn't know if she should.
The Red Tabs were often mentioned in the papers, and what *Die
Transvaler* wrote about them was especially bad. She didn't want
Meester to think badly of Gerbrand.

So she just took a good look on the wall map to see where
Kenya was.

From a distance she saw a commotion at the little house on
the ridge. Mr. Fourie's pickup was parked among the orange trees
on the riverbank. There was another pickup, covered at the back.

Then she saw Lewies Pieterse come out of the house. His
arms were flailing, he was shouting, but she was too far away to
make out the words. She froze to the spot.

Another two men came out of the house. One of them grabbed
Lewies Pieterse by the arm. Lewies looked furious. He pulled and
tugged, but the man was stronger.

Over to one side stood Mr. Fourie, smoking his pipe.

Hannapat came rushing around the corner. She raced down
the footpath to the river. Pérsomi stood motionless on the opposite bank.

"Pérsomi!" Hannapat shouted. "They've come for Pa, the police
have come to fetch Pa!"

25

The police?

"And some ladies are talking to Sissie! Ma says you must come!"

Pérsomi felt her legs get ready to run.

"Pérsomi!" Hannapat screamed. "Ma says don't run away again! You must . . ."

But she was already running.

From the mountainside she watched them: two policemen held Lewies Pieterse and threw him into the back of the pickup. A strange lady and Mr. Fourie walked on either side of a sobbing Sissie, helping her across the stones. Hannapat and Gertjie stood on the bank, watching. She could make out her ma's forlorn figure at the side of the house, Baby on her hip.

They drove off, taking Lewies Pieterse and Sissie along. Pérsomi hoped they'd remember to give Sissie her medicine.

❦

The next day when she came home from school, the ladies were back. Sissie wasn't with them. They were talking to her ma.

Her ma looked dazed and sat staring into the distance. "Mr. Fourie is going to chase us away," she mumbled. "If Lewies goes to jail, Mr. Fourie will chase us away."

One of the ladies turned to her. "You're Pérsomi, aren't you?"

"Yes?"

The lady gave her a friendly smile. "I'm Mrs. Marie Retief from the Department of Social Welfare. I've come to give you a hand. Mrs. Fourie tells me you're a smart girl?"

Pérsomi didn't know how to respond.

"Walk with me, and we'll talk," the lady said.

They walked on the footpath down to the river and sat down on the bank. "Sit here beside me," the lady said.

She spoke about all kinds of things, like the sun on the water and the oranges, so colorful in the trees, and the hadeda's shrill call. After a while Pérsomi began to relax.

Then the lady said, "Pérsomi, do you know why we're here?"

"Not really, Aunt Marie," Pérsomi admitted.

"You know what happened to Sissie?" the lady asked.

Pérsomi hesitated. "Yes, she's going to have a baby."

"And do you know how that happened?"

"No." She was too scared to say what she was thinking.

The lady was silent for a long time, then she said, "You all sleep together in the front room, don't you?"

"Yes," Pérsomi said cautiously.

"Tell me what happened at night," the lady said.

Pérsomi sat quite still. Could she tell? And what should she tell? "Only some nights," she said.

"What happened some nights?"

Pérsomi licked her lips. "Sissie cried," she said.

"Why did Sissie cry?"

"I think she had bad dreams," she said. She closed her eyes. "Or maybe he hurt her."

"Your father?"

Pérsomi said nothing.

"Pérsomi, look at me. Did your father ever hurt you?"

"I can run fast," said Pérsomi.

The lady nodded. "That's good," she said. She thought for a while, then asked, "Pérsomi, do you know how your father hurt Sissie?"

Pérsomi bit her lower lip. She didn't know how to say it. After a while she said, "Was he . . . making out with her?"

The lady nodded. "Tell me, does Sissie have a boyfriend?"

"No, Aunt Marie," Pérsomi answered.

"Thanks, sweetheart. You're a very smart girl." The lady got up and dusted off her skirt. "Come, that's enough for today. But we'll talk again. And if there's anything you want to tell me, anything you think isn't right, you must go ahead and tell me, understand?"

"Okay," said Pérsomi.

When they were walking back, the lady said, "You're in standard six now, aren't you?"

"Yes," said Pérsomi.

"What will you be doing next year?" the lady asked.

"Looking for work. In Joburg."

"Wouldn't you like to go to high school instead? Finish Form III, at least?"

"Yes," said Pérsomi. "But we don't have any money."

"Social Welfare gives grants to needy children who do well at school," said the lady. "If you want me to, I'll see if I can arrange something. And if your grades are good enough."

"My grades are good. And I want to," said Pérsomi. "But my ma and pa want me to find a job."

"I'll talk to them," the lady said.

❧

The next day Aunt Marie Retief was back, and two days later she was there again. She brought sweaters for them all and medicine for Gertjie's cough.

"Sissie is fine," she said. "She's at a special home, where she'll stay until her baby is born. Then she can come back."

"Sissie should have stayed here," said Pérsomi's ma.

"And the baby?" asked Hannapat.

"We'll talk about the baby later," the lady said. "There's going to be a court case, Jemima. You and Sissie will have to give evidence, and possibly Pérsomi as well."

"Court?" Pérsomi's ma asked, alarmed.

"Yes," Aunt Marie said. "Jemima, what do you feed Gertjie and Baby? Besides porridge, of course?"

"Give . . . evidence?" asked her ma.

Aunt Marie put her hand on her ma's arm. "It's nothing to be worried about, Jemima," she said calmly. "But Lewies Pieterse will have to stand trial and you—"

"He's going to kill us," Ma said, shaking her head wildly.

"The law will protect you," said Aunt Marie.

But her ma kept shaking her head. "The law is in town, Mrs. Retief. Lewies Pieterse is here, in this house."

Long after Aunt Marie had left, when darkness was closing in, her ma was still sitting at the kitchen table. "Lewies Pieterse is going to kill us," she kept saying.

❧

At the end of the week, Lewies Pieterse was back. That same afternoon, Ma's sister, Sis Els, and Sis's husband, Attie Els, walked up the hill to visit. They lived with their daughter Faansie in the bywoner house on Freddie le Roux's farm. They wanted to hear the stories.

"I knew there was going to be trouble," Auntie Sis gasped. "I had a vision last Sunday."

Jemima nodded. Auntie Sis had premonitions, and they came from another world, visions that called for great respect.

"You were right, Sis," Lewies Pieterse said somberly.

Auntie Sis nodded and lowered her heavy bulk onto the tea chest. "My visions are always right," she said.

"Well, see," Lewies began, "they took me to town in the van, to the police station. In the back, never you mind, like a dog. Yanked me out when we got to town. Man, I'm telling you, my blood was boiling."

"And then?" Oom Attie leaned forward in his chair.

"Pushed me and shoved me, I'm telling you, all the way inside. I thought: Watch out, you buggers, watch I don't lay into you with my fists. But I kept calm, because I didn't want to cause trouble, you know it's not like me. But when a snot-nosed constable gave me lip, I let him have it."

Pérsomi held her breath.

"Good for you!" said Oom Attie, punching the palm of his left hand with his right fist. "They think they can bugger us around just because we're poor!"

"And Sissie?" asked Auntie Sis. "I saw her, too, poor girl, with a—"

"Man, I punched him on the chin, lights out," Lewies said. "Later I heard they took him to hospital, couldn't bring him round at all."

"You don't say!" said Oom Attie, impressed. "What happened next?"

"What about Sissie?" asked Pérsomi's ma.

"The other policemen stepped away"—Lewies was demonstrating with hands and body—"when they saw I wasn't going to be messed with. When the little sergeant gave me a piece of paper to sign, I said, 'What do you mean, sign? Lewies Pieterse doesn't sign anything without his lawyer.' The weak-kneed little chap stepped back when he realized I know my rights."

"Did you punch the little sergeant as well?" asked Oom Attie.

"No, by then the whole lot of them were like putty in my hands," said Lewies, spreading his fingers. His hands were big and hard. "When I said, 'Where's the coffee?' they brought it chop-chop. I'd say, 'I want meat with my samp,' and there would be meat. I've never seen so much meat. No, I had them eating from my hand. They won't bother Lewies Pieterse again, that's no maybe!"

"What did you see, Sis?" Pérsomi's ma kept saying.

Auntie Sis asked, "Where's Sissie now?"

Lewies said, "If I get hold of that boyfriend of hers, I'll choke his last breath out of him. I'll cut off his—"

"Did you bring us a little something from town?" asked Oom Attie.

Lewies held up a bottle of amber liquid.

Pérsomi walked out through the back door. This time she remembered to take a blanket.

At the crack of dawn the next morning Pérsomi watched Mr. Fourie stride to the little house on the riverbank. He was wasting his time. Lewies Pieterse was still sleeping it off.

But within minutes both men appeared from the house. Mr. Fourie led the way, walking fast. Behind him came Lewies, rushing. He didn't even have his *veldskoens* on his feet.

On the other side of the Pontenilo Mr. Fourie turned and grabbed Lewies by the throat. Pérsomi was startled. What if Lewies punched Mr. Fourie like he punched the policeman? Then they would definitely be chased off the farm.

But Lewies didn't do anything. Mr. Fourie shook him, then slapped him soundly around the ears, swung his finger under Lewies's nose and shoved him so that Lewies fell on his backside. Lewies threw his hands in front of his face and shook his head and began to cry.

Then Mr. Fourie turned and strode back to the Big House.

Maybe they could tell Mr. Fourie if Lewies wanted to kill them, Pérsomi thought.

She didn't go home before the sun went down behind the mountain.

Early in September the police came again for Lewies Pieterse. They came in the morning, when Pérsomi and Hannapat were at school.

When they returned, he was gone. And Sissie was back, her eyes swollen from crying.

"Where's your baby?" Hannapat asked.

Sissie burst into tears. "They took my baby!" she moaned.

"How can they take your baby?" Hannapat demanded. "It's *your* baby, they can't just take him!"

Sissie cried harder. "They told me to write my name on a piece of paper, then they took my baby!"

"Where's Ma?" Pérsomi asked. "And Gertjie and Baby?"

Sissie cried so much she could hardly get a word out. She sounded just like the female baboon who had howled about her dead baby for days, carrying him around until he looked like a piece of dry biltong.

"They took Gertjie and Baby, too," she managed to say at last. "That Aunt Marie smiles, but you can't trust her."

Pérsomi grew afraid. The friendly lady who had said she would try to arrange for Pérsomi to go to high school next year had taken Gertjie and Baby? And was her ma gone too?

"Where's Ma?" she asked again.

"With Oom Freddie. He's talking to Ma," Sissie sobbed. "Ma and I are just the same. They took our children!" And she began to wail again.

Oom Freddie was an important man, a member of the Provincial Council, a leader in the district. And he was always very friendly. If anyone could help, it was Oom Freddie. Provided Old Anne didn't have her way.

Pérsomi went out and gathered some wood. She blew on the fire and fetched water from the river. She stirred maize flour into the water and put the heavy lid on the pot.

"Oom Freddie will help," said her ma when she returned at

dusk. "He gave us this chicken to eat, and money too. Freddie le Roux is a good man."

The next morning, while Pérsomi was doing sums and the standard threes were reading to Meester, the students heard a car stop outside.

"The welfare woman is here, Meester," Irene said, stretching her neck to peer out of the window. "I think she wants to speak to Pérsomi because her pa is in jail."

Humiliation washed over Pérsomi like a sudden shower, soaking her, chilling her to the bone.

Meester sent Pérsomi to find out what was happening.

Slowly she walked over to Aunt Marie's car.

They sat down in the thin shade of a thorn tree.

Aunt Marie talked and talked, and the more she talked the better Pérsomi understood. She didn't want to understand, but her mind did.

Gertjie was very weak. If they left him with Ma, he would die. He had TB.

And Baby—Aunt Marie called her Johanna, which was Baby's real name—wasn't getting the right food, so she was bound to get sick as well. Once the two little ones were better and the situation at home improved, Aunt Marie would bring them back.

"Sissie can't stop crying," Pérsomi said.

Aunt Marie explained about Sissie. Everything. And that Sissie's baby wasn't quite right. Then Pérsomi understood that Aunt Marie and the Department of Social Welfare had also made the right decision about Sissie.

"There's going to be a hearing about your father, Pérsomi," said Aunt Marie. "I think you'll be our strongest witness, because you're a clever girl. It all depends on whether you think you're up to it."

"Yes," said Pérsomi. "I'll do it."

"Your father will be in the dock. He's going to be looking at you all the time you're in there. He's going to hear everything you say," Aunt Marie warned her.

"I'll do it."

"And the defense attorney, the man defending your father, is going to ask you a lot of questions. Hard questions, to try and prove you're lying."

"He won't be able to, because I'll speak the truth." Then she raised her eyes and looked straight at Aunt Marie. "I can definitely do it."

At the car, Aunt Marie said, "I have some good news. The department approved my application. You can go to high school next year. They'll pay your full board and your books as well."

For the first time in many, many weeks, maybe for the first time in months, happiness filled Pérsomi's heart, warming her entire body, making her ears ring. "Thank you very, very much, Aunt Marie. I promise to study really hard."

When the welfare lady drove away, Pérsomi kept waving long after the dust cloud had disappeared around the corner.

🌿

That afternoon after school Pérsomi tried to explain to her ma about Gertjie and Baby. "Gertjie is sick, Ma, he must get better first, he's got TB," she explained.

"Yes, I know," said her ma, staring into space.

"And Baby must just get strong and get the right food, then she'll be coming home too."

"Yes," said her ma. "Next year when you're working in Joburg we'll be able to afford good food."

Pérsomi felt a chill run through her. "Aunt Marie said I can go to high school next year, Ma. Welfare will pay for me, for my books as well."

"No," said her ma and for the first time in a long while she seemed determined. "You're going to get a job in Joburg next year, or I won't be able to buy good food for Gertjie and Baby. That's what your pa says too."

A huge dark cloud moved in front of the sun. But not the kind that brings rain.

❧

When Pérsomi fetched the newspapers at the Big House in the middle of November, there was mail: a brown envelope without postage, just a rubber stamp that read: Official. Censored.

The letter was addressed to her ma.

Gerbrand's handwriting was on the envelope.

Pérsomi ran home like the wind. She raced through the orange trees, stopped for a split second to leap across the pool, then sprinted up the hill to the house.

"Ma! A letter from Gerbrand!" she gasped, throwing the letter on the kitchen table.

"Oh, heavens above, Pérsomi!" her ma said, startled. "Open it, child, read it! Heavens, see how I'm trembling!"

Carefully Pérsomi opened the letter. She took out a pound note and handed it to her ma.

"Thank you, thank you, God!" said her ma, tucking the note into her bosom.

Pérsomi unfolded the letter and began to read:

30 OCTOBER 1940

Dear Ma and Pérsomi,

I am well. We haven't gone to battle yet and the food is good. I've made good friends here. My best friend is a guy we call Jackal.

We traveled by ship from Durban to Mombasa in Kenya. Our officer reads all our letters before we can mail them so I can't tell you everything. It was a big ship but it was very crowded. We slept in hammocks in the hold and we couldn't use any lights and it was very stuffy and we got a bit seasick. So most of us slept on deck. The sea was wild and we threw up. But we're in Kenya now.

I am in the Royal Natal Carbineers, C Company, the best Company.

We eat a lot of venison because we shoot buck with our machine guns. We fry the liver when we get a chance. The cooks make stews from dried vegetables like cabbage and carrots and potatoes. The potatoes are okay because they get mashed but the other vegetables are awful. For breakfast we get maize porridge. Worst of all are the powdered eggs. No one wants to be a cook in the army.

We drive around in three-ton trucks. Each section has a truck. A few times we heard that the Italians are close but so far I haven't seen one. We call them Eyeties.

We have a lot of fighter planes. They are the Junkers JU 86, the Hurricane, the Hartbees, the Fury and the Fairey Battle light bomber. When I come home, I'll bring photos. Jackal has a camera.

Our commander is Brigadier Dan Pienaar and I have a lot of respect for him.

The English ladies in Cape Town send us parcels with hand-knitted socks that shrink when you wash them.

I think I'm going to stay on in the army. I would like to fly a fighter plane.

Write to me Pérsomi. Write down what Ma says. And read my letter to Ma.

Gerbrand

Carefully Pérsomi folded the letter. "Read it again," her ma said. "I want to hear it again."

She unfolded the letter again. "Gerbrand didn't give his address," she said, dismayed. "How can I write to him if he doesn't give his address?"

"Ask Klara when she comes again, she'll know," said her ma.

Pérsomi thought of something else. "Ma, if Lewies Pieterse isn't here anymore—"

"Heavens, Pérsomi, since when do you call your pa by his name?" her ma scolded.

"Lewies Pieterse is not my pa and you know it."

Her ma's head snapped up, her eyes wide. "Child, what story are you making up now?"

It was too late now, the words had been spoken.

"If Lewies is no longer here to take Gerbrand's money, you can use it all to buy healthy food," Pérsomi continued. "It will be enough. I won't have to go and work next year."

"Heavens, Pérsomi, stop making up stories. You're going to work next year and that's the end of it," said her ma. "Now read the letter again."

🌿

Aunt Marie came to speak to all three of them about the hearing. She explained what to expect: the oath they would have to take, the magistrate sitting at the front on a kind of stage, the prosecutor who would try to prove Lewies Pieterse was guilty, and the defense who would be on his side. She made a sketch of where all of them would be sitting, and where Lewies would be.

"You needn't be afraid, we'll be there to protect you," she kept reassuring them.

But that night, when Aunt Marie had left and only the four

of them remained, her ma said, "Lewies Pieterse is going to kill us. They can lock him up now, but one day he'll be out. And then we'll all be dead."

Two days before the hearing, Pérsomi went to fetch the papers at the Big House and found Boelie and De Wet in their kitchen, home for the December vacation.

"Hello, Pérsomi," De Wet said through the open kitchen door. "Come in, I want to talk to you."

Hesitantly she stepped into the Big House.

"Hello, Pérsomi," said Boelie. He looked strange. His hair was longer than usual and there was a dark shadow on his chin and jaw.

"Hello," she said from the doorway.

"Sit down," said De Wet. He got up and went to the stove. "Would you like some coffee?"

She didn't know what to say. Her legs were tingling with the desire to run.

"Sit," said Boelie, pointing at a chair.

She sat. De Wet put a cup of coffee in front of her.

She took a cautious sip. It was hot, but it was the most delicious coffee she had ever tasted.

"Rusk?" De Wet asked and pushed a tin full of the dry cookies across the table.

She shook her head. She was afraid it would stick in her throat.

"My mom tells me you're a witness, Pérsomi," De Wet said in a friendly voice.

She nodded.

"I just want to make sure you know what to do," he said. "I'm a law student, see? One day I'll be a lawyer. So I thought I could help you."

"Oh," she said. She didn't know if she should tell him Aunt Marie had already spoken to them. He looked so eager to help. So she listened to everything again: the oath, the magistrate, the prosecutor, defense, accused, everything.

"And I'll be going with you," he said. "I'll be there, in the courtroom, if you need help."

"Thanks," she said.

"You're thirteen, Pérsomi, is that right?"

"Yes."

"You can give evidence in camera, if you wish. It means it'll be only you, the magistrate, the prosecutor, and the defense attorney. No one will look at you, especially not your father."

Aunt Marie had explained it to her. "No," she said, "I want to speak where everyone can hear, so that they'll know Lewies Pieterse is a pig. Gerbrand thinks so too . . . that he's a pig."

De Wet nodded. "Very well," he said. "I just hope you realize what you're letting yourself in for."

"She knows," Boelie said from his chair. "I told you: this one knows what she's doing."

Pérsomi turned to Boelie. "Are you coming, too, Boelie?"

He thought for a moment. "Yes," he said, "yes, I think I'll go to court after all."

On Sunday Auntie Sis came round to help pick out their clothes. They had to look decent in court the next day. They might be dirt poor, but it was no reason not to be clean, she said.

Pérsomi had three dresses. All three had once belonged to

Sissie, so they were a bit too short and much too wide. "You're so tall," Auntie Sis said almost crossly.

"Wear Ma's belt or people will think you're pregnant," said Hannapat.

"Heavens above, Hannapat," her ma said, startled, "where do you hear such talk?"

"You're so thin," said Sissie. "People will think you don't get food."

"A good thing you're going, too," Hannapat laughed, "so people can see we've got food."

Pérsomi went down to the river with her green dress. She washed it as clean as she was able and flattened it on the rocks. While the hot bushveld sun baked the dress dry, she washed her hair in the pool. Then she washed herself all over. She put her clothes back on and combed her long hair with her fingers.

She wished she had a ribbon to tie it with. But she didn't. All she had was some underwear elastic to tie her braids with.

When her dress was dry, she walked home slowly.

🌿

Monday morning, Boelie and De Wet drove the family to town. The veld flew past the car, much faster than any man or horse could run. It was far, much farther than she had imagined.

Pérsomi clung to the door handle, but after a while she began to relax.

In town the road surface changed from gravel to tar. She had heard about tarred roads at school. They drove along the smooth road with houses on either side. She saw a church with a spire reaching into the sky.

"This is the high school, Pérsomi," De Wet said.

Pérsomi looked through the window. The school was a big

building with hundreds of windows. She had never imagined a school could be so large.

It was the school Gerbrand had gone to as well.

"I take it you'll be coming here next year?" De Wet said.

"She's going to work. In Joburg," her ma said brusquely.

"Oh." He sounded surprised.

Past the school and the church there were stores, all in the same street. They drove past Smit's Garage, where there was a picture of a winged horse on a signpost that said Pegasus Petrol. Next door was Cohen Tailor and on the other side of the street, Thom's Liquor Store. She tried to take in everything: the Grand Hotel, the Bosveld Butchery, Johnny's Café & Bakery, the red-and-white striped pole with the barber sign swinging in the wind, Dr. Louw: Surgery, and the Bosveld Pharmacy next door—but it was too much. She could easily get lost in this town.

"Shall I take you to the General Dealer for the shoes?" Boelie asked her ma.

"Shoes?" Pérsomi asked, looking down at her bare feet.

"No," Ma said to Boelie, "to Ismail's. The General Dealer is too expensive."

"Where did you get money for shoes?" Pérsomi asked.

"Heavens, Pérsomi. Don't embarrass me. You need shoes for court."

Boelie and De Wet seemed not to hear. They drove past a row of buildings, each with a veranda. Boelie stopped the car. "Here you are. I'll pick you up in a while," he said, and waited for them to get out. "Don't be long, we have to be in court at nine."

Pérsomi followed her ma and Sissie inside. After a while her eyes got used to the dark.

The store smelled of tobacco and maize flour and other things she didn't recognize. There was a high, wide counter, and the shelves behind it were filled with tins and bottles. Large bags of maize flour and sugar stood on the floor. A man with a black beard and a strange hat was scooping sugar from one of the bags and pouring it into a brown paper cone.

To the left of the door was the haberdashery department. She saw fabric and lace and cotton, as well as blankets, coats, dresses, hats, and shoes. Pérsomi stood transfixed. She had never seen such pretty dresses. She wanted to keep looking, but her ma and Sissie were already heading for the shoes.

"Ma, look!" said Sissie.

"Can I help?" a dark-skinned young boy asked politely.

"I'm looking for Mr. Ismail," said her ma.

"He's still at home. I'll send someone to call him," said the boy. He gestured to a younger boy, who disappeared through the back door.

Sissie and her ma lingered beside a showcase full of shiny things. "Ma, look at the necklaces!" said Sissie.

Pérsomi wandered off to where the shoe boxes were stacked almost to the ceiling. The boy followed her.

"We live behind the store," he said. "My grandpa will be here shortly. What have you come to buy?"

"Shoes," said Pérsomi.

"Okay," said the boy. "What size?"

"I . . . don't know," said Pérsomi.

The boy looked at her, taking in her bare feet and the faded green dress that was too short and too wide. He nodded.

She said, "My brother is in the army. He sends us money."

The boy looked up, surprised. "My brother is in the army too," he said. "He's in Kenya. They're on their way to Abyssinia."

"So is my brother! He wrote a letter to tell us. I didn't know coolies fight in the war."

"Don't call us coolies, it's insulting," the boy said earnestly.

"Oh, I thought you were coolies," said Pérsomi. "You look like coolies."

"Call us Indians," said the boy. "We're Indians, we're originally from India."

"Okay," said Pérsomi, "I'll remember."

"Are you looking for school shoes? Or what?" the boy asked. "Your feet are long and narrow, I think you'll take a number five."

"I'm looking for . . . ordinary shoes," Pérsomi said uncertainly.

"Wait, I'll take them down, then you can look. My brother is a stretcher bearer in the medical corps," the boy said.

"Gerbrand is in the Royal Natal Carbineers. Gosh, those are pretty shoes!"

The next moment an old man spoke behind her. "I'll take it from here, Yusuf," he said. "No, no, those aren't the right ones. You can choose from these." He took three pairs of shoes from a shelf and held them up to Pérsomi.

"Oh," she said.

"Here, try these."

She pushed her foot into the shoe. It was pretty but it felt strange and hard. "Did you bring socks?" the old man asked.

"No," said Pérsomi.

"Well, you should wear socks, or you'll get blisters," said the man.

"Okay," said Pérsomi.

The man took the shoes and wrapped them in a piece of newspaper. "There you are," he said.

"Can we buy these two necklaces as well?" her ma asked.

"I'm sorry, Mrs. Pieterse, the money isn't enough." He shook his head regretfully and clicked with his tongue. But then he smiled broadly and said, "But for you, Mrs. Pieterse, for you, it's a present today." He put the two necklaces in her ma's hand.

When Boelie stopped in front of the store, they were waiting: Pérsomi with her hard new shoes on her bare feet, her ma and Sissie each with a shiny new necklace around their necks.

"Mr. Ismail is a good man, that's for sure," her ma said.

"Watch out, Aunt Jemima," said Boelie from the front seat. "He's a sly old fox."

The magistrate's court was a big gray building with thick pillars at the front. Two flags hung limply from scruffy flagpoles: the Union Jack and the Union flag.

Pérsomi felt her stomach contract. The nice new shoes felt strange on her feet.

Aunt Marie was waiting on the steps. "All set?" she asked.

"Heavens above, Mrs. Retief, I'm all in," her ma said. "My nerves are shot."

Sissie burst into tears.

"Don't worry, you'll be fine," said Aunt Marie. "Sissie, stop crying now, or you won't be able to speak."

Sissie gave a long, hard sniff.

"How about you, Pérsomi?" asked Aunt Marie.

Pérsomi looked up, straight into Boelie's dark eyes. He gave her an almost imperceptible nod. Then she looked at Aunt Marie. "I'm ready, thank you," she said.

"We're going in. We'll meet you here afterward," said Boelie.

Pérsomi, her ma, and Sissie were not allowed to go inside, because they were witnesses. They had to wait on a bench in the passage.

They sat down. People walked by, some quickly, some slowly. They stared straight ahead.

They waited on the bench in the passage outside the courtroom for a very long time. They didn't speak, just waited.

Someone brought them coffee and bread. Then they waited some more.

Pérsomi's nice new shoes began to pinch her feet.

Sissie was called in first. When the policeman came to fetch her, she looked petrified, but at least she wasn't crying.

Her ma crumpled and wrung her gray handkerchief.

After a while they came to fetch her ma as well, but Sissie didn't come back.

It was a long passage with a lot of doors and lights high up on the ceiling. The bench got harder the longer she waited.

Her feet felt warm in the shoes. They were sweating.

At last they came for her. She followed the policeman. Her feet hurt so badly she could barely walk.

She put her hand on the Bible and swore to tell the truth, as Aunt Marie and De Wet had instructed her. Then she was told to sit on a small platform just below the magistrate.

She looked at the prosecutor, like Aunt Marie had told her to. He was a young man with green eyes, almost like De Wet's.

"Pérsomi," said the prosecutor in a friendly voice, "we're here to find out what happened in your home at night. You know what this is about, don't you?"

"Yes," said Pérsomi, "it's about Sissie having a baby."

At a long table behind the prosecutor sat a man with a thin nose, the defense attorney. Lewies sat beside him, but she avoided his eyes.

"Can you describe to us what your home looks like?" the prosecutor asked.

"There are two rooms. My parents sleep in one room, we sleep in the other," she said.

She took a peek at the courtroom. It didn't scare her. Behind the man with the thin nose was a railing, and behind it were rows of people who had come to listen. She didn't look directly at them, but she saw them.

"So you and Sissie sleep in the same room?"

"Yes, that's right."

She spotted Aunt Marie among the people. Aunt Marie smiled and nodded.

"Pérsomi, did your father sometimes come into your room? When your mother was asleep?"

Pérsomi drew a slow breath. On one side of the courtroom, near the aisle, sat De Wet and Boelie. De Wet was writing on a piece of paper. Boelie nodded when she looked at him.

"Yes, some nights, and always when he drank brandy."

"What happened then?"

Pérsomi licked her dry lips. Wolf stories wouldn't help her now. "He lay down on Sissie's mattress, with Sissie."

The prosecutor spoke softly now. "And then, Pérsomi? I know this is hard, but you must tell me everything."

"Then . . . Sissie cried."

"Why did Sissie cry?"

"I think . . . he hurt her. He . . ." She hesitated a moment, then she said very softly, "He made out with her."

The prosecutor nodded and smiled, and she felt better. "Pérsomi, did Sissie have a special friend? A boyfriend?" he asked.

"No," Pérsomi answered.

"Maybe she had one you didn't know about?"

"No," Pérsomi answered firmly. "No one ever came to visit us, except Oom Attie and his family, and Sissie never went anywhere. Except to Oom Attie's house."

"And who is Oom Attie?"

"My uncle. My ma's sister's husband," Pérsomi explained.

"Thank you," said the prosecutor and smiled again. He turned to the magistrate. "No further questions, Your Honor."

Pérsomi looked up at where Aunt Marie was sitting. She nodded. Everything had gone well. Pérsomi looked to Boelie but he was reading what De Wet was writing.

The man with the thin nose got up and gave her a friendly smile. "Your name is Pérsomi, is that right? May I call you Pérsomi?"

"Yes," Pérsomi said cautiously. He was the man who was going to ask her trick questions, Aunt Marie had said.

"How old are you, Pérsomi?"

"Thirteen."

"And you and your sister sleep in the same room?"

"Yes," Pérsomi answered, "we all sleep in the same room, except my parents."

"Your mother sleeps in the room next to yours?"

"Yes."

"Hmm." The man with the thin nose looked down at his papers, then he looked up again. "You said the accused, your father, came to Sissie at night?"

"Yes."

"Could you see, or just hear?"

"I heard," Pérsomi said cautiously. "It was dark. You can't see in the dark."

Pérsomi heard a rustle from the gallery as if people were whispering.

"Yes, quite right," the man said. "And did you hear what was happening in the bed next to yours? Did you hear your sister cry?"

Pérsomi's eyes narrowed. "That's what I said, yes. Only, we sleep on mattresses, not in beds."

"Very well. And you said it happened often during the past"—he looked at his notes—"the past year and a half? At least two or three times a month?"

Pérsomi felt tension gnaw at her. Inside the hard shoes her feet were tingling. She had a feeling that the thin-nosed man was setting a trap for her. But she knew how to look out for snares on a goat trail. So she looked at the magistrate and said clearly, "That's what I said, Your Honor. That's what happened."

The magistrate wore thick glasses with black frames. He nodded solemnly.

"I see," said the defense attorney. He tapped on his notes with his pencil. "Then how is it that your mother testified she never heard anything?"

Pérsomi hesitated a moment. She knew what her ma and Sissie had discussed when Aunt Marie wasn't present. But she couldn't get her ma into trouble, so she said: "My ma was sleeping in the other room."

"But there's only a thin curtain between the two rooms? Surely one can hear what is happening in the room next door?"

How could he know this? He'd never been in their home. "My ma didn't even wake up when Gertjie was coughing," she said. "And sometimes he coughed all night."

"Do you mean to tell me all these things happened without your mother ever waking up?" She could see the man with his clever ways didn't believe her at all.

She lifted her chin and looked him in the eye. At that moment she didn't care—she wouldn't allow him to make out that she was stupid. "That's what I said, yes," she said loudly and clearly. "That's what happened," she said, turning to face the magistrate. "And it's the truth, Your Honor."

"I hear what you're saying," the man with the black-rimmed glasses assured her. His eyes were serious.

The man with the thin nose walked back to his table and looked at his papers for a long time. Pérsomi felt in her legs the impulse to run. If only she could get her feet out of the shoes.

But then he looked up. He stared at her for a long time. She stared back at him.

He removed his thin spectacles. Now he looked a lot friendlier. "Pérsomi, Lewies Pieterse isn't your biological father, is he?" he asked quietly.

Pérsomi was startled. She looked past him at Boelie. She could see by the surprise in Boelie's eyes that he hadn't known.

Aunt Marie's hand had flown to her mouth. She hadn't known either.

No one had told Pérsomi she was going to be asked that question. And she had made a cross-my-heart promise to Gerbrand.

"I asked whether Lewies Pieterse is your biological father, Pérsomi."

She could just say yes, it would be easy. But she didn't want to say yes, because she didn't want Lewies Pieterse as her pa.

And the oath on the Bible was probably stronger than the cross-my-heart promise.

She raised her head and said, "Lewies Pieterse isn't my father."

She heard a ripple go through the courtroom. "Silence in court!" the magistrate said sternly.

Thin Nose looked satisfied and nodded. She kept looking straight at him.

"And . . . do the two of you have a good relationship?" he asked. "Do you get on well with him?"

"No," said Pérsomi, "I don't."

"Why not?"

Pérsomi took a deep breath. "Because he wastes our money when we have it." She turned to the magistrate again. "My brother Gerbrand is in the army, he sends us money every month. But if Lewies Pieterse gets hold of the envelope first, he buys brandy, Your Honor, and gets drunk and then we don't have money for food, Your Honor."

"I see," said the magistrate.

"What else does he do that you don't like?" asked Thin Nose.

"He beats us, with his hands or the strap, my ma as well." She turned to the magistrate again. "And he doesn't help us in the fields when we have to plant mealies or pumpkins, even though he's strong enough to push the plow into the soil, Your Honor."

The magistrate nodded.

"I understand," said the attorney, looking down his nose. "I also understand that you do well at school. Your teacher tells me that you've been awarded a grant to go to high school next year?"

"Yes," said Pérsomi. What did that have to do with anything?

"But Lewies Pieterse has arranged for you to go and work in Johannesburg. I understand your brother Piet has already got you a job?"

"At a laundry, yes," Pérsomi said uneasily.

"So," said Thin Nose, fumbling with his papers, "it would suit you if your stepfather were found guilty? If he were removed from your lives for a few years? Isn't that right, Pérsomi?"

She realized where the bloody crook's questions had been leading. She jumped to her feet at the same time the prosecutor did.

"Objection, Your Honor. The defense—"

"I can speak for myself," she announced. "I have a head that's not just for keeping my ears apart. I can see what he's doing." She turned to Thin Nose and looked at him. "Yes, it would be good if Lewies Pieterse was found guilty, not because I want him out of the house"—she turned to the magistrate—"but because he *is* guilty, and that's all there's to it, Your Honor."

"I see," said the magistrate.

"I have one more thing to say, Your Honor."

"All right," said the magistrate, "but first you must sit down and remain seated."

"Okay, Your Honor," said Pérsomi and sank back onto her seat. Her feet were burning in the hard shoes.

She faced the magistrate and spoke directly to him. He was the one who had to know the truth. "My ma and Sissie decided beforehand that they would say Sissie has a boyfriend, because they're afraid Mr. Fourie will chase us away if Lewies goes to jail, and then we won't have a home. But ask who that boyfriend is? They'll say he's a married man, they can't tell you his name. But there's no such person, Your Honor. And also, says my ma, if we say anything against Lewies Pieterse"—for the first time she looked at the man in the dock—"he'll kill us the day he gets out." She drew a deep breath and turned her gaze back to the magistrate. "And, Your Honor, I'm not a liar like that man with the thin nose makes me out to be. Everything I've said is the truth."

❦

Boelie was waiting for her in the hall. "Can she come with me?" he asked the policewoman who escorted Pérsomi out.

"Yes, she's finished," the woman said.

"I'll fetch the others later," said Boelie. "Please tell them to wait here. Come, Pérsomi."

She followed him to the car. The shoes hurt her feet. He opened the passenger door. She got in and sat close to the window.

When they were driving down the main street, Boelie said, "You did the right thing to tell the truth, Pérsomi."

She nodded but didn't say anything.

In front of Johnny's Café he parked and got out. "Come," he said over his shoulder as he walked into the café.

Pérsomi followed uncertainly. He walked to the rear and sat down at a table. "Sit," he said and pointed at the chair facing him.

"What kind of soda would you like? Coca-Cola? Hubbly Bubbly? Sparletta?"

She shrugged. She had no idea what he was talking about.

The room smelled of food. Her stomach contracted. Anger still filled her entire body.

She wished she could free her feet from the shoes. Her toes were crammed together.

"Two Sparletta Cream Sodas, please," Boelie said to the woman standing next to them. "And two pies with gravy and chips."

Pérsomi sat up straight and looked around. At the entrance was a two-tiered glass display cabinet. Each tier consisted of about eight glass cubicles containing a variety of sweets, hundreds of thousands of sweets, it seemed.

A fat man with a red face was leaning against the counter. Behind him was a shelf stacked with bread and cigarettes, and on the opposite side a stand with newspapers and magazines.

Red-and-white checkered tablecloths covered the tables. Each table had four chairs.

But the prettiness didn't make the anger inside her go away. When her soda came and she raised the glass, her hand was still trembling.

"Why are you trembling?" he asked. "Were you afraid?"

"No. Boelie, I was so bloody angry!"

He began to laugh. "Young ladies shouldn't use language like that."

"You do."

"I'm a man. But never mind, you put him in his place," he said, still laughing. "And De Wet says you were a credible witness."

"What does that mean?"

"It means you spoke so well that everyone believed you."

"Well, I spoke the truth," she said.

"Yes," he said. "Look, here are our pies and gravy. I'm bloody hungry, how about you?"

"I'm *very* hungry too," she said and smiled at him. "Thank you for the food."

"I just wanted to tell you," he said, "I'm proud of you today." He came out with it as if it was nothing, but every word settled in her mind to stay.

"You know what, Boelie? That's what I want to do one day."

"What?"

"Work in court."

"Like De Wet."

"Yes."

Boelie gave her a slow smile. "I don't know whether women can become lawyers, but if they can, I'm sure you'll make a success of it," he said.

THREE

Lewies Pieterse was found guilty and sentenced to jail for six years. Mr. Fourie did not chase the women off the farm. In fact, he convinced Ma that she should let Pérsomi attend school.

Early in January 1941, it rained for days on end. The roof leaked like a sieve. They put the bucket and the two pots on the floor to catch the water.

"At least we don't have to fetch water at the river," said Hannapat.

But the bucket and pots weren't much help. The house became wetter and wetter. After a while, even the mattresses were soaked. And the wood—the fire was more smoke than flames. "We can't even make a fire anymore," said Pérsomi.

"This rain must stop now," said her ma.

"We'll starve if we can't make porridge," said Hannapat.

"The flour is almost finished anyway," said their ma, tucking her frizzy red hair behind her ear.

They had no news from Gerbrand, even though Pérsomi had written. They still got an envelope with money every month, but he didn't write.

"Men don't like to write letters," Klara said when she came home from university with her brothers.

"But he writes to you?" Pérsomi asked.

"Not often," Klara answered vaguely. "He doesn't really have time. But I think he's doing fine."

Ma took Pérsomi back to town to get what she needed for high school at Mr. Ismail's store. Karla and Irene's ouma had agreed to make a new white dress for Pérsomi to wear to church. Pérsomi wished someone else could have made the dress. Anyone except old Mrs. Fourie.

The day after it finally stopped raining, Pérsomi woke long before sunrise. She got up and walked to the Fouries' to try on her dress. If she didn't try on her white church dress today, Irene's ouma might not finish it before she left for school on Monday.

Because the Pontenilo was a rushing brown mass of water, she had to go over the mountain. The ground was wet and slippery, the rocks slimy, but she knew her mountain. She knew every path and every rocky outcrop and every dangerous cliff.

She avoided the Big House, passing around the back to the Old House, where the Fourie grandparents lived.

The back door was open. Uncertainty burned a hole in her stomach. Grumpy Oupa Fourie, Mrs. Fourie, and Boelie were having coffee at the kitchen table. Her legs tingled with the desire to run away.

Resolutely she raised her hand and knocked on the door. "Good morning Mrs. Fourie Oupa Fourie Boelie I've come to try on my dress," she said in a single breath.

"Child!" Mrs. Fourie said, surprised.

"Pérsomi!" Boelie stood up. "How did you get here? Surely you didn't cross the river!"

"I came over the mountain," she replied. "I've come to try on my dress."

"But . . . it's half a day on foot." He still seemed astonished.

"I got an early start," she said.

"Would you like some coffee?" he asked, opening the door. "Come inside."

"I'm covered in mud."

"Yes, you look as if you rolled in mud," said Mrs. Fourie, sounding annoyed. "Wash at the trough, then come and try on your dress."

Later, when she put the dress on, Pérsomi couldn't help saying, "It's a lovely dress, Mrs. Fourie."

"Yes," muttered Irene's ouma, her mouth full of pins, "you must look decent when you go to church. Don't you have a bust bodice?"

Before Pérsomi could answer, Mrs. Fourie said, "You must have a panama hat as well. I'll see if Klara's old one is still around somewhere."

"Thank you," said Pérsomi.

It was the first new dress Pérsomi had ever had. It was her first dress that wasn't way too wide and too short. Pérsomi couldn't stop looking at it.

"Come and fetch it tomorrow or the day after, when the river has gone down. Don't come over the mountain again, it's too dangerous."

"Thank you," said Pérsomi.

When she passed through the kitchen, Boelie was no longer there. She smelled the coffee but no one had poured her a cup.

She walked past the Big House and past the barn, heading for the mountain. When she passed the kraal, Boelie came round the corner.

"Are you going back over the mountain?" he asked.

"Yes," she said.

He shook his head. "And I suppose you haven't eaten? What time did you start walking?"

"Early," she said.

"Wait here," he said and walked back to the Big House.

He returned with two rusks. "Here, eat," he said and fell into step with her in the narrow footpath.

"Pérsomi, do you know what to expect? At boarding school, I mean?" he asked after a while.

"Not really," she admitted past the crumbs in her throat.

"Hmm." His gaze was fixed on the path ahead. "You'll have to make your own bed and eat at the table with a knife and fork."

She felt humiliated that he knew what life was like in her home. "I know," she murmured. "I'll watch what the others are doing."

"Yes," he said. For a while they walked in silence, then he said, "Do you have things like soap and a toothbrush and a towel?"

A wave of embarrassment engulfed her. Boelie knew everything. Gerbrand had probably arrived at boarding school without a towel.

When she didn't reply, Boelie said, "I'll see what I can do."

"Thank you," she said softly.

A while later he asked, "What news do you get from Gerbrand?"

"Not much," she answered. "He's only written once."

"Hmm," he said.

She summoned up enough courage to ask, "Why do you think Gerbrand joined the war?"

He stopped and turned to face her. For the first time he looked her in the eye, his expression serious. "It's this bloody government of ours, Pérsomi," he said. "They're a bunch of Khaki lovers led by that traitor Smuts." His hands formed fists at his sides. "You know, Pérsomi, our Afrikaner boys, like Gerbrand, are being bought by our biggest enemies, by England and the powerful Jews with the money."

She did not know what he meant.

"Young men who are suffering hardship join the armed forces

for financial reasons. The blood of Afrikaner boys is being spilled to help build the British Empire!"

She was startled at the bitterness in his voice.

"Have you ever heard of the *Ossewabrandwag*, Pérsomi?" he asked.

Pérsomi didn't want to admit that she knew hardly anything about it. "I've read about it in the paper," she said.

"I belong to the OB. It's a good Afrikaner organization that's dead set against our participation in the war. I just wish they'd become more militant, or they won't make a difference."

She frowned. She had no idea what he was talking about. "Yes," she said.

"You know, Pérsomi, we must stop all the talk, talk, talk, the attending of meetings and singing of songs. We must start to act, blow things up. That's what we must do."

"What do you mean?" she asked cautiously. It sounded a bit like war to her.

"We must sabotage things, like the telephone exchanges, the railway lines, troop trains, harbors—everything that's needed to take our men up north." His anger seemed to turn into enthusiasm, as if he saw a solution. "You know, Pers, at least half the police force would join us, and with the majority of our armed forces up north, a takeover would be easy."

The more he talked, the less she understood. But she just nodded.

In the future she would read the newspaper articles that dealt with the OB as well.

Late that night, when Hannapat was fast asleep and Sissie was snoring softly, Pérsomi got up and went outside.

Boelie's words haunted her. England and the mighty Jews with the money bought Gerbrand, Boelie had said. Gerbrand was a traitor. Gerbrand was a Khaki lover.

He was also her big brother who was looking after them. The money Gerbrand sent home was keeping them alive. It was the porridge they ate every day, it was the new bloomers and bust bodice packed in the flour bag, ready for her to take along to boarding school.

She undid her long braid. It was tugging at her scalp.

Where did Boelie fit into the picture if he wanted to blow up railway lines and sabotage telephone exchanges?

A cold breeze came up. She rubbed her bare upper arms with her hands. Then she went back into the house. She lay down on her mattress and drew the thin blanket over her head. She didn't want to think about everything Boelie had said.

But even in her cozy nest under the blanket Boelie's words kept coming back to her: "The blood of Afrikaner boys is being spilled to help build the British Empire!"

❧

Monday morning the Pontenilo was considerably lower, yet Pérsomi was still drenched when she reached the other side. She washed the mud from her legs, waited for her dress to dry, then walked slowly to the Big House. There was more than enough time. Mr. Fourie would only be taking them to school at ten.

The flour bag she carried contained her new hairbrush, an extra bloomer, her two old dresses, the brand-new church dress Irene's ouma had made, as well as the towel, soap, and toothbrush Boelie had brought. She was wearing the other bloomer and the bust bodice under her green dress.

The bust bodice felt strange and tight.

Aunt Marie had said she would bring her uniform to the school in the afternoon.

When Pérsomi reached the barn, she put on her courtroom shoes. She hoped Aunt Marie would bring socks, because the shoes gave her blisters.

She waited outside the barn for a long time before the door of the Big House opened. Mr. Fourie came out, carrying a suitcase. Irene carried a basket and a leather satchel, and her mother, Aunt Lulu, followed with two cookie tins. Oupa and Mrs. Fourie also came out. Mrs. Fourie was carrying Irene's brand-new panama hat, and her husband hobbled after the rest of them, leaning on his cane.

When they had almost reached the barn, Mrs. Fourie noticed her. "Oh goodness, I forgot to find the child a hat," she said. "Lulu, is Klara's old panama hat still around here somewhere?"

Now Aunt Lulu also noticed her. "For Pérsomi? Don't you have a hat of your own, Pérsomi?" she asked, sounding surprised. "And do you have all your things in that little bag? Irene, see if you can find Klara's hat in her closet. And fetch that old suitcase in the storeroom. The child can't arrive at school with her belongings in a flour bag."

"The latches are broken, Ma," said Irene.

"We'll tie a rope around it. Go now," said Aunt Lulu.

"Hurry, I want to leave," Mr. Fourie said.

Pérsomi felt herself shrinking. Her mouth was bone-dry, and her legs tingled with the desire to run. But she swallowed and stood motionless. And she didn't look away.

When at last they drove over the causeway and left the farm behind, Pérsomi felt a strange sadness in her heart. For a long time she gazed at her mountain, until it disappeared behind the hills.

The room the prefect took Pérsomi to had two iron beds that stood against the walls like railroad tracks. Each bed had a coir mattress, a pillow, two stiff white sheets, a gray blanket, and a blue bedspread embroidered with the letters *T E D* for Transvaal Education Department. Under the window two small tables had been pushed together, and in the corner stood a small bookcase. The other corner housed a steel locker with four shelves, two for her and two for her roommate, the prefect explained. There was hanging space for four items of clothing each.

The room was at the back of the building and overlooked a row of garbage cans, several long clotheslines, and a sad thorn tree surrounded by concrete.

In the distance lay the wide expanse of the bushveld. She couldn't see her mountain.

When she heard the door open behind her, she turned. "This is Beth Murray, your roommate," the prefect said. "What did you say your name was?"

"Pérsomi Pieterse."

"Well, show her the ropes and bring your mugs at four," said the prefect before hurrying away.

Pérsomi's new roommate was small, with white-blonde hair and a pale face. Her long dress had long sleeves and a frill around the high neckline. She wasn't a welfare child, Pérsomi decided, but she looked as if she might burst into tears at any moment.

They stood looking at each other uncertainly.

Pérsomi realized that Beth was afraid. She smiled and asked, "Which bed would you like?"

Beth shook her head, her blue eyes big and shiny.

"Okay, I'll take this one," Pérsomi decided. She turned to the locker. "You have two shelves, and there's hanging space for your clothes. I put my towel over—"

"I don't have a mug," Beth said, her eyes wide. She spoke with a strange accent.

"I don't have one either," said Pérsomi, "but it doesn't matter, we just won't have coffee."

"Oh," said Beth, as if that option hadn't occurred to her.

"Why don't you unpack now?" said Pérsomi.

At four o'clock a bell rang and they went down to the dining hall. They were told to line up according to their room numbers. Pérsomi and Beth were in room 27. Irene and her roommate were in room 31. The girls were assigned the same table. A matric girl took the place at the head. She was the table captain.

There was a stiff white tablecloth, and each place was laid with a plate, knife, fork, spoon, and small coarse cloth. They stood behind their chairs until the teacher had said grace. Then they were allowed to sit.

The matric girl lifted the lids of the four serving bowls and began to dish up. She passed along the plates. "Put your napkin on your lap, Pérsomi," Irene said.

Pérsomi bundled the stiff cloth onto her lap and looked at the food in front of her: samp, chunks of meat in gravy, and cabbage leaves. There was enough meat on her plate for her entire family. Her mouth watered, but nausea pushed against her throat. She wished she could run away, far away.

Carefully she picked up her knife and fork. All the other girls handled the cutlery easily, as if their hands knew exactly what to do. Furtively she watched the girl sitting opposite her and tried to copy her movements. The knife and fork felt awkward in her hands. Her feet were burning inside the school shoes. The strange food got stuck in her tight throat.

She longed to be back on the farm, seated at the table where her ma and Hannapat and Sissie were eating their porridge at this moment.

Gerbrand had done this. She could do it too.

Pérsomi forced down the food. It was quiet at the table, the only sound the clink of cutlery.

After supper the teacher rapped on the table. "Let us pray," she said.

Then they were summoned to the study hall to listen to the rules. There were hundreds of rules, and if you did something wrong, you would not be allowed to go home on free weekends.

Next the Form I and II girls took showers. The prefect hurried them along. "You have fifteen minutes before you must be in your rooms for quiet time."

Pérsomi grabbed her soap, toothbrush, and small towel and followed the others to the bathroom. Beth was nowhere to be seen.

Clouds of steam hung in the bathroom. Pérsomi stopped in the doorway, uncertain of what to do. "Next, next!" the prefect called. "Come, girls, come, out of your clothes and under the water!"

Pérsomi saw the girls take off their clothes, put them in neat piles on the bench, and disappear behind a curtain. "Come along, get undressed!" the prefect scolded.

She stepped under the shower. It felt strange, the hot water gushing from above and running over her body. She raised her face. The hot water ran down her neck, over her hair and down her back, forming warm puddles at her feet.

"Come along, out, out," the prefect cried. "Goodness, why did you wash your hair? You'll never get it dry! You'll get a terrible cold."

Confused, Pérsomi grabbed her towel and tried to dry herself. The other girls had big towels that they wrapped around themselves. Still wet, she put her clothes back on. "Next time, bring along your nightdress and dressing gown," the prefect said crossly. "Come, back to your rooms!"

Beth was in the room, clad in a suffocating pink nightdress with long sleeves and a stiff frill around her neck. Pérsomi decided to wear her yellow dress to bed. It was her oldest dress and very short. Its floral pattern was faded and worn with washing.

A shrill bell rang. "Quiet time!" a prefect roared down the corridor.

Beth went to the locker and took out a Bible. Quietly she began to read.

Pérsomi sat motionless on her bed.

Then Beth knelt beside the bed and rested her head on her folded hands.

Pérsomi had always thought only Meester Lampbrecht prayed in the mornings before he told the class a Bible story. She had never realized ordinary people also prayed.

Suddenly it struck her: Like Gerbrand, she was among real people, as if she herself was a real person too. Tomorrow morning when she put on her school uniform and went down to breakfast with the others and then to the new school, no one would know she was a bywoner child. Unless Irene . . .

When another bell rang, Beth remained on her knees. "Lights out!" the prefect called.

Pérsomi got up and switched off the electric light. It was another strange and wonderful privilege for real people, these electric lights. Then she drew back the bedding carefully so that she would be able to make it neat the next morning.

Later that night Pérsomi lay motionless between the stiff sheets in the strange bed, listening to her new roommate crying softly into her pillow. She realized she hadn't used the soap Boelie had given to her.

Pérsomi walked from the dormitory to the school with the other girls. They all looked the same in their white shirts, black jumpers, white socks, and black lace-up shoes. Pérsomi's jumper was a bit short, but it was the best Aunt Marie could find for her.

"My jumper is very long," Beth said when she saw Pérsomi's. "Mrs. Reverend says it's a sin to wear short skirts. Not that I mean yours is a sin, I just mean . . ." She didn't finish her thought.

Aunt Marie had promised to look for a longer one, but her success would depend on the welfare donations.

In the school hall the students sat in rows, hundreds of children, all clothed exactly the same. Then they were divided into classes. Pérsomi found herself in a class with twenty-four other Form IIs. She was in the B class. Both Irene and Beth were in the A class. She knew that as a bywoner child she had automatically been placed in the B class.

But after first recess she was moved to the A class.

Thirty strange pairs of eyes regarded her. In the second row, Irene sat next to the window. Pérsomi stood in the doorway.

"This is . . . er"—her new class teacher searched for her name on a piece of paper—"Er . . . Pérsomi Pieterse." He looked at the children over his glasses. "Yes . . . er . . . is there an empty desk somewhere? Reinier, is the desk next to you open?"

A tall, thin boy at the back of the class extricated himself from his desk. "Yes, sir," he said reluctantly.

The school shoes pinched her feet as she walked the long aisle to the back. She noticed Beth in the second row from the back. Beth gave her a slight smile.

Her chest opened up a little as she sat. But the strange boy's tall figure was uncomfortably close to her.

"Take out your math books," said the teacher.

The children dug into their satchels and put their books on their desks, along with their new pencils, pens, rulers, compasses— everything.

Pérsomi had nothing.

"Open your books to page five," said the teacher. Pages were turned. Pérsomi sat motionless.

"Turn to exercise four. Who can tell me . . ." He stopped.

Pérsomi kept her eyes fixed on the bare wooden desk.

"Girl, where's your book?" The teacher sounded annoyed.

She looked up slowly. He was looking at her. She began to stand. Everybody was looking at her.

"Oh, sir," Irene spoke loudly. "Pérsomi is a welfare child, she must get free books."

The words hung in the air. Welfare child.

There was nowhere she could run.

"Well, why didn't you say so?" the teacher said. "How did you think you were going to do the work? Or didn't you think? You people . . ." He shook his head. "Fetch a book at the office. And come straight back to class, don't make any detours, understand?"

Outside, the sun blazed down on Pérsomi's hot head, but the warmth didn't reach her heart.

The thin woman in the office grumbled, "You can't just come and beg for books any time you want. You should have come after school. Here, take all your books. And look after them properly, understand? Another welfare child must use them next year. There's no end to you lot."

When Pérsomi got back to class with the pile of books, the boy in the seat next to hers said, "Did you get all your books? That was clever."

That was clever. A small spot thawed somewhere in her cold, stiff body.

After school everyone went to the rugby field and was sorted into athletic teams. Pérsomi was with the Impalas. She joined her team members in line without knowing exactly what they were going to do.

The Form I's were first to take their places behind a white line.

A teacher said: "On your marks, get set, go!" The girls ran as fast as they could to the opposite side of the field.

Next the Form IIs lined up. "On your marks, get set, go!" said the teacher before Pérsomi had even got to the white line. The other girls ran.

Pérsomi stood dismayed. "Run!" the teacher roared.

She ran, her long legs flying across the field. Within seconds she had passed the girls bringing up the rear. Her legs felt liberated, her feet free. Halfway across the field only three girls were still ahead of her. She ran away from the welfare humiliation, from her too-short school jumper, from her shirt with the missing buttons and the threadbare dress she slept in. She ran away from free school books and the hard bed she struggled to make and the strange napkin at the dinner table.

Five yards before the white line at the opposite end she flew past the girl in the lead. "Goodness, child, you can certainly run!" said the teacher as he wrote her name on a list. "Do you do long jump and high jump as well?"

Long jump was easy. She ran, took off, and jumped the way she jumped across the pool in the river.

High jump was strange to her. "You'll find it easy, you'll see," the teacher assured her. "You've got long legs. Just scissor your legs when you go over the crossbar. But you can't do it in your school uniform. Wear your gym clothes tomorrow."

At shower time that evening she remembered her soap. It had a lovely smell, and it felt nice too. She tried not to get her hair wet again.

Beth read from her Bible at quiet time, then passed it to Pérsomi before kneeling beside her bed. Pérsomi opened the English Bible to a random page. She had no idea what she was supposed to read.

"Trust in the Lod with all thine heart," she read, "and lean not unto thine own understanding. In all thy ways acknowledge him, and he shall direct thy paths."

She looked up, frowning slightly. Was that what Beth was doing? And others who read the Bible and prayed every night?

Beth was still on her knees, moving her head slightly at times, and even her hands. She seemed to be talking, not praying.

Then the bell rang for lights out. She got up quietly and switched off the light.

When Beth was lying under her sheet, the warm blanket neatly folded back, she whispered, "You run like the wind, Pérsomi. Not like me. I came in stone last."

"But I don't have any gym clothes," Pérsomi whispered back.

"Neither do I," whispered Beth. "Mrs. Reverend would never allow me to wear anything like that. So it's just as well I'm not on the team."

Pérsomi couldn't ask who Mrs. Reverend was, because she heard the prefect doing her rounds after lights-out.

Late that night, still awake in the hard bed, she heard Beth quietly sobbing in her pillow again. It was a strange sound, not like Sissie's crying or Gertjie's wails or Hannapat's whining. It sounded . . . lonely. "Don't cry, Beth," she whispered.

"I'm so homesick," Beth said softly.

"Me too," said Pérsomi.

"I miss Mrs. Reverend," Beth sobbed, "and everyone at the mission station."

"I miss my brother," said Pérsomi, "and my ma and our home on the farm."

At last they fell asleep.

The coach who had been at the high jump the day before was also the science teacher. "You're the girl who runs so fast," Mr. Nienaber said as he stood beside her desk. "Come directly to the high jump this afternoon. What did you say your name was?"

"Pérsomi Pieterse," she replied.

"She's Gerbrand Pieterse's sister, sir," said Reinier de Vos, who sat next to her in this class as well in math. "Remember, sir, the rugby player?"

"Yes, yes, the redhead. He was in your sister's class, wasn't he?"

"Yes." Reinier smiled. "That's him, sir. He was in Annabel's class."

When the teacher turned his back, Reinier whispered, "Your brother was a very good rugby player."

Pérsomi felt a warm glow of pride inside her. Gerbrand had never mentioned it. "I didn't know," she said quietly and carried on with her work.

The next day, when the children went out for first recess after their science lesson, Mr. Nienaber said, "Pérsomi, just a moment."

She stood at his table. She knew what was coming.

"Why didn't you come to the high jump yesterday?"

She lifted her chin and looked him in the eye. "I don't have the right clothes, sir." She said it as if it was nothing, as if she couldn't care less.

"Oh," he said. He walked to the door and called down the porch. "Reinier! Reinier de Vos, come back for a moment!"

Pérsomi's face flushed. She stared at the table as Reinier returned.

"Sir?"

"Reinier, I'm looking for gym clothes for Pérsomi. Won't you ask your mother if she still has Annabel's somewhere? They should fit Pérsomi."

"Yes, of course, sir. I'll bring them tomorrow." He glanced at Pérsomi before leaving.

"Thank you," Pérsomi said to Mr. Nienaber.

Why did it have to be Reinier, just about the only person who had shown her any kindness?

Friday afternoon, Pérsomi went to the library.

"I want to look at the newspapers," she said to the librarian. When she noticed that the woman was glaring at her, she quickly added, "Please."

"Please, who?"

"Please, miss?"

"See that you keep the papers tidy! They're on the shelf over there."

But the shelf contained only the papers from the past two days. Pérsomi went back to the counter. "May I please have the week's papers, miss?" she asked.

The woman sighed and reached under the counter. "What are you looking for?" she asked, pushing the pile of papers toward Pérsomi.

"I want to read about the war, and about the Ossewabrandwag," said Pérsomi.

"Why?" asked the librarian.

"My brother is fighting in Kenya," Pérsomi said without thinking, "and my—"

"Your brother is fighting in . . . Is he a Red Tab?" Pérsomi heard the disgust in her voice.

She stuck out her chin. "Yes, miss," she said, outwardly calm. "Gerbrand enlisted in the armed forces, and I want to read what's happening." She felt her stomach tighten.

"Gerbrand Pieterse? I should have known. It's people like him who are willing to aid our archenemies for a few pieces of silver." She turned her back on Pérsomi and continued with her work.

Pérsomi picked up the papers and walked to a table, her back stiff. Her hands were trembling. That woman had no idea what every copper penny and silver tickey meant to her family.

💐

The interhouse track and field meet took place on the second Saturday of the first term. Pérsomi was awake long before the sun was up. She was so excited she could hardly eat. After breakfast she put on Annabel's dark-blue sleeveless bodysuit with buttons at the back and elastic around the leg openings. Over the body suit she wore a short white pleated skirt. It fit her perfectly.

By eight o'clock the field around the athletics track was crowded with people: farmers from the neighboring farms, townsfolk, parents and grandparents who had come to support their children.

Saturday turned out to be the best day of Pérsomi's life. She crouched behind the white starting line and shattered every record. Her long legs flew down the narrow lane and across the sandpit. She tucked her short skirt into the elastic of her bodysuit and sailed over the crossbar. Time after time she climbed to the top of the podium. She was the last one to be handed the baton in the relay race and was still first through the white tape. The rest of the Impalas team cheered wildly.

"My sister was fast, but you'd leave her standing," Reinier said.

Pérsomi's cheeks glowed with pride. She wished Gerbrand could be there to see her. He would have been so proud.

When they walked back to the dormitory in the late afternoon, Beth said: "Pérsomi, you were so good. God has blessed you with a wonderful talent."

Pérsomi tried to make light of her embarrassment. "But your team won." Beth was in the Kudus team.

"It was fun," said Beth. There was a blush on her cheeks and she was hoarse from shouting. She shook her head anxiously. "I don't know what the Reverend and Mrs. Reverend would say about all this. I'm afraid it might be a sin."

"What?"

"Well I didn't behave with decorum," said Beth.

"Why should you?" asked Pérsomi.

"I don't know. It's just . . . right," answered Beth. "A girl should behave with decorum."

"Oh," said Pérsomi. "I know a girl shouldn't swear."

"No one should swear!" Beth said, wide-eyed. "The Reverend says it's a terrible sin."

"Who's the Reverend and Mrs. Reverend?" she finally asked.

"The people who raised me," said Beth.

Pérsomi had never been to church, but she didn't mention it to anyone.

"Listen, they're calling 'Come, Sinners, Come,'" Beth said the first time Pérsomi heard the Sunday morning church bells. That

January morning in the sweltering bushveld the minister wore a pitch-black cassock. The organ notes dripped like sticky syrup from the walls and ceiling and the people dragged behind the music, as if the organ were drawing their voices out of their throats. She looked at the row of elders with their shiny pates and wrinkly necks dozing in the pews and the deacons in their black suits and snow-white bow ties, passing along the collection plates. She didn't have a tickey to put in. In truth, she didn't even have a penny.

She was shown to a Sunday school class and given a booklet from which she had to learn a Bible text by heart. It looked quite easy.

Sunday lunch included dessert. And chicken. She wished she could put away some food every day to take home during the vacation.

After lunch on Sundays there was quiet time until five. They couldn't do any work, especially homework; they couldn't jog around the track or practice the long jump; they could sing only hymns; they couldn't read anything but the Bible.

There was another church service after supper on Sundays. Then they went to bed.

Sunday was the longest day in Pérsomi's week.

At assembly on Monday morning six big trophies stood on a table in front of the stage, and the principal read the names of all the athletes who had been selected for the school team.

Irene's name was read. She was in the relay team. Pérsomi's name was read, and so was Reinier's. The pupils applauded.

Then the principal said: "And now for the highlight of the day. Everyone knows the Kudus were the winning team. Will the captains please fetch the trophy?"

The Kudus cheered enthusiastically to celebrate their victory.

When the cheering died down, the principal said, "The trophy for the best singing goes to the . . . Impalas!"

The Impalas almost raised the roof. The cheerleaders proudly went up to receive the trophy, taking their places next to the captains of the Kudus. Pérsomi wondered what the other four trophies were for.

"And now for the stars of the event," said the principal. He picked up one of the remaining four trophies. "You won't be surprised to learn that our junior *Victrix ludorum* is Pérsomi Pieterse of the Impalas!"

Pérsomi heard her name through a haze.

The Impalas erupted with joy.

Gradually it dawned on Pérsomi—she had won a trophy.

Beth nudged her. "Go to the stage!" she shouted over the cheering voices.

Pérsomi climbed the steps. Everyone applauded. The principal shook her hand.

"Congratulations, Pérsomi," he said, "we're looking forward to seeing you compete against the other schools."

She stood next to the other trophy winners, the big trophy in her hands.

She gazed over a sea of faces in identical school uniforms, all of them looking at her, holding the trophy. Her classmates smiled at her.

All day long she felt like a real person.

❦

"Why don't you wear a nightgown?" Beth asked one evening after lights out. If they whispered softly after the prefect had done her rounds, they could talk in the dark for a long time.

"I haven't got one," Pérsomi answered.

"Yes, I know, but why not? Why doesn't your mom make you one?"

"Where would my ma find fabric? And I don't think she can sew," said Pérsomi.

It was quiet for while, then Beth whispered, "Why are you so poor, Pérsomi?"

"I don't know. We don't have any money, that's all."

"Doesn't your dad earn any money?"

"No, he doesn't work." She didn't explain everything. Beth wouldn't understand. Beth was a real person who had grown up with the Reverend and who had dresses and nightgowns and a satchel and two school jumpers. "Beth, why do you live with the Reverend and his wife?"

"My mom died. At the mission station, just after my birth," said Beth.

"Oh," said Pérsomi. "I'm sorry."

"It's all right, I never knew her," said Beth. "And Reverend and Mrs. Reverend really love me."

After a while Pérsomi asked: "And your dad?"

"I don't know who my dad is," said Beth. "No one knows, except my mom, I suppose. But she's dead."

Pérsomi didn't say that she didn't know her pa either.

A few moments later she heard Beth's even breathing. This coming vacation, she resolved, she would try to find out who her real pa was. Her ma would just have to tell her. She would have to.

❧

"This afternoon I'm going to town," Pérsomi told Beth one Friday. "Mr. Nienaber gave me a tickey for looking after his children."

It was the first money Pérsomi had ever had just for herself.

"Really?" said Beth, pleased. "What will you buy?"

"I don't know, I'll see," said Pérsomi. She had no idea what you could buy with a tickey. She'd thought of sweets, but maybe she should buy a nightgown, if one could be had for a tickey.

In town, after the other girls had scattered, they found themselves in a wide street with shops and a butchery and a post office. Farther down the street Pérsomi recognized the magistrate's court with its two wilting flags.

"There's the General Dealer," said Beth. "I think that's where we should go."

"Why don't you get what you need from Ismail's?" Pérsomi suggested. "They're a lot cheaper than the General Dealer."

"Reverend says it's a sin to buy from coolies," Beth said.

"Why?" Pérsomi said. "And don't call them coolies. It's a very bad word, almost like swearing."

"Oh, I didn't know. But still . . . They're Mohammedans, not Christians, that's why we mustn't spend our money with them."

"My ma says they're cheaper, and Mr. Ismail always gives her a bargain."

"I can't go there," Beth said, wide-eyed.

"Okay, go to the General Dealer and I'll meet you here afterward," Pérsomi suggested and set off down the street.

At the door she took a deep breath. The store always smelled the same. She didn't know what it was, but the mixture of smells made her feel welcome.

She walked slowly through the shop to the ladies' wear department. Everything was pleasantly familiar.

"Hi," Yusuf said behind her, "what can I help you with today? And by the way, I don't know your name."

"Pérsomi," she said, "Pérsomi Pieterse."

"Pérsomi," he repeated. "Unusual, but nice."

"I'm just looking," she said. "Where are your nightgowns?"

He crossed to a drawer, opened it, and spread out the night-gowns—a frilly pink one, a light-blue one trimmed with lace and bows, and a yellow one with tiny embroidered roses. She stroked the fabric. It was soft and almost slippery to the touch. "They're all so lovely!" she said.

But when she saw the prices, she turned away. "Actually I just want to buy some sweets," she said, embarrassed.

He gave her a reassuring smile. "It's still nice to look, isn't it?" he said, folding the nightgowns and returning them to the drawer. "How are you doing at school?"

"Fine," she said. She wished she could tell him about the athletics, but he probably wouldn't be interested. "And you?"

"Fine," he said.

"Where's your school?" she asked.

"Right behind the store, next to the mosque," he said. "We don't have such a big school, because there aren't many Indians in town. We have our lessons in English, you know."

"English? Why?" she asked, surprised. "You speak Afrikaans."

"All Indians go to school in English," he said, "even if they speak Afrikaans."

"It makes no sense," she said. "Why don't you just come to our school?"

He laughed. "That wouldn't work," he said. "You're Boers, we're Indians."

"Yes," she said, "and you're Mohammedans and we're Christians."

They had reached the sweets counter. "We call ourselves Muslims, not Mohammedans," he said. "What kind of sweets do you want?"

"A tickey's worth," she said, pointing.

He deftly folded a cone from a piece of newsprint and poured in a handful of sweets. He added a few more and folded the top over. "Please look in again, even if you don't buy anything," he said, handing her the paper cone. "I'd like to hear your brother's news."

"Thanks, I will, but now I'm afraid I'm going to be late," she said and left to meet Beth.

Outside the sun was blazing down on the tarmac.

"Did you know that Indians are Muslims and not Mohammedans?" she asked as they filed back to the dormitory with the rest of the boarders.

"No," said Beth. "Who told you so?"

"Yusuf, Mr. Ismail's grandson. You should go with me to Mr. Ismail's store. You don't have to buy anything. It's just . . . nice inside, special."

❧

At the end of February Pérsomi read in *Die Transvaler* that the first Italian prisoners of war captured in Italian-Somalia and Abyssinia had arrived in South Africa. Gerbrand was in Abyssinia. She wished they would send him back to South Africa too.

On March 2 she read that it was forbidden now for government officials to belong to the Ossewabrandwag. She didn't know what that meant or whether it was important, but she would try to remember it when she talked to Boelie during the vacation. In just a few short weeks Mr. Fourie would be waiting for Irene and her at the station.

Maybe she could also talk to Boelie about the athletics. He and De Wet had taken part when they attended the school. She had seen De Wet's name on the honors roll in the hall.

She put away the packet of sweets to share with her ma and sisters.

Soon she would be back on her mountain. She missed her ma and their home and the farm. But most of all her mountain.

FOUR

PÉRSOMI ARRIVED AT THE FARM WITH THE FOURIES LATE
Saturday evening. When the car stopped in front of the house,
the dogs barked themselves into a frenzy, beside themselves
with joy at seeing Irene again. The front door opened, and light
streamed out over the porch. Irene's mother and grandma came
out, laughing and opening their arms to Irene. "You must be
dying of hunger," said Aunt Lulu. "Come in, your ouma made a
milk tart."

"Have Klara and the others come?" Irene asked, picking up
the smallest dog. "Hello, Courage, did you miss me? Gosh, it's
good to be home!"

Pérsomi picked up her suitcase and quietly made her way to
the orange grove.

The dark swallowed her. Behind her the windows of the Big
House were brightly lit. The path through the trees was barely
visible in the starlight.

At the Pontenilo she bent down for a moment, scooping up
handfuls of water to drink. I'm back, she thought as she prepared
to cross to her family's side. The river was also a part of her.

The little house on the ridge loomed in the dark.

She pushed open the back door. It creaked loudly in the quiet
night.

"Who's there?" Hannapat mumbled.

"Me, Pérsomi."

"Oh," said Hannapat as she sat up on her mattress. "Why did you take so long? We were waiting for you yesterday."

"I had to go to a track meet," said Pérsomi. She looked around the dark room. "Where's the candle? Is there any food?" she asked.

"Look in the pot," said Hannapat, "but I think it's empty."

She struggled to light the short wick of the candle. The porridge pot was empty. She turned away from the cold stove. "Where's my mattress?" she asked.

"Sissie is sleeping on your mattress. She sleeps on two mattresses. Did you bring anything from town?"

"Yes, but I'll give it to you tomorrow when Ma and Sissie are awake. Move over, I'm exhausted."

She lay behind Hannapat's back under the rough gray blanket, Sissie's soft snores in her ears and the sour smell of her home pricking her nostrils. She had forgotten what it was like.

A scurrying woke her. Ma stood in the doorway. She had opened the curtain between the bedroom and the kitchen. "Fetch some water, Hannapat," she said.

Pérsomi slowly opened her eyes. "Look, Ma, Pérsomi's here," said Hannapat.

"Heavens, child, where did you spring from?" her ma asked. "We thought you'd be here Friday."

"I took part in a track meet," said Pérsomi. "Ran races, you know?"

"How would I know?" asked her ma.

"Ma, my tooth hurts," Sissie complained from under her blanket.

Pérsomi sat up, throwing off the threadbare cover. "It was a big meeting," she said. "All the schools were there. We went to Potgietersrus by train."

"Potgietersrus?" said her ma.

"Ma-a, my tooth," said Sissie.

"Yes, Ma," said Pérsomi and got up. "The whole team went by train. We left yesterday morning at four."

"Oh," said her ma, "that's early. Hannapat, fetch water."

"I took part in a number of events," Pérsomi continued. She was keen to tell her ma everything. She felt sure her ma would be so proud.

"Oh," said her ma.

"In the 100 yards, the 200 yards, the high jump, the long jump, and the relay."

"Oh," said her ma. "Hannapat, fetch the water now."

Hannapat did not budge.

"I did very well. I was the best junior girl of all the schools present."

"Oh," said her ma, "that's good. Hannapat, will you fetch the water now? Or must I fetch the strap?"

Reluctantly Hannapat picked up the bucket and sauntered to the door.

"Ma-a, my tooth!" Sissie groaned.

"Oh, Sissie, shut up," said her ma.

"I thought you'd be proud," said Pérsomi.

"Yes," said her ma. "Here's a letter from Gerbrand. Hannapat read it but she can't read very well. You read it to me." She produced a crumpled envelope from the front of her dress.

"He only writes to you and Ma anyway," Hannapat said sulkily from the door. "Let me fetch the water."

Pérsomi had wanted to bring the trophy home, to show her family. But Mr. Nienaber had said it would be better if it stayed at school. Then he locked it in the glass case in the foyer.

She took the much-handled letter from her ma's hands, unfolded it carefully, and began to read the familiar round writing:

10 MARCH 1941

Dear Ma and Pérsomi,

I'm sorry I can't write more often we are very busy. We're in Italian-Somaliland now. The roads are terrible. We just about had to rebuild the road. We drove through thick sand and sometimes we had to take detours through dense bushes because we have to look out for land mines.

We have made contact with the Eyeties. I got my hands on an Italian water bottle it's a lot better than ours because our water bottles hold a pint and the Italian bottles hold three pints.

I want to spend the rest of my life in the army. It's a good thing I came.

A guy in our C Company is very ill malaria, they say. He was sent back to the Union.

We have taken quite a lot of Italians prisoner.

I want to tell you about the bridge we had to build across the Juba River because the enemy blew up the bridge and it's a wide river so we built a bridge. We tied drums together and tied them to trees. Then we rowed across in boats and tied the ropes to trees on the opposite bank and pulled the drums and the chains right up against the trees. Then they I mean we put wooden boards on top of the drums.

"Gerbrand is very smart, building a bridge like that," said her ma.

"Yes, he is," said Pérsomi and read on.

The Dukes that's another of our groups also came to help. The enemy opened fire every now and then. It is called a floating bridge. We built it in three days. First our infantrymen walked across then our vehicles followed. Don't you think that's good?

It's so hot I can't sleep but I must sleep because we have to make progress tomorrow. The mosquitoes are a nuisance.

Best wishes.

Your son and brother,

Gerbrand

"The mosquitoes are everywhere," her ma sighed.

"Yes," said Pérsomi, folding the letter. A sudden longing for Gerbrand formed a lump in her throat.

Carefully her ma returned the letter to the envelope and tucked it back into her bodice.

Pérsomi swallowed hard against the lump. Deep inside her was an unfamiliar emptiness.

"We must get Sissie something for her toothache," she said and looked around. For the first time she noticed the shambles. The back door swung from a single hinge; there were holes in the dung floor hollowed out by feet over the years; the oven door was missing, and through the gaping hole you could see the flames inside the stove. The two front legs were missing too. Gerbrand had propped it up with stones.

Her shiny trophy would have been completely out of place.

"I don't have anything for toothache," said her ma. "The hospital gave Sissie stronger medicine because the fits come more often these days. It makes her sleepy. She'll have to take some of it for her tooth."

Pérsomi folded her blanket. Sadness was growing inside her.

She felt as if she was about to lose something, or maybe she'd already lost it.

When Hannapat came back with the water, Pérsomi said, "I brought you something from town." She knew they would be happy about the sweets. Everyone would laugh.

But when she turned to her suitcase on the floor, she saw that the string had been removed. She hadn't untied it herself.

She opened the suitcase. Her ma and Sissie stepped closer, curious. Only Hannapat kept her distance.

The suitcase contained only her three dresses, her bloomers, her two school shirts, her hairbrush, and her toothbrush. The sweets were gone.

"What did you bring?" asked Sissie.

"A packet of sweets, but it's gone," said Pérsomi. She turned to Hannapat.

"Where are the sweets?" she demanded.

"How am I supposed to know?" Hannapat replied. "You must have left them at the dormitory, or maybe you're lying."

"I didn't leave it and I'm not lying," Pérsomi said.

"Are you saying I stole it?" asked Hannapat, screwing up her eyes.

"Someone removed the string and it certainly wasn't me."

"Are you saying I—"

"Hand over the sweets!" Sissie launched herself at Hannapat. "Give them here!" she shouted, tugging at Hannapat's hair.

Hannapat screamed and fought back. "Ma! Ma! Sissie is killing me!"

Sissie fell over a chair and pulled Hannapat to the floor. Hannapat kicked and scratched and bit her way out from under Sissie's fat body. "Give the sweets!" Sissie screamed.

"Ma, she's killing me," yelled Hannapat.

Pérsomi walked through the back door and up her mountain.

The sun was high in the sky the morning Pérsomi helped her ma carry a load of washing to the river. It was always better to talk to her ma when she was busy. It was as if her ma could listen better.

They sat down beside the pool. Pérsomi scraped together some clean sand and began to rub it into the collars of her white school shirts. Her ma threw one of Sissie's dresses into the pool and slowly began to wash it, without sand.

"Ma, do you know how to make soap, from fat?" asked Pérsomi.

"Heavens, Pérsomi, what kind of question is that?"

"I'm just asking if you know how to make soap," Pérsomi repeated as reasonably as possible.

"Yes, yes, I suppose I do," said her ma, still rubbing the same spot on the dress. "But I'd have to buy caustic soda, and it costs money."

"What else do you need?" asked Pérsomi.

"Well, child, what shall I say?" Her ma frowned. "A fire, of course, and a soap pot, and fat. Heavens above, I don't remember anymore."

"Have you ever made soap?" asked Pérsomi.

"Stop asking questions, child. You're confusing me," said her ma.

Pérsomi rinsed her white shirt until it looked reasonably clean. "At the dormitory we hand in our clothes on Wednesday and we get them back on Friday, washed and ironed," she said.

"Yes," said her ma.

"I like school. The work isn't too hard. And I do well, at sport and at my schoolwork."

"Yes," said her ma.

Pérsomi licked her dry lips. She had to send the conversation in the right direction, so that she had a reason to ask about her pa.

"I have a roommate, Beth Murray," she said. "She's an orphan. Her ma died when she was born. So she stayed behind at the mission station with the reverend and his wife."

"Oh," said her ma.

"She knows who her ma was, because the reverend could tell her," Pérsomi continued. "But no one knows who her pa was."

"Yes," said her ma. "Mind that the river doesn't take your bloomer."

Pérsomi fished the bloomer out of the pool and began to rinse it. "I don't know who my real pa is either, but you do," she said.

Her ma's hands stopped moving. She looked straight ahead at the water but said nothing.

"Ma." Pérsomi spoke softly. "I really want to know who my pa was. Or is."

Her ma slowly shook her head.

"It's important to me. It's . . . as if a part of me is missing. As if . . ." She was almost pleading now. "As if there's a hole inside me, do you understand?"

But her ma was still shaking her head. "I'll never tell you. I'll never tell anyone," she said in a flat voice.

"Ma, please! I promise, on my word of honor, not to tell anyone, I promise."

"I can't tell you." Her ma kept shaking her head. "I promised I'd never talk. I might not be educated and I'm miserable and poor and a bad mother whose children were taken away. But I promised I'd keep my mouth shut. And that's how it will stay."

Pérsomi felt disappointment choke up her chest, push up in her throat, bitter as gall. She closed her eyes for a moment and swallowed hard. She would wait, but not forever. Sooner or later she would find out.

She looked across the pool at the orange trees covered in blossoms. She drew the sweet smell deep into her lungs. "I don't think you're a bad mother," she said. "Gertjie and Baby didn't get the right food, that's all. Once they get strong again, the welfare will bring them back."

"Yes," her ma said. She picked up Sissie's dress again and began to rub.

Tuesday morning, Pérsomi said, "I'm going across to the Big House to fetch the papers."

"Ask Aunt Lulu if we can borrow a bowl of sugar while you're there," said her ma. "And if she can spare a spoonful or two of coffee, that would also help. And maybe something for Sissie's tummy, tell her she's got a blockage. Say I haven't been able to get to town, but I'll give everything back as soon as we've got plenty again."

"I really don't like to beg," said Pérsomi.

"Heavens, child, it's not begging!" her ma said indignantly. "I just want to borrow a few things!"

"Yes, Ma," said Pérsomi. But she knew very well that nothing Ma borrowed was ever returned.

She washed her face and feet at the river and dried them in the sun. Klara and Irene would be at the Big House, and De Wet. Maybe even Boelie, though he might be at the kraal. Boelie loved the farm, just like his pa and oupa.

When her feet were dry, she walked slowly through the orange trees. She breathed in the sweet smell that filled the air.

At the back door of the Big House she paused for a moment. Inside she heard girls' voices, laughing. Somewhere deep inside the house she heard real people talking and laughing.

She knocked timidly. Only the housekeeper Lena was in the

kitchen, stoking the fire in the stove. "I just came to fetch the newspapers," said Pérsomi.

"Wait here, missy, I'll fetch them in the pantry," said Lena.

"I must also ask for some sugar and flour. No, wait, coffee," Pérsomi hastened to add.

"You'll have to ask one of the family," said Lena. "I can't give it to you. Wait, I'll call Miss Klara."

Pérsomi looked down at her bare feet. Klara would be better than Irene or Aunt Lulu.

But Klara wasn't alone when she entered the kitchen. Two girls followed her in, all three of them laughing.

Klara wore a pale-yellow summer dress. Her brown hair had glints of gold in the shaft of sunlight that fell in through the back door.

Behind her was Christine le Roux, Oom Freddie's daughter. She was small, with curly blonde hair and big blue eyes, like a doll.

The third girl was striking: tall and slender, with long legs and a sun-kissed complexion. Her dark hair fell down her back, shiny and silken. Her dark eyebrows were neat arches, her full lips a deep red color.

"Hello, Pérsomi," Klara said cheerfully. "Are you also home for the vacation?"

"Yes."

Klara said to her friends, "This is Gerbrand's little sister, she's Irene and Reinier's age."

"Yes," said Christine, "I know her, but she's growing up so fast!" She turned to Pérsomi. "What do you hear from Gerbrand?"

"He's well. They built a bridge across a river," Pérsomi answered awkwardly. Her green dress felt extra short.

Klara laughed. "They should have sent him here to build a bridge across our Pontenilo," she said merrily. "I doubt it will ever happen! Did you want some sugar?"

The tall girl's dark eyes seemed to be assessing Pérsomi. She was the girl who swam in the pool with Gerbrand and the others, the girl with the big sunglasses. Pérsomi wondered whether she was Reinier's sister, Annabel.

"Just sugar, Pérsomi?" Klara asked.

"And . . . flour. Please."

On her way back, Pérsomi's thoughts kept returning to the three pretty girls. They had lovely clothes and elegant sandals. The kitchen had been filled with sunshine, and the smell of coffee had hung over everything.

At home Hannapat asked, "Did you bring the sugar and the coffee?"

"Coffee? I brought sugar and flour."

"Oh, you are stupid," Hannapat said, annoyed. "Are we supposed to drink flour? I was so looking forward to a sip of coffee!"

❦

Wednesday evening Pérsomi's ma said, "Mr. Fourie said they need help with the meat. They slaughtered a cow."

"As long as they give us meat as well," Hannapat said, "and not just the innards."

"Poor people can't pick and choose," said her ma.

"I'll eat anything that looks like meat," said Sissie. "I'll help too."

Pérsomi thought about eating meat nearly every day at the dormitory.

But the next day as they were leaving, Sissie felt sick. She didn't get up from her mattress. "My tummy aches," she said, drawing up her knees, "and my head."

"Oh, Sissie, just shut up," said her ma.

"Auntie Sis said we must pick some burstwort," said Sissie.

"She said we must boil it with wild dagga and white turmeric for my tough tummy."

"Oh heavens above," said her ma.

"You forgot about your tooth, you lazy lump," Hannapat scolded as they went out.

Things were hectic at the barn. Boelie and De Wet were hoisting up the heavy cow with a block and tackle, Mr. Fourie was sharpening a knife on the whetstone, Klara came walking toward them with an armful of bowls, and Lena was scrubbing the tables, making sure they were spotless.

"Hello, Pérsomi," De Wet said. "Any news from Gerbrand?"

"He says he's fine," said Pérsomi.

"Oh, here you are," said Aunt Lulu, coming from the kitchen with a bowl of water. "Go wash your hands. Klara, call Irene to come and help."

"Here she comes, Mommy," said Klara.

Boelie looked up from where he was cutting up the carcass with a big knife. "Hello, Pérsomi, are you also on vacation?" he said, as if he hadn't expected her there.

"Yes," she said, but he didn't seem to hear.

"Hannapat, bring the wheelbarrow so that you can take the entrails," Boelie said. "Do you want any of it, Ma?"

"Only the liver and kidneys, and of course the guts for the sausage casings, the rest can go," said Aunt Lulu. "There's no time today for scraping offal."

Pérsomi saw Hannapat's eyes narrow before she turned and went over to the wheelbarrow in the corner, swinging her hips impertinently.

With one deft stroke Boelie cut the carcass open along the stomach from top to bottom. The entrails spilled out—bundles of guts, the stomach and its contents, the gall bladder and pluck and lungs—and landed in the wheelbarrow. "Oh, yuck, I'm going to be sick!" Irene screamed and ran back to the house.

Boelie looked up, disturbed. "High time someone taught that little girl a lesson," he said as he removed the last of the entrails.

"She'll come and lend a hand later," said his mother. "There isn't much for her to do at present."

Boelie raised his eyebrows, but said nothing.

"Hannapat," said Aunt Lulu, "take the entrails home. And make sure you cook them today, or they'll attract the jackals. Boelie, keep the feet to make brawn."

"Hold here for me, Pérsomi," said Boelie as he pulled on the cow's foreleg.

The sun was high and the entire forequarter had been cut up into biltong and meat for dried sausage by the time Irene's ouma brought a pot of coffee. Behind her followed Lena with a tray laden with cups and a large plate of sandwiches. There was no sign of Irene or Hannapat.

"Cut the biltong into thin strips and salt it well," said Irene's ouma. "Bring the tongue, Klara, I want to pickle it."

Aunt Lulu said, "Jemima, when you've finished your coffee, go home and and deal with the innards. I'm worried about the heat, maybe we should have waited a week or two with the slaughtering."

"Then you would've had to do without the slave labor, Ma," De Wet teased her.

"Slave labor, my eye," said his mother. "When I was a child—"

"Yes, yes," said Boelie.

When Aunt Lulu disappeared into the kitchen to start making the brawn, only De Wet, Boelie, and Pérsomi remained.

"So they drop out, one by one," De Wet said. "Only the three of us are left and the hindquarter is still hanging from the hook."

"Hmm," said Boelie. "Ma will have to get Irene in line. What good is it Ma telling us how hard she had to work as a child, while that young lady sits around reading stories like Queen Victoria?"

"Pérsomi, I think you should start cutting up the sausage meat," said De Wet. "Here, cut the cubes this size. And try to remove as much of the sinewy bits as possible, or we'll be cleaning the mincer more often than we'll be mincing."

Pérsomi drew the bowl closer and began to cut. She did her best, because she didn't want to disappoint Boelie and De Wet.

"Oupa irritates me a bit with his English ways," Boelie said suddenly.

"Goodness, you're in a bad mood today," said De Wet.

"He still believes in Smuts, can you believe it?" Boelie complained. "And this knife is bloody dull."

"You seem to have your knife in for everyone," De Wet said calmly.

"Oh, De Wet, stop being witty. Oupa won't hear a word against Smuts, can you deny it?"

Pérsomi felt herself grow tense. What if Boelie and De Wet began to fight?

"What has Smuts done now?" asked De Wet.

"I swear Smuts and Van Rensburg are hand in glove," Boelie said crossly. "I don't trust Van Rensburg anymore."

"Why not?" De Wet asked and put another large chunk of meat on the table. "This is the last piece," he said to Pérsomi, "then we can begin mincing it for the sausage. How're you getting along?"

She just nodded.

"Smuts and his spies are everywhere," said Boelie. "I'm beginning to believe Van Rensburg was planted by Smuts to keep the OB in check. Why isn't Van Rensburg doing anything useful?"

"Who's Van Rensburg?" Pérsomi asked.

"Leader of the OB," De Wet answered. "I'll set up the mincer. He's a lawyer. Used to be Tielman Roos's private secretary, later he became Secretary of Justice, and in 1936 he was appointed Administrator of the Free State. In January this year he became Commandant-General of the Ossewabrandwag."

"Must you always deliver a bloody lecture when someone asks you a question?" Boelie asked.

"Now she knows," De Wet said coolly. "You're the one who always says she's so bright."

Pérsomi's hands stopped moving for a moment. A warm feeling rose up inside her—Boelie had said she was bright. He had told De Wet, who was very bright, that she, Pérsomi, was bright.

The warm feeling settled somewhere deep inside her.

❦

"It's nice being back at school," Pérsomi said to Beth the first evening. She was drying her hair, her body still tingling after a hot bath.

"I suppose so," said Beth, "but it's much nicer at home."

No, Pérsomi thought, no. But she didn't say it out loud.

"I brought you a present," said Beth, smiling timidly. She took something out of her suitcase. "It's a bit old and unfortunately it's in English, but it's all we have at the mission," she said, handing Pérsomi a Bible.

Pérsomi ran her hands over the worn leather cover. Then she opened the Bible and drew a deep breath. She was aware of the vaguely moldy smell of the closed pages in her nostrils. "Thanks, Beth," she said.

"Mrs. Reverend also made cookies," Beth went on. "Here, have one."

Pérsomi had nothing to share with her. "I'll have one later, thanks, Beth," she said. "First I . . . want to write to my brother."

At home there had been no paper and no pen.

"At our church Reverend prays for the soldiers at every service," said Beth. "They're fighting in Abyssinia now, I think."

"Yes," said Pérsomi, carefully tearing a page from the middle of her math book, "that's where my big brother is."

Beth was the only one at the school she could tell. To everyone else the Red Tabs were traitors, fighting for the enemy.

She unscrewed the inkpot, dipped her pen, and began to write.

22 APRIL 1941

Dear Gerbrand,
    It's the second school term now and I'm back at the dormitory. I find high school

She shouldn't have written *Dear Gerbrand*. He wouldn't like it. But she couldn't very well put a line through it and write *Hello*. What would that look like? And she couldn't afford to tear another page from her book.

So she carried on.

very nice. I am good at the schoolwork and also at athletics, I was the junior Victrix Ludorum and at the Potties meeting I was named best junior female athlete.

She worried she was boasting. But Gerbrand was the only one who would understand, and she was dying to tell him.

The athletics season is over now, but the teacher said I should come and play hockey, she will find me a stick and boots.
    The boy who sits next to me in class is Reinier de Vos. He says you were a very good rugby player. His sister Annabel was in your class.

I have a very nice roommate, Beth Murray is her name. She brought me a Bible, because she's from a mission station. I'm glad, now I have a Bible as well.

Everyone is fine at home, Ma and Hannapat and Sissie. You know about Lewies Pieterse, I wrote to you about him. It's much better now that he's gone.

I think Ma misses Gertjie and Baby. And you, especially, I know she does.

Gerbrand, I really want to know why you enlisted. I'm not saying it's right or wrong, I just want to know why. There's no one here who can tell me, so I'm asking you. Please don't take it the wrong way, I just want to know. So that I can understand.

In the vacation I saw Boelie and De Wet. They slaughtered a cow. And I saw Klara and Oom Freddie's daughter, Christine, too. They send their best wishes.

We also have a lot of mosquitoes here, but soon it will be winter and then they'll be gone.

She couldn't think of anything else to write. She wished she could tell him to come home, but he wouldn't like it. So she ended the letter.

Best wishes.

Your sister,
Pérsomi

❧

"You've never watched a movie?" Reinier asked her one Wednesday, astounded. "Everyone has been to the bioscope."

"Not me," she answered. "And I won't get there anytime soon, because it costs money and that's something I don't have."

"I can't believe it," he said. "I'll give you money, then you can go, on Saturday evening."

"I won't take your money, Reinier, and you'd know that, if you knew me at all."

"Must you always be so pigheaded? I suppose I'll have to ask you on a date then. We can't let you go through life unbioscoped."

"Date?"

"Ask you to go with me. Whatever."

So that Saturday she stood in front of the town hall with the rest of the dormitory girls, dressed in their school uniforms.

"It's so stupid that we have to wear our uniforms to bioscope," said Irene somewhere behind her. "The town children wear day clothes. I can't believe we boarders have to wear our jumpers!"

Pérsomi spotted Reinier at the door, waving their tickets in the air. She joined him.

"Let's get good seats at the front," he said. "The kids who want to make out sit at the back."

"I don't want to make out!" said Pérsomi.

Reinier laughed. "Don't worry, I won't even try."

The hall was dimly lit, the curtains drawn. A white screen had been erected against the heavy dark-blue velvet stage curtains.

"The movie is *The Wizard of Oz*," said Reinier. "But first there's a Western, a serial. There's a new episode every month. And then there's *African Mirror*, the news program."

Pérsomi sat quite still, but excitement made her entire body tingle. She wondered if Gerbrand had ever seen a movie.

The wonders of modern technology unfolded in front of her eyes. She gazed at the screen, enchanted. She watched the cowboys on their horses, heard them shoot, heard the girl in her beautiful dress scream, saw the wagon tumbling over the cliff, the wheels still turning.

"To be continued" appeared on the screen.

"Oh, no!" said Pérsomi. How was she ever going to find out whether the poor girl survived the accident?

"She'll live," Reinier assured her. He went to the movies nearly every Saturday, he would know.

There was the sound of trumpets from the screen. *African Mirror* . . . The words grew bigger and bigger.

Images of the war on a distant continent came to the bushveld, stirring the hearts of the people who saw what was happening.

The flat voice of the commentator went on and on, as if the news he was reading was nothing special. "On May the tenth the British House of Commons suffered damage during an air strike," he said. The image of a ruined building, once part of the Houses of Parliament, flashed on the screen.

"On May the twentieth Germany invaded Crete," said the commentator. Planes dived low over buildings, dropping bombs on their targets. Ships steamed out of a bombed harbor. "Britain is withdrawing from Crete," said the voice.

Pérsomi sat riveted, watching, her hands pressed to her cheeks.

But Gerbrand wasn't in Europe, he was in East Africa.

Then the scene shifted to a different part of the world. "On May the nineteenth the Duke of Aosta with five thousand men surrendered to Brigadier Dan Pienaar at Amba Alagi."

Pérsomi leaned forward. That was where Gerbrand was. Maybe she would catch a glimpse of him. But all the soldiers looked the same in their uniforms.

"South African soldiers are being sent to North Africa." Pérsomi watched as rows and rows of soldiers boarded a warship, cheerily waving at the cameras, their big bags slung over their shoulders.

"And since the first of May, families on the home front have been eating only standard government bread," said the commentator. On the screen a father, mother, two little boys, and two little girls sat at a neatly laid table, eating bread. The boys' hair was slicked down on their foreheads. The girls wore frilly dresses and ribbons in their hair.

After intermission the actual movie began. It started with black-and-white pictures, just like the cowboy serial and *African Mirror*, but then it changed and everything was brightly colored. Pérsomi's jaw dropped. Hastily she closed her mouth without taking her eyes off the big screen.

The movie drew Pérsomi in. Fear gripped her when the tornado flattened poor Dorothy's home. She laughed at the stupid scarecrow, at the stick-like tin man, at the cowardly lion. The jolly songs swept her along to a strange and wonderful world.

"Did you enjoy it?" asked Reinier when the lights came back on.

"It was absolutely . . . amazing," said Pérsomi. "It was so . . . real. Thank you."

They walked back to the dormitory with the others. In the cloudless sky overhead the moon hung like a big ball. Ahead of them a group of girls were giggling about something. Far behind them the prefect and her boyfriend came sauntering along. The streetlights cast long shadows that became shorter as they approached, then vanished until the next streetlight drew the long shadows from under their feet again.

Pérsomi said, "You only actually realize how bad the war is when you see it on the screen, larger than life. And especially when you hear it."

"I don't care too much about the war," said Reinier, shrugging.

"The Khakis went looking for trouble and they're getting what they deserve. Serves them right."

"But those are *people* whose homes are being blown up, Reinier."

He shrugged again. "I'm an OB man," he said, "I'm against the war."

"My brother is a Red Tab," she said, almost defiantly.

"That's his business," said Reinier.

"I wrote him a letter to ask why he joined but he hasn't replied."

"Hmm," said Reinier and kicked at a pebble. "What matters is how *you* feel about it."

"I don't like war. I think it's stupid and cruel," she replied, "and a waste of money."

He laughed. "Seems to me you're an OB man yourself."

"I'm a girl, and I don't belong to the OB. I think for myself, thanks very much."

He laughed so loudly that the girls walking ahead of them looked over their shoulders. "You're strange for a girl, Pérsomi," he said affably. "But I could tell you a thing or two, if you wish."

"Things I don't already know?" she teased.

"Things you definitely don't know," he said. "Many people inside the OB feel that the movement isn't doing enough, that they should protest more openly against the war."

She thought of Boelie.

"I know that," she said.

"At the beginning of the war," Reinier eagerly continued, "Smuts issued a decree that authorized the police to confiscate firearms. One guy got his hands on a number of the police's receipt books, and he drove around the bushveld confiscating people's firearms. And he wrote out receipts—"

"How did you hear such a thing?" Pérsomi asked skeptically.

"I listen when my dad and his friends are talking," said Reinier. "Dad's a lawyer, didn't you know? You pick up a lot of things if you keep your ears open."

"Well, I think you should be careful what you repeat," said Pérsomi.

"I'm only telling *you*," said Reinier. "You're not like other girls. You won't gossip, I know that."

"Oh," said Pérsomi. Not like other girls?

"Anyway, he wrote out receipts under a variety of false names, and he gave himself any rank he felt like that particular day. Apparently he got his hands on seven hundred rifles to be used when they take over the government, see?"

"I see," said Pérsomi. How was she not like other girls? "But I really think you should be careful who you talk to about these things."

He smiled. "I'm telling you because I trust you. I won't tell anyone else," he said.

The week before the start of the June exams, Reinier whispered to her in class, "There was news about the OB on the radio last night. It didn't sound good."

"Why?" Pérsomi whispered back.

"The police are raiding the houses of OB members and arresting the residents."

"Arresting?" she said, startled. She imagined Boelie being arrested at the Big House. "But isn't it just a . . . cultural organization?"

"It's not illegal, that's what my dad says. But he also says some of their members are suspected of sabotage. They blow up railway lines and stuff, you know?"

Slowly her hands went to her mouth. She clearly remembered Boelie's words: "We must sabotage things, like the telephone exchanges, the railway lines, troop trains, harbors—everything that's needed to take our men up North."

"And . . . will they go"—she hesitated to say the words—"to jail?"

"Shh, not so loud. My dad says they're being sent to internment camps."

"Bloody English!" she said.

"Don't swear!" he said. "And lower your voice! My dad said last night that more than 3,700 people were sent to the camps last month."

She shook her head, dismayed.

"It doesn't look good, Pérsomi. I'm a bit worried about . . . my dad."

"Why?" she asked. "Are you afraid he might blow up the station? Or the post office?"

He laughed softly. "No, man, he wouldn't do that!"

"Well, is he an OB member?"

Reinier nodded. "Definitely, and he feels strongly about the cause. I'm afraid he'll help the guys who get into trouble, the OB guys."

"Help in what way?" she asked.

"Defend them, in court. And if you defend the wrong people, it can be very dangerous, says my mom."

That evening she realized that she had never heard Reinier mention his mom before. He often spoke about his dad, but never his mom. She wondered why.

FIVE

PÉRSOMI STOOD WITH HER MA AND HANNAPAT IN FRONT OF the rundown outhouse. The hole of the longdrop had collapsed while Pérsomi was in school. The sides just caved in.

"Must be because of all the rain," said her ma.

"And then a piece of the wall also fell." Hannapat pointed. "And the door came off its hinges. See how it hangs?"

"We must fix the longdrop," said Pérsomi, upset. "We can't keep going behind the bushes!"

"Impossible," said Hannapat.

"Then we'll have to build a new one," said Pérsomi. She sighed. Of course she didn't know how. Welfare had taken Sissie somewhere that she could work, and although her stepbrother Piet had returned from Joburg, unemployed, he was unwilling to lift a finger.

"And who do you think is going to dig the hole?" asked Hannapat. "You know how hard the soil is. But you've probably forgotten, because you live in town now and it's up to us to plant the pumpkins."

"Piet must help," said Pérsomi. "We must—"

"Do I look like an aardvark to you? Or a springhare, huh?" Hannapat objected. "I don't dig holes, and neither will Piet."

"But we *must*—"

"If you're too hoity-toity to go behind a bush, why don't you ask Mr. Fourie to send a farmhand?" said Hannapat and began to walk away. "It's their job to dig holes."

The last time the roof of the longdrop blew off, Gerbrand fixed it. Mr. Fourie gave them two sheets of metal and some nails, and Gerbrand took off his shirt and stood on top of the walls to fix the roof. He worked for three days, chopping new crossbeams and plastering the walls. She helped him. She carried the axe, mixed cement, passed the nails, and searched for a flat rock to use as a hammer. He didn't really speak to her, but when the roof was on and they stepped back to look, he said: "You worked hard, too, Pérsomi. Good."

But now Gerbrand was gone.

"Heavens, Sis, what's wrong?" her ma asked outside the kitchen door.

"I knew it," Auntie Sis panted, dabbing at her face with a gray handkerchief. "Sunday afternoon I was walking round the back, to the outhouse . . . Man, what's wrong with your outhouse?"

"What did you know?" asked Pérsomi's ma.

"Can I have a sip of coffee? I have heart palpitations from the long walk."

Pérsomi went inside and shoved a log into the mouth of the stove. Piet sat at the table, scraping dirt from his fingernails. He got up and went outside. The wisps of smoke trickling through the broken oven door made her eyes water and filled the entire room.

She added a little water to the coffee pot. The grounds had been used over and over. They were gray as dishwater, but the coffee tin was empty.

She heard Auntie Sis sigh deeply outside. "I saw a vision . . . oh man alive!"

They waited. She sighed again and said, "I saw coffins piled one on top of the other, piles of coffins. And people with the coffins, but behind bars."

Breathless silence.

"That's all," said Auntie Sis.

"Lewies?" Pérsomi's ma whispered.

"Man, I couldn't make out any faces, you know how the visions work. But this morning when I got the news, I knew."

"Who, Auntie Sis?" Hannapat asked impatiently.

"It's Boelie," Auntie Sis gasped, still short of breath, "it's Boelie and De Wet!"

Alarmed, Pérsomi went to stand in the doorway.

"Oh heavens!" said Pérsomi's ma. "Has there been a death?"

"Man, what are you saying! Worse, worse, I'm telling you! Piet, bring me a chair. My back won't last on this bench."

"Worse than death?" Ma sank down on the old car seat at the back door.

Auntie Sis kept wiping her face with her big hankie. "You're telling me," she said. "It's police business!"

"Police!" Ma and Hannapat said simultaneously.

"Put that chair over there, Piet," said Auntie Sis. "What happened to your longdrop?"

"What . . . what about the police?" Ma asked.

"Man, don't ask!" sighed Auntie Sis, lowering herself onto the straight-backed kitchen chair. "The police raided their room in Pretoria—at the university where they're studying!"

"The police raided their room?" her ma repeated.

"Listen to what I'm saying: The police raided their room, I'm telling you."

"But . . . why?" her ma asked, dismayed.

"They must have been looking for stolen goods," said Piet.

"Man, I didn't want to say it, because I don't talk behind

people's backs, but that's what I thought, too, and so did Attie," sighed Auntie Sis. "And to crown it all, your longdrop is falling to pieces."

"Stolen goods!" her ma said, shocked.

Pérsomi poured the coffee, knowing that wasn't why. But she didn't try to explain the police raids on members of the OB.

"And the coffins?" asked Hannapat.

"What coffins?" their ma asked, startled.

"The ones Auntie Sis saw."

"Oh, that? No, that's probably still coming." Auntie Sis gave another deep sigh. "But death is waiting, it's waiting."

Pérsomi gave Auntie Sis and her ma their coffee. Then she turned and walked away. She managed to walk away calmly, not to break into a run. But the moment she found herself behind the first hill, the running just happened. It came into her legs like a release and took over her entire body.

She stopped only when the burning in her chest became worse than her fear for Boelie. What if they caught him and put him behind barbed wire in a concentration camp?

She had to speak to Boelie herself, hear from him what was going on.

This bloody, bloody war.

🌿

When Mr. Fourie saw the state of their longdrop at the end of the week, he was furious. "When did this happen?" he asked. "Please don't tell me you're going in the veld!"

"Oh heavens, it's the rain, Mr. Fourie," said her ma, frightened. "I'm sorry."

"But why haven't you done anything about it, Jemima?" he scolded as he walked around the longdrop. "My goodness, you could have told me! I can't smell it if something is wrong down here!" Then he stopped. "I believe Piet is here."

Silence.

"Where's Piet?" he asked.

Pérsomi could see the trouble coming.

"He's feeling a bit out of sorts this morning," said her ma, crumpling her hankie.

"Where is he?"

Silence.

"He's . . . inside," Hannapat said.

"Still asleep at this hour?" roared Mr. Fourie, and he strode toward the house.

"O Lord, help us," said Ma.

Mr. Fourie entered their home. Moments later Piet came stumbling through the back door, his neck drawn down between his shoulder blades, his arms covering his head. Mr. Fourie was right behind him.

"Start digging!" shouted Mr. Fourie. He picked up the shovel next to the back door. "Take this. Go dig the hole higher up. We'll have to move the entire outhouse. And you two girls, go sweep that kitchen and clean up the place. It looks like a pigsty. And before the vacation is over you plaster that floor with dung. Do you hear me?"

Red-hot shame flooded Pérsomi's body.

Mr. Fourie strode away, stiff with anger. "When I come back this afternoon, that hole had better be halfway done and the house spotless, is that clear?" he said over his shoulder.

As soon as Mr. Fourie could no longer be seen, Piet threw down the shovel, fuming. "Who does he think he is, talking to me like that?" He spat on the ground beside him.

"Mr. Fourie treats us well," Pérsomi said firmly. "What use are we to him? It wouldn't take much for him to chase us away!"

"O Lord, help us," groaned her ma.

"No one speaks to Piet Pieterse like that!" Piet panted, his face bright red. "I'm not a laborer who digs holes! I don't know why I ever came back here. With Pa gone, you women are pathetic. You can't even keep the house clean. Pigs! Ma, give me back my pound. I'm leaving. I'm going back to Joburg."

"Oh heavens, Piet," her ma tried to protest, "I thought you said—"

"Give me back my pound or I'll beat the living daylights out of the lot of you. You're asking for it."

"Give him his pound, Ma," said Pérsomi. "The sooner he leaves, the better." She turned to Piet. "Do us all a favor and stay in Joburg forever."

"Oh heavens above," groaned her ma.

"*You* can clean the house," said Hannapat, plonking herself down in the winter sun with her back against the wall. "I'm always doing it while you live like a lady at school."

When Mr. Fourie returned that afternoon, he was even angrier. "That lazy lout," he said when he learned Piet had gone. He ran his hand over his face and shook his head. "I'll send someone on Monday to fix the outhouse." He turned and began to walk away.

"Mr. Fourie?" Pérsomi called.

He stopped and turned, his face a thundercloud.

She looked him in the eye. "Thank you, Mr. Fourie," she said. "You're good to us, even if we can't help you on the farm anymore."

He looked at her steadily.

"Thank you," she said again.

"It's okay," he said and turned to go.

But for a moment, just before he turned his back on her, she thought she saw a strange expression in his eyes.

The vacation was almost at an end before Pérsomi got a chance to speak to Boelie. She happened to see him walk slowly up the mountain. He had his rifle in his hand but didn't look as if he was planning to hunt.

She took a shortcut around the back of the baboon cliffs and reached the wild fig before him. She sank down onto the flat rocks and stretched out her legs. From up here she could see the road leading to the town, to the world where Irene lived in a room that looked the same as hers and ate the same food that Pérsomi did.

She watched as Boelie approached slowly, raising his hand in a kind of greeting. He sank down beside her. Carefully he laid his rifle on the rocky ledge between them.

"Hello, Boelie."

They sat quietly, gazing into the distance. His rifle lay next to her.

"You can see almost all the way to town from up here," she said.

"Hmm," said Boelie. He sounded tired. Or maybe he just didn't feel like talking.

Maybe she should go, it was no good trying to talk to him if he didn't want to. And she didn't want him to think her a nuisance. But it was her last chance to speak to him before she must go back to school.

"Are you looking forward to going back?" he asked, as if she had spoken aloud.

"Yes. I like school, but I do miss the farm sometimes, and the mountain."

"Yes," he said.

Silence.

"And you?" she asked. "Are you looking forward to going back to Pretoria?"

"I don't know, Pérsomi," he said. Then he shook his head slowly. "No, I'm not."

"I hear the OB is more active nowadays, especially around Pretoria," she began.

"Hmm," he said.

She licked her lips. "I hear they're blowing up stuff. And sometimes they get caught."

"You shouldn't listen to stories."

"Almost four thousand have been arrested and sent to camps, Boelie," she continued. "They're not just stories."

He made no reply.

"Almost every day I read about more people being arrested. Two students from the university just before the vacation, and an Afrikaans school principal from Helderberg, and a composer or something. I read it in the newspaper, Boelie."

"Heidelberg. The principal is from Heidelberg," he said, gazing into the distance. "Yes, Pérsomi, you're right."

"I know," she said. "There's a group, they call themselves the Stormjaers. They work with the OB. Tell me about them, Boelie."

He frowned.

"I . . . just want to know more," she said, "so that I can understand."

He was still not looking at her. "I can tell you, yes. But remember, Pers, I'm not saying I belong to them, I'm just telling you about them. And it's better not to mention these things to anyone. It's . . . safer to say nothing."

"I can keep a secret," she said.

"Okay. The Stormjaers are an ultraconservative militant group inside the Nazi party in Germany."

"Oh."

"The Stormjaers have a lot of members. In the Transvaal alone there are thought to be about eight thousand, fully trained and armed. These include members of the police force. They say some of the most senior police officers are Stormjaers."

"Who are *they*?" she asked.

"What do you mean?"

"Who are the people who say so?"

"Just . . . you know . . . the people who know," Boelie replied. "The Stormjaers are very serious about the cause. You know, Pers"—for the first time he looked at her, his dark eyes burning and intense—"a Stormjaer has to be willing to lay down his life for the freedom of his people. And if he betrays the ideals of the Stormjaers, they'll target him."

She frowned. "Is it worth it, Boelie? Laying down your life for the freedom of your people?"

"It's what soldiers of many countries in Europe and North Africa are doing at this moment . . . thousands, millions of them," he said.

"So the Stormjaers are also fighting in a kind of war. They're also soldiers."

"I suppose so," he admitted. "They stand up and fight for what they believe is right. They have their own convictions."

"It's important to have your own convictions, isn't it?"

"Yes, or you're nothing but a piece of clay," he said.

"And . . . you agree with them?" she made certain. "With the Stormjaers, I mean?"

"Let me put it this way: I completely understand how they feel. Something must be done! South Africa won't solve its problems by talking."

"Oh," she said. "So you do support them?"

"Why do you want to know?"

"I hear what I hear, Boelie. I know your room was raided, your room and De Wet's."

"So?"

"I worry about you," she said. "I don't want them to put you in a concentration camp."

"Internment camp."

"Same thing."

"Why not?" he asked.

"Why not what?"

"Why don't you want me to be put in a camp?"

"Because . . . you're my friend," she said.

He gave her a strange look. "You saw me walk up here, so you waited for me, didn't you?"

"Yes, I did."

He nodded slowly and smiled. It was the first time she had seen him smile since she'd come home for the vacation, and his face looked a little less tired. "You're a remarkable girl," he said. Then he got to his feet. "I'm going back now. Don't worry about me, I know what I'm doing."

She watched him walk downhill until his strong figure became one with the veld in the distance.

She felt even more afraid.

❦

"Go buy what you need at Ismail's," her ma had said just before she went back to school. "There's money there."

Pérsomi thought Gerbrand must be sending money directly to Mr. Ismail's store.

"I don't need Gerbrand's money, Ma," she tried to protest. "Why don't you buy food instead—coffee and sugar and flour and stuff? And soap?"

"Oh heavens, Pérsomi, the money is for you and that's the end of it!"

Pérsomi pondered this as she walked to the store alone. How

had her ma known about the money? If Gerbrand had explained it in a letter, Pérsomi would have seen it.

As always, the store was dimly lit after the bright sunlight outside. And it smelled exactly the same. Good.

"Well, hello!" Yusuf's cheery voice greeted her. "I thought the war had swallowed you."

"Hello, Yusuf." She smiled. "The vacation swallowed me."

"Now it's back to jail, isn't it? What can we do for you today?"

"My brother sent some money, I want to buy soap and toothpaste," she said.

"Wait, I'll ask my grandpa," he said. "Look at the nightgowns while you're here. There aren't many left and with the war and everything, we won't be getting any new ones."

She went to the drawer and opened it. For a moment she stood looking at the soft pink fabric.

"Take it out," he said behind her. "There's enough money for soap and toothpaste and that nightgown."

She gave a puzzled frown. "How much money is there?" she asked.

He gave her a mischievous smile. "Pockets full," he said.

"Yusuf!" she threatened.

He laughed, his teeth white against his dark skin. "A pound!" he said.

Gerbrand couldn't have sent that much. What about their ma? And Hannapat?

"It's all yours, girl," said Yusuf. "Spend it."

"I could never spend that much money."

"Well, buy what you need and leave the rest on the book," he suggested. "I'll get the soap and things, you pick a nightgown. The day after tomorrow they might all be gone."

The drawer represented a new world—the world of real people. She took the nightgowns out one by one and spread them on the counter. Each one was more beautiful than the last. They were all around ten shillings.

"What's your favorite color?" Yusuf asked.

"I could never spend this much on a nightgown," she said.

"I can show you day dresses for the same price," he said.

She shook her head. "We wear a uniform all day. And I've got a dress for church."

"Come on, Pérsomi, spoil yourself," he said. "The soap and toothpaste come to less than a shilling. If you buy the nightgown, you'll still have almost ten bob on the book."

She put her hand out and touched the pink nightgown. Her hand on the soft fabric was red and chapped, like her ma's hands. "You're a shrewd salesman, Yusuf Ismail," she said.

"You have to sleep in something," he smiled, carefully folding it. "What do you hear from your brother?"

"He doesn't write very often," she said.

"My brother is in Egypt now. He went there in June. To think he has actually seen the pyramids, and the Red Sea and the River Nile! I feel like joining up myself. 'Join the army and see the world,' you know? Anything else for you?"

She hesitated a moment. "Do you have . . . cream? For . . . the skin?"

"Oh yes, all kinds," he said and took her to another counter. "Different colors, scents, everything. They say soap and cream and stuff will soon be in short supply, but at the moment we still have lots."

"I think I'll buy some cream too," she said.

"I can give you an expensive cream," he said, "but the best cream is the kind my granny mixes herself, and it's better value for the money."

"Maybe you're not such a great salesman after all, Yusuf. I would have bought the more expensive cream!"

Monday morning during math Reinier passed her a page from a newspaper. She looked at the date at the top of the page: Friday 18 July 1941. "Daring Theft of Dynamite—Nocturnal Incident in Stone Quarry."

Relief flooded her. The story was about South Africa, not Gerbrand's Abyssinia.

Wednesday morning a large supply of dynamite and explosives was stolen from a quarry belonging to Iscor seven miles outside Pretoria. The quarry is protected by armed guards.

During the night nine men arrived in three cars. They overpowered the guards and locked them up. Dynamite was removed from a storeroom and detonators from another. The stolen items were loaded into the cars and the perpetrators drove off.

She looked up, shrugging. "Read on," whispered Reinier.

Soon after they left, one of the cars left the road and landed in a ditch. The occupants stopped a passing truck and asked the driver to assist them. The three cars disappeared without a trace.

The police are looking for the truck driver to help them identify the offenders. The guards were relieved of their firearms and one of them was slightly injured.

She gave the paper back. "And?" she asked softly.

"They were OB members, Pérsomi, Stormjaers," he whispered.

She understood. "They stole dynamite to blow things up?" she said, shocked.

"Shh! Yes, I think so. My dad says with the Nazis achieving one victory after another, the antiwar faction in South Africa is gaining ground."

"If they steal," she whispered earnestly, "they'll go to jail." She feared for Boelie. The incident was so close to Pretoria.

"And if they blow up things."

"Reinier and Pérsomi, stand!" the teacher said.

Guiltily they got to their feet.

"Didn't I tell you to carry on with your work?"

"Sir, we've finished our work, sir," Reinier said.

"Well, do some more," the teacher said.

"Yes, of course. Right, sir." said Reinier.

"Yes, sir," said Pérsomi.

All day long worry gnawed at her belly.

When they were walking back to the dormitory after school that afternoon, Pérsomi heard Irene say to her friends: "Imagine! Sitting at the back, chatting away with Reinier. Mr. Van Wyk had to tell them off. With Reinier, of all people! I wonder if she really thinks she has a chance. With those grasshopper legs?"

Pérsomi slowed down. But Irene's voice still came to her on the wind. "She crawls out of a hole, man, believe me, I know. Why my dad didn't chase the whole lot off the farm years ago none of us can understand."

❧

That evening she wrote Gerbrand a long letter. She wrote as small as she could because she didn't want to tear more than one page from her exercise book.

Gerbrand,

Thank you very, very much for the pound you sent Mr. Ismail. I bought soap and toothpaste, and a pink nightie. Maybe you think I should have bought a day dress, but see, we wear our uniform all day and I already have a dress for church. And a girl likes to feel good when she goes to bed. And I bought cream to make my hands soft.

She told him about the farm and their ma and Hannapat, and about Sissie who was working now and living in a kind of hostel. She made no mention of Piet and the longdrop.

She wished she could tell him about Boelie and how worried she was, but she couldn't, because she had promised not to say anything. And Gerbrand had said their letters were censored.

At the end she wrote:

Gerbrand, will you please write to me? Please tell me what you are doing and please tell me why you joined the army and if you are happy.

Look after yourself. Because I really miss talking to you.

Best wishes.

Your sister,

Pérsomi

She folded the letter neatly, wrote the address on the envelope, and put a stamp on it. She would mail it on Friday.

Then she took her Bible and read from the gospel of Luke.

But when she finally fell asleep she didn't dream of Gerbrand behind the rolls of barbed wire with his rifle and round tin hat. Her mind turned to Boelie, sitting in a barbed-wire cage, his face like a mask, his eyes staring straight ahead without any expression.

Just after the short recess Tuesday morning the school secretary came to their history class and spoke to their teacher. The teacher frowned slightly. Her hand went to her mouth, and she shook her head.

"Irene, please go to the office with Mrs. Olivier," the teacher said. "Take your books along."

Pérsomi felt her entire being sink to the pit of her stomach.

"It's Boelie," she whispered to Reinier.

"Boelie?" Reinier asked, puzzled.

OB, Pérsomi penciled in her history book.

Stormjaers? Reinier wrote.

Pérsomi nodded and took care to erase the words.

She was right. Rumors soon spread throughout the school.

That evening she said to Beth, "Now I know that prayer doesn't help. I prayed so often for Boelie not to get into trouble, especially during the past few weeks. Now look what has happened."

"We don't understand the ways of God," said Beth, "but He knows what He's doing."

"I won't pray anymore," said Pérsomi firmly.

"Whether you pray or not, He is in control," Beth said. "He will always be there for you."

There was a long silence. Then Pérsomi asked: "Beth, will you please pray for Boelie to get through this thing? And . . . for Gerbrand, too, for his safety, and happiness. I really miss him."

On the last day of school she received an award for being the top achiever in Form II. She beat Reinier by a whopping 2 percent. She'd worked hard for it, so she walked proudly to the stage, stood tall among the other achievers, and looked out over the sea of black-and-white uniforms and upturned faces in the school hall. She shook the headmaster's hand before returning to her place among the other Form IIs. Afterward, Beth put her arm around Pérsomi, and Reinier came over from the boys' side to congratulate her.

But when she walked into the dormitory, she overheard Irene say: "Not bad for the daughter of a jailbird."

"Jailbird?" one of her friends asked. "Who's in jail?"

"Her father, more than a year already," said Irene.

"And you're only telling us now?"

No one spoke of Boelie's arrest.

"Oh, you know." Irene replied sweetly, "one doesn't like to speak about that kind of thing. They *are* our bywoners, after all."

SIX

THE FLIES BUZZED LAZILY AGAINST THE WALLS, BUNCHED together on the tabletop, whirred aimlessly around the mattresses under the table, huddled black on the burnt porridge scrapings.

The early morning sun blazed down on the exposed tin roof, mercilessly scorched the open plains around the small house, trapped the occupants in a bottomless oven.

"It's very bad at the Big House," said Hannapat the first day. "Aunt Lulu cries all the time and Mr. Fourie is very cross, worse than ever. It's because of Boelie being in jail, that's why."

"It's an internment camp, not a jail," said Pérsomi.

"Oom Attie and Auntie Sis say it's a jail," Hannapat argued. "Boelie was in court, Auntie Sis told me, and now he's behind bars. Are you saying Oom Attie and Auntie Sis are lying? Huh?"

Pérsomi had no idea how long Boelie would be interned.

She walked down to the Pontenilo. It was a muddy, shallow pool. The rocky ledges, submerged when it rained, were dry.

Pérsomi waded in, ankle deep. The water was lukewarm and slimy, the bottom slippery. She kicked away the slimy threads, bent down, and washed her face. In the late afternoon, when it was cooler, she would go upriver to find a cleaner pool to bathe in.

Slowly she waded to the opposite bank. At its deepest, the water reached just below her knees. More than ever she missed the clean dormitory, the dishes filled with cabbage and samp and pumpkin at lunchtime, the bathrooms, and her bed with the stiff white sheets. She missed the library with its books and newspapers, the town, and Mr. Ismail's store. She missed Beth and their whispered conversations after lights-out. She missed her conversations with Reinier, who thought she was different from other girls.

It felt as if she no longer belonged here.

From the front of her dress she took the gray envelope. She knew the words of the two letters by heart. She always kept them close to her heart and held the words in her heart. She read the letters almost every day, because they were *her* letters, something tangible to which she could cling.

Dear Pérsomi,

I can't write much because we're at the front now and very busy. But you must keep writing because we look out for mail every day it's nice to get a letter.

I'm still in Abyssinia, near Adis Abeba it's their capital city. We have defeated the Eyeties completely in Abyssinia and we have put Emperor Haile Selassie that's their leader back on the throne so we're their liberators. The Abyssinians I mean. He's not much to look at you know that Haile Selassie he's a short thin little man with a face like a raisin. We take all the Eyetie prisoners to the harbor but we don't have to guard them. They guard us because they want to reach the harbor safely to get out of the country they're so afraid of the Abyssinians from here they go to the Union. Tonight they sang to us they sing really well almost like on the records.

Last night we drank an awful lot. My friend Jakkals and I and two more guys had a keg of Aquavit we took from the Eyetie prisoners. It looks almost like water but it burns all the way to your stomach and it has a good kick. This morning my head was bloddy sore but now I'm alright. Don't tell Ma this I'm only telling you.

We're done here in East Africa at the end of the week we're going further north to Egypt. That's where the pyramids are and the River Nile. Our headquarters will be in Cairo I'm looking forward to it.

I'm going to hand in the letter now it will go to the Union by ship. Tell Ma I send my best wishes.

Oh and don't thank me for the pound I didn't send old Ismail a pound for you I don't trust him.

I like it in the army now I'm going to hand in the letter.

Your brother,

Gerbrand

Pérsomi smiled. She could hear Gerbrand speak. The words went from his round handwriting to her eyes and straight to her ears.

If Gerbrand didn't send Mr. Ismail a pound, where did it come from? She had asked her ma but she only said, "Heavens, Pérsomi, stop asking so many questions."

Carefully she folded the letter, put it back in the envelope, and unfolded the second letter. The handwriting was also round, but smaller and easier to read, though it was harder to hear the words. Boelie sounded more formal than her brother.

KOFFIEFONTEIN

10 OCTOBER 1941

Dear Pérsomi,

Thank you very much for your letter that I received yesterday. I'd appreciate it if you write again, it's good to get news from outside the camp.

We are treated well. The food is reasonably good, a lot like the food you get at school.

Yes, Pers, I might have been expecting it, but it was still a shock when the police arrived. The trial was unpleasant. Because I believe in the Afrikaner cause, because I fought for my convictions, I was treated like a criminal. Not only me—thousands of other Afrikaners, many in the highest positions in our country, were arrested and locked up like criminals.

But we are not bitter, Pérsomi. We talk a lot—there's not much else to do—and we inspire each other.

Today was Kruger Day. One of the men here, John Vorster (he's an attorney in Port Elizabeth and very involved with the Purified National Party), wrote a short play that we put on tonight. Some of the men recited poetry and we even have a choir. Tonight I realized again what our people are made of. Like the men behind barbed wire in camps in Ceylon forty years ago who refused to take the Red Oath of allegiance, our national pride will never allow us to be forced to swear allegiance to the enemy's dynasty.

I want you to know, Pérsomi, that I am not ashamed, or sorry for what I did. I do regret the grief I've caused my family, but if I had a choice today, I would do it all again. I can't do anything else.

I've been interned because I'm an Afrikaner and I'm proud of it.

Your friend,
Boelie

He wrote to her as if she were a grownup, though she was only fourteen. He talked to her as if she knew what was happening in the world away from the farm.

She missed Boelie, too, she realized. She had seldom seen him during her vacations but she had always known he was somewhere on the farm. Yes, she missed Boelie, just as she missed Beth and Reinier. Because he was her friend.

But most of all she missed Gerbrand.

One sweltering morning in the second week of the vacation, Auntie Sis, breathless from her walk to the house, plopped down on the old car seat and announced, "Christine le Roux has enlisted in the war."

"Christine?" Pérsomi's ma asked. "To the war? Heavens, but she's a girl!"

"She won't fight, they don't give girls guns, I know that," said Oom Attie, arriving behind his wife. "When I was in German South-West during the Great War, where I nearly lost my knee, the girls were nurses."

Pérsomi's ma pressed her hands to her face. "Heavens, what does Freddie say, and Old Anne?" she asked.

"Well, what can they say? Christine is twenty-one, and girls don't know their place anymore," Auntie Sis answered. "Freddie le Roux walks around like a dog that's lost its tail and Old Anne lies in a darkened room all day with a wet cloth on her forehead. What's the use of being rich if you're going to lie with your eyes shut all day?"

"Do you think Christine will see Gerbrand at the front?" Hannapat asked.

"There are thousands of people at the front," said Oom Attie. "The chances of their running into each other are probably small."

"But still," said Hannapat.

"Ye-es, maybe."

"Look at this," said Reinier about two weeks after school had resumed. He handed Pérsomi an article he had torn out of the paper. "Police Force Cleaned Up," said the headline.

> January 20 a special police parade took place at Marshall Square. The National Volunteers' Brigade was summoned to help. The names of police members who were being interned were read out one by one.
>
> Then the Minister of Justice, Dr. Colin Steyn, made a public announcement.
>
> "It is with great regret that I announce today that we have had to relieve a large number of policemen of their duties because of their treacherous actions," Steyn said. "But now we know: the police force has been purged, the people of South Africa can sleep easy."

"Hundreds of policemen, my dad says," Reinier whispered.

"What now?" she asked.

He shrugged.

"Boelie said hundreds of policemen support the Stormjaers," she whispered. "He said about half the force—"

"Shh." Reinier motioned with his head in the direction of the teacher's table.

She lowered her voice. "I think you must believe in a cause and fight for it if it's expected of you."

He nodded earnestly, but said nothing further.

Just before lunch he said: "I want to talk to you, about something else."

"Well, go ahead."

He took his time to secure his satchel on the carrier of his bike before turning to her. But still he said nothing.

"Speak. I don't want to miss lunch."

"It's hard," he said, blushing.

"Hmm," said Pérsomi, "so it must be a girl."

Reinier gave her a lopsided smile and nodded, embarrassed.

"And I must play Cupid?"

He nodded again.

"Is the girl Beth?" she asked.

His jaw dropped. "Beth?" he asked. "Beth? Pérsomi, she's a real goody two-shoes, and besides, she's fat! Have a heart!"

Pérsomi felt annoyed. "Don't speak that way of Beth! She's a lovely girl!"

He shrugged.

She felt like leaving right away. But she wondered who the girl could be who had Reinier in such a state. "Well, if it isn't Beth, who is it?" she demanded.

"Irene," he said.

"Irene!" she exclaimed. "Reinier, have you lost your mind?"

"She's beautiful," he said. "She's small and . . . very pretty, and cheeky as well. And she's not afraid of anything."

"Irene! You don't know Irene!"

"I'd like to get to know her better." Reinier smiled.

"Well, it'll be without any help from me." She turned and headed for the dormitory.

"Pérsomi!" Reinier called after her.

She stopped. "What?" She put her hand on her hip.

"Please?"

"You won't get any help from me." She turned and hurried back to the dormitory.

❦

Letters came for Pérsomi frequently. Most were from Boelie, impersonal accounts of what they were doing in the camp and how he felt. Pérsomi wrote back every time. Klara had given her a pile of envelopes and stamps, probably under the impression that Pérsomi would be writing to Gerbrand. In her letters to both Boelie and her brother she wrote about school and athletics and how dry the bushveld was this year.

Klara didn't know Boelie was writing to her. Neither did Irene. Only Beth knew. Oh yes, and Reinier.

But best of all were the rare letters from Gerbrand.

Dear Pérsomi,

I am near Tobruk that's in North Africa. We have to guard the harbor which is full of oil from the sunken ships and a railroad that gets supplies and things to our men further along. The only reason why we're fighting in the desert is the Suez Canal. At night it is ice cold and by day it is very hot. It's winter now in summer we're going to die and not because of the bombs. There are many snakes and scorpions here just like in the bushveld but no buck to shoot so we eat Spam. There are swarms of flies buzzing around us and crawling up our nostrils looking for moisture. There is very little water but we have to shave every morning even if we're going into battle the army has strange rules.

We do nothing all day long it's very boring. I get really burnt by the sun because you know I've got red hair not like you who don't mind the sun.

At Christmas I went to visit Christine le Roux in Cairo it was very nice. You know she's here too. I hope she can make it in the war and here in the desert but I don't know. She's soft and really fair.

The leader of the Germans and the Eyeties is a German called General Rommel and our leader is General Montgomery he's our commander he's an Englishman from England but good. There was a battle at Sidi Rezegh where they captured more than 3 000 of our guys and sent them to camps in Italy or Germany. Pérsomi I'll die if they put me behind barbed wire or in a prison behind bars like Boelie then they must rather shoot me.

I'm finding out what to do to learn to fly planes. It seems I need to have passed matric but I'll study to get it because it's what I want to do. You must also learn hard.

Did you know America is also in the war now well now you know.

Give my best wishes to Ma and tell her I'm fine.

Your brother,

Gerbrand

Her longing for Gerbrand flared up and burned behind her eyelids. When he came home again one day, she would talk to him. Really talk, the way she talked to Reinier, or sometimes to Boelie. She was bigger now. She could talk to Gerbrand now, almost like an equal.

After he returned, the two of them could live together in Joburg and find jobs and both pass matric. Gerbrand could look after her and she could cook for him and help him with his schoolwork. He could help her figure out how to become a lawyer.

She read the letter over and over before she folded it and started with her homework.

❧

The war became a series of loose incidents somewhere distant where the sun always shone and where her brother lay behind rolls of barbed wire, shooting, with a steel helmet on his head. The war was fragments of reports from a week's newspapers, scraps of stories from Gerbrand's unpunctuated letters, frozen images from newspaper photos, flat sounds from a visit to the movies.

"I can't imagine what the war is really like," Pérsomi whispered to Beth late at night.

"It must be terrible," Beth whispered back. "We must pray for them, for our men."

"Depends on where you are," said Reinier the next day. "I think there's a big difference between being in the Sahara desert, or in Russia, where the soldiers freeze to death in the snow, or at sea, where a submarine can move in under your ship and sink it."

"There are terrible sandstorms in the desert, dust storms," wrote Gerbrand in one of his letters. "You have to wear a dust mask or you die. Everyone looks like meerkats, or aardvarks with long blunt snouts. But inside the mask you suffocate anyway."

In the paper Pérsomi read about thousands of Italians taken prisoner. Some of them were sent to the Union. She read about air strikes in Europe and North Africa. She read how the German Stuka dive-bombers and the Messerschmitts strafed the Allieds from the air.

"It's terrible," she wrote to Gerbrand, "in the desert you must have nowhere to hide."

"Yes," he replied, "but after a while you get used to being scared. The sun is actually worse than the planes, at least the planes go away sometimes."

"It's not too bad in the camp," Boelie wrote. "I help some of the older men with math and science. Many of them are using the opportunity to write matric. You won't believe it, Pérsomi, I play in the camp orchestra."

In his next letter Boelie wrote that he had taken up boxing. In fact, he was the camp champion.

"Boxing!" Pérsomi said to Reinier. "That's rather brutal."

"Well, you think men are brutes anyway," he said.

He might be released before the end of the year, Boelie wrote shortly before the June exams began. But he'd be confined to the farm, which meant he would have to stay on the farm and report to the police every day.

At least he would be home.

She was at the point of heading for the dormitory to fetch her sandwiches when Reinier said, "Pérsomi, please, you *have* to help me."

"I don't *have* to do anything," she warned him. "What do you want?"

"Please don't bite my head off like last time," he said.

"Reinier, what are you talking about?"

He sighed. "Irene."

She gave him an earnest look. "No," she said.

"Pérsomi . . ."

"No."

She turned and set off for the dormitory.

"Stubborn mule," he said to her back.

After break she ignored him. At the end of the day she didn't say good-bye.

The vacation of April 1942 was still sizzling hot and dry, and Persomi felt beaten. Boelie remained in the camp. Gerbrand had not written recently.

The house on the farm was in a worse state than ever. The dung floor was worn through in places. It hadn't been plastered in months. Fly specks covered the mouldy curtain separating the front room from the bedroom.

Pérsomi stared at the filthy mattresses, the dirty gray blankets. "We must plaster the floor," she said the first day, "and wash the bedding."

"Oh heavens, Pérsomi," said her ma.

"I'm not going to plaster the floor with dung," said Hannapat.

"I'll do it if you'll wash the blankets," Pérsomi offered. "We really can't live like this!"

"Just listen to Miss High-and-Mighty!" Hannapat sneered. "If our house is no longer good enough for you, why don't you stay at the dormitory? It will suit me."

"Oh heavens above," said their ma.

It was probably better that Gertjie and Baby had been taken away and not returned.

She pulled herself together. Tomorrow she would go to the kraal to collect dung for the floor. She would wash everything inside the house. She would hoe the little field next to the house and remove the weeds and sweep the yard.

When everything was spick-and-span, Ma's and Hannapat's spirits might lift a little.

In the second week of the vacation Pérsomi went to the bywoner house on Freddie le Roux's farm. Oom Attie wasn't home, and before Auntie Sis could start talking, Pérsomi came to the point.

"Auntie Sis, I know Lewies Pieterse is not my pa."

"Child, don't say such a thing!" Auntie Sis wiped the sweat from her round face with her gray hankie. "Your ma told me you said it in court. You shouldn't have done that. What must people think of her?"

"I have to find out who my pa was . . . or is."

"Let it go, Pérsomi. Winter is a long time coming this year. Strange, isn't it?"

"Auntie Sis, it's important to me."

"It's still so hot."

Pérsomi took a chance. "You know who my pa is."

Silence.

"Auntie Sis?"

"Pérsomi, you're looking for trouble."

"You must know who was courting my ma at the time?"

"I don't know who your pa is, Pérsomi. It's no use snooping. I wasn't living at home then. I was married, with children of my own."

"But you and Oom Attie always lived nearby. Surely you know something?" Pérsomi persisted.

"Child, I don't know a thing, and your ma never spoke, of that I'm sure."

A kind of despair took hold of Pérsomi. "Ma must tell me, Auntie Sis. I have a right to know who my own pa is. Do you promise you don't know?"

"I know nothing, child. And your ma won't tell. The cows will come home before she'll say anything. I knew when she began to show and our pa beat the living daylights out of her. She refused to talk even then. He thrashed her so that she had to stay in bed for three days. I thought both she and you would die protecting some good-for-nothing bum."

Pérsomi drew a deep breath and closed her eyes for a moment. The picture in her mind wouldn't go away.

"The only people in the house at the time," Auntie Sis said, "were your late oupa, your ma, and Gerbrand. Gerbrand was just a little boy, but he must have seen something. Someone who came to fetch your ma, or something."

Her ma must have loved the man. Her ma must have loved her pa so much that she protected him with her life.

"Auntie Sis, I wonder if Oom Freddie might be my pa."

Auntie Sis looked the other way. "You're looking for trouble."

Pérsomi waited. Sometimes waiting led to answers.

Auntie Sis gave a slight nod. "You said it, not me."

"What do you think?"

"No, I'm not saying a word," said Auntie Sis, and sniffed loudly. "I like living on this farm, and Freddie le Roux is a good man. I'm not saying a word."

"Someone gives Mr. Ismail money for me, Auntie Sis, so I can buy soap and stuff, and even school shoes when mine are worn through."

"Must be Gerbrand," said Auntie Sis.

"No, I know it's not. I think it might be Oom Freddie. I've seen him give Ma money."

"I'm not saying a word, Pérsomi."

"But you agree, don't you, Auntie Sis, that it could be Oom Freddie?"

"Pérsomi, stop prying. I don't know who your pa is."

❧

"Oh, by the way, a letter came for you," Klara Fourie said when Pérsomi went to the back door of the Big House to collect the old newspapers for the new longdrop. "It's Gerbrand's handwriting. He must know you're on vacation. I had a letter from him yesterday. Does he write more often now?"

"Yes, he does. He probably misses home," said Pérsomi.

"I hear the troops are given a pass when they've been at the front for eighteen months," said Klara. "Maybe Gerbrand will be home before Christmas."

"That would be nice."

Pérsomi walked to the river with the letter in her hand and the pile of old papers under her arm. She sat down on the warm rocks and stretched her legs in front of her before she carefully opened the envelope.

30 JUNE 1942

Dear Pérsomi,

Thank you for your letters when I read them it almost feels as if I'm home.

I've just written to Klara and told her about the Gazala Gallop but it's too much to write again so if you see her ask her to give you that letter then you can read about the Gazala Gallop to Ma. It was bad with bombs and planes overhead and tanks. We started out with 300 tanks after two days we had only 70 left now you know how bad it was. Then they told us to retreat then there was terrible chaos getting back to Egypt because Tobruk is in Libya. Then during the night a terrible thunderstorm came up the storms are terrible here like in the bushveld but there's no place to hide from the lightning. But we could see a little because of the lightning in the dark and so we got out.

Our entire division retreated to a small station called El Alamein. It's much smaller than our station at home so now you know. It was such a hurried operation the troops panicked and the commanders too. Now they call it the Gazala Gallop because we started at Gazala.

General Dan Pienaar is still our commander he is very good. El Alamein is on the coast and just about 40 miles to the south lies the Qattara depression they say it's a harsh sandy wilderness. We hold a line now from the coast up to that wilderness no one can get through anyway. But we lost a lot of ground because the Germans and Eyeties want to get to Cairo and we're only 100 miles from Cairo now.

We're not fighting at all just building camouflaged shelters and having parades in the sand and digging ditches for trenches all day long. Instead of charging and overpowering them. It's hotter than blazes here that's why I think it's better to fly planes.

I saw Christine in Cairo again she's very well and tell Ma I'm fine and I don't know who gave old Ismail money for you again but it was definitely not me must be Father Christmas. I would have told you if it was me.

Best wishes.

Your brother,

Gerbrand

Pérsomi confronted her ma late in the afternoon. "Gerbrand told me again he's not the one who's giving Mr. Ismail money for me,"

"Heavens above, Pérsomi . . ."

"Stop saying that. I want answers. I'm fifteen."

Her ma pressed her lips together.

"I know it's my pa who's paying the money."

Silence.

"I'd like to thank him."

Silence.

"It's a lot of money. It's just good manners."

"Oh heavens, child, please stop." Her ma was almost pleading.

"If you won't tell me who he is, just tell me why he didn't marry you when you got pregnant."

Silence.

"Did he know about me? Did he know you were pregnant?"

"Heavens above. Yes."

"Well, if he was a decent man, he would have married you."

"He *is* a decent man, Pérsomi. Heavens, child, he couldn't marry me, or he would have."

Pérsomi looked up quickly. Her ma's face had changed, become softer. Pérsomi felt tenderness well up inside her. She reached for her ma, but didn't touch her.

"You loved him?" she asked.

"Yes."

"Was he already married? Is that why he couldn't marry you?"

Silence.

"Married men can leave their wives and marry the woman they made pregnant," said Pérsomi.

"He couldn't. His wife was also . . ." She stopped.

Pérsomi narrowed her eyes. "Also pregnant?"

Her ma got up. "Pérsomi, stop stepping all over me with dirty feet," she said. She turned and walked off into the veld—a thin, lonely woman in a threadbare dress and worn shoes.

Pérsomi did some math in her head. If the man's wife was pregnant, Freddie le Roux couldn't be her father. Christine was his only child, and she was six years older than Pérsomi.

❧

"Auntie Sis, why did my ma marry a man like Lewies Pieterse?"

"Don't speak of your pa like that. Show some respect!" Auntie Sis scolded.

"Why did my ma marry him?" Pérsomi insisted.

"Your ma's time for picking and choosing was over, Pérsomi. She didn't have a roof over her head, she didn't have food to eat. She was pregnant and Gerbrand was young. Lewies Pieterse was the answer. In return she looked after his children. Especially Sissie, with her falling sickness and all. Your ma was trapped, Pérsomi, she was trapped."

There were so many things she knew nothing about, Pérsomi thought later, on her way back to Mr. Fourie's farm.

So many things.

One afternoon Pérsomi told her ma, "Come with me. I want to show you something wonderful."

Her ma got up from where she had been sitting at the kitchen table. "Now?" she asked.

"Yes, come."

"Is it far?" her ma asked when they turned toward the mountain.

"No, not really, and it's lovely," said Pérsomi.

On a ridge some distance from the house was an enormous wild fig tree. "I hope they're still here," said Pérsomi as they approached. "Come and see."

"Look, Ma," she whispered. "Bushveld parrots. They're after the ripe fruit."

They looked up into the branches. Small birds with hooked beaks swarmed all over.

"I see them," her ma said softly.

The parrots were dark on top, with green and blue undersides. "They're . . . pretty," said her ma.

They fluttered on bright yellow wings from one fig to the next. "Pretty," her ma whispered.

Pérsomi turned her head slowly and looked at her ma. Her entire face had gone soft. Her eyes had come alive.

"Let's sit for a while and watch them," she said.

Gently they sat down among the ripe figs that had fallen. "They don't eat the rotten ones," her ma whispered.

They sat, silently looking up into the tree.

Pérsomi wanted to put her arm around her ma, or stroke her hair. But she couldn't do it. Maybe this was what it was like to have a conversation with someone close to you.

"Ma, everyone always wants to know where I got my name. Will you tell me?"

"I just thought it's a grand name," said her ma, almost inaudibly.

Above their heads the parrots screeched and called out, *chee-chee-chee.*

"It's the best name you could've given me," she said. She kept talking softly, not wanting to spoil the moment. "No one else has a name like it."

"I . . . had nothing," said her ma. She didn't look at Pérsomi. She wasn't looking at the parrots anymore either, but at her feet. "But I knew one day you'd be smart and pretty, because . . . he's smart, and good-looking, see?"

Pérsomi's heart was thumping in her chest, in her throat.

"And when Auntie Sis—she came to help me when it was my time—when she said, 'Jemima, it's a little girl,' I just knew your name would be Pérsomi. I wanted to give you a grand name."

"You have a pretty name too—Jemima."

"Yes, I always liked it. But your pa says it's a . . ." She fell silent.

"Lewies Pieterse is just jealous. What does he know about anything pretty? Forget about him."

"Yes," said her ma.

The parrots twittered overhead.

"Where did you first hear my name?"

Her ma was silent for a long time. A ripe fruit thudded on the ground close to them. "From him," she said at last.

My father, Pérsomi thought breathlessly, slivers of information about my father. She kept quiet, waiting.

"He told me about the name one evening. He came courting, just like a gentleman, in his motorcar. He's rich. He came at night.

"He always wore smart clothes. And he gave me a necklace, and often he brought chocolates. Then that night he told me about the play. He said everything was so beautiful, with candles and everything, and he said the man on the stage said, 'Pérsomi, light the candle,' and then he died. The man on the stage. 'Pérsomi is a beautiful name, isn't it, Jemima?' he said. He always spoke to me like a man should speak to a girl.

"By that time I knew I was expecting. But I couldn't say anything."

Her ma was quiet for a long time. Pérsomi couldn't let her stop talking. "Why not, Ma?"

Her ma's voice changed slightly. "Men, rich men, don't like their girlfriends to be expecting."

Pérsomi almost said, *You have to fight for your rights. A woman must be able to stand up for herself in this unfair man's world.* But she remembered her ma saying, "Pérsomi, stop stepping all over me with dirty feet," and she remembered the lonely figure walking away across the bare veld.

So she just nodded and said, "Yes, that's true. And then?"

"So I thought now I must speak, because I saw he . . ."

Her ma just shook her head slowly from side to side.

"You saw he loved you," Pérsomi said softly.

Her mother nodded.

The smell of the fruit was all around them.

"And then, Mama?"

Her ma looked up. There was a deep desolation in her eyes, a loneliness like nothing Pérsomi had ever seen before.

"Then he never came again."

"El Alamein is just a tiny station, even smaller than our own station in town," Pérsomi said a week after the school had reopened.

"If you read the papers you'd know El Alamein is an important strategic point," Reinier said. "Do you know of the battles that have been fought there by the British and the Germans? Just yesterday I read that the Eighth Army captured more than seven thousand Germans and Italians there and—"

"It's still a tiny station in the middle of the desert," Pérsomi said. "Gerbrand says so and he should know. He's there."

"Bloody Red Tab," said Reinier.

"Oh, I thought it was his business?" Pérsomi said.

"He's still a Red Tab," said Reinier.

At the beginning of September Reinier brought a newspaper clipping to school. "Take a look at what's going on at your tiny little station," he said, slapping the clipping down in front of Pérsomi.

She took her time ironing out the creases and began to read:

> During the past week Rommel launched another offensive against the strategic station El Alamein. He is estimated to have no more than 200 serviceable tanks and a few substandard Italian armored vehicles to deploy against the 700 tanks of the British Forces. It is also alleged that the Germans have very little fuel and that their food rations are almost completely depleted.

"Poor Germans," said Pérsomi, frowning.

"You're supposed to be against them," said Reinier.

"I'm on no one's side," Pérsomi said firmly. "War is a dumb game thought out by men when they became too old to play cowboys and crooks. They don't think about the people caught up in the war."

"It's a lot more than that!" Reinier cried, outraged. "There are politics involved, ideologies that—"

"That's what your dad says, I know. But if people are suffering because of their own ideologies, it's dumb. Be quiet so I can read the rest."

"You're impossible," Reinier muttered.

> Allied fighter planes are constantly attacking the Axis forces,

Pérsomi read on.

> General Montgomery had expected Rommel's forces to advance northward to the sea and that's why he went to great trouble to fortify the Alam el Halfa ridge—a clever strategic decision. The British 2nd Armored Brigade could therefore stop Rommel's 2nd Panzer Division just before the ridge. On September 3 Rommel ordered a withdrawal.

"So actually they didn't achieve anything, except to kill a lot of people," Pérsomi said, returning the clipping to Reinier.

"I'll never understand you women," Reinier said.

❧

A letter was waiting for her back at the dormitory.

EL ALAMEIN

OCTOBER 1942

Dear Pérsomi,

Thank you for your letters I also get letters from Klara it's always very nice to get news from home.

Pérsomi we're preparing for a major offensive that's why I'm writing now because we're going to be very busy. We're going to chase the Germans and the Eyeties from El Alamein into the sea on the other side of the desert not just drive them back like at Alam el Halfa where we just stopped them. We have plenty of reinforcements and supplies now I feel certain we're going to win because we are preparing very thoroughly it's very good.

This is the best time of my life because we're all friends no matter what language we speak and we have lots of fun. Tell Ma as well.

Sometimes we get a pass then we go to Cairo then I sometimes see Christine. I saw her in September when we were in Cairo but I don't think I'll visit her again even if I'm in Cairo because she's getting to be a nuisance. She seems to think I have to come and visit her when I'm there but I'm not her boyfriend. Pérsomi if you get a boyfriend one day you mustn't be a nuisance and don't cry men don't like it. But you mustn't get a boyfriend now only later.

Maybe I'll be home soon maybe even before Christmas.

Pérsomi I'm going to learn to fly planes and when the war is over I'm going to stay in the air force. One day I might even come home in a plane.

Best wishes.

Your brother,

Gerbrand

"Gerbrand may be home before Christmas," Pérsomi told Beth that evening.

"You'd like that, wouldn't you?"

"It would be the best Christmas in the whole world," Pérsomi smiled in the dark.

❦

Monday morning was hot. The English teacher was reading in a monotonous voice. A bluebottle buzzed against the windowpane next to Pérsomi. Reinier was leaning back, the book propped on his desk to hide the fact that his eyes were closed.

Two rows in front of her Beth sat up straight, following in her book. Diagonally in front of her Irene was drawing hearts on her desk.

The principal's secretary entered and everyone looked up. She spoke to the teacher, then shrugged her shoulders.

"Pérsomi, please go to the principal's office with Mrs. Lubbe," the teacher said.

She followed the secretary. Her feet felt heavy, her heart was thumping in her chest, her mind was blank. The principal got to his feet when she entered and came walking around the desk. His eyes looked strange.

His lips moved.

She saw his lips move.

His words bounced off the ceiling and the white walls and the windowpanes. Her mind did not hear the words.

Her feet began to run.

SEVEN

HER MOUNTAIN WAS ANCIENT. UNCHANGING.

Her mountain had deep crevices and tall, hard cliffs. The crevices lay sheltered in cool shadows, the cliffs stood proud and warm in the last rays of the sun.

Her mountain was always there. Always. The river could run dry, the moon could darken, the trees could shrivel and become firewood and vanish into ashes—her mountain would remain.

Beth had said the same about God.

Beth had lied.

Pérsomi had come through the veld, avoiding the road. She had climbed through paddock fences and boundary fences, she had angled toward the setting sun in the direction where she knew the farm to be. She had jogged and sprinted and stood doubled over to regain her breath. She had looked at the ground for springhare burrows and up at her mountain, a beacon on the horizon. She had drunk from reservoirs at wells and from troughs.

Just before sunset she had reached her mountain.

She had prayed, every night during quiet time. Only in the vacation she had sometimes forgotten.

God hadn't heard.

No God of love would have taken Gerbrand.

It couldn't be true.

Her mountain's soil was under her bare feet. Her mountain's

dry grass turned into powder under her feet, its sharp stones hurt her feet. Only her feet could feel. And her bone-dry mouth and throat.

Near the cave she sat down on the lukewarm rocks. The sun was gone.

Her mountain was completely silent.

Her mind knew the truth, but her heart refused to hear.

Nothing around her stirred.

With the dark came deeper thoughts. The Defence Force could have made a mistake. Hundreds of soldiers fell on the battlefields every single day.

"We wear dog tags," Gerbrand had once written, "so that the army can identify us if we can't tell them who we are. The trouble is that sometimes the dog tag is also shot to pieces."

"Don't swear," she had replied. "What does the army do in a case like that?"

"They send the family a telegram saying *Missing in action*," Gerbrand had answered. "But in the end the army identifies everyone, then there will be another telegram that says *Fallen at the front* or something like that. I don't know exactly. I have never received a telegram like that."

Pérsomi knew exactly.

The night was pitch-dark, there was a dark moon, even the stars were obscured by fleece clouds.

The ache inside her began to overshadow every possible doubt. The ache inside her chilled her heart. Because she knew. She knew that she knew.

Sometime in the middle of the night the cold crept up on her. Just before daybreak it was at its worst. The pain broke down all her defenses. Her heart lay stripped naked on the cold rocky ledge, helpless.

She didn't cry, she broke apart.

She would get up and go to her ma, she thought just before day-break. Her ma would open her arms and wrap them around her. She would open her arms and hold her ma tightly. She would hold Hannapat too. Their arms would make a circle around all of them.

Her body was stiff with cold. Her heart ached and ached.

When the sun had thawed her body, she got up and walked slowly home, down the side of her mountain.

❧

Her ma was a thin woman with dry, empty eyes.

"Mama?" she said.

"Mr. Fourie went to fetch you," her ma's voice spoke, "but you were gone."

"I walked," she said.

Auntie Sis was overpowering, her enormous bosom stifling hot, her eyes swollen and red, her embrace suffocating. "Child, child, where were you all night?"

Oom Attie was prickly and wheezed. "Your Auntie Sis knew," he sighed. "She hasn't slept for months. She saw the coffins. This thing will be the end of your auntie."

Hannapat bawled with snot and tears. "I heard yesterday, at school," she moaned. "I've been crying all the time, I couldn't even sleep."

She turned back to her ma. Her ma's face was empty.

❧

School consisted of uniformed arms and legs and eyes.

"Shame, Pérsomi," and they clicked their tongues. "We'll pray for you, d'you hear?"

"What happened, Pérsomi?" they asked.

"When are you expecting the body, Pérsomi? I don't suppose you'll be able to see him."

Sometimes she heard *Red Tab*. Sometimes *renegade* or *Khaki lover*.

She didn't listen. She breathed and ate and did her schoolwork.

"Pérsomi, tell me about him," said Beth, her eyes gentle.

Pérsomi shook her head.

"Well, sit here on my bed, and I'll pray for you," said Beth.

"Pérsomi, I'm really very sorry about your brother," Reinier said with serious eyes.

"Thanks," she said and bent over her work.

"Pérsomi, you and your family are in our thoughts," said Mr. Nienaber beside her desk. "If there's anything we can do, if we can help in any way, please tell me."

"Thank you, sir," she said. She looked down, didn't want to see any more eyes.

Three days later everyone had forgotten. They no longer looked at her. They did their math and ate their sandwiches and laughed.

She did her math. "The teacher is focusing on trigonometry. I'll bet we'll get loads of questions on it in the exam," Reinier whispered.

She nodded.

She ate her sandwiches. "I know I shouldn't eat so much bread," sighed Beth, "but I'm so hungry!"

Pérsomi nodded again.

Gerbrand had been the breadwinner in their home.

The bread stuck in her throat.

On Friday Mr. Nienaber asked her, "Can you watch the kids tomorrow evening? My wife and I would like . . . Oh wait, you're probably going home for the weekend."

Home?

"I'll look after the children, sir," she said.

The days and the weeks and the minutes dropped into a black hole. If she worked hard enough, ran far enough, showered quickly enough, and washed her clothes daily, she didn't hear the desperate cries of the minutes and the seconds.

But the night became a menace.

At the bottom of the darkness lay a pain that gripped her, a loneliness that kept her chained to the bottom. Because at night the memories came unbidden. And with the memories came the longing, harsher every time, and more painful.

She had never hurt so much, or been so alone.

"Fallen on the battlefield, laid down his life in the service of his people," the local paper said. She cut out the small article and put it in her Bible. Maybe she would open the Bible again one day.

Each dark night the treacherous thought returned: Gerbrand was dead. Her big brother. And the family's sole breadwinner.

She did not want to attend the funeral with Ma, who had still not cried, and Hannapat, who hadn't stopped. But she did go home.

The night before they brought him back there was a half moon, but the sky was cloudless, the stars bright. She walked slowly to her mountain, to her cave. She knew the way, knew every stone and every tuft of grass and every crevice.

She had known the cold would come. The cold night was more bearable than the cold fire burning her up from the inside, freezing her.

She rolled into a ball. Nothing eased the black pain that was everywhere. The broken moon limped through the dark sky.

The morning of November 12, 1942, the sun rose as it had done for millions of years.

The blinding pain was back in a flash.

She got up, she walked all the way down to the fountain, she drank water, she washed her face. She walked aimlessly back to the cave.

Much later she moved to a place where she could see the Big House. There was a bustle around the kraal. Smoke rose from the chimney. The Fouries would be having coffee at the kitchen table, eating those long rusks Irene's ouma baked in the outside oven. Everyone had returned for Gerbrand's funeral.

"Mr. Fourie has put chairs in the barn, and a table in front for the minister," Hannapat had said when Pérsomi arrived yesterday. "Aunt Lulu sent us this pudding."

"Oom Freddie gave us this chicken," her ma had said. "Freddie le Roux is a good man."

But in the end only Hannapat had eaten some of the chicken and the pudding.

When the sun had climbed a quarter of its way up the sky, Pérsomi saw a dust trail. A khaki-colored truck labored along the farm road to the Big House. She knew: it was the soldiers who had brought Gerbrand home. Someone pointed the driver toward the barn.

Her throat began to burn, she kept swallowing. She drew her knees to her chest, she wrapped her arms tightly around her knees, she lowered her head onto her knees, she kept her eyes closed.

She couldn't watch. Her heart ached too much.

A while later she opened her eyes.

The truck was parked at the barn. The yard was dead quiet, nothing was alive.

She saw Boelie coming from a distance. He nearly walked past her to the cave, but then he saw her.

She looked away. She didn't want to see the pity in his eyes.

"I thought I'd find you here," he said when he reached her.

"Hello, Boelie," she said.

He nodded. "I was released from the camp last week," he said.

"Oh, I didn't know," she said.

He was staring out over the farm.

"Would you like to sit?" she asked.

He looked at her. His eyes were dark, unreadable. He sat down on the rocks beside her.

"The . . . people came," she said.

Boelie nodded.

There was a long silence before he said: "Thanks for writing."

"Okay," she said.

"And . . . I'm sorry about Gerbrand."

"Okay," she said.

There was still no movement in the yard below, no sound in the veld.

A lizard moved across the rocky ledge, its head raised high. "He'll have the fright of his life when he notices us," Boelie said softly.

The lizard scurried away, startled.

"Are you glad to be home?" she asked.

He shrugged. "I suppose so," he said.

She saw the tension in his clasped hands, in his averted gaze. "It must have been terrible for you," she said.

He didn't answer.

It was an easy silence, calm. For the first time in weeks she experienced a kind of peace. Her pain was no less intense, but her body felt softer, the way it felt when she was very, very tired.

Another half hour passed, maybe an hour. Then the yard

below came to life. People emerged from the barn, the truck moved slowly backward.

Pérsomi felt the iron fist grip her again. The truck would follow the bumpy path through the orange trees down to the river. They would have to cross the Pontenilo and continue up the ridge on foot.

The grave had been waiting a short distance from the bywoner house since the previous day, open and raw.

The truck moved slowly until she could no longer see it. "Let's sit where you can watch," said Boelie.

"I . . . don't want to watch," she said.

"Let's move anyway. You don't have to watch if you don't want to."

He got up and walked down to the left. He sat down in the thin shade of a wild plum.

After a while she followed. "Sit," he said.

She remained on her feet. From there they could see the river. And the bywoner house on the barren ridge. "Why aren't you down there?" she asked.

He paused before he answered. "Those are Red Tabs, Pers."

She nodded and sat down beside him.

People appeared at the river. It was too far to make out who they were.

Six soldiers lifted the coffin from the back of the truck. They carried it on their shoulders. At the river they lowered the coffin and carried it between them over the rocks. Then they put it back on their shoulders and carried it up the hill.

A small procession followed slowly—a handful of people who had come this sweltering summer's day to bury Gerbrand Pieterse on the barren ridge next to his family home.

The small group stood motionless around the grave for a long time.

After a while a soldier brought an instrument to his lips. Through the silence of the veld Pérsomi heard the thin sounds of the trumpet. She began to shiver, her entire body trembling as if she were cold. Boelie put his arm around her shoulders.

The sounds of the trumpet died down.

The six soldiers raised their rifles. She saw the rifles jerk as they fired the ceremonial salute. The shots reverberated through the languid silence of the bushveld.

She jumped when the sound reached her. Her body jerked, the hard cocoon around her heart burst apart, her heart bled out into her body, filled her entirely with mournful blood.

Boelie's arm tightened around her shoulder.

The sun blazed down. She was shivering from head to toe.

Boelie said nothing. He stared at the ground and kept his arm around her.

They sat without moving until long after it was all over, until the grave was filled, until everyone was gone and her ma had disappeared into the house alone.

Boelie lowered his arm and leaned back. "It's over, Pérsomi," he said.

"Yes," she said. She felt utterly empty, exhausted. The lump in her chest was still pushing up into her throat.

He dug into his pocket and said, "Here, take this, I brought you a rusk. Let's go to the fountain, I'm thirsty. It's bloody hot, isn't it?"

"Yes, it's *very* hot," she said, getting up slowly.

❧

"Aren't you going back home?" Boelie asked when the sun began to set.

"No," Pérsomi said.

"You'll have to go home in the end," he said.

"Tomorrow, not today," she said. "Aren't you going home, Boelie?"

"No," he said.

There's a time after sunset and before the light has gone when the world holds its breath for the arrival of the stars.

Boelie and Pérsomi lay back, gazing up at the night sky.

The familiar ache began to fill the emptiness in her heart.

"Why are you staying?" she asked.

"I need time," he said, "and quiet."

After a while he said, "I didn't mean I don't want you to talk. Your words are quiet. You can talk if you want."

"I don't really want to," she said.

The stars became brighter. "You can almost touch the stars," she said. Maybe that's where Gerbrand was now.

Much later she said, "Tobruk is a place with small white flat-roofed houses, all shot to pieces, Gerbrand wrote in July. And the harbor is full of oil from the sunken ships."

Sometime during the night Boelie said, "I'm not angry with Gerbrand, Pers, I just want you to know. Gerbrand was my friend, he always was, will always be."

She nodded in the darkness. "You're angry with the government," she said, "for what they did to our Afrikaner boys."

"Yes. You understand."

Somewhere high up in the cliffs a baby baboon screamed. The rest of the troop barked, upset about the nocturnal disturbance. "They're a rowdy lot," said Boelie.

"Gerbrand once wrote that he often thinks of you in that camp," she said. "He said they must rather . . . shoot him before they keep him captive behind barbed wire." She felt the pain flooding her again, growing, becoming wider and thicker. "It's just so . . . final," she said.

Suddenly the pain intensified, and she put up a strong barricade against it. She had to think of something else. "What will you do now?" she asked.

"I hope to build a dam on the Pontenilo. For the dry seasons. If I can convince my dad to part with the money," he said. "I'm not allowed to leave the farm anyway. I'll have to do something to stop myself from going crazy. Actually the plans for the dam are ready. I worked on them at camp. But I'll have to get an expert blaster to excavate the cliffs in places. Yesterday when I went to take a look at the terrain . . ."

"Pérsomi?"

The barricade burst as if it had been blown apart with dynamite. Rubble shot up in the air. She felt the impact, felt her body being ripped apart. She heard the sobs erupt, take over uncontrollably.

Somewhere during this eternity she felt Boelie's strong arms around her. She turned and clung to him.

Much later there were no more tears left, just random sobs sporadically finding their way out from somewhere deep inside.

"How do you feel now?" he asked.

"Empty," she said. "I'm sorry."

"That's okay," he said.

They sat in easy silence for a long time. "What are you saddest about?" he asked.

"There are so many things I still wanted to ask Gerbrand," she said quietly. "He was my . . . big brother."

"Such as? Ask me if you like, I'm a big brother, too," he said.

"Such as"—she hesitated a moment—"who my real father is."

"That I can't answer," he said. "Ask your mother."

"She refuses to say. But Gerbrand was old enough. He might have remembered who called on my ma at the time."

"Hmm." Silence. "What else?"

"What do you mean?"

"What else did you want to ask Gerbrand?"

"I can't remember." Pain began to seep back. "I wanted to go to Joburg with him next year," she said. "He wanted to learn to fly planes, but he had to pass matric first."

Boelie thought for a while before he asked, "Why did you want to go to Johannesburg?"

"To find a job," she muttered past the lump in her throat.

The sobs began to tear through her again. They came from somewhere very, very deep. "I'm sorry, I can't help it," she sobbed. "I really . . . never . . . cry."

"It's okay, Pérsomi," he comforted her clumsily and put his arm around her again. "It's okay, Pers."

After a while she calmed down, though an occasional shudder still passed through her body. Boelie raised his hand. With one finger he pushed a strand of hair out of her face and tucked it behind her ear. Then he cupped his hand around her head and stroked her hair. "It's okay, Pers, it's okay," he said and kept stroking.

After a time he said, "You're not going to Joburg, you're going to write matric here at the town school."

She shook her head, exhausted.

"You are a top achiever and an excellent athlete. You can definitely get a grant."

Exhaustion almost paralyzed her. "We don't even have food at home."

"Your mother will get Gerbrand's army pension."

She kept shaking her head.

"But it won't be much," he said.

She nodded mechanically. Wearily.

"Pérsomi, I promise we'll think of something. I understand, I truly understand. But I promise you, next year you'll be in Form

IV, and the year after that you'll be writing matric at our local school."

Exhaustion took over. But she believed him. She believed him the way she had always believed her big brother.

❦

"I have to report at the police station before ten this morning," Boelie said when they had quenched their thirst at the fountain. The sun was blazing down from a cloudless sky.

"Then you'd better go," she said.

"Will you be okay?"

She looked up into his dark eyes. "Yes, Boelie. I'll be okay."

PART II

EIGHT

"OUR RESULTS WON'T BE OUT UNTIL THE DAY AFTER NEW Year," Pérsomi said to Yusuf in his grandfather's store. "I've come to say good-bye. I don't suppose I'll be in town anytime soon again."

"In that case, let me make some tea," said Yusuf, leading her to the kitchen. "What did you think of your last paper?"

"English essays? How hard can it be?"

"Hmm. What time is De Wet fetching you?" He took two mugs from the shelf.

"Boelie is fetching me. He and . . . his friend have to buy materials for the dam they're building."

"You speak of Antonio," Yusuf asked cautiously.

Pérsomi set her lips in a thin line.

"Have you made peace with the Italian?" he asked.

"No," she said, "and I never will."

"You don't know that it was an Italian who shot your brother," he said, pouring milk into a saucepan, his back turned to her.

"Please don't start with that again," she said. "Why an Italian prisoner of war should be stationed on the farm where I live I'll never understand. And please don't make my tea with boiled milk, and hold back on the sugar."

"You can't carry so much bitterness inside you, Pérsomi."

"I don't like sweet—"

159

"I'm not talking about the tea. I felt the same toward the Germans after my brother was killed. But war is war and our brothers knew what they were getting themselves into."

"I'll leave if you don't stop lecturing." She rose to her feet.

"Sit," he said. "Here's your tea, made with water, not milk, and only half a teaspoon of sugar."

She took the cup. "When do you have to be at Wits?" she asked, referring to the research university he would attend in Johannesburg.

"The end of January," he said. "Just think, in a few years' time you'll be addressing me as Dr. Ismail and I'll call you the Honorable Judge Pieterse."

Pérsomi laughed. "I'm going to be a lawyer, Yusuf, not a judge! But let's drink to our futures anyway."

Yusuf got to his feet and raised his tin mug. "To Counselor Pérsomi and Dr. Yusuf!"

Pérsomi got up, too, and clinked her mug against his. "To us," she said.

"I'm going to work," Hannapat told Pérsomi and their ma just after Christmas. "Piet has contacts, he can organize a job for me."

"Work!" Pérsomi said, dismayed. "But you only have standard six!"

"I'll be sixteen next month. I'm not staying in school any longer."

"It's not too late to change your mind."

But Hannapat was adamant. "Piet says there are a lot of rich men in Joburg who drive smart cars and buy their girls perfume and necklaces and things. If I can catch one of them, even if he's a bit older, I'll be well away. Then I'll leave you lot behind and never come back again."

Pérsomi watched with sadness when her younger sister waved good-bye in Pérsomi's faded white church dress. Hannapat was a shapeless child with her hair bleached bone-white, her face smeared with rouge, her dreams of the future built on a train ticket to the bright lights of the City of Gold. She had never even switched on an electric light.

🌿

Pérsomi and her ma were alone in the house for the first time in their lives.

During the day Ma went over to the Big House or the Old House to do the ironing or other chores. On Tuesdays and Fridays she went to Oom Freddie's house to iron.

The day after they heard Pérsomi had been granted all the scholarships she'd applied for, her ma said, "Klara says you must come to the Big House tomorrow."

She went reluctantly the next afternoon. Klara had company in the kitchen.

"Pérsomi, you remember Annabel, Reinier's sister?" said Klara, pointing at the beautiful girl with the long black hair.

"Hello," Pérsomi said. She remembered seeing the beautiful creature a few years earlier in this very kitchen with Klara and Christine, though she had never seen her with Reinier.

"So you're Gerbrand's little sister?" Annabel asked, tilting her head. "You don't look anything like him."

Pérsomi stood motionless. The dark eyes studied her, sizing her up. She felt as if her skirt was shrinking, as if the old school shirt was suddenly tighter around her chest.

"We heard yesterday that Pérsomi was awarded scholarships," Klara said. "She's going to study law at Tukkies."

"I hear poor whites don't have any trouble getting scholarships," said Annabel. "You're right, Klara, my old clothes will fit her." She turned from Pérsomi. "My closet is crammed with clothes I never wear. In my profession you can't afford to be seen in last year's styles. You're always in the public eye. I'll put a few things in a bag and send it over with De Wet."

"De Wet works for Annabel and Reinier's father at his law office now," Klara explained.

Pérsomi flushed and felt her cheeks grow hot. Her bare feet felt even more exposed in her shabby clothes. "Thanks," she said softly.

Annabel looked her over from head to toe. "Well, I hope you manage if you plan to study law," she said skeptically. "My dad would probably have liked me or Reinier to follow him, but neither of us was drawn to it." She tossed her long loose hair over her shoulder.

Pérsomi turned and quietly left through the back door.

One day, she told herself, no one would treat her like rubbish again.

"What will you do when Lewies Pieterse comes out on parole?" she asked her ma one evening.

"Heavens, child!" Her ma's hands flew to her face. "Don't say that!"

"You should think about it," she said seriously. "He's been in jail four years already. It's going to happen, sooner or later."

"Oh heavens above," said her ma.

A few mornings later she was walking to the Big House with her ma for newspapers when Klara called her. "Annabel has sent her clothes, Pérsomi. But you'll have to iron them. They've all been stuffed in a bag."

"There aren't enough irons in the Old House for us both," her ma said at once.

"Come and do it here in our kitchen," Klara said to Pérsomi. "We've finished our breakfast."

"Thanks," said Pérsomi.

She entered the Big House filled with a strange mixture of dread and anticipation. She had taken note of Annabel's beautiful clothes, but she was afraid of being humiliated. What if Boelie or, even worse, Irene, came into the kitchen while she was ironing Reinier's sister's castoffs?

The overflowing bag sat on a chair.

Pérsomi took out the pieces one by one.

She was glad she was alone.

They were the most beautiful clothes she had ever seen: dresses, skirts and blouses, a jacket, a sweater, four nightgowns, even two pairs of pedal pushers and a pair of kidskin shoes.

She ironed the pieces one by one and folded them neatly.

At the bottom of the bag she found two evening gowns. She drew in her breath. The first one was a deep-red satin cut on the bias. It was made to cling to a tall, slender figure and accentuate every curve.

She shook out the dress carefully and held it in front of her. The glossy fabric draped softly over her chest. With one hand she held the waist of the dress to her own waist and lifted her leg. The deep-red fabric rested elegantly on her rough, bare feet.

Pérsomi was Cinderella, in the kitchen where she belonged.

The second evening gown was a sophisticated black dress with a long slit at the back and a plunging neckline. She held it up.

"That's pretty," Klara said from the doorway.

"I'll never wear it," Pérsomi mumbled, stuffing it back into the bag.

"Pity," Klara smiled. "You'd look ravishing in it."

"Ask De Wet if you can go into town with him tomorrow," her ma said one morning.

"What for?" Pérsomi asked.

"To open an account."

"What account, Ma?"

"At the bank."

Pérsomi frowned. "Ma, I don't understand, what account must I open at the bank?"

"Heavens, Pérsomi, don't be stupid! It's for money." Her ma handed her an envelope.

Pérsomi carefully opened it. "Ma, where does this money come from?" she asked.

"How much is it?" asked her ma.

Pérsomi did not count it. She folded the envelope and put it in the pocket of her dress. "Do you mean a savings account? Must I open a savings account at the bank and deposit this money?" she asked.

"That's what I said," her ma said, annoyed.

Pérsomi sighed. "Okay, what bank?"

"Heavens, child, stop asking so many questions."

"Okay, I'll decide. Is my mysterious father going to deposit money in it for me?" she asked directly.

But her ma turned and walked away.

Pérsomi walked to the kloof where Boelie was building his dam. She stood for a while, surveying the activity down below. The Italian, Antonio, was nowhere to be seen. Slowly she walked down. Boelie saw her and met her halfway.

"Your dam is coming along nicely," she said, looking at where a laborer was scraping the dam with four donkeys.

"If only my dad wasn't so tightfisted with money and diesel, we could have been finished. But by the time he realizes the value of the dam, the rainy season will be over. So, you're just about on your way to Tukkies?"

She gave a slight smile and nodded.

He nodded as well. "I think you'll enjoy it."

"I have no idea what to expect," she said.

"Oh, it's a lot like a big high school and a big dormitory, just with more freedom and no uniform," said Boelie. "You also go to classes and write tests, but it's just . . . I don't know, better than high school, so much better. You'll like Pretoria." He thought for a moment. "You realize you'll be initiated during the first few weeks?"

"Yes."

"I don't think initiation is so bad in the women's residences," Boelie said, "but I don't suppose it's very nice."

"They say during the first two weeks we'll have to wear the same dress every day," Pérsomi said. She laughed. "It won't be anything new to me."

"No, you're used to getting by with very little," he said. "Stand over here and I'll show you how the dam will work."

She stood beside him on a slight rise. "Look over there." He pointed at the wall taking shape from mounds of soil. "When the wall is as high as that post I planted over there . . . Do you see it?"

"Yes," she said.

"When the wall is that high, it will catch all the rain that presently flows away to the sea. And the water will rise until it reaches that rock I marked with paint. See?"

"It's going to be quite a puddle."

"Of course there will have to be good rains first," he said. "But with all that water we'll be able to irrigate some of the dry land as well, besides the citrus trees. We'll be able to plant additional grazing."

"Won't the dam wall be washed away?" she asked.

"We'll shore it up with stones," he said.

They stood looking out over the terrain. She wouldn't come back before April, maybe even July. She was going to be homesick, she realized.

"I love the farm," she said.

Boelie nodded. "Me, too," he said.

They stood together in a cocoon of silence.

"Why did you choose to study engineering and not agriculture?" she asked. "Don't you want to farm rather than . . . build bridges and dams, or whatever it is that you're going to build?"

"Yes," he said, "I do."

"And De Wet won't be a farmer, so why don't you come and help your dad on the farm?"

He stood looking out over the farm for a long time. "I won't be able to work under my dad, or even with my dad. We're just . . . too different."

"Or maybe too similar?"

He shrugged. "I hope the war ends soon," he said. "I'd like to finish my studies and begin to stand on my own two feet. The sooner the better."

He broke through the cocoon and went back to his dam. She turned and headed in the direction of the bywoner cottage where the sun set against the ridge.

The first weeks at the university were a relentless turmoil of new people and English textbooks and noisy nights. The hours rushed past, the days stampeded through the week.

"We're going to die of exhaustion," said Lucia, Pérsomi's roommate, when they were ordered by their seniors at midnight to sleep *under* their mattresses.

"I have to write an exam tomorrow," Pérsomi groaned. "I won't be able to think clearly."

"I think I hate res," said Lucia. "I definitely hate the seniors."

The next Tuesday Pérsomi ran into Reinier at the library door. "Are you surviving?" he asked.

"No," she said, "how about you?"

"Not a chance!"

But after a few weeks things began to fall into place. Most of the seniors had grown bored with the initiation, or maybe they simply had too much work.

The lounge in Pérsomi's res had big leather couches where the senior girls could sit and read. Every day the newspapers were placed on a big table under the window. The freshers were allowed to read the papers, as long as they remained on their feet and didn't sit on the couches.

Pérsomi read standing at the table every day.

On May 1 the Germans surrendered in Italy. Berlin was in the hands of the Red Army, and on the bridge across the Elbe River the American and Russian soldiers drank a toast to victory.

On May 8 all the girls in the women's residence sat in front of the wireless, listening to the victory speech of the British prime minister, Winston Churchill, broadcast directly from England. He ended with the words: "God save the King!" Trumpets clamoured, sirens wailed, cars blew their horns, trams sounded their bells. People cheered, shouted, and sang.

Some of the girls, including Lucia, got carried away, raising their hands and singing along: "Send him victorious, happy and glorious . . ." But most got up and left. "Bloody Khaki lovers!" they sneered.

"Everyone has lost, not only Germany," said Pérsomi, back in their room. "It was all so terribly unnecessary."

"The first returning troops will be parading down Church Street on Saturday morning," said Reinier when she ran into him between classes on Thursday. "I feel like going. I'd like to see the troop carriers."

"I don't want to go," Pérsomi said at once. The gaping wound of Gerbrand's death had slowly healed, but the scar remained.

"Okay," he said, kicking at a stone. "Come to bioscope with me on Saturday? It's a kind of war movie, but I don't think there'll be too much fighting, because it's a musical. It's called *Anchors Aweigh*, with those two guys who sing and dance, Gene Kelly and Frank somebody."

"Sinatra," she said.

"Yes, that's right. What do you say?"

She hesitated.

"Come on, Pérsomi, we can catch up like in the old days. It feels as if we haven't spoken for years."

"Oh, all right." She began to laugh. "You make it sound as if we're very old."

He smiled. "Studying is making me old," he said and shifted his books to his other arm.

Saturday night she spent a long time in front of her closet. She would have to wear her kidskin shoes. She couldn't go to bioscope in her old school shoes. Pérsomi picked a full skirt and a blouse that more or less matched.

"Are you going out tonight?" Lucia asked behind her.

"Yes," said Pérsomi.

"Where?"

"Bioscope."

"With a guy?" Lucia asked, surprised.

"Yes."

"Who is he?"

"Just someone who went to school with me."

"Is he handsome?" asked Lucia. "If he is, you must introduce him to me."

"The girls at school thought he was good-looking," she answered. "But to me he's just a good friend."

"You can't wear those shoes with that skirt," said Lucia.

"They're all I have," said Pérsomi and began to brush her hair.

❧

Boelie was granted the chance to finish his studies. At the beginning of the third term, Irene and Pérsomi drove back to university with him. They drove in Boelie's small new Chevy Deluxe, a secondhand car his oupa had bought for him. They drove across the Springbok flats to Pretoria, past the dozens of small platforms where the train stopped for milk cans and mail-bags.

"Next Saturday we should take a look at how the Voortrekker Monument is coming along," Boelie said when they stopped to eat the cold sausage and thinly sliced venison and the sandwiches his ouma had packed for them.

"Count me out," said Irene. "The cornerstone ceremony was one of the worst weeks of my life. I ripped the horrible Voortrekker dress I was forced to wear and Ouma pretended it was nothing."

So only Pérsomi stood waiting for Boelie in front of her residence Saturday morning. It was still early and the air was fresh and nippy. Pérsomi rubbed her hands together to warm them. When Boelie stopped next to her and leaned over to open the door, she got in quickly, knocking her head against his.

"Ouch!" she said.

His dark eyes were laughing, inches from her face. "Wild thing," he teased her.

"It's cold," she protested and quickly closed the door.

Suddenly the car felt different, smaller than it had a week ago. It felt strange to be sitting beside Boelie. The gum trees threw long shadows across the road in the feeble winter sun.

"It's a nice car," she said to fill the awkward silence.

"Hmm," he said, "I'm very happy with it."

She looked at his hands on the wheel: the broad fingers; the short, square nails; the dark hairs on the back of his hands. She remembered how those hands had stroked her hair in the darkest night.

"It's been nearly seven years since I last visited the monument," Boelie said.

She looked at his strong profile as if seeing it for the first time. "I've never been there," she said.

"I'll never forget the cornerstone ceremony," he said. Even his voice sounded different. "There were thousands of people, all of them Afrikaners. That week I realized, Pérsomi, that I could never be anything but an Afrikaner. It's in my marrow and in my blood."

She nodded.

When they arrived at the national symbol, she had even less to say. She was faced with a colossal roofless block, a huge cube with granite walls—like ruins—doggedly clinging to the rocky soil, its bare walls surrounded by stark scaffolding.

She stood motionless, staring.

"This place is almost sacred," said Boelie. "Here we are reminded of the Covenant the Voortrekkers made more than a century ago in the face of death. Here we know that God planted our nation at the southernmost tip of Africa for a reason."

"Yes," she said.

The strangeness remained: a strange place, a strange conversation, a strange Boelie.

"Do you feel it, Pérsomi?" Boelie asked beside her.

She didn't know what she felt. She was scared of what she thought she felt, so she said nothing.

"What do you think of the monument?" he asked after a while.

"It looks like"—she had to be honest—"a half-finished building."

"It will be a great church to honor God and our ancestors, a reminder of the great courage of our forefathers. It's where we Afrikaners come from, Pers, remember that and be proud."

They walked across the uneven terrain surrounding the building. Boelie looked at the half-finished monument from every side, talking and waving his hands. If Reinier had been here, he would have joined in the conversation, Pérsomi thought.

That evening Lucia asked: "How was your morning?"

"Interesting," Pérsomi replied. "Actually . . . weird."

"Yes, I also find the obsession with the monument weird."

But Pérsomi had not been referring to the monument.

"Pérsomi! Visitor for you!" a fresher yelled down the passage one evening.

"It must be that Reinier pal of yours," said Lucia. "You must really introduce me to him. Tonight, if possible."

Pérsomi hastily ran a comb through her hair. "And Japie?" she asked over her shoulder.

"Japie doesn't dance. I'm going to be left all alone at res when everyone else goes to the year-end ball!" Lucia groaned.

"I'll be here too," said Pérsomi as she left.

It wasn't Reinier waiting at the front door, however.

"Boelie?" He was standing in the dim light of the porch, casually leaning against a pillar.

"I've come to find out how you're doing," he said, stepping forward. "Let's go out for a soda."

Happiness welled up inside her. "I have to be back at seven thirty."

"We'll be quick," he said and set off. She fell into step beside him. He walked with long, easy strides.

They didn't talk, just walked quickly and quietly to the café.

"How are you?" she asked.

"Fine," he said, "fine."

At the café they sat down at a table set slightly apart from the others. "Two Sparletta Cream Sodas, please," Boelie ordered.

When the waiter had left, Pérsomi gave a slow smile. "How do you know I don't prefer Coke or Hubbly Bubbly?" she asked.

"Do you?" he asked, surprised.

"No, I'm just pulling your leg."

"Oh," he said. "I just wanted to find out how you are."

"I'm fine, Boelie," she said. "I like living in res. I have a weird roommate, but she's okay, and I'm starting to enjoy my studies. I've found my feet now. Actually you already know all of that."

"Good," he said.

The waiter brought their sodas. They drank, sipping the green liquid through long, thin straws. Persomi thought something was bothering him.

"So, how does it feel being back?" she asked.

"Okay," he said.

"You were gone a long time. Has the course changed much?"

"A little, yes," he answered. "It's just, well, there are two new lecturers."

"But you'll pass, won't you?" she asked. "It's all that matters in the end, isn't it? That you get your degree?"

"Yes, you're right. That's something you need to remember too," he said earnestly.

"No," she said, "I must pass with distinction, or else I'll lose my scholarships."

"But you must enjoy student life as well. How often do you go out? Do you join in the fun?"

"I went to the intervarsity match against Wits," she said.

"The freshmen have to go," he said. "What else?"

"I've gone to bioscope with Reinier. And we serenade."

"How often?"

"Did you bring me here to take me to task about my social life?" She smiled.

"It's important for you to experience every aspect of student life. Have you been to a ball?"

"No," she said.

"Do you have a dress?" he asked.

"Of course I have a dress," she said, annoyed.

"I mean a ball gown."

"Yes, Boelie, I have a ball gown."

"And have you been invited to a ball?"

She felt her irritation growing. "I was invited, yes, and I didn't feel like going."

"Well, when someone invites you to the year-end ball, you're going, understand? Have you finished your soda? We must go, or you'll be late."

He got up, paid at the counter, and walked out. She fell into step beside him, fuming.

"I'm serious, Pérsomi," he said.

"Why?" Her inner irritation broke loose piece by piece and pushed up into her mouth. "Why should I go to a ball? Why are you sticking your nose into my business? You have nothing to do with me."

He stopped and turned to her. "You're angry," he said, surprised.

"I'll be the one to decide what I want to do," she said.

"I don't doubt it for a moment," he nodded. "But I know you. If you have a choice, you'll stay at res and study. Varsity is about so much more than academics."

She maintained an obstinate silence. When they had almost reached her residence, he said, "If *I* don't tell you to be more social, who will?"

She felt her irritation slowly evaporate. "I'll think about it," she reluctantly agreed. "Thanks for the soda, Boelie."

She didn't *want* to be a bluestocking, she thought just before she reached her room. She wanted to take part in student life, like a real person. And she had a gown, a beautiful red gown that fit her like a glove.

All she needed was a pair of shoes.

❦

"Gosh, girl, you look lovely," Lucia said as she pushed the last hairpin into Pérsomi's hairdo. "You look . . . regal."

Pérsomi turned to the full-length mirror on Lucia's closet

door. The satin gown hugged her tall, slim figure. Her bronzed shoulders were bare, and a glimpse of her shapely legs was visible through the long slit at the back. Her dark hair was done up in an elegant French roll. The dainty shoes that she had purchased with money from her new bank account felt strange on her feet. The sensation of feeling pretty took her by suprise.

"I still think you should put on a little lipstick and a necklace," Lucia said.

"No, thanks." Pérsomi headed for the door. "Enjoy the movie."

Lucia groaned. "I'm desperate to find a new boyfriend," she said just before Pérsomi closed the door.

The passage smelled of 4711 Cologne and Wellaflex hairspray. "You look lovely, Pérsomi," one or two girls said as she walked by.

"Thanks, you too," said Pérsomi and went down the stairs to the foyer to meet Petrus, a classmate. His bulky figure looked uncomfortable in the dark suit.

"My, Pérsomi, you look stunning," he said in his deep voice. His thick neck seemed intent on escaping from the unfamiliar bow tie.

They walked to the venue in silence. Just before they reached it he said, "I don't dance very well."

"I can't dance at all. I did warn you," she said.

They shared a table with his friends from the men's residence. Pérsomi didn't know anyone. "Can I get you a drink?" asked Petrus.

"Coke, thanks," said Pérsomi.

When he had left, the guy opposite her asked, "So, I hear you're doing law with Petrus?"

"Yes."

"He says you're top of the class."

"Well . . . sometimes," she said uncomfortably.

"And I believe you're a first-rate athlete?" the girl next to him said.

What else had Petrus said about her? "I . . . take part, yes."

"I like sports, too," the girl said, "but I play netball. Have you ever tried it?"

"No."

"You should. You're tall. Where are you from?"

Pérsomi felt her legs begin to itch. "The bushveld," she said, wishing Petrus would return.

When the music began it was mercifully loud, drowning out all further attempts at conversation. "Let's dance," said Petrus and got to his feet.

It was a struggle.

When the first dance was over, Pérsomi saw that Reinier had entered—tall and handsome in his dark trousers and white tuxedo jacket. And on his arm was Irene, striking in a soft green gown. She looked confident all evening, in control. Reinier looked like a sheep who had been awarded first prize at the farmers' market.

The evening did not improve.

🍃

"Let's go for coffee," said Boelie when she came out on the veranda. He set off at a brisk pace.

"Are you well?" she asked, falling into step at his side.

"Yes," he said.

But he seemed distracted. The streetlights lit up the street, the cars' headlights threw long beams across the tarmac.

Halfway to the café, he said, "I hear you went to the ball."

"Yes."

"I'm glad." Boelie didn't look at her.

"I didn't enjoy it."

"I'm still proud of you for going," he said.

Proud of her? Perhaps he understood more than she suspected. "Who told you I went?" she asked.

"Irene," he said.

Of course, Irene.

They entered the same café and headed for the same table at the window. He pulled out her chair. "Coffee?" he asked when they were seated, "or would you prefer a soda?"

She smiled. "Sparletta Cream Soda, please," she said.

He also gave a slight smile. "Then we'll stick to it," he said.

They talked about the farm and the approaching exams and Boelie's plans for the following year, about De Wet's job with Reinier's father, Mr. De Vos, and about Boelie's oupa, whose health was rapidly declining. He avoided talking about Klara.

Pérsomi waited.

"Christine le Roux is back," he eventually said.

"Finally back from the war? Oom Freddie and Old Anne must be very happy." Was this what Boelie had wanted to tell her?

"Yes, they've been very worried."

Silence. He played with the straw in the glass. Outside, a tram rattled past.

"De Wet went to fetch her," he said.

"From Egypt?"

"Italy. She was in Italy."

"Oh."

More silence. The only sound was the cars driving by.

"They're kind of together now."

"De Wet and Christine?" she asked, surprised. "That's . . . interesting."

She didn't know where Boelie was heading with the conversation, but she got the feeling there was more. "Your families must be pleased."

"Yes, I suppose so."

Silence.

"Boelie, what do you really want to tell me?"

He looked up. His expression was very serious.

"Boelie?"

"Christine has a baby boy, Pérsomi."

"A baby?" she said. "She married?"

How did De Wet fit into this?

"No." He looked past her at the street where the sound of cars came from.

Suddenly she understood the consequences, the disgrace awaiting Christine's homecoming. "Old Anne can't be very impressed."

Boelie shook his head. "There's something else," said Boelie.

She waited, her heart pounding.

"Pérsomi, the baby's father is Gerbrand."

His name shocked through her, picked at the scar. Disbelief shot through her like an angry flame. She got to her feet. "I don't believe it," she said.

"Sit down," he said.

She stalked out of the café. Outside, cars were still driving down the street. A tram rattled past noisily.

She began to walk as fast as she could. In a few moments Boelie fell in beside her. "They've named him for your brother," he said. "I didn't want you to hear it from someone else."

"It's not true!" she said. She kept walking. "Gerbrand would have told me if he had planned to marry Christine. He said she was a nuisance."

"Pérsomi, listen to me. I believe it's true. Leave it until you get home and see the child. And don't say anything about what Gerbrand wrote."

She entered her res without saying good-bye. To Lucia she said, "I can't believe how people spread lies about someone who isn't even here to tell his side of the story."

But late that night, when the rest of the world was asleep, she took the pile of letters from the bottom of her closet, untied the string, and began to read.

All through the December vacation she avoided the Big House. She avoided Oom Freddie's farm. She didn't even pay Auntie Sis a visit. And one Saturday when she saw De Wet heading for the bywoner cottage on the ridge, holding the hand of a redheaded little boy, she set off for the mountain. Boelie found her there late in the afternoon.

"You can go home now, they've left," he said and sat down beside her on the rocky ledge.

"Hello, Boelie."

"Yes, hello. Gosh, it's hot, isn't it?"

She nodded. "I wish it would rain," she said.

The sun began to vanish behind her mountain. "What are your plans for next year, Boelie?"

"I got a job with the Department of Agriculture in Pretoria, as an engineer," he said.

She smiled. "I'm glad you're still going to be close," she said.

He got up. "You must go back now, it's getting dark."

"I will," she said but she didn't get up.

When he had gone a few paces, he turned. "You won't be able to avoid the child for the rest of your life, Pérsomi," he said. "He's just a little boy and you're his only real aunt."

She didn't go back home before the moon was high in the night sky.

On Christmas Eve Hannapat and Piet arrived from Johannesburg. Lewies Pieterse was with them.

He brought two bottles of brandy, and clearly had more than a few glasses inside him.

"Out on parole last month," he lisped. A whole year before the end of his sentence. "Good behavior. Monday I have to get back, to book in with the cops."

"Pa found a job with the municipality," Piet said, rather unsteady on his feet himself.

"Good behavior," Lewies repeated. "Pérsomi, don't you greet your pa?"

She left the house and returned only once she was certain Lewies Pieterse and Piet were asleep. "How are you?" she asked Hannapat softly.

"Fine," Hannapat answered. "I've got a boyfriend. As soon as he gets a job, I'm going to quit my job and get married."

"Hannapat, you're so young!"

"Oh, shut up!" Hannapat said, annoyed. "So what? Ma was thirteen when Gerbrand was born." She turned her back on Pérsomi and pulled the gray blanket over her head.

On Christmas morning Pérsomi's ma was up earlier than usual. "Auntie Sis and Oom Attie are coming over," she said, "and Fya and her children."

"And her husband?" Pérsomi asked.

"No, he left her, the rubbish," her ma muttered.

It's going to be a very long day, Pérsomi thought.

When Lewies woke up, the three-legged pot was already perched over a fire in the blazing sun. "Freddie le Roux sent this cake, and the chicken," her ma said nervously, "and Mrs. Fourie sent the potatoes."

Shortly afterward Auntie Sis and Oom Attie arrived, with a down-at-heel Fya and four snot-nosed kids in their wake. Auntie

Sis brought a loaf of bread she had baked, Oom Attie carried a pot with more food. And a bottle, firmly tucked under his arm. "Today we'll eat enough for the whole year," he said contentedly.

"Come, brother-in-law," said Lewies hospitably, "Christmas comes but once a year." He threw the cap of the brandy bottle over his shoulder.

The sun blazed down on the tin roof. Not a blade of grass stirred. The cicadas shrilled endlessly.

Pérsomi felt herself grow cold.

In the late afternoon Pérsomi saw De Wet and Christine approach through the citrus trees on the other side of the Pontenilo. The child was with them.

Auntie Sis and the rest had left, but Lewies Pieterse lay passed out in the kitchen doorway. Piet sat propped against the wall, clutching his head. Hannapat lay sideways on the car seat, fast asleep, and their ma slept slack-mouthed on the rumpled bed in the bedroom.

A wave of humiliation washed over Pérsomi. De Wet and Christine mustn't come near the house now.

She walked down to the river. She was of two minds: she really didn't want to see the child, but she was even less willing for these real people to see what was going on in her home. She waded through the shallow water to the rocky ledge on the opposite bank and waited for them.

The child's hair was copper-colored in the sunlight. He pulled away and began to run ahead. "Wa-tel! Wa-tel!" he cried.

Pérsomi stood frozen, watching.

De Wet let go of Christine's hand and hurried after the little boy. "Don't go into the water on your own, Gerbrand," he said.

The child came running along, barefoot, on sturdy little legs. He looked so . . . wholesome. Like Mr. Nienaber's children.

As the child reached her, De Wet picked him up. "This is your Aunt Pérsomi," he told the boy. "Say hello to Pérsomi."

"Wa-tel, wa-tel," said the child, struggling to get down.

"He's interested in nothing but the water now," De Wet apologized.

"He'll say hello after a while," said Christine. "Happy Christmas, Pérsomi."

"Yes, sorry, happy Christmas," De Wet smiled. "Easy does it, Gerbrand!"

"Thanks, the same to you," said Pérsomi. She tried to avoid looking at the child. "Everyone's asleep, I'm the only one awake."

"Gerbrand wanted to bring his ouma a gift," said Christine, "but if she's sleeping, maybe you'd better take it."

"Thanks." Pérsomi took the parcel. "I don't know whether Ma has anything for him," she said, embarrassed.

"I hope not," De Wet said easily. "He got so many presents, he'll need a year to play with them all."

"Permi!" the little boy called.

"Listen, he's trying to say Pérsomi!"

"Are you calling Pérsomi, big boy?" asked De Wet.

"Permi! Permi!" the child called out again.

She no longer had a choice. She turned to where the child was sitting flat on his behind in the water that ran over the stones. "Permi! Come play," he called.

"I can't believe he's saying your name," Christine said proudly.

Pérsomi looked down at the little boy, his eyes shining, his teeth sparkling white in the sunlight. "He's beautiful," she said.

"I . . . think so too," Christine said.

The child grabbed the dark mud in his fists and plastered it onto his face. "Mind you don't get mud in your eyes," Pérsomi warned. "Wait, wait, don't throw it like that."

Before she realized it, she had joined him in the muddy pool, bewitched by his charm. The child wasn't an incarnation of her brother. He was a little person in his own right.

"Gosh, he's quite a handful," she said after a while.

"Yes, he is," said Christine.

"Tell us how you're doing at varsity," De Wet said. "Are you still top of your class?"

She sat down on the rocky ledge. The sun threw long shadows around them. Her eyes were fixed on the child in the water. "It's been an . . . adjustment," she said.

"Yes, I know, but it's good, isn't it?" De Wet asked.

"Oh, yes, very good."

He cleared his throat. "Did you hear? Antonio plans to stay in South Africa."

She looked down at the child playing in the water and tried to ignore her bitterness toward the Italian. "Whatever for?"

"He's a nice fellow, Pérsomi."

"I haven't seen Klara so happy in years," said Christine.

Klara! Pérsomi didn't want to hear it.

"Come, Permi, come!" little Gerbrand called, throwing a ball into the muddy pool.

"We must put the past behind us and look forward," De Wet said calmly.

Pérsomi looked at Gerbrand. She saw his chubby little body, his strong legs, his coppery red hair. She saw him charging fearlessly into the water after the ball.

This was her brother's child. There was no doubt about it. "It hurts," she said.

"I know," said De Wet in his rich voice. "But you know,

Pérsomi, neither little Gerbrand nor Antonio had any direct part in your pain. I believe Antonio will make Klara very happy. And little Gerbrand is already the greatest source of pleasure to us all."

Pérsomi looked at Christine, whose blue eyes were brimming with tears.

The boy slipped and his head disappeared under the muddy water. Pérsomi dashed forward and lifted him out. "Gosh, look at you swim!" she said.

Gerbrand wiped his face with his hand and squirmed out of her grasp, back into the water. "Swim, swim," he said.

NINE

IN THE VERY FIRST WEEK OF HER FOURTH YEAR AT TUKKIES
Pérsomi had to choose her research assignment.

"We're to pick a law that is less than two years old," Pérsomi
explained to Reinier as they walked between classes, "then analyze its potential long-term consequences. Many of them are
really interesting."

"Hmm," he said. "That's what's called an oxymoron."

"What?"

"The words *law* and *interesting* side by side in the same sentence. The language of law is so pretentious that I'm completely
turned off."

"It's just legal jargon," she said. "Anyway, they're still much
more interesting than the bunch of old buildings you dragged me
to last year."

"But you said you found them interesting!"

"Well, not the last two hundred."

"We didn't look at more than fifteen historic buildings in
and around Pretoria!" he protested. "And it was *my* big research
assignment of the year."

"That's why I'm asking you now," she replied. "I helped you
survey and take photos. Now it's your turn to help me choose an
interesting law."

"Do you have one in mind?"

"Kind of. In 1946 Parliament passed the Asiatic Land Tenure and Indian Representation Act. I think it wants to restrict the locations where Indians can live and trade. There's also something about their right to vote."

"Indians can't vote," Renier said.

"I know, but what else could *Indian Representation* mean? I have to study it, then I'd like to speak to Yusuf's family and find out how it will affect them."

"Sounds like you don't need my help to decide," he said.

"Why this act, Pérsomi?" the professor asked. "The Asians don't play an important role in our society."

"In my town we know them all by name. Mr. Ismail and Mr. Ravat and the Moosas, all of them," she said. "They are storekeepers. One of them, Mr. Ravat, owns the only hardware store in town. That's besides the co-op, of course. But they don't carry as much stock as he does. And he's cheaper than the co-op and the General Dealer."

The professor frowned. "Well, as background, you'll have to examine the government's official Asian policy before you analyze the content of the act. You know they're not considered part of the South African population, don't you? They're to be repatriated to their fatherland as soon as possible. I really think you should choose another act. Stay away from politics, look at education instead, or housing, health, social legislature—there's such a wide choice."

"I'll stick to this one, thank you, professor," said Pérsomi.

Early one Thursday evening at the end of February, before the dinner gong, there was a soft tap on her door. "Miss Pérsomi," a timid fresher said, "there's someone at the front door for you."

"Someone?"

"Yes, miss. A man, miss."

"Thanks," said Pérsomi and pulled a brush through her hair.

Outside a soft drizzle was falling. The dense green trees looked gray behind the misty rain curtain.

There was no one on the veranda. Pérsomi went out and looked down the street.

She saw his car first, shiny with moisture. Then she saw him. He was waiting just outside the gate. There were fine raindrops in his dark hair and his wet shirt clung to his body.

Her heart gave a leap. Boelie.

She closed her eyes for a moment, got her heart under control. Then she walked to him.

He turned toward her. His face was closed, dark.

She knew at once. She put her hand on his arm. "Your oupa?" she asked.

He nodded. "This afternoon, suddenly. My dad phoned."

"I'm really sorry," she said.

He nodded. They stood in the soft drizzle, but he seemed unaware of the damp.

"Er . . . would you like to go for coffee?" she asked.

He nodded again and began to walk to his car.

They drove in silence. Persomi didn't know what to say. She didn't know if she should comfort him or just talk as if everything was normal.

They didn't go to the usual place. They drove past the shops and the blocks of flats and houses, through an unfamiliar part of the city. They didn't speak. But when they drove down a street with Indian stores, Boelie said, "They'll have to clean up this slum."

Pérsomi frowned. "What are you talking about? Who are *they*?"

"The municipality, the government," said Boelie. "Just look at it. The natives are taking over the city center."

"The natives are here anyway," she said calmly. "They work here, that's why they live here. And the whites need their labor. Without it our economy won't survive."

"Don't make a political argument out of every remark," he said.

Under different circumstances she would have accused him of starting it. Instead she simply asked, "Where are we going?"

"Out of the city, where it's quiet," he said.

She nodded. The streetlights began to come on. The streets were black and wet. The windows of the apartment buildings were shut.

"He had improved, he was doing fine," he said suddenly. "When my ouma came into his room, he was just gone."

Oom Fourie was dead. It was so final, she realized. "It's a good way to go, Boelie, just like that, quietly."

"Yes," he said.

They drove past the last houses. Boelie switched on the headlights. The drizzle had stopped and the headlights threw shiny silver beams across the wet road.

On a hill outside the city Boelie pulled off the road. The sun had gone down, and the clouds began to disperse. A few stars were visible. "Let's walk up here," said Boelie and headed off.

She followed. They were accustomed to walking in the dark, had been since childhood. Their feet knew how to step carefully.

It was quiet. But it wasn't their mountain. Their mountain had a bigger silence, a deeper peace.

"Look, there are a few stars," said Boelie.

She gazed up. "It's beautiful, but not as beautiful as our stars on the farm," she said. "Ours are much brighter. Still, the city lights are also beautiful from up here."

"The city has too many lights. They steal the glow of the stars."

"You should have been a poet." She smiled.

"I don't know about that," he said.

They sat down on the wet rocks and looked out over the sparkling city.

She was intensely aware of him beside her and missed the easy silence that used to enfold her when they sat close. She wished everything could be the way it used to be, before that winter morning in her first year, when he had taken her to the monument.

"The funeral will probably be on Monday or Tuesday," he said. "Would you like to come?"

She shook her head. "I have a test on Monday. I'll have to stay."

He gave a deep sigh. "You know, Pers, he and I were always at loggerheads, especially about politics."

She nodded.

"And yet I feel so . . . I don't know." He kept silent.

"Sad," she said.

"Yes, sad."

She nodded again. "I don't believe disagreements break the ties of love. The members of your family have always had different opinions on politics, still there's a strong tie between you."

"Yes," he said, "you're right, you understand. When I think of them now, I feel the things we disagreed on were so . . . temporary, so trivial."

"How you feel in your heart, your convictions, are never trivial," she said.

"I just wish I could . . ." He shook his head.

She reached for him, then withdrew her hand.

Suddenly he got up. "Let me take you back, or you'll miss supper," he said. "Come."

"Irene is angry with her oupa," Reinier told her as they waited for the film to start at the biosphere.

"Because he died so suddenly?" Pérsomi asked.

"Must you always be so nasty about Irene?" he asked, annoyed. "It doesn't suit you at all."

"I'm sorry," she said. "Why is she angry?"

"Haven't you heard about the will?"

"No."

"Would you believe Boelie inherited the farm and everything on it? In other words, the farm where Irene's father worked so hard all his life now belongs to his son."

After a moment she realized the implications of his words. "I don't suppose Mr. Fourie is very happy."

"He's furious, Irene says. He'll get a little cash, but that's all. Her ouma inherits some cash and various items. De Wet gets the old Daimler and a house they keep in town. He left Irene and Klara nothing. All the rest goes to Boelie. Gosh, Irene is upset with my dad too."

"Why is she upset with your dad?" asked Pérsomi.

"She thinks he should have persuaded her oupa to draw up a different will, or at least have warned her father in advance."

"A lawyer can advise his client, but in the end he must do what the client wants," Pérsomi said. "And your dad couldn't have discussed the will with Mr. Fourie in advance, it would have been unethical."

"I know, but try explaining it to Irene. She can be rather . . . unreasonable," he said.

"You said it, not me."

He sighed. "Yes, Pérsomi," he said. "Just promise me one thing. The day you fall in love, choose someone uncomplicated, who doesn't find a crisis behind every bush."

She gave a slight laugh. "Someone like you?"

He gave a crooked smile. "Why not?" he asked.

"Maybe I should fall in love with you," she said when she and Reinier sat eating sandwiches between classes a few days later.

Reinier burst out laughing. "Pérsomi, you're one of a kind! You've clearly never been in love. You don't have a clue what you're saying. Listen, Annabel gave me two tickets for a show by some theatrical company. It's in the old city hall on Saturday night, I think. Afterward they're taking the show on tour through the bushveld or the Lowveld, or somewhere. Want to come along?"

"You're not being very specific," she said. "Perhaps you mean André Huguenet? What's the name of the play?"

"I don't know, *Shattered by His Idol* or some such thing."

"Gosh," she laughed, "it sounds dramatic enough. Yes, okay, let's go take a look at those shattered idol worshippers."

On Saturday she stood in front of her closet for a long time. She didn't have much to wear. Her clothing supply from Reinier's sister had dried up in her second year, and she wasn't sure what to wear to an event at the city hall anyway. She had never seen a play, only the school's operetta. She took her three evening gowns out of her closet. Her favorite was the deep-red satin dress, but she had worn it on many occasions, including Klara's wedding to Antonio and the ball she'd gone to with Reinier earlier in the year.

She spread out the second dress. It was a glossy deep-blue taffeta gown with a sweetheart neckline. She felt pretty in it. She had worn it only twice, and never with Reinier. But she decided it was too extravagant.

All that remained was the sophisticated black velvet dress with the plunging neckline and the long slit at the back. She had never had the courage to wear it, but she remembered Klara's words: "You'd look ravishing in it."

Dress, it's you and me tonight, she finally decided. Behave yourself and stay up, d'you hear?

She put on her new strappy shoes and studied her image in the mirror.

When she went down to the front door half an hour later, she knew she looked good. Reinier stood waiting for her, in a dark suit and bowtie.

"Wow!" he said as they headed for his car. "Which fairy tale did you step out of?"

"You choose: *The Ugly Duckling, Cinderella*—"

"Not *Cinderella*, or old Bucket might leave us in the lurch tonight like that pumpkin carriage," he protested. "What about *Pérsomi, Princess of Tukkieland*?"

"There's no such fairy tale," she laughed.

"Seriously, you look beautiful."

"Thanks," she said. It was always good to be with Reinier— relaxed, easy. Fun.

At the city hall there was a sea of cars. She felt a thrill of excitement. Tonight she was going to see a play with real people in it, well-known actors.

Twenty-one years ago her father went to see a show, and left with her name.

In that moment she realized she didn't want to know her father's identity. It would be better if she never knew. There were too many things she wanted to say about how he had treated her mother.

The foyer of the old city hall was packed. Some of the women were in fur coats or fur cloaks, some had ornate opera glasses with which they could watch every movement on stage. The men wore dark suits and spoke in droning voices.

She saw a beautiful woman standing on the first step leading to the balcony, her hand in a long black glove resting elegantly on the ornate railing. Pérsomi recognized the style of her dress from the fashion plates in the latest *Brandwag*. It was Dior's New Look: the full, wide floral silk skirt reaching almost to her ankles, the snug top with the shoestring straps over her bronzed shoulders, the short black velvet jacket draped nonchalantly over one shoulder.

It was Annabel.

Boelie stood beneath her on the steps, broad-shouldered in his dark suit. He was looking at Annabel and the two of them were laughing.

Pérsomi felt a sharp pang pierce her like a lightning bolt.

"Why, there's Annabel," Reinier said cheerfully. "Let's say hello, we're probably sitting together."

Pérsomi felt her skin crawl with the urge to run. She drew a deep breath and stayed with Reinier. She saw Boelie's eyes darken when he noticed her. Was her neckline too low? Was the gown too snug?

Her gaze shifted and she saw Annabel's disapproving look, as if she wanted to say, Reinier, don't tell me you've dragged her along! And that dress—please, it's a war model, six or seven years behind the fashion!

"Evening, you two," Reinier said. "Nice and warm in here after the cold outside, isn't it?"

Pérsomi lifted her chin. "Good evening," she said.

"Yes, evening," said Boelie, sounding formal.

"Hello," said Annabel. She didn't look at Pérsomi. "Shall we go in?"

❧

On her way home for the April vacation, Pérsomi paid a visit to Yusuf.

"Miss Pérsomi Pieterse!" Mr. Ismail said, surprised when she appeared on the stoop of his shop. "Have you come to buy everything in my store?"

She laughed. "Just wait till I've finished my studies, Mr. Ismail, and I'm earning bags full of money. Actually I came to talk to Yusuf. Is he here for the vacation?"

"He's inside, please go in," said Mr. Ismail, opening the door wide.

The shop was still dark inside, still smelled of tobacco and maize flour and curry powder and new leather. And strange incense. The huge bags of maize flour and sugar still stood on the wooden floor, the piles of blankets still reached to the ceiling.

"In all of Pretoria there's no store that comes close to yours," said Pérsomi as she entered.

Yusuf was equally surprised to see her. They talked for a while, sharing stories about student life and their studies. Then she said, "I'm actually here to do some research."

"Research?" he asked, puzzled.

"Yes. You see, we have to analyze a recent law for its possible long-term consequences. I've decided on the Asiatic Land Tenure and Indian Representation Act," she said. "Do you know anything about it?"

His expression changed. "Every Indian in the country knows about it."

"Good, because it's what I want to speak to you about," she said.

"I don't know what you want from me," he said, almost aggressively.

"I just want to know how you feel about it."

"Well, how do you *think* we feel?"

"I suppose you . . . don't feel good about it," she said warily.

"That's putting it mildly. People are angry."

"I understand. Tell me exactly why?"

"Many of our people have been in this country for generations, some longer than the people who are pushing these acts through parliament."

"It's a good point, I'll look into it," she said, making a quick note.

"Would you like a cup of tea?" He began to light the Primus stove.

He's in a better mood now, she thought. "I'd love some, thanks," she said, "And remember, don't—"

"I know about the milk and sugar," he said.

"How do you feel about the restricted land ownership?"

"It's the real reason why my people are so angry." He slammed the kettle down on the Primus stove. "We Indians have never had complete freedom of movement in the Union, but now we're being restricted even further in where we're allowed to live and trade! Dr. Naicker calls it the Ghetto Act. It's pure Hitler racism, Pérsomi—that's what it is."

"Who's Dr. Naicker?"

"Dr. G. M. Naicker, one of our leaders. The other one is Dr. Yusuf Dadoo."

She wrote down the names. "Leaders in what?"

"The Indians have a tradition of satyagraha, passive resistance, the heritage of Mahatma Gandhi. In 1913 he—"

"I know his story."

"We have two political organizations, the Natal Indian Congress and the Transvaal Indian Congress," Yusuf continued. "The membership numbers of the Natal Congress are rapidly increasing. Here in the Transvaal we don't have any registered members, but our congress is also very active, especially among the students at Wits."

"How active, besides passive resistance?" she asked.

"Very."

"How?"

"Pérsomi!" he warned her.

"Well, answer me," she insisted.

"Except for boycotting things, which you'd probably classify as passive, we also arrange meetings to inform people. Lots of people attend, not all of them Indian."

"Are *you* active as well?" she asked.

"Yes, of course," he said.

"Just don't get interned like Boelie," she warned him, "or you'll also have to wait four years before you can finish your studies."

"No," he shook his head, "I'm more like De Wet. Active, but on the right side of the law."

"Better be careful," she warned.

"When the law was first introduced, thousands of people, I think more than fifteen thousand, held a march in Durban. A group pitched tents on a piece of land in the traditional Indian business district, now rezoned for whites. A group of white hooligans began to harass them every night, later by day as well, and quite a few Indians died, mostly of their injuries. The police did nothing."

"Impossible, Yusuf," she said firmly. "The police wouldn't stand by and watch while people were being killed."

"It didn't happen under the noses of the policemen," he said. "Dead people in the streets aren't something the police can overlook, yet no one was prosecuted."

"Hmm," she said, "I'll see what I can find out."

"I can give you the name of one of my friends, Benny Sischy. He was there. He was an eyewitness. I don't know his address, but he's at varsity with me. If you write a letter, I could give it to him."

"Yes, perhaps I should, thanks," she said.

"There's also a cleric, Michael Scott," Yusuf said. "He could give you a lot of inside information."

"You've been a great help, Yusuf," she said, pleased. "What's the story about certain Indians getting the vote?"

"Only those who qualify will be able to vote for a few white representatives in parliament, not our own people," he said.

"But you've never had the vote, have you?"

"Some Indians did. In the Cape, I think."

"I don't know, I'll make sure." She made a note.

"I believe it's so, and they're going to lose the right to vote now. The law is an insult to Indian people. We've sent representatives to India, England, and America to state our case. There's more tea in the pot. Shall I pour you another cup?"

🌿

From Mr. Ismail's store Pérsomi dropped in to see De Wet at the De Vos law offices. He had suggested they might have work for her to do through the vacation.

The carpet in the reception area was thick, and there were two leather armchairs and a table with books. A corseted lady with purplish gray hair sat behind the desk. To her left was a big window on which was written De Vos and De Vos, and in smaller letters underneath: Attorneys, Notaries, Conveyancers, Agents, Auctioneers.

Was it possible she might work in an office like this next year?

De Wet introduced her. "Ms. Steyn is our secretary. She says she has plenty of filing you can help with if you wish?"

The secretary nodded. Behind her hung a large painting of impala drinking from a muddy pool. On the desk stood a vase with fresh flowers.

"Yes, I'd like to," Pérsomi said. "Thanks."

"Have you met Mr. De Vos?" De Wet asked.

"I know what he looks like. I've seen him with Reinier and Annabel, but I've never met him in person," said Pérsomi. "But surely there's no need, De Wet?"

"I think he'd like to meet you," De Wet said easily. "Come along."

She followed him down a short passage, also carpeted. On the walls was a collection of old photographs, including one of Reinier's grandfather, the town's first lawyer.

At the end of the passage De Wet tapped on a door before opening it.

Half the space was taken up by a large desk made of dark wood. The polished top glistened in the overhead light. Mr. De Vos sat behind the desk. He was a big man with a ruddy complexion and a bald head. He peered at them over his spectacles. He didn't seem very pleased by the interruption.

"Oom Bartel," said De Wet, "this is Pérsomi. I told you about her. She's come to help us over the vacation."

Mr. De Vos rose halfway to his feet. He was not only broad but tall as well. And he was frowning. "Yes, I believe she was at school with Reinier," he said.

"That's right," said De Wet. "She's studying law at Tukkies."

Mr. De Vos lowered himself back onto his chair.

When De Wet closed the door again, he said apologetically, "He must be very busy. Usually he's much friendlier."

Pérsomi was glad Reinier didn't take after his father, but Annabel's personality now made more sense.

❧

Klara insisted Pérsomi attend Irene's coming-of-age party. She meant well but didn't understand. Because while Pérsomi and Reinier mingled with guests in the decked-out barn, Auntie Sis and Ma were in the kitchen in their Cinderella outfits, washing the dishes. And Annabel was on the dance floor, glued to Boelie, wearing an incredible emerald gown that would no doubt end up in the welfare pile next year.

"Come on," Reinier said, "you can't hang around the food all night, it's time for dancing."

She held back. "You know I don't really dance."

"Well, it's your choice," said Reinier. "Either you come willingly, or we make a scene."

"That's not a fair choice!"

"Who said life is fair?" He took her firmly by the hand and led her to the dance floor, where he gave her a playful twirl. He laughed and began to move in time with the music.

Because it was a waltz, the only dance she had mastered, she stayed.

"Stop being so unwilling. It's quite nice, don't you agree?" Reinier persisted.

He didn't understand either. After all these years Pérsomi still didn't belong here. But she noticed that no one gave her strange looks. Everyone kept right on dancing as if she did belong. Maybe it was her own fault that she still felt like a barefoot child among real people.

But as they danced past Boelie and Annabel, she felt Annabel's ice-cold, critical gaze on her. The fighter in Pérsomi came to the fore, and she returned the stare. She knew she looked good in Annabel's cast-off dress.

She couldn't look at Boelie, however. It was hard for her to see how comfortable Annabel seemed in Boelie's arms, how they moved as one in the dance.

Someone put a new record on the grammophone, and everyone gathered in a circle. "Tango!" they cried. "Where's Annabel?"

A laughing Annabel floated into the circle. "Come, Boelie, no excuses, I've shown you how," she said coyly.

Boelie laughed and stepped into the circle. Smiling, he held out his hand to Annabel.

They danced the tango. The way it should be danced.

The other guests clapped to the beat of the music.

Pérsomi stood at the outer edge of the circle. It was clear there was an established bond between the man and the woman on the dance floor.

She turned away.

For the rest of the evening she stood in the shadows. She saw Oom Freddie dance with one woman after another. She saw Old Anne's neck stiffen and her mouth turn into a thin, straight line. She saw the eyes of all the young men following Annabel in her revealing dress and noticed that Boelie did not stray from her side all night. She saw Reinier dance with Irene. She saw Mrs. De Vos, Reinier and Annabel's mother, down one glass of brandy and Coke after another.

Close to midnight Pérsomi began to gather dishes from the

tables to carry them to the kitchen. Someone touched her arm and spoke softly into her ear.

"My turn." Boelie steered her toward the dance floor.

"Boelie," she said anxiously, "I really don't dance well. Actually I can only waltz. This is certainly not a waltz."

He didn't answer, just gripped her arm more firmly.

"Boelie, please!"

"Just follow my lead," he said. On the dance floor he put his arm around her waist. She felt his hand rest lightly on her back, his other hand folding around her own. Slowly, without speaking, he began to dance. Her body was tense as she tried to follow his movements.

"Relax, Pers," he said softly.

She made a deliberate effort to relax, as she had learned to do on the track. She allowed the lilting music to sweep her along, she followed where he led, she was acutely aware of his proximity.

"It's not so hard after all, is it?" he spoke into her hair.

She nodded, too afraid to say anything.

In the morning she was in the barn before daybreak to finish cleaning. She prayed that Boelie wouldn't be there to help. The barn looked like it had been struck by a tornado. She pushed the empty trash can to the door and began to fill it.

Her thoughts turned to her assignment. There were so many facts she wanted to include, so many loose threads to be tied up before it was due in a few weeks. She had finished the letter to Benny Sischy. She would give it to Yusuf when she and De Vos went to town this morning. And she'd write to Michael Scott. She just wasn't sure where to get hold of his address.

Two empty wine bottles landed in the can with a clang.

She would have to search in the university library for old newspapers, maybe—

"Gosh, you're an early bird!"

Boelie's voice at the door made her jump. Her heart was in her throat.

He laughed.

"Jumpy?" he asked as he entered the barn. "What were you thinking about?"

"My . . . assignment." Her voice sounded strange. She swallowed. It was only Boelie.

But her heart didn't listen.

He began to pull the straw bales away from the wall. "You don't have to help clean."

"I promised your mother I would," she said.

"Can you believe it? There's a whole nest of glasses behind this bale. Bring the basket," he said. "What's your assignment?"

"It's about the Asiatic Land Tenure Act," she said, passing him the basket.

"Yes, I know about it," he said. The glasses clinked as he put them in.

"I had a very interesting conversation with Yusuf Ismail last Monday."

"You didn't have to talk to him. You could just read about the repercussions in the papers," he said.

"I did that too," she said. "The Indians are up in arms, and I think they have a valid point. Careful, you're going to break those glasses."

"Valid point?" he asked skeptically. "You're wrong there. The Indians ought to know their place in this country. They should behave, or they should return to India. They shouldn't try to act like whites."

Carefully she put the basket with the dirty glasses on a chair. "Boelie, if the traders are restricted in where they're allowed to trade, or the doctors and lawyers are told where they may practice, how can they run their businesses properly?"

"In this country," Boelie said emphatically, "we must look after ourselves, Pérsomi. The interests of the whites, specifically the Afrikaners, come first. Do you realize how many clients the General Dealer and the Farmers' Co-op have lost because Ismail sells his inferior products at a cheaper price? For once, the Khaki government is acting strictly, and it's a good thing. Lawyers and doctors and teachers and traders, the whole caboodle, are being arrested and chucked into jail, hundreds of them, if not thousands."

She straightened and looked him in the eye. "Doesn't that sound familiar to you?"

He frowned, puzzled.

"What did you fight for? Why were you and a whole caboodle of lawyers and doctors and teachers willing to be imprisoned behind barbed wire five years ago?" she asked earnestly.

"For the God-given rights of the Afrikaner nation."

"For the rights of your people?"

"Yes," he said. "And if I had to choose again today, I'd choose the same route."

"And isn't it the same route these people are also choosing? Aren't they also standing up for what they believe are the rights of their people?"

"For goodness' sake, Pérsomi, this is not their country! They're visitors, laborers. India is their fatherland! They should go back there."

"And if their fathers and their fathers' fathers were born here? Our forefathers came from Europe. Why is the Union our fatherland but not theirs?"

Boelie swore. "Don't be so naive to believe the curried hogwash Yusuf Ismail feeds you. The whole lot are Communists, including Yusuf Ismail."

"Why do you say that, Boelie? Do you have proof?"

"Heavens, woman, must you always have proof of everything?"

"Don't *heavens, woman* me!" she snapped.

He looked up, a strange expression on his face. It passed swiftly.

"When the National Party gets voted in, their attitude is one of the first rotten apples that must be got rid of."

"*If* the National Party gets voted in," she said.

"You're trying my patience this morning," he said. "I'd better leave."

He strode out of the shadowy barn into the bright sunlight. She followed him with her eyes as he strode toward the kraal, his broad shoulders stiff, his head high.

A deep sadness grew inside her. She stood alone in the chaotic barn. Alone she took the burned-out lanterns from the wall hooks, alone she packed the last dirty glasses in the basket.

Alone she folded one tablecloth after another.

Her mother came through the barn door to help.

"Pérsomi, you must stay away from boyfriends, you're looking for trouble," her ma said.

"What?"

But that was all her mother was willing to say.

The Indians refer to this act as the Ghetto Act,

Pérsomi wrote in the conclusion of her assignment.

I doubt whether it's possible to apply the law successfully. To date no Indian has agreed to serve on the Land Tenure Advisory Board.

Furthermore, it is my opinion that the consequences of this law will be more far-reaching than the lawmakers could ever have foreseen.

In the first instance, it has made people who were favorably disposed toward whites for decades turn against them. It deeply upset families who lost a brother or son in the recent war—relatives of young men who lost their lives serving the same government who now wants to restrict their parents' opportunities to trade (see interviews and letters, addenda one and two).

Furthermore, the Asiatic Land Tenure Act gave rise to closer cooperation between the various Indian Congresses, the ANC and the Coloured population's African People's Organisation (APO), as is clear from recent pronouncements by the President General of the ANC, A. B. Xuma, in the press (see addendum three).

On their part, the Indians have developed sympathy with the black population, as was evident during the black miners' strike of August 1946 (see reports in addendum four).

The Indian people have won considerable support from the white population, culminating in the establishment of the Council for Asian Rights in Johannesburg (report and photographs, addendum five).

The law also had international repercussions when India tabled the matter for discussion and action at the UN, and opposed South Africa's application to incorporate Southwest Africa with the Union (see addendum six). If the application is denied, it could be considered a direct consequence of the act.

In conclusion, I am of the opinion that the Asiatic Land Tenure Act has never been a viable proposition and is presently leading to anarchy rather than good order.

When her assignment was returned a week later, there was no grade on it. Neither were there any comments. Only a message: *Come and see me.*

She made her way to the professor's office, her heart heavy. What could be wrong?

The professor looked up when she entered, then back down at the documents on his desk.

Gently she laid the assignment on the desk between them.

He picked up the assignment and paged through it.

She waited.

"Your elucidation and analysis of the finer legal points, and your research, are excellent," he said at last.

Her heart was in her mouth.

"Your command of language is admirable, also the structure of the assignment and your referencing."

Her blood seemed to flow slowly, heavily.

The professor looked at her. "The problem I have is with the conclusion you reach."

Her blood no longer reached her brain. Her head ached.

"Pérsomi, our university endorses lofty Christian National principles. Our department has a specific culture, an ethos, of which we are proud."

She licked her dry lips. "I don't understand, professor," she said.

He picked up the assignment and turned to the last two pages. "This conclusion," he said and tapped on the words, "borders on the propagation of Communism. I won't have it in my department."

The professor took his time to remove his spectacles. At last he said, "I'll give you the opportunity to change the conclusion. You can hand in your assignment at the end of the week, after which it will be graded."

He put his spectacles back on his nose. The conversation was clearly at an end.

"Professor, what grade will you give me if I don't change my conclusion?" She forced the words past her constricted throat.

He looked up, troubled. "Fifty percent. Fifty-five at most," he said.

She felt the words pierce her body. Her throat closed up. "Then I won't get a distinction," she said. She would lose her scholarships.

"It's your choice. I can't accept the assignment as it is." He removed his spectacles again. His smoky blue eyes seemed rimmed with gray. "You're my top student, Pérsomi. You've passed every year with distinction. It would be a pity if you don't graduate cum laude because of two pages of one assignment. I warned you at the outset to pick another law. I told you it's a sensitive matter, but you insisted on having your way. We dare not underestimate the onslaught of Communism in our country."

She remained silent for a long time before she said, "I know very little about Communism, professor, and it's the last thing I was trying to propagate. What I do know is that I can't change my conclusion. It is my honest opinion."

"Then I can't change your grade," he said.

She thought for a moment. Then she lifted her chin. "When is the absolute deadline for the assignment?" she asked.

"The test series begins on Monday," he said. "I can't give you more than two weeks' deferment."

"I'll hand in another assignment on a different law. In time," she said.

She turned on her heel and walked out, gently closing the door behind her.

She left the assignment lying on his desk and didn't mention it to anyone.

TEN

THE ENTIRE MONTH OF MAY 1948 STOOD IN THE LIGHT OF THE
upcoming election, or maybe in its shadow. The United Party
incumbent, Jan Smuts, who had been prime minister since 1939,
was on the verge of being ousted. His accommodating positions on
racial integration were increasingly unpopular among Afrikaners
who feared the economic, religious, racial, and political repercussions of growing minority groups. The opposing Reunited
National Party, also known as the HNP, quelled such anxieties
with promises of total segregation.

"Is the election all you guys can talk about?" Pérsomi asked
Reinier as they walked between classes.

He gave her a surprised look. "Gosh, Pérsomi, what else do
you want to talk about? Surely not the approaching exam, or our
respective love lives, or the drought in the bushveld?"

"Well, Christine and De Wet had a baby girl. That's exciting
news," she challenged him.

"Oh, Pérsomi, that was last week."

"Okay. And . . . er . . . what about . . . ?"

"The election," he suggested cheerily. "The National Party's
chances are a lot better than in '43."

She sighed, shrugging. "And you think they're going to win?"

"You must learn to say we, not they. Aren't you going to vote for them?"

"I'm not sure I'm going to vote at all," Pérsomi said.

"Of course you are. Pérsomi, have you seen where the United Party is heading? They pretend to reject integration, but at the same time they say total segregation is impossible. If they have their way, our cities will be black before long."

"But segregation *is* impractical. If Blacks are no longer allowed to live in the cities, who's going to work in the mines? Or the factories?"

"That's why we have migrant workers," Reinier said irritably. "They come in to work in the mines and industries, then they return to the reserves. It's the logical solution."

"Maybe. But I don't know whether this new term *apartheid* is just another kind of discrimination."

"Where would you get such an idea?" His tone was uncharacteristically annoyed. "Apartheid just means that the whites and the natives will live separately—we in our cities and towns, they on the reserves. And it's not a new concept. Total segregation has been NP policy since 1934. They want to develop the reserves so that the natives can retain their tribal identity."

"In other words, keep them unschooled and in their place?" she asked.

"Heavens, Pérsomi, their culture and traditional way of life are just as important to them as our culture is to us. Who are we to try and make them more like us?"

It sounded logical and fair, but it bothered her.

She received top marks on her second assignment, and kept that to herself as well.

On May 24, two days before the general election, *Die Transvaler* reported that the HNP was worried about the political cooperation of the minority groups.

> Last Saturday, Black leaders met with their Indian and Coloured counterparts, and even a number of whites, demanding full franchise rights for all, after which they signed a Joint Declaration of Cooperation.
>
> This development came shortly after Dr. A. B. Xuma, president of the ANC, had thanked the Indians for their part in the struggle against racial discrimination.
>
> If the Nationalists come into power, they will have to take strict steps against the Indians who are trying to influence all non-white groups against the whites.

The evening before election day, a group of seniors was sitting in the lounge listening to a special broadcast. Dr. Malan, candidate of the Reunited National Party, was first to speak. "Bring together what belongs together," he said. "The future of the white population lies in the cities and towns and on the farms, where we carry the economy of the country. The future of the natives lies in the reserves. They must develop at their own pace in their own areas. We recognize the threat of the endless flood of natives entering the cities. We will undertake to protect the white character of our cities."

His voice droned on over the airwaves. "We intend to put a stop to mixed marriages, there will be no natives in parliament, job reservation will be applied more strictly, Indian immigration will be stopped, Indians will be repatriated . . ."

Quietly Pérsomi got up and left the lounge. The other girls sat listening, captivated.

Everyone gathered at Boelie's place to listen to results come in over the wireless. Boelie was writing down the results in a notebook when Pérsomi arrived. He called over his shoulder, "You'll find the Primus and the kettle over there. Why don't you make some coffee? And there are rusks in the tin."

"It doesn't look good for the National Party, does it, Boelie?" said Pérsomi, studying the results he had written down.

"Just you wait, our results are still coming," he replied.

Reinier joined them after completing a test, and Annabel arrived shortly after.

"Do I hear my brother's voice?" Annabel said chirpily.

"We've just got another seat!" Reinier reported, putting his hands around her waist.

Annabel laughed. "Every little bit helps, doesn't it? Wait, Reinier, let me say hello to Boelie."

She floated across the room to where Boelie was standing at the window, snuggled up against him, and raised her face. "Hello, Boelie."

He gave her a lopsided grin. "This is a surprise," he said. "Have you come all the way from Joburg?"

"It's not that far," she laughed. Only then did she turn to Pérsomi. "Oh, you're here too? Hello, Pérsomi."

"Good afternoon, Annabel."

"You take the pen, Pérsomi," Boelie instructed as another series of beeps came over the wireless. He handed the notebook to her. She felt the weight and quality of the pen in her hands. "I have news," he announced.

"News?" Pérsomi asked.

"Yes, I . . ." Boelie hesitated, then looked at her. "I won't be here much longer. I resigned at the Department of Agriculture, Pers, I'm going back to the farm at the end of June. Permanently."

Annabel drew a sharp breath. "Resigned?" she cried. "Are you mad?"

"No, I've given it a great deal of thought." He reached out and took her hand.

Pérsomi nodded slowly. "Will you be farming with your dad?"

"Surely you can't waste your qualifications on farming!" said Annabel, withdrawing her hand from his.

Boelie ran his fingers through his hair. "I'm going to try," he said. "I hope it works."

"And if it doesn't?" Reinier asked.

He shrugged. "The bottom line is that the farm belongs to me, no matter how unfair it may seem."

The wireless interrupted their conversation.

"Write!" said Boelie and turned up the volume slightly.

"Here is the result of the constituency of Losberg, Transvaal."

"The Transvaal rural areas. Now things will get moving," Reinier said.

"It's Louis Botha's former seat," Annabel warned, linking arms with Boelie, "and the UP has put up a strong candidate there, Bailey Bekker. I don't know . . ."

She knows so much more than me, Pérsomi thought briefly. No wonder Boelie—

"G. P. Brits, Reunited National Party . . ."

"We've got it!" Reinier roared.

"Quiet!" Pérsomi scolded. "I can't hear."

"We've got it! We've got it!" Reinier rejoiced. He grabbed Pérsomi by the waist and spun her round and round.

"We've bloody well got it!" Boelie said, amazed.

"One swallow doesn't make a summer," Annabel said, taking

over Pérsomi's seat and pen. "Pérsomi, make some fresh coffee, I'll write. Or do you have something stronger, Boelie?"

"Yes, I think there's a bottle of wine. Look in the bottom of the cupboard, Pers." He crossed the room and opened the window.

Pérsomi filled the kettle and found the bottle of wine in the cupboard. "So, you chose the farm?" she asked, handing the wine and corkscrew to Boelie.

He nodded. "Yes, I'm thirty, I want to settle."

"Thirty?" Reinier cried, shocked. "Boelie, that's old! You'd better drag my sister to the altar soon or you'll both be left on the shelf!"

Pérsomi felt the words pierce her heart.

Annabel's laugh was bright. "Steady, brother," she said, "I don't think I'm quite ready to tie the knot."

"You're an old maid, Annabel," said Reinier.

Annabel raised her brows. "That's your opinion. I see myself as a successful career woman." She took a glass of dark red wine from Boelie and snuggled against him. "I'll tell you what. If I get that job as foreign correspondent in London, you'll have to wait another year or so to be a groomsman. If not, wedding bells might chime sooner than you think."

"Mom and Dad won't be very excited if you get the job," Reinier said earnestly and took a sip of wine. "What do you think, Boelie?"

Boelie shrugged. "I suppose she can make up her own mind."

"She's been doing exactly as she pleases since she was seven," Reinier said. "No one could ever tell my sis what to do."

"You're right, brother," said Annabel, "you're quite right. Pérsomi, are you actually having coffee? What a little goody two-shoes you are!"

At quarter to ten that evening the HNP's victory was official. Smuts was out. D. L. Malan would be South Africa's next prime minister. And by half past seven the next morning, the HNP and

Afrikaner Party had taken a majority of seats in the House of Assembly, paving the way for apartheid to become more than an idea.

In the last days of her exam, a fresher came to call her. "Miss Pérsomi, there's someone at the front door for you."

"Someone?"

She noticed the girl's inquisitive expression. "Yes, miss. He says he's your father."

Pérsomi was stunned by the possibility. But the next moment she realized it could only be Lewies Pieterse.

She felt herself turn cold. It was early evening. There would be students in the foyer, the garden would be full of dating couples.

She knew what Lewies Pieterse would look like, act like, at this time of day. She had to get rid of him as quickly as possible.

She hurried down the stairs. He'd want money. It was the only reason he would come to see her. But if she gave him any, how would she ever get rid of him again?

He was standing in the middle of the foyer, even drunker than she had expected.

Many eyes were watching.

"Come outside," she said brusquely and led the way to the garden, her back stiff. She walked some distance, to a point far from the gate.

"Don't you say hello to your pa?" he asked when she turned to face him.

"What do you want?"

"Pérsomi, Pa's little girlie, I wanted to come and see for myself how you are," he lisped. "I just—"

"I'm fine. Go, before I call the police."

A sly look flitted across his face. He shook his head. "Lewies Pieterse doesn't fall for your bluff." He took a step closer. He smelled of old sweat and his breath was sour. "I'm a free man, I've done my parole. The cops can't touch me, because I'm toeing the line. Lewies Pieterse knows his rights. I've come to visit my daughter, what's—"

"It definitely isn't love that brought you here, because there's no love lost between us. None, do you hear me?" She kept her voice very low and looked him in the eye. "And I'm not your daughter, you know that as well as I do. So leave." She turned back toward the res.

He caught her arm in a painful grip. She tried to free herself, but he held on. "I won't go before you give me money," he said loudly.

She turned, facing him again. Her entire being radiated scorn. "I don't have any money."

"I'm not going anywhere." He lurched, then found his feet again. He raised his voice. "I'm not going. Go find money."

She was overcome by despair. He'd make a scene.

"Stay here," she said. "Don't move. I'll see if I can borrow money. If you move, I won't give you a cent."

He shot her a sly look. "I'll wait five minutes, then I'm coming in to look for you. And no one will stop Lewies Pieterse, not one of these girls." He hooked his thumbs in his braces and stepped back, full of bravado, pleased with himself.

Pérsomi went back inside and took the stairs two at a time. She couldn't borrow money. She couldn't give him money. She couldn't phone the police either; he hadn't done anything wrong.

She yanked open her bedroom door. He would certainly come inside.

She pressed her palms to her flushed face. *Dear Lord, help!* she prayed. *I don't know what to do.*

Her hands took a tickey from her purse. Her feet walked to the phone booth. Her fingers found the right numbers. Her voice spoke without her having thought about what she would say.

"Boelie, please come and help me. Lewies Pieterse is here at res, in the garden."

She was trembling from head to toe.

A dark eternity later there was a soft knock on the door. "Miss Pérsomi, there's someone at the front door for you."

It was long after visiting hours.

"Are you all right, miss?" The fresher sounded anxious.

Slowly Pérsomi came out from under the blanket. "Yes," she said. Her voice sounded strange, hoarse.

"Miss, the man says his name is Boelie Fourie. He says you must come quickly, he won't be long."

Boelie. Her oasis in the wilderness. Her anchor in a stormy sea.

She went downstairs.

"Who was the man who was here earlier?" the fresher asked.

"Just a no-good bywoner from the farm where I live," Pérsomi answered.

"He said he was your father."

"He was drunk," Pérsomi said. "He's no more my father than the man in the moon."

"Oh, that's what we thought."

In the foyer Pérsomi said, "You can go to your room. I'll lock up."

She waited until the girl had left, then stepped outside. Boelie was standing just below the veranda, in the path leading to the gate. "Are you okay, Pers?" he asked.

She nodded, then her head began to shake involuntarily.

He opened his arms.

She walked into his embrace.

His arms folded around her. Tight. Hard as steel.

Safe.

She was trembling all over.

He clasped her firmly to his chest while his other hand stroked her hair. "All right, Pers, he's gone now."

She stood motionless in his embrace. "Where is he?" she whispered almost inaudibly.

"Gone," he said. "He won't be back."

She felt his calmness, his strength, gradually enter her being.

"I was so . . . afraid," she murmured.

He held her more tightly. She felt his heart beat against her chest, heard him breathe in her ear. "I don't want you ever to be afraid again." His hand kept stroking her hair, her neck. "Never again."

She stood electrified, petrified. His hand slid down her neck, her back, pressed her more tightly to him.

His lips were on her hair.

She felt his wild heartbeat.

"Pérsomi!" His voice was hoarse.

She lifted her head.

For a moment she saw his face in the dim streetlight, then he stepped back and turned away. "Just . . . go back in," he said, his voice choked. "Go."

ELEVEN

THE LOCOMOTIVE BEGAN TO HISS AND BLOW, THE WHEELS screeching on the iron tracks, the wagons jerking into motion. Pérsomi saw the white steam billowing and the black smoke rising into the blue sky. The acrid smoke burned her nostrils and the back of her throat. Her white blouse was covered in specks of soot.

She gave herself up to the rocking motion of the train and took her last ride home from Tukkies. The Springbok Plains slept peacefully, as they had been doing for ages, under the scorching sun. Not a cloud was in sight.

Sleepily Pérsomi leaned back in her seat. She would miss her life as a student, but she was excited, not sad. Monday she would start as an articled clerk at De Vos and De Vos, where she had worked with De Wet in April. Reinier would qualify as an architect at the end of next year. Annabel was in London, having secured the correspondence position she wanted.

Over the slight melancholy and the vague excitement lay a deep uncertainty.

Boelie.

She had felt something in him that night. She had heard something new in his voice when he spoke her name, knew she had seen something in his eyes that fraction of a second before he turned away.

But after he left, he did not contact her again.

During the July vacation she'd caught the odd glimpse of him on the farm. She knew he was very busy. He and his father had things to sort out—hard things, painful things.

In her last few months at varsity she was often called to the phone.

It was never Boelie.

Ma's little house on the ridge had given up. One wall was collapsing, and the roof had sagged until one window was almost completely obscured.

"Are you a lawyer now?" Oom Attie asked Pérsomi the first Sunday.

"I've completed my studies, but I still have to do a two-year internship in a lawyer's office," Pérsomi explained.

"But she's getting paid," her ma added at once.

"You'll be getting a lot of money now," said Auntie Sis. "I suppose you'll be too good for us."

"I'll be earning very little. I'm actually still being trained," said Pérsomi. "But the first thing we must do is fix this house."

Monday morning she drove to work with De Wet. At the office, Ms. Steyn was still behind the reception desk with the same purple hairdo and stiff corset. She gave Pérsomi some filing to do.

"I'm glad you're back," she said. "I hope you know how to type."

In the afternoon Mr. De Vos called her into his office. She closed the door behind her, alone with him for the first time.

He looked up without getting to his feet. Behind the thick lenses of his spectacles his eyes looked large. "I hear you fared well at varsity," he said. "Congratulations."

"Thank you, sir," she said.

"You were strongly recommended by De Wet. We don't usually take interns. Ms. Steyn also says you are reliable."

"Thank you," she said.

He began to shuffle the papers on his desk. "The next two years I'll be acting as your principal," he said, "which means that you'll be working under my direct supervision."

"Thank you," she said again, fearing she sounded like a fool.

"At the beginning you'll help chiefly with administration, but gradually we'll introduce you to other tasks." He focused on the papers. "A lawyer, especially one in a small town, is also an estate agent and auctioneer at cattle sales and especially at liquidation sales. We draw up contracts, supervise farm rentals, deal with wills and inheritances. It's not only court work."

"Yes, I understand," she said. That much had been made clear to her during her April stint.

"Fine." He seemed slightly taken aback by her acceptance. "In time I'll take you along to hearings. For now, you can carry on here at the office."

"Thank you, sir," she said and closed the door behind her.

❦

When she and De Wet got into the car after work, he said, "I want to show you something."

He turned into a side street. After another block he turned onto an untarred road and stopped at the third house from the corner. "This is our townhouse, the one that was left to me by my grandfather," he said, getting out. "Come, take a look."

The house had a small porch almost on the curb. The peeling paint on the green front door revealed that once it was gray. The brass doorknob and letter drop were tarnished green.

De Wet unlocked the door. The linoleum floor in the dark passage was scuffed down the center. He flicked on the light switch. "Come see," he said again.

To the left of the passage was the sitting room, with a bench and two big chairs, their seats threaded with rawhide and their cushions faded. To the right was a dining room with a table, six chairs and a sideboard. "My grandma always kept her linen in there," De Wet said.

"Oh," said Pérsomi.

They looked into the next two rooms. "These are the bedrooms," said De Wet. To the left was a room with a double bed, a wardrobe, and a washstand with a basin and jug. To the right was a second bedroom with two iron bedsteads and a sloping table.

The passage ended in a kitchen. "This is the kitchen," said De Wet.

"I see." Pérsomi smiled.

"Yes, I suppose it's pretty obvious," he said, slightly embarrassed.

In the middle of the kitchen floor stood a table and three chairs. A stove and a crate for wood were pushed against the wall. A shelf next to the back door held a kitchen sink with two taps. The only other piece of furniture was a green dresser with two shelves, stacked with plates, bowls, and dishes. Cups were suspended by their handles on hooks. Several rusty tins were on display on top of the dresser. "This is where the supplies are kept," De Wet said, opening a door.

His pride in the house struck her as strange, considering the grandness of the Big House he had grown up in.

There was a bathtub on clawed feet in a small room off the kitchen. A flimsy curtain strung on a cord covered the window.

"And here's the backyard, as you can see," De Wet said, unlocking the back door to reveal a bare patch of earth with a single pepper tree, a dilapidated clothesline, and an outhouse. Khaki bush sprouted in the gray soil.

Pérsomi didn't know what to say. Surely De Wet and Christine weren't planning to live here. Not after Oom Freddie and Old Anne had built a smaller, more modern house on the Le Roux farm. Christine and De Wet had been living in the original farmstead.

"This was your grandparents' home?" she asked politely as they prepared to leave.

"Yes, before they moved into the Old House," he said, locking the door. "After my oupa bought the Daimler, they seldom used it. That's why it's so run down."

It was dilapidated, in fact. They stood at the car, looking at the house. The downpipe hung at an angle, the walls needed paint, a piece of cardboard covered a window with a missing pane.

"We'll have to fix it up as soon as possible," said De Wet and got back into the car.

When they had left the town behind, Pérsomi asked, "Are you thinking of selling the house?"

"No," said De Wet. "Actually, Christine and I have a plan we'd like to discuss with you."

Surely De Wet wasn't going to ask her advice?

"Gerbrand will go to school in January. He'll be six in June."

"I can't believe how he's grown!" said Pérsomi.

"Yes," De Wet nodded, "and you remember our little farm school closed down two years ago. Boarding school is out of the question. So we have a problem. He can travel into town with me in the mornings, but Oom Freddie can't fetch him every afternoon and Christine doesn't drive. And he can't wait for me until five without supervision, you can imagine how impossible that would be."

Pérsomi smiled. "Yes, he'll demolish the school, or the office."

De Wet drove the car with his left hand on the wheel and his right arm propped in the open window. When he had to change gears, his right hand took over for the left one. "If we fix up the townhouse, you and your mother could live there. At twelve, Aunt Jemima could fetch Gerbrand at school, give him lunch, and look after him until I fetch him. He and his ouma get along well. And it would be better for you too. You can walk to work, it's close enough."

Pérsomi sat motionless as the proposal slowly sank in. The house had a bathtub, and hot water. She'd have her own bedroom and bed. There was a stove, running water in the kitchen, and a neat outhouse at the back.

"They use the bucket system," De Wet explained, as if he were reading her mind. "Every second night the night cart picks up the buckets and exchanges them for clean ones."

"Do you really think my ma could handle Gerbrand?" she asked.

"I do," De Wet answered. "Especially once Gerbrand realizes the only alternative is boarding school. I'll make it quite clear to him."

Pérsomi was quiet for a long time. When they crossed the bridge just before the farm, she said, "It's a wonderful offer, De Wet. Have you seen our house recently?"

"Yes, I have," he said seriously. "But remember, both sides would win if your ma feels up to it. Discuss it with her, and we'll all go and look at the house over the weekend."

They moved in the Saturday after Christmas.

Early in the morning, Pérsomi woke and found her ma standing at the shallow grave next to the crumbling bywoner house, her face expressionless, her hands limp at her sides. She stood like that until Boelie's pickup approached through the orange trees on the other side of the river. Then she returned to the house to wait inside.

Boelie came with two laborers to help carry their possessions across the river. It was the first time she had seen him since finishing at varsity. She saw him from a distance, felt anticipation build.

"Hello, Pérsomi, so you're up?" he called when he was within hearing distance.

Neutral.

It hurt.

"We were up at the crack of dawn," she smiled. "Hello, Boelie."

He turned away from her and immediately began to give orders. They carried out the boxes filled with clothing and a few kitchen things. Her ma insisted on taking the wagon chest and the tea chest, as well as the rickety table. When Pérsomi attempted to stop her, Boelie said, "There's enough room on the pickup. Let her take her things."

Pérsomi, Ma, Boelie, and the workers carried all their earthly possessions to the pickup in one go. An enormous wardrobe was already on the pickup. "My ouma says one of the rooms doesn't have a wardrobe, so she made us take this monster," Boelie explained. "How we're going to get it inside, goodness knows."

On their way to town she and her ma sat in the cab with Boelie. She was intensely aware of his presence, of the casual brush of his shoulder against hers, of his hands on the steering wheel. She couldn't think of a single thing to say.

He didn't say much either.

Her ma didn't speak at all. She sat pressed against the door, clinging to the handle.

De Wet was already at the townhouse. He unlocked the front door and handed Pérsomi the keys. "Oom Freddie and Christine had a team of cleaners in here yesterday," he said. "Well, I hope the two of you will be very happy. I must go, I have an auction today."

"Thanks, De Wet," Pérsomi called after him.

"We'll speak on Monday," he said over his shoulder.

Boelie stayed only long enough to carry their things inside.

At dusk there was a knock on the front door. Her ma's hands flew to her face. "Heavens, who can it be?"

"I'll go see," Pérsomi said.

At the door was a short, stout woman with a high bosom, her hair in a severe bun. Behind her stood a sinewy little man with a moustache like a shoe brush, his sparse hair slicked back, a turkey neck, and an overactive Adam's apple. In the woman's hand was a basket covered with a cloth.

"Evening I'm Aunt Duifie and this is my husband Oom Polla we're your neighbors and we've come to present you with this freshly baked loaf welcome in our part of town," she said without taking a breath.

"Good evening," said Pérsomi.

Oom Polla reached past his round wife to shake her hand. "Polla Labuschagne, a privilege to meet you," he croaked.

"Pérsomi Pieterse." Pérsomi shook the proffered hand. "Would you like to come in?"

They headed straight for the sitting room, where they sat down on the *riempies* bench, ramrod straight.

Pérsomi hovered in the doorway. "I'll . . . call my ma," she said. "Can I offer you some coffee?"

"That would be nice," said Oom Polla.

Her ma stood in a corner of the kitchen, eyes wide, hands wringing her apron. "It's just the neighbors," said Pérsomi as she filled the kettle. She popped another log in the mouth of the stove. "Take off your apron and come with me."

Oom Polla and Aunt Duifie jumped up when they entered. "This is my ma, Jemima Pieterse," Pérsomi introduced them.

"Polla Labuschagne," said the man.

"Duifie Labuschagne," said the woman.

"Good heavens," said her ma.

"We're your neighbors," said Aunt Duifie, "and we've come to present you with this freshly baked loaf and hope you'll be very happy and please tell us if you need any help."

She spoke the way Gerbrand used to write, without punctuation marks, Pérsomi remembered. "Thank you very much, Aunt Duifie," she said.

"To my knowledge and if I'm not mistaken you're the new agent," said Oom Polla. His watery eyes blinked as he looked at Pérsomi.

Agent?

"At Mr. De Vos's office," the man helped her.

"Oh, that's right, I'm the new clerk."

"And you're from Mr. Fourie's farm I saw the Fourie boy brought you what a shame that the farm went to him and not to Mr. Fourie himself"—Aunt Duifie took a quick breath—"and the other Fourie boy got this house but my lips are sealed it's none of my business." She pursed her lips and piously folded her chubby hands in her lap.

"You seem well informed," Pérsomi said cautiously.

"Around here we know everyone's business because anyone's

business is everyone's business in our part of the world," said Aunt Duifie.

"We look after each other," Oom Polla said, nodding earnestly.

"I think the coffee is ready," said Pérsomi. "Thank you very much for the bread, Aunt Duifie. I'm sure it'll be delicious. I'll put it away in the kitchen."

When she returned, Aunt Duifie was holding forth, with Oom Polla adding an occasional word. Her ma sat frozen, her eyes darting from one to the other.

After coffee, Oom Polla solemnly got to his feet. "Don't worry about a thing, my girl," he said. "Aunt Duifie over here and I will look after you and Polla Labuschagne is a jack of all trades, even if I have to say so myself."

But the sentence had been too long for his short breath and he succumbed to a violent coughing fit. "Phthisis," Aunt Duifie whispered, "from years on the mines. He's on his last legs, Oom Polla."

When they had left, her ma said, "Heavens, Pérsomi, that woman makes my head spin."

🌿

Early in March 1949 Mr. De Vos roped Pérsomi in to help with a hearing. "It's time you learned how to do an investigation, collect facts, prepare your witnesses for court," he said. As a habit he avoided looking at her and fumbled with his papers. "The most important thing is to find out whether your client is lying or not."

"And if he's lying?" asked Pérsomi.

"Then you must decide whether you want to continue being his lawyer," said Mr. De Vos.

"What do you do in a case like that?" Pérsomi asked.

For a moment he looked up, then lowered his eyes again. "I don't continue," he said gravely.

She nodded. She was glad. She wouldn't want to either. "And if the state appoints you to defend the client? If you have no choice?"

"Those cases are channeled to lawyers according to a specific formula and we deal with them free of charge. It's generally considered a kind of charitable action and is handled with integrity." He stacked his papers neatly. "A case like that can sometimes escalate without the lawyer being remunerated, but it's an exception to the rule."

"Can a lawyer refuse an appointment like that?" she asked again.

"I suppose, but a refusal would be frowned upon."

"So if you know the person is lying, you have to choose between your conscience and being frowned upon by the rest of the legal community?"

"Your conscience doesn't have to play a role. You work according to legal criteria," Mr. De Vos replied, slightly impatient now. "Here, take this correspondence and work through it so that you know the background of the case."

That night she told her ma, "Today I helped prepare for a trial."

"Oh. Gerbrand has a book now, he can read words. He's teaching me to read as well. He's very clever, just like his daddy."

"He's bright," Pérsomi agreed. "Next week I'll make my first court appearance," she said.

But her ma had already gone to her room.

Boelie brought firewood once a week, sometimes eggs as well, and vegetables for Gerbrand's lunch. De Wet brought fresh milk every day. Gerbrand had a mug of milk when he came home from school. But there was always enough for Pérsomi and her ma as well.

One Saturday morning in April she heard a knock on the back door. She had just washed her hair, and it was plastered to her scalp. Her feet were bare, her housedress too short. The coffee had just begun to percolate on the stove. Expecting Aunt Duifie, she opened the back door.

Boelie stood two steps below her. His khaki shirt was stretched across his shoulders, the sleeves almost too tight for his tanned forearms. "I put the wood next to the door," he said.

"Come in, I've just made coffee," she said on the spur of the moment. "The neighbor brought rusks."

He gave a slight smile. "Sounds like an offer I can't refuse," he said. "I just want to fetch a box of oranges from the pickup."

Pérsomi's heart was beating uncontrollably as she poured two cups of coffee. She took four rusks out of the tin and put them on a plate.

Boelie put the oranges on the table. "Sit, drink your coffee," Pérsomi invited him.

"Thanks." He sat down facing her, put three spoons of sugar in his cup, and stirred and stirred.

"How are things on the farm?" she asked.

"Fine. We've had good rains this year."

"And your dam?"

He looked up, smiling. "Almost full."

"It must be a beautiful sight."

They dipped their rusks in their coffee.

"Lovely rusks," said Boelie.

"Not quite as good as your ouma's," said Pérsomi.

"Hmm. Ouma doesn't bake anymore." He sipped his coffee. "She seems to have lost her spirit, with Oupa gone."

"Pity," she said.

"Yes," he said. He looked her in the eye. "How are *you*, Pérsomi?"

"Fine," she said, "just fine."

He stared into his cup, nodding slowly.

"You know, Boelie, we never talk anymore," she said.

When he looked up, his eyes seemed wary. "I thought . . ." he began, but fell silent.

"What did you think?" she asked.

"Nothing." He stirred his coffee again. "I miss talking to you too," he said.

"Maybe it's because there's no mountain here," she said, keeping the conversation light.

He gave a slight smile. He was still not looking at her. "We kept talking during all those years in Pretoria, without a mountain."

"True," she said. "You'll have to show up for coffee now and again."

He looked up. His eyes were inscrutable, pinning her down. "I will, thanks."

But the conversation remained stilted, unfinished, and he left soon after.

❦

"What can we do here except see a movie?" Reinier asked cheerfully when he came home for the July vacation.

She shrugged. "Wait for a party on one of the farms, go dancing in the hotel, make out under that tree on the riverbank. Reinier, there's really nothing to do here except see a movie."

"Dancing at the hotel sounds like a plan," he said.

"Decent girls don't go dancing at the hotel," she said, "so I don't know where you're going to find a partner."

He gave an exaggerated sigh. "Pérsomi, can you forget about your reputation for just one night and go dancing with me at the hotel?"

"No."

"Okay, maybe that sounded a little racy. One *evening* then, just until pumpkin hour?"

"No."

"Fine." He pretended to be deep in thought. "Would you like to make out under the tree on the riverbank?"

"Okay."

He laughed. "Really?" He sounded incredulous.

She laughed as well. "No, Reinier, I definitely don't want to make out with you. Why don't you find another candidate?"

"Because I want to spend time with you. Maybe I could come for coffee at your house, and we could talk until the early hours?"

She shook her head slowly. "That won't work. My ma nearly had a fit the other day when Boelie brought an old school friend for coffee. A guy named Braam."

He nodded. "And my home has its own problems, so we can't go there either."

She'd heard the rumors about his mother's heavy drinking. Though Reinier had never spoken of it, Ms. Steyn often did, when Mr. De Vos was out of earshot.

"Of course, I couldn't visit you at home," she said. "What if Mr. De Vos fetched a glass of milk in his nightshirt and nightcap while I was sitting in his kitchen?"

Reinier burst out laughing. "He doesn't wear a nightgown and nightcap!"

"I said *nightshirt!*" Pérsomi protested. "Anyway, I prefer not to know what he sleeps in. I don't want to know anything about him outside the office."

"I suppose not," said Reinier. "Shall we brave the hard town-hall chairs and the fidgety kids and the randy schoolboys and the problems with the prewar projector on Saturday night and go see a movie?"

"Sounds irresistible. I'll meet you at the town hall at seven."

❧

"Reinier is thinking about opening an architect's practice in town next year," Pérsomi told her ma the following week.

Her ma gave her a puzzled look.

"Reinier, Mr. De Vos's son? He was at school with me? He studied to be an architect. He's going to draw plans for people who want to build houses, or offices and shops and things."

Her ma raised her forefinger. "You must stay away from boyfriends, Pérsomi."

"Oh, Ma, please! Reinier is just a friend, he's never been a boyfriend."

"Stay away from boyfriends," her ma repeated.

"Yes, Ma," said Pérsomi.

She wondered what her ma would say if she knew Braam had phoned to say he'd be passing through over the weekend and wanted to drop in. Because she had seen the look in Braam's eyes the night Boelie introduced them.

❧

"Louis Kamfer came to see me," Mr. De Vos said one Monday morning in September. His gaze was fixed on De Wet as if only the two of them were present, though Pérsomi sat in the office as well.

De Wet gave a slight frown. "Is he the man who farms with chickens on a plot outside town?" he asked. "The one who's married to the Indian woman?"

"That's the one. He wants us to make sure his marriage is still legal."

"Interesting," De Wet said. "He's worried about the new Prohibition of Mixed Marriages Act."

"The act doesn't impact preexisting mixed marriages," said

Mr. De Vos. "I think he just wants to make sure of possible future implications."

Pérsomi said, "I read in the papers that the government might force different racial groups to live in separate areas."

"Yes, we should take a look at that," said De Wet. "I would imagine he's also worried about the Immorality Act that is being amended."

Mr. De Vos nodded.

"Amended how?" Pérsomi asked.

"In its new form it will outlaw extramarital intercourse between any European and non-European," De Wet said.

"But they're married already," Pérsomi said. De Wet shrugged.

Mr. De Vos continued to address De Wet. "We can look into the matter, but it would take time and it won't bring in much money."

"I'm already swamped," De Wet said, shaking his head. "I won't have time for the research."

Mr. De Vos glanced at Pérsomi, then turned his gaze back to De Wet. "I wonder if Pérsomi could do it?" he said.

"How about it, Pérsomi?" asked De Wet. "Is it something you'd like to do?"

"I would," she said immediately.

"Okay," said Mr. De Vos, "it's settled then."

❧

In December 1949 Pérsomi unlocked the office door and sat down at the reception desk. The rest of the staff was gone to Monument Hill to celebrate the opening of the Voortrekker Monument.

The sun blazed down on the tarred street outside, the ceiling fan chopped hopelessly at the thick air, and the cicadas had taken up their shrill cry.

Just after nine there was a knock on the front door.

A boy stepped in apologetically, his rough bare feet turned slightly inward, his cloth hat clasped to his chest, his eyes timid.

"Can I help you?" she asked.

He raised his head slightly. "I'm looking for the lawyer," he said.

She got up from behind the desk. "I'm the lawyer," she said. "Come inside."

He stayed put. He was used to the back door. She understood the hesitancy.

"Why do you want to see a lawyer?"

His eyes were a grayish green, his worn clothing clean. He couldn't be much older than fourteen. "My ma told me to come and speak."

"Okay," she said, "let's go to my office."

She led the way. He followed at a distance. "Sit," she said, pointing at a chair. "Start by telling me your name."

"Kosie Barnard."

"Age?"

"Pardon?"

"How old are you?"

"Seventeen."

"Seventeen?" she asked, surprised.

"Yes, Your Honor."

"You can call me miss."

"Pardon?"

"Never mind. Tell me why you want to see a lawyer."

"Mr. Gouws's dog caught our chicken."

"Is Mr. Gouws the farmer on whose farm you live?" she asked.

"It was the chicken my ma was going to slaughter at Christmas."

"I see," she nodded. She saw much more than words could ever say. She got the full picture. "And then?"

He lowered his head. She waited. He didn't speak. "You'll have to tell me, Kosie, or I can't help you. What happened then?"

"I took another chicken."

"One of Mr. Gouws's chickens?"

Kosie nodded. "He has a lot of chickens," he said, almost defiantly.

She understood every word. She knew every argument, every emotion.

"What did Mr. Gouws do then?"

"He went and told the court."

She knew in advance how Mr. Gouws would argue. "What you did, Kosie," she said, "is theft. You stole Mr. Gouws's chicken, and for that you can go to jail."

His eyes took on a dumb, almost vacant expression. "His dog ate our chicken, the chicken my ma was going to slaughter for Christmas."

"Even so, it's no reason to steal his chicken. I think you know that."

His eyes remained dumb. He didn't follow her argument.

"What do you want me to do, Kosie?"

"You must come with me to court. My ma says the government pays Your Honor to come to court with me."

"No, the government won't pay, it's a service we render. Did you see Mr. Gouws's dog catch the chicken?"

"I saw the feathers, everywhere. It was our chicken he—"

"Yes, I know. When must you be in court?"

"Now."

"*Now?* Today?"

He nodded. "This morning."

She saw the fear in the young man's expression. The vacant look in his eyes had turned into a kind of despair.

"Please, Your Honor."

She got up, took her robe from the hook, and locked the office door behind her.

In the street stood a brown donkey with a stumpy tail and four white legs. Kosie untied the donkey, stroked lovingly between his ears, and said, "Come, Alvier."

They walked to the magistrate's office. "Is this your donkey?" Pérsomi asked.

"Yes, Your Honor."

"What happened to his tail?"

"He rolled in the fire and it fell off, Your Honor," said Kosie.

When they reached the magistrate's office, he pointed timidly at Mr. Gouws, who was smoking under a tree.

"Wait here," said Pérsomi.

Kosie tied his donkey to the hitching post in front of the building and sat down with his back against the wall, waiting.

She walked over to the tree. Mr. Gouws looked at her with a frown.

"Mr. Gouws?" she asked when she reached him.

His frown deepened. She saw him take in the robe over her arm, the briefcase in her hand.

"Yes?" He sounded defensive, or maybe just uncertain.

"Good morning, I'm Pérsomi Pieterse. Can we talk?"

"About the . . . court case?"

"Well, I'm hoping we can avoid going to court," she said. "Do you know what time you have to go in?"

"They'll call us around eleven," he replied.

She pointed at a bench under the tree. "Shall we sit?"

"What do you want, Miss Pieterse?"

She sensed he was on the attack because he was unsure of himself. "Kosie says you've charged him with theft?"

"He stole my wife's rooster."

"He says your dog killed their chicken?"

"It was a genet, if you ask me," said the farmer. "If I've told those people once to lock up their chickens at night, I've told them a hundred times!"

"I see," she said cautiously.

"No, miss, I don't think you do," he said. "The government think they solved the poor-white problem with the war, turning hundreds of them into cannon fodder for the British Empire." It still hurt her to hear it said. "But those who remained behind are even worse off. They're actually good for nothing. And we farmers are stuck with them, because we believe it's our Christian or patriotic duty to take care of our fellow Afrikaners. Then something like this happens, and your wife has a fit about her best rooster, and you feel like chasing the whole lot off the farm."

She had wondered for years why Mr. Fourie had never chased off her family. But here she was, still living in one of the family homes.

"You're convinced Kosie stole the rooster?" she asked.

"He admitted it, in the presence of witnesses."

"And you're convinced it wasn't your dog that caught their chicken?"

"Two of my dogs sleep inside, the third one is tied up at night," he replied.

"Mr. Gouws, even if you're convinced he's in the wrong, I'd still like to know—why are you taking him to court?"

"The boy must be taught a lesson," said the farmer. "Thrashing him won't do any good. His father has been beating him to within an inch of his life since he was a boy. The youngster is a good worker, but this way of his . . . It's not the first time."

"Do you want him to go to jail?" she asked directly.

"No." The farmer frowned even more deeply. "Surely he won't go to jail for stealing a chicken?"

"He might get a fine that he won't be able to pay," she explained. "But the most probable sentence for theft is jail time."

The farmer shook his head. "Can't the police just give him a beating?"

"You said yourself a beating won't do any good," she said.

"Heavens, miss, you just don't know. These people have me at my wits' end."

"If we can think of something, a punishment that will satisfy you, something that would really affect him so that he realizes the consequences of his actions, would you be willing to withdraw the case?"

"Like what?"

"Like . . ." She had no idea. She needed the wisdom of Solomon.

Kosie was still sitting on the ground, his legs stretched in front of him, his back against the wall. A few meters away the donkey stood quietly, leaning against the railing, its head lowered.

"Like . . . having his donkey impounded for a while, say two weeks?" Pérsomi suggested. "We can explain to him that it's his punishment, that the donkey will be impounded for longer the next time he does something wrong and will finally be taken away completely if he doesn't listen."

The farmer considered this. "It might work. What can we do to stop the case from going ahead?"

"Leave it to me," she said and got to her feet.

That night she told her ma, "I handled my first case today, all on my own."

"Oh," said her ma.

The year 1950 passed swiftly. Reinier opened the town's first architecture office across the street from De Vos and De Vos. A week later Mr. Ismail paid Mr. De Vos a visit, and the men spent a long time behind closed doors. The following week, Mr. Ismail hired Reinier to build him an extension onto their house for his wife and himself. Pérsomi wondered how much Mr. De Vos had to do with it.

Christmas came without fail.

Jemima's eyes were shining. "We're going to spend Christmas week with Auntie Sis and Oom Attie," she said when Pérsomi came home from work. "De Wet and Boelie are going to pitch their Nagmaal tents so there's room for us," her ma said.

Pérsomi agreed to stay for only one day.

The Pontenilo still followed its age-old course. The orange trees stood half-wilted in the late afternoon sun. The ridge was baked dry. Behind it all loomed her mountain, untouched, anchored in the dry shrubs, its gorges deep and dark, its cliffs reaching for the sky.

She avoided the old house, where Lewies now lived, and the new house, where Old Anne and Oom Freddie lived. She had no wish to see Oom Freddie. Auntie Sis and Oom Attie's children and grandchildren were already at the bywoner cottage. Sometime in the small hours a car roared into the yard, carrying Piet. He and Lewies and Oom Attie and the other men, including Hannapat's smarmy new boyfriend, drank until dawn. Just before noon on Christmas day the festivities resumed, albeit a bit halfheartedly, as if the heads were woozy.

But after the Christmas meal and an afternoon nap, Piet brought more to drink out of the trunk of his car.

Quietly Pérsomi rolled up her blanket and walked away. She reached her cave just before dark.

A deep peace enveloped her. She spread her blanket on a sandy patch on the uneven rock floor. Then she sat down just outside the mouth of the cave and watched as darkness descended on the veld, listened to the muted night sounds, saw the stars increase in number. The peaceful feeling deepened, filled her entire being.

After a while she lay back, the stars wide and bright overhead, the firmament stretching to infinity.

A soft sound close by woke her. She sat up anxiously.

Boelie was sitting just a step away. "Sorry, I tried not wake you."

"How did you know I'd be here?" she asked.

"I knew."

"What's the time?"

"Around midnight," he replied.

"How did you get here?" She was confused, disoriented. "Gosh, I can't believe how I slept!"

He laughed softly. "You look a bit tousled, yes, especially your hair."

She pushed her fingers through her long, loose hair. "How did you get here in the dark?" she asked again.

"I used a flashlight. My days of walking in the dark are over. It's a lovely evening, isn't it?"

"Night," she said. "It's a lovely night."

Together they looked at the stars, as they had done so often in the past.

The deep peace she had felt before had been replaced by an overwhelming joy. No, not replaced, because the peace was still inside her. Her entire being seemed to have expanded to embrace the joy of his presence and a peace she would cherish and remember.

"I brought us a picnic," he said and began to dig in his pockets. From one he produced a small flask and from the other a piece of biltong and a knife.

"What's in the flask?" she asked warily.

"Sweet wine."

"I don't drink wine."

"Then I'll have it all," he said calmly and began to carve. He held the biltong in his right hand and carved thin slices with his left, the knife stopping when it reached his thumb.

"Don't cut yourself," she said, "you're using the wrong hand."

"I won't. I'm an experienced carver, even with my left hand," he said and held out a small sheaf of sliced biltong.

"You're left in everything you do, Boelie," she smiled. "Thanks, it looks lovely." She took the biltong, felt the light touch of his fingers ripple like a shock wave through her body.

They chewed in silence.

"Klara and Antonio are going to have another baby," Boelie said.

"A third! Oh, that's good news!"

"I don't know how she'll cope with another one. Why don't you taste the wine, Persomi? It's really nice."

"I'll have a small sip. Were you all together today?"

"Yes." He opened the flask, wiped the top with his handkerchief and handed it to her.

She sipped. "Gosh, it burns my throat!" She shuddered and handed back the flask. "Why aren't you at home with them?"

"Same reason as you," he said.

"Our situations aren't exactly alike," she said.

"They're probably equally unbearable," he said with a slight shake of his head. "Here, have some more biltong."

"Thanks." She hesitated a moment, decided to ask after all. "Unbearable with your father?"

"Yes, Pers. And of course it affects everyone else." He snapped the knife shut and returned it to his pocket. Then he leaned back on his elbows.

She was aware of his right arm behind her back.

Her heart was thudding.

"I feared we wouldn't be able to work together. We really can't. I tried." His rich voice came from slightly behind her in the dark.

Her heart was beating wildly, like it used to before an important track meeting. She drew a deep, slow breath. If she leaned back about three inches . . .

She didn't move. "What's the chief problem?" Even her voice sounded strange, as if she were speaking in a tunnel.

Then she felt it—he had moved his arm slightly. His right arm was touching her back.

"It's not just our personalities," he said evenly. "My father can't accept that the farm belongs to me, that I have a say in important matters now."

Maybe he was unaware that he was touching her. "Can't you share the responsibilities, so that you don't get into each other's hair?" she said, just as evenly.

"I don't know, Pers. He shoots down all my proposals before I've even explained them. Maybe I'm introducing too many new ideas at once. He's ultraconservative, not just with money, in everything. I believe in taking the odd risk. Pérsomi?"

"Yes?"

"Relax." It was the calm, steady voice of someone in control.

She tried to. She was sitting almost in the crook of his elbow.

"You have no idea how we clash, about everything, even petty things."

She had to concentrate hard to follow the conversation. "And . . . it's affecting the rest of the family?"

"Yes, especially my mom and ouma. The right thing is probably for me to go back to Pretoria and find a job as an engineer for the next few years, until my father is ready to hand over the farm."

Slowly she began to relax. She felt it not only in her shoulders and back, but also in her soul. The joy had turned into excitement, flooding her. He was definitely aware that his arm was touching her back.

"It might be a solution, but I think the city would stifle you," she said.

"You're right. And I can't just abandon the farm. It's my career, my future!"

She shook her head slowly. "No, Boelie, you can't. And you can't tell your father to give up farming. He's done it all his life, and he's still your father. It's . . . I don't know."

They were quiet for a long time. Even the veld was silent. Only the stars flickered light years overhead. Age-old currents.

They found themselves on an island in an infinity of space and time.

An island of quiet camaraderie.

"You listen to me," he said at last, "and you understand so incredibly well."

She laid her head gently on his shoulder. "You, too, Boelie."

He drew her head toward him, stroked her hair and rested his lips on the crown of her head. "You're an exceptional person, Pérsomi," he said. "A truly exceptional person."

TWELVE

"I'LL FETCH YOU ON SATURDAY NIGHT TO GO TO THE MOVIES," said Boelie when he came in to sign a document.

Her little office was filled with his presence. Her heart leaped, she blossomed with joy. She tried to rein herself in. It was just a movie in the town hall, where she and Reinier went at least once a month.

"I'll meet you there. You know how Ma feels about my going out," she said calmly.

"It's not my style not to fetch a girl at home."

"Boelie, if you come for coffee in the middle of a Saturday, it's bad enough. To arrive at my home at night is a mortal sin."

He smiled slightly. "Compromise. I'll wait across the street."

Long after he'd left, wild horses were still galloping inside and around and through her. All that night and the next day and night the joy remained.

Saturday morning she drew money from her savings account and walked over to Mr. Ismail's store. She wanted to buy something new. She wanted to look pretty.

As always, the store welcomed her with the familiar scents of brown sugar and garlic and leather saddles and incense. And as always, everyone was glad to see her. "Miss Pérsomi herself!" cried Mr. Ismail, "and more beautiful than ever! My, the lads of the district must be lining up at the door! Ossie, bring Miss Pérsomi a cup of tea."

His grandson hastened to the little kitchen at the back.

She bought a green sundress with thin shoulder straps and a full skirt. And a new pair of strappy sandals with high heels. In the afternoon she washed her hair and rinsed it with vinegar as she had seen the girls at Tukkies do. She was almost too excited to eat. "I'm going to the movies, Ma," she called over her shoulder as she left the house.

"With a boyfriend?" her ma's voice followed her, but she closed the door.

She saw him immediately. His Chevy was parked diagonally across the street. He was leaning against the car, his feet crossed, watching her. A small smile played around his mouth. When she reached him, he shook his head.

"You look lovely."

"Thank you." Compliments usually made her feel awkward, but Boelie's words turned her into the most beautiful girl in the world.

They drove the few blocks to the town hall and parked under a jacaranda tree on a side street. Boelie bought their tickets.

Every time she and Reinier came to watch a movie, he would ask, "Do you want to watch or make out?" Then they would laugh and sit in the fourth row from the front.

It was different with Boelie. He bought the more expensive balcony tickets. His hand was on her elbow as they went up the stairs.

Like he had held Annabel's elbow the night of the play.

Forget about that night! she told herself for the umpteenth time. Annabel was still far away in London.

The balcony had only four rows of seats. They sat down in the middle of the back row. "There's a good view from here and usually no kids," said Boelie.

"Yes, these are good seats," she said.

"Yes," said Boelie.

Silence.

The lights went down. A single beam came from behind their heads, narrow and full of flurrying dust particles. It funneled wider and wider until it filled the entire screen at the front of the hall with images.

The sound also came from behind their heads, loud enough that the people right at the front could hear.

In the short silence between the end of the serial Western and the start of *African Mirror*, Boelie said, "It's a real pity the sound is so loud."

There were only three other couples on the balcony, all of them older people, all of them in the front row.

A trumpet announced the start of *African Mirror*. Fighter planes soared from a runway into the sky until the entire sky was filled with planes.

Boelie's arm lay on the back of her seat.

"There was high acclaim this week for the South African Air Force and their fighter pilots' brave performance in Korea," the metallic voice said. Would the world never stop making war?

Gently Boelie's hand began to stroke her bare shoulder. She froze.

Rows of long-legged girls clad in bikinis moved from left to right across the screen. They stopped at the edge of a pool, neatly in line, one leg slightly in front of the other. "In London, Kiki Håkansson of Sweden was crowned as the first Miss World this week. Eric Morley and his wife, Julia, founders of the competition, believe that the pageant has come to stay," the announcer said.

He stroked so gently that she didn't know if it was really happening. Her lungs seemed to have frozen as well.

The screen was filled with rugby players. There was a crash tackle right in the middle of the field. "Big things are expected from the center partnership between Ryk van Schoor and Tjol Lategan in the upcoming Springbok tour to Great Britain and France," the newscaster said.

Her body was tense, hard as stone.

His hand stopped but he didn't remove it.

"Bobby Locke became the first person in the history of the South African Open Golf Championship to achieve a score lower than sixty-five," the announcer said enthusiastically.

When the lights came on for intermission, Boelie turned to her. "Am I making you nervous, Pers?" he asked.

She looked at him. The expression in his dark eyes was serious. She gave a slight nod. Don't stop, she wanted to say. But her throat had turned to stone.

The corners of his mouth turned up in a small smile. "It's not my intention," he said and briefly stroked her hair. Then he went to buy them drinks.

The lights went down again, the film began. It was an old-ish movie, nearly fifteen years old—*Maytime*, with Jeanette MacDonald and Nelson Eddy in the leading roles, a tale about an overambitious opera singer who chooses her career over love.

They watched in silence. Sadness welled up inside Pérsomi, filtering through the stone and filling her body.

It wasn't the movie that was making her sad.

Too late the opera singer realized that success could never make her happy, that she was standing in the spotlight alone and terribly lonely.

How could she tell Boelie to put his arm back? Please put his arm back? Please stroke her shoulder again?

The two actors on the big screen at the front of the hall got another chance: the young hero got the opportunity to perform with the famous opera singer. The audience sat entranced.

Should she just say, Put your arm around me again, Boelie? Should she rest her head on his shoulder?

The lovestruck singers declared their undying love. They would run away together that very night. But the opera singer's husband appeared, producing a revolver from his pocket.

Pérsomi couldn't move. She sat staring at the screen.

The husband fired a shot. The young hero died in the arms of his beloved.

For a few seconds the audience was silent. Then someone gave a deep sigh.

It's so sad, so unnecessary, Pérsomi thought. People should just talk to each other, listen.

"God Save the King" blared from the sound system overhead. Reluctantly the moviegoers got up. Boelie and Pérsomi remained seated. They waited until almost everyone had left before they walked to the quiet side street where the Chevy was parked. He opened the door for her, then got in on the driver's side.

I must do something, she thought, panic-stricken.

When he was about to put the key in the ignition, she said: "I don't want to go home yet."

His hands stopped moving. He turned to her. "What would you like to do?"

"Just . . . talk, like we used to." She thought for a moment. "About anything, like . . . how things are on the farm."

Both his hands rested on the wheel. "Fine, Pérsomi."

"I'm glad. Could you sort out matters?"

"No, I meant fine, we can talk. The situation at home has gone from bad to worse."

"Oh, I'm sorry," she said.

He shrugged.

The streetlight cast a feeble glow through the branches of the big jacaranda tree.

The conversation petered out to almost nothing.

All she had to do was reach out and touch him, she knew. It couldn't be too hard, it couldn't. If it were Reinier next to her, she would have no problem placing her hand on his arm.

Slowly she reached out and laid her hand on his arm. Carefully she forced the words past the stone wall inside her. "I . . . didn't want you to . . . take away your arm."

He took her hand and gently pressed it to his cheek, which was rough and slightly prickly. "It's my fault, I want . . ." He stopped and moved her hand back to her lap. But this time his big hand covered hers.

When he spoke again, his voice was husky. "Pérsomi, I know we've been good friends in the past, or maybe like . . . brother and sister. But . . . I feel more than that for you."

She heard herself gasp.

"The last thing I want to do," he said, removing his hand, "is to upset or frighten you. I don't want to do anything to harm our friendship. It's one of the most precious things in my life."

She had to speak. "Mine, too, Boelie." There was a pleading note in her voice.

He turned to her with a hint of a smile. "We'll try, Pérsomi," he said confidently, "and if anything bothers you, if at any stage you think our friendship is suffering, please tell me. I don't want to lose you as a friend and confidante."

"Me . . . neither," she said. Why was she so tongue-tied tonight?

"Are you going to make me a cup of coffee before I go back to the farm?" he tried to ease the tension.

She shook her head. "My ma," she said.

He nodded and started the engine. "I plan to speak to your mother, Pers," he said. "I don't want to wait in the street like a criminal every time I come to pick you up."

"Wait until it's . . . absolutely necessary," she said.

"I'll wait, with everything," he promised, as he reversed the car. "But it's one of the first things I want to do."

When they were in the street, he said, "Come sit beside me, please?"

She moved closer. He put his arm around her shoulders and drew her to him. "This is where I want you," he said, smiling down at her.

She focused on relaxing her shoulders.

Close to home, she moved away. "I'll get out here," she said, reaching for the door handle.

He nodded. "Thank you for a lovely evening, Pérsomi. We'll do it again soon. Okay?"

"Yes. Thanks, Boelie."

He waited in the car until she had closed the front door behind her. Then he drove away.

She sank down on a chair in the sitting room. Her heart was beating wildly. Her cheeks were burning. Her breathing was shallow and jerky.

An impossible dream was coming true. And all she wanted to do was run away.

❧

"Pérsomi, I'm a man who knows my politics, as you well know," Oom Polla said importantly one Tuesday evening. They were having coffee in the sitting room. Aunt Duifie's cup was neatly balanced on her ample bosom. Pérsomi's ma sat bolt upright, proud as a peacock in her new frizzy hairdo given to her by Aunt Dufie. She seemed afraid to move her head, as if the stiff curls might drop off at any moment.

"I know you know your politics," said Pérsomi.

"But this thing in *Die Vaderland*?" Oom Polla handed her the paper. "Look, it's not that I don't know what's going on, I just want to . . ." He began to cough.

She had seen the headline. Mr. De Vos and De Wet had discussed it at the office. She had listened, not in total agreement, but said nothing. She looked at the front page again: "UP Drags Government to Court," said the headline, and in smaller print below: "Separate Registration of Voters Act violates entrenched Coloured franchise."

". . . make a hundred percent sure of the legal aspects," Oom Polla completed his sentence.

"Oom Polla, when the South Africa Act came into being in 1909 and the Union was established, there was a clause entrenching the Coloured vote. This could only be changed if a two-thirds majority was achieved in a joint sitting of both houses of Parliament."

"Yes, I know," said Oom Polla, but his eyes told a different story.

"The Coloured people are almost all Smuts supporters—"

"Yes," he nodded, "like me, and Aunt Duifie here."

"—so they voted for the United Party in the previous election."

"Yes, that is so," Oom Polla agreed.

"Don't you think your ma's hair looks nice, Pérsomi?" Aunt Duifie interrupted.

"Yes, Aunt Duifie," said Pérsomi. "It's lovely. Anyway, Oom Polla, I believe the National Party wants to get rid of those UP votes before the next election, so they introduced a bill that will place the Coloured people on a separate voters' roll." If Mr. De Vos and De Wet heard her now, they'd have a fit. Not to mention Boelie.

"Oh," said Oom Polla, nodding gravely.

"Do you think we should have used bigger rollers, or maybe dixies for the side whiskers?" Aunt Duifie persisted.

"No, it looks fine, Aunt Duifie," said Pérsomi. "The UP is challenging the validity of the act to determine whether the government acted unconstitutionally. That's all, Oom Polla."

"Exactly what I thought," said Oom Polla.

"Don't you think next time we should use a bit of color, Pérsomi?" asked Aunt Duifie.

"We're going to be slaughtering this weekend," De Wet said one Wednesday in June. "Boelie was wondering if you and your ma would lend a hand?"

Ma and me? Pérsomi hesitated.

"But if you have other plans . . ." De Wet had noticed her slight hesitation.

"No, no, we'll come," she said at once.

"I'll pick you up Saturday morning early."

Now De Wet, Boelie, and Pérsomi stood at the sausage table— alone. Aunt Lulu and Pérsomi's ma were busy with the offal in the kitchen. Irene's ouma had gone to lie down hours ago, and Mr. Fourie had set off for the fields after an unpleasant incident with Boelie.

"I wonder how many yards of sausage the three of us have churned out of this machine," De Wet said at three that after- noon.

"If we don't succeed at our careers we can become professional sausage fillers," Pérsomi said.

"I'm already a professional toiletrician," Boelie said.

"A what?"

"I don't know what kind of toilet Oupa fitted in that bathroom in the Old House," he muttered, "but I fixed that thing yesterday for the very last time. Next week I'm replacing it. Turn that handle, brother, there's a mountain of meat to process."

"No, your turn, my arm is about to fall off," said De Wet, stepping back.

"I'll turn if someone else will unravel the casings," Pérsomi offered hopefully.

"No, thanks," the two men chorused.

They worked in silence for a while—a comfortable silence between people used to working together. Then Boelie said, "I see the bill to remove the Coloureds from the combined voters' roll was passed."

Here we go again, thought Pérsomi.

"Yes," said De Wet, "but I wonder whether the NP hasn't overplayed its hand. The decision has been taken on appeal. What do you think, Pérsomi?" De Wet asked.

"I think we're going to see a lot of opposition and protest action," she said. "Apparently fifty thousand people took part in marches last week."

"Their flame will soon be doused," Boelie said.

❧

When they finished and De Wet had left, Boelie smiled at her. "Come," he said.

She felt her throat constrict again. "Where to?" she asked.

"Somewhere I can have you to myself for a while," he said.

"Boelie?"

"Relax, Pérsomi," he said and headed for the river. "Or wait, tell me what's making you so nervous."

"I'm afraid . . . You want to speak to my ma." Her voice sounded thin in the chilly afternoon air.

"I promised it would be our secret until you're ready, didn't I?" He walked calmly beside her, his large presence comfortingly close—disturbingly close.

Their shoes left prints in the loose sand.

"That's not what you're afraid of, Pérsomi. You and I both know it."

She made no reply.

At the river he stood looking at the water. "Look at the Egyptian geese," he said, pointing. "You'd swear they don't feel the cold."

She began to relax. "Of course not! They're wearing thick feather coats." She held up her hand to screen the westerly sun. "What are those long-legged birds on the sandbank?"

"Plovers," he said, sitting down on a dry tree trunk.

"And that's a heron, isn't it?" She pointed and sat down beside him.

"Yes, a gray heron, probably looking for a juicy frog."

They sat watching the whirligig beetles swim in quick circles. A dragonfly hovered over the pool and the Egyptian geese waddled out onto the sand.

"Pérsomi?"

"Hmm?"

"Are you afraid I might touch you?"

Was she afraid? She turned her face to him, then slowly shook her head. "I like sitting close to you," she said honestly.

He opened his arm. "Well, sit close to me then. It's your place," he said.

She snuggled under his arm and he held her against him. His body was warm.

The sun went down, the Egyptian geese flew away, the whirligig beetles and dragonfly disappeared, the plovers had gone in search of their nests. "I'm afraid you'll kiss me," she said, her voice choked.

He held her more tightly, stroked her hair. "I'll wait," he said. "Don't be afraid, I'll wait."

In July 1951 Minister of Native Affairs Hendrik Verwoerd launched the Bantu Authorities Act, whereby a system of tribal authorities was established on local and district levels.

Yusuf was more than skeptical. When he came home for a visit from Joburg, he said, "This Verwoerd is bad news for everyone who's not lily-white."

"Boelie says he's absolutely brilliant," said Pérsomi, sipping tea Yusuf had made for her.

"He's a brilliant orator, I'll give him that," said Yusuf. "When he proposes a new law, one that's utterly racist and discriminatory, he makes it sound as if the natives should thank him for his perception and far-sightedness."

"I do believe he has good intentions. He seems to want to develop the reserves. He even wants to move the industries there," she echoed Boelie's words.

"It sounds good on paper, Pérsomi. But developing the reserves will cost the taxpayers—his voters—a fortune. Do you honestly think the government can afford to lose votes at this stage?"

"I suppose not. But I think the idea of decentralizing the industries is good. It's a global trend, isn't it?"

"In this case it's a smokescreen, Pérsomi," Yusuf said earnestly. "You know, sometimes I wonder whether there's a future for me in this country."

The next time Boelie sang Verwoerd's praises, sitting in her kitchen drinking coffee, Pérsomi said, "Yusuf Ismail doesn't seem to share your enthusiasm for him."

He frowned. "Pérsomi, stay away from those Indians. You shouldn't be socializing with them," he said.

"I have always been a customer at their store, Boelie," she said calmly. "There's no way it's going to change now."

"It's unacceptable. Especially with that Yusuf Ismail. He's a Communist, a true Wits troublemaker."

"Yusuf Ismail is a dedicated Muslim. He's an excellent student and is loyal to his family. He wonders what will happen to them under the new regime. That's not being a Communist, Boelie."

"Next time he's so worried, tell him to use the money he earns in Joburg to buy them all tickets back to their fatherland."

"South Africa is his father's land and that of his grandfather and *his* father before him," she snapped.

"Heavens, woman, we've had this conversation before!"

"And I've told you not to 'heavens, woman' me!"

Boelie softened and shook his head. "You're beautiful when you're angry." He gave a deep sigh and reached for her hand. "I don't want to fight with you," he said.

She took his hand. "I don't want to either, Boelie, not at all. But you can't tell me what to do."

"I'd appreciate it if you respect my feelings," he said earnestly.

"And you mine. Mr. Ismail is part of my life, has been for years. Yusuf has been my friend, since forever, and it's going to stay that way."

Somewhere their hands lost each other. "But they're Indians, Mohammedans, Pérsomi!"

"Muslims," she said. "And we are Christian Afrikaners. So what's your point?"

"We don't fraternize!"

She shook her head. "Here we go again."

"I know." He sighed and ran his hand through his hair. "We'll have to reach an agreement, you and I," he said earnestly.

She thought for a moment. "We could agree to disagree," she said.

"Maybe two independent parties could do that, but not two rational people in a . . . steady relationship."

"You're right," she said. "But I can't see either of us changing."

THIRTEEN

Pérsomi looked critically at her own image in the mirror. Her simple red dress was snug around the waist, hugged her hips, and fell in soft folds to her ankles. The skin of her arms and slim neck glowed in the late afternoon light. She turned sideways and looked at the low back line. Tonight she would feel Boelie's hand on her back as they danced at his friend's wedding in Pretoria.

She bent down and put on her new high-heeled shoes. She had always been the tallest in her class. But Boelie was tall as well, and even in high heels she would still be the shorter partner.

She picked up her evening bag and went to the sitting room.

Boelie stood looking through the window, his back to the door. His dark suit fitted his broad shoulders like a glove. His bronzed skin contrasted sharply with the white shirt, his dark curls just touching the collar.

Boelie, waiting for her.

He turned. Their eyes met across the length of the room. She gave a hesitant smile.

For a moment he stood motionless, his eyes taking her in. "You look . . . ravishing."

She felt every word.

Slowly he closed the distance between them. Then he put out

his hand and stroked her hair. "You must never . . . cut your hair," he said.

"I won't," she promised softly.

They drove to the church. He opened the car door for her. She entered at his side, saw heads turn. She sat next to him in the pew, her heart thumping.

At the first chords of the wedding march, everyone got to their feet and turned to look at the double doors at the back of the church.

Anticipation rose in Pérsomi.

The bride appeared in the doorway, her face veiled, a bouquet of pale yellow orchids in her hand. She walked down the aisle on her father's arm, the hem of her lace gown trailing behind her over the red carpet. Slowly she made her way between the pews, down the aisle, to the front of the church, where the groom was waiting.

The blond man at the pulpit was waiting for his bride, his blue eyes fixed on her, his gaze intense.

Next to her she felt Boelie's body close to her, touching her.

They sat. Sometime during the sermon her hand ended up snugly in Boelie's big palm.

For the first time ever she listened to the marriage service and grasped its sacredness. You must really love your partner with all your heart to make such promises before God and His congregation, she realized.

Afterward, as they were waiting outside for the bridal couple to make their appearance, Pérsomi said, "I don't think people should ever get divorced, Boelie."

"I agree, Pers. You take a vow before God. No court can ever free you from it," Boelie said.

The reception was at a nearby hotel. The room was festively decorated, the tablecloths starched and snowy, the flowers profuse. Pérsomi found it all very stylish, very tasteful. But then again, what did she know?

The guests sat at their allotted places, talked stiffly, sipped sherry, waited for the bridal couple.

"It's all so elegant," she said to Boelie.

"Too elegant," he said. "Give me a good old farm wedding anytime, like Klara's, or De Wet's. The guests enjoy it so much more."

Champagne corks popped, toasts were made. They laughed at familiar jokes, they serenaded the bride and groom. Servers brought wine to the tables.

A festive atmosphere reigned. They ate and ate. The empty wine bottles disappeared into the kitchen along with the dirty plates, and fresh bottles appeared.

The festivities intensified.

The bride and groom opened the dance floor. Pérsomi followed the couple with her eyes, watched them speak softly to each other, laugh. She felt Boelie's arm on her back. She leaned into it. His hand gripped her shoulder gently.

Other couples joined the bride and groom. The dance floor filled up with people floating in each other's arms.

Boelie got up and held out his hand. "Dance with me, my lovely," he said.

She put her hand in his and he led her onto the dance floor. His hand folded over hers. She felt the music pulse through her, gave herself up to his closeness, relaxed, followed where he led. It didn't matter that there were few waltzes.

They danced in silence, to one melody after another, round and round, in a world of harmony and captivating music, where two bodies moved as one.

Boelie said, "I love you very much, Pérsomi."

She looked up at him. There was a smile on his lips. The

expression in his eyes was gentle, almost vulnerable. Everything and everyone else faded away, until only the two of them remained.

Without a doubt she knew she loved this man. For this man, she would take those unbreakable vows.

She nodded slowly. I love you, Boelie, said her heart.

But the words did not pass her lips.

Monday night her ma said, "Boelie brought wood this morning, and lemons and tangerines."

"Oh, good." Pérsomi's mind was occupied with a letter Mr. De Vos had given her earlier. He wanted her opinion.

"He went to their farm on the other side of Messina today, he and Oom Freddie."

"Yes, he . . . De Wet told me," she said, deep in thought.

"He wants to come and talk to me on Saturday morning. What about, I wonder?"

Pérsomi looked up. "I guess we'll have to wait until Saturday."

"But heavens, Pérsomi, he said you must also be here. I'm worried. Heavens, what if—"

"There's nothing to worry about, Ma. Listen, I have a lot of work to finish before tomorrow. Will you call me when supper is ready?"

She took the letter up to her room.

Reinier popped his head into her office later that week.

"Pérsomi, even if I'm right and you *do* have a secret lover, tonight you're going to celebrate with me!" he said.

"Depends what we're celebrating," she said cheerfully. The

conversation with Mr. De Vos about the letter had gone exceptionally well. He had almost complimented her.

"For me to know and for you to find out!"

"Judging by your expression, you seem to have won a thousand pounds."

"Something like that. I'll tell you tonight," he said. "See you at seven, okay?" He disappeared into the passage.

"Reinier, stop! I don't know what or where!" she called after him.

He laughed. "I'm treating you to dinner at the hotel. I'm off to book us a table. A champagne dinner, because I have something to celebrate."

"You've already said so. Did she agree at last?"

"I haven't met her yet. Still looking. Have to go now!"

That night her ma was extra difficult.

"Ma, I'm going out for supper, that's all," Pérsomi said.

"In that smart dress? With a boyfriend?" her ma asked suspiciously.

"No, Ma, not with a boyfriend!" Reinier was definitely not a boyfriend in the sense that her ma used the word. "And even if it was with a boyfriend, I really can't see why it would be so terribly wrong."

"Pérsomi!" Her ma raised a warning finger. "You must stay away from men!"

"Oh, Ma, please! I'm going now, sleep well."

Reinier was waiting for her at the corner, where he always picked her up.

In mutual recognition of their respective family skeletons they had never been in each other's homes.

"Come on, out with it," she said when she'd got into Bucket.

"No, I'll tell you over a bottle of champagne," he said. "But here's a clue: Bucket's days are numbered."

She considered his words. "Reinier, did you get such a big contract that you can buy a proper car?" she asked. "I know you're building Yusuf's surgery—but surely it's not such a huge project?"

"My lips are sealed. Only champagne can unseal them," he said.

"Come on, tell me!"

He motioned that his lips were under lock and key.

"Oh, you're spiteful!" she said.

He parked at the hotel and opened the door for her. She got out and they walked up the three steps to the veranda.

She thought of something and stopped in her tracks. "What are you going to do with Bucket?"

"Probably try to sell her—though I think I might have to pay someone to take her off my hands. Come, let's go in."

A waiter pulled out their chairs. When they were seated, she said, "If the price is right, I'll buy her."

He frowned. "What are you talking about?"

"Bucket, of course."

He shook his head. "She's really not reliable anymore. I can't sell her to you." He turned to the waiter. "An ice-cold bottle of champagne, please."

"Well, I won't be able to afford anything better," she said when the waiter had left. "At least I know Bucket."

He turned to her. "Pérsomi, you don't even know how to drive."

"You can teach me," she said.

"Gosh, you turn everything into a debate," he said.

"Well, just sell Bucket to me!"

"I won't sell her to you, but you can have her. Wait, here's the champagne. I'll pour it myself, thanks. Have you decided what you want to order?"

She looked at the menu, then up at the waiter. "I'll have

everything on the menu," she said. "It all sounds good: soup, fish, meat, vegetables. Yes, I'll have it all, thank you."

Reinier laughed. "Bring me everything as well, thanks," he told the waiter.

When the waiter had left, she said: "I don't want Bucket for free. I'll pay you."

"You're full of nonsense," said Reinier. "Here, hold out your glass for some champagne."

"Tell me now, what are we celebrating?"

"And a typical nosy woman too."

"Speak!" she said menacingly.

His expression became serious. "Pérsomi, I submitted a rough draft for the new municipal buildings. I never thought I stood a chance or that they'd even consider me for the job."

"You didn't tell me," she said.

"No, I didn't . . . tell anyone." He still looked earnest, slightly uncertain.

This side of Reinier was new to her. "And?"

He shrugged and the familiar smile was back on his face. "I was assigned the project."

"Reinier!" She held out both hands to him. "It's . . . wonderful! I'm so proud of you!"

"Champagne?" he asked, embarrassed.

She raised her glass. "To Reinier de Vos, architect of the year!"

"Well, maybe not quite," he laughed. "Cheers!"

She took a large gulp. The ice-cold bubbles danced in her mouth, tickled her throat, warmed her stomach. She shuddered. "Gosh, it's strong!" she smiled.

He laughed again. "Remind me to teach you how to drink," he said.

"And drive a car," she said.

The next afternoon Boelie was waiting for her in front of the office. "What brings you here?" she asked, surprised.

"I missed you. Tell your mother you'll be late tonight, then I'm taking you out to the farm."

"Boelie, she'll have a fit. I was out last night as well," she tried to stop him.

"I'll wring Reinier's neck," he said, but his smile contradicted his words.

"He just wanted to celebrate. He got the contract for the new municipal buildings, can you believe it?"

"I'm very happy for him, but even so, he must stay away from my girl." Boelie was still smiling. He stopped in front of her home. "Go tell your mother, and come back at once."

Her ma was nowhere to be found, but soon enough Aunt Duifie appeared, so Pérsomi left a message with her.

"That was easy enough," she said as she got back into the car.

"Come, sit closer, you have no idea how I missed you," Boelie said and drew her to him.

"You were gone only four days," she smiled.

"Actually I don't want to be away from you at all," he said, holding her closer. "I want you near me forever."

"Oh, Boelie," she said happily.

They drove the nine miles to the farm. They spoke about this and that, but even their silences were happy.

"Let's go down to the Pontenilo. I'll get the picnic basket," said Boelie as he stopped in front of the Big House.

"Not to the cave?" she asked.

"No, too far and too late. I have to toe the line, at least until I speak to your mother on Saturday morning."

She smiled and nodded. She was so incredibly happy that not even the thought of that conversation could spoil it for her.

When he had fetched the basket they walked down to the river, then carried on upstream, almost to the kloof. The late afternoon air began to cool down, and a light breeze came up.

At a big old willow tree he stopped and spread the blanket on the grass. She unpacked the food: savory biscuits, sliced biltong, cubed cheese, fruit. He poured two glasses of red wine.

"To the prettiest, smartest, dearest girl in the world," he said, raising his glass.

"To you, Boelie," she sat next to him. "I'm getting used to the taste of wine," she said after a while.

"Hmm. Hand me another biscuit with cheese, will you?"

"Please?" she said.

He smiled. "Please. And put your head on my lap, please?"

She did as he asked and looked up at the branches overhead. He stroked her hair. "The branches make patterns, like lace," she said.

He looked down at her. "I love you more than words can say, Pérsomi," he said softly.

"Boelie . . ."

He put his finger on her lips. "Don't say anything, I know you're still getting used to the idea," he said. "I don't want you to say anything now that you may later regret."

"I . . . okay." She wanted to say *I love you*. She loved him so much.

"There's just one more thing I want to say, Pers," he said. His hand brushed the hair from her face, then he resumed stroking her hair and her face.

"Boelie?"

"Before I . . . we . . . speak to your mother on Saturday, I want you to know that I'm very serious. I want to be with you for the rest of my life." There was a moment's silence. "One day, when you're ready, I'm going to ask you to be my wife, Pérsomi."

❦

Pérsomi was drunk with happiness when she softly closed the door behind her. She couldn't wipe the smile from her lips.

"Where have you been all this time?" her ma asked from the dark sitting room.

She jumped. "I . . . I told Aunt Duifie I'd be late, to tell you not to worry."

"Were you with a boyfriend?"

She didn't have the energy for an argument on the happiest night of her life. But neither could she explain. Boelie would be here Saturday. "I went out to the farm with Boelie, Ma. I'm tired, I'm going—"

"Boelie?" Her ma sounded anxious. "Boelie?"

"Night, Ma," said Pérsomi and headed for the bathroom. She turned on the water to fill the basin, washed her face, and brushed her teeth.

"Pérsomi?" her ma whined when she stepped into the passage.

"No, Ma, I'm going to bed. It's past midnight and I have to work tomorrow," she said firmly and shut her bedroom door.

❦

But sleep evaded her. Bubbling anticipation, exuberant happiness, overwhelming joy coursed through her veins, putting sleep completely out of the question.

Why had she never been able to tell Boelie she loved him?

She knew he was waiting to hear her say it. She knew she loved him with all her heart. She knew she wanted to make him happy.

Was she so jaded, so dulled by her childhood that she couldn't lift her head and offer him her lips? That she couldn't say the simple words *I love you*?

❦

Her ma was waiting in the sitting room when she came in from work the next afternoon. "We must talk," she said.

Pérsomi felt suddenly exhausted. She knew what it was about. Maybe it was a good time to try and resolve the issue, before Boelie turned up the next day.

"I'll just fetch a glass of cold water, then I'll be with you," she said.

When she was sitting opposite her ma, she asked, "What's bothering you?"

"You must stay away from men. Stay away completely, d'you hear me?"

It was just as she had expected. It was time to put the matter to rest.

"Ma, I'm sick and tired of this old story," she said firmly. "Give me one good reason why I should stay away from men."

"Heavens, girl, stop asking questions. Haven't you seen what a man does to a woman?"

"Not all men, Ma. Look at De Wet and Christine. Or Oom Polla and Aunt Duifie. They've been married for donkey's years and they're perfectly happy."

"Don't be cheeky!" her ma snapped.

"I know it's your way of protecting me, I know you've had bad experiences with men. You've had a hard time," she tried a gentler approach. "But I'm careful, Ma, I know what I want in life, where

I'm going. And it includes a real family, a husband, and later children as well."

"Pérsomi . . ." Her ma was almost pleading.

Pérsomi knelt before her ma, covered the rough hands with the broken nails with her own manicured fingers. "I'm going to get married one day, Ma, sooner than you think."

Pérsomi saw her ma's fear. She watched her grow noticeably paler. Her hands flew to her face. "You can't!" she said.

"Yes, Ma, I can," Pérsomi said and got to her feet. "I'm twenty-four, and if the right man asks me to marry him, I'll do it."

"Heavens, child, that's what I keep saying. You can't!" Her ma looked desperate, panic-stricken.

"But why not, Ma? You keep saying I can't have boyfriends, but it's natural for a man and a woman to be together. It's how God created us. And you'll always be cared for. I won't leave you alone, don't worry," she said.

"It's not that."

"Well, what is it then, Ma?" She heard the impatience in her own voice.

Jemima wrung her handkerchief into a tight ball. "I promised not to talk and I never have."

Pérsomi felt herself grow cold. Her ma was dead serious. Suddenly she realized: all these years her ma wasn't just being possessive, as she had thought. Her ma's warnings were more than the awkward, naive attempts of a simple woman to protect her attractive daughter against life's hardships. Something was seriously wrong, and her ma's promise "not to talk" had been standing in the way of the truth.

"What is it, Ma?" she asked again.

"If you want to find yourself a boyfriend, you've got to go away from here, far away," said her ma.

"Ma?"

"You can't have a boyfriend from around here, you can't! Go find a boyfriend somewhere else, somewhere far away," her ma pleaded.

"I can't go away, Ma. My work is here, my home is here, it's where I want to live," she tried to reason with her. "And there are many nice young men around here to choose from."

Her ma closed her eyes. "But heavens, Pérsomi, what if you marry your own brother?"

FOURTEEN

THE FURTHER THE NIGHT PROGRESSED, THE MORE EVERYTHING made sense. That was why Mr. Fourie had never chased them off the farm. That was why he kept helping, even after they could no longer work for him. That was where the pounds had come from at Ismail's, and her pocket money in her student days.

She poured herself a cup of milk and shook a headache powder out in her palm. Her head was about to burst.

She should have seen the likeness between herself and De Wet. How could she have been so blind? They excelled at the same subjects at school—they chose the same field of study. She should have understood the rivalry with Irene—a girl born within a few months of herself.

Blood knows without words. Blood *knows*. Only she had been too stupid—deaf and blind to the logical, clear evidence.

She was tall, with dark hair and dark eyes, like Mr. Fourie.

Like Boelie.

"Boelie?" her ma had said the night before when she'd come home. "*Boelie?*"

Blood knows without words. That was why her usually glib tongue had been silent.

Because Boelie was her brother.

🍃

For weeks he kept trying: *Pérsomi, it can't be—something must have happened—your feelings for me couldn't have changed overnight—for heaven's sake, just talk to me.*

"Please accept it, Boelie. I've given it a lot of thought. You're like a brother to me." It was terribly, terribly hard to see his pain, to hide her own pain.

It's your childhood, he said. *It's because of what you saw and heard and experienced when you were too young—I know, I understand. Together we'll overcome it. I love you, Pérsomi.*

"It's not that, Boelie, please believe me. No, I don't need time, this is final."

He tried a different angle. *I shouldn't have been so hasty. I shouldn't have mentioned marriage. Can we try again, please? Heavens, Pérsomi, I love you! I know you love me, too, I know it. I know you.*

"You came into my life when Gerbrand left. You've always been there for me. I appreciate it more than words can say," she said. Her tone had been unemotional, matter-of-fact. Debate and argument were second nature to her. "Of course I love you, Boelie, but not the way a woman should love a man. I love you like a brother. I've only just realized it, I'm truly sorry."

Then he stayed away. Completely.

By day she knew it was better to have no further contact, preferable by far to the arguments and conversations that kept going round and round in her head. Her mind began to accept the finality.

At night her heart wept like never before.

Then, when her words had driven him away and she had escaped from the futile arguments, she learned the meaning of the word *self-contempt*. She had fallen in love with her own brother. The horror choked her.

The nights became a black bottomless pit.

Night after night. After night.

Annabel returned from London, her contract finally over. She was elegant and stunningly beautiful and brilliant. The town couldn't get enough of her.

And she set her sights on anything she liked.

In January 1952 Yusuf Ismail moved into the surgery Reinier built for him in the center of town, close to Mr. Ismail's store. He was as excited as a child before his birthday.

"These rooms are in the perfect location," Yusuf said when she went to call on him one lunchtime.

"Where do you think your patients will come from, Yusuf?" she asked.

"Well, apart from the Indian community, which is not really that big, I hope to have a lot of black patients. I have so many ideas, Pérsomi," he said, switching on the kettle in his small reception room. "Most of my work will be in the nonwhite hospital. My first priority is to see if we can get better equipment for the theatre. Lettie, Dr. Louw's daughter, has joined her father's practice and she said she'd help me. She also studied at Wits, you know?"

"That's right, yes."

"I want to put up a shelf for patent medicines, mostly traditional Eastern medicines. I met a girl, Jasmine, she's . . . er . . . she . . ." He hesitated, seemed embarrassed.

"Is she your girlfriend?" Pérsomi asked.

"Not really. In our culture the two of us don't have much say in those matters. But let me put it this way: if our parents and grandparents can reach an agreement, she might become my girlfriend, yes."

"Affairs of the heart are always complicated," said Pérsomi. Yusuf nodded. "Maybe more than we realize."

❧

"Yusuf's surgery is a fine-looking building. You've made your mark, Reinier," said Pérsomi the following day at lunchtime.

He frowned. "Have you been there?"

"Yes, I called on him yesterday at lunchtime. Yusuf showed me . . ."

"You can't do that," he interrupted her.

She gave him a puzzled look. "Can't do what?"

"You can't just walk in and pay him a visit!"

"It was lunchtime, Reinier," she said. "Besides, he's not all that busy."

"Pérsomi, he's an Indian."

"I know he's an Indian. A Muslim as well," she said, losing her patience. "Next you're going to say he's a Communist."

"I don't know whether he's a Communist," Reinier said calmly, "but I know you can't just walk in there for a social visit. It's not proper."

"Don't be ridiculous," she said. "What difference does it make whether I walk into his grandfather's store to buy clothes, or into the surgery *you* designed for him?"

"There's a huge difference, Pérsomi, and you know it."

❧

At night she didn't know what was worse: the scorching self-contempt, or the intense pain that forgave and longed and yearned for him, all at the same time.

Annabel de Vos popped into her father's office at all hours. She arrived with a fanfare. Could Ms. Steyn make her a cup of tea? This town was wearing her out. She tossed her long, shiny black hair over her shoulder with the flick of a hand.

Could one of the typists type this letter for her? She had to get it in the mail, but first she had to discuss something with her father. She held the teacup to best show off her manicured hands.

Could the other typist pop out to the post office and buy her some stamps? She really didn't have time to stand in line. She stood in front of the mirror, dabbing on lipstick, and wiping the corners of her mouth with her little finger.

Could Ms. Steyn cut out these articles for her and file them? Ms. Steyn was such a darling.

Annabel wrapped her father around her little finger. "It's so lovely to be home again," she purred like a kitten. By day she drove around in Mr. De Vos's new Mercedes-Benz, until he bought her a brand-new DKW.

Even De Wet didn't get off scot-free. "Coo-ee! De Wet, are you here?" And the office door closed behind her.

Pérsomi was the only one who had little contact with her. Annabel seemed to deliberately ignore her.

But one morning she ran into Pérsomi in the reception room. Mercifully the waiting client was already in Mr. De Vos's office. But both typists were at Ms. Steyn's desk, discussing the day's tasks.

When Pérsomi turned to go into her office, Annabel said, "No, wait a moment."

Pérsomi stopped.

Annabel took a step back and tilted her head. Everyone's

attention was focused on her. "You know, Pérsomi, you could be quite an attractive girl, but I'll have to take you in hand," she said, regarding Pérsomi critically. "We must get rid of that hairstyle, it makes you look old. And we must really do something about your wardrobe, not to mention your shoes."

Pérsomi lifted her chin. "I'm sure you mean well, Annabel, but I'm quite happy with my appearance, thanks," she said calmly.

"You can't think only of yourself," Annabel said dismissively. "This is my father's firm. Over the years it has always projected a particular image."

The typists' eyes were like saucers.

"The image I want to project to the world," Pérsomi said coldly, forcing herself to stay calm, though she was seething inside, "is one of professionalism. I think my clothes and hairstyle are quite suitable."

"And I think you look like a prude," Annabel countered.

An icy anger froze the flames inside Pérsomi. "Everyone is entitled to an opinion," she said. "Now you'll have to excuse me. I've got work to do." She turned and closed her office door behind her.

At teatime she avoided the typists' shiny eyes and eager tongues.

"I wish she'd go back to England," one of the typists said a few weeks later.

"Or to Russia. Then she might never come back," said the other.

Only Ms. Steyn couldn't stop talking about Mr. De Vos's lovely daughter. "She's like a beautiful, gleaming black racehorse," Ms. Steyn sighed, "but not broken in." She closed her eyes for a moment. When she opened them, they were dreamy. "There's only one man who can rein her in, and that's Boelie Fourie. The sooner he puts a ring on her finger, the better."

For the pain Pérsomi knew no remedy. Weeks later it was still a malignant tumor, threatening to devour her life from the inside.

For the pain Pérsomi knew no remedy. Weeks later it was still a malignant tumor, threatening to devour her life from the inside.

Two or three times she saw the Fourie pickup drive down the street. She turned her head the other way. She didn't want to know whether it was Mr. Fourie or Boelie behind the wheel. She didn't want to see either of them.

She buried herself in her work. She immersed herself in factual conversations: legal aspects and political intrigues and topical events. During the day it worked.

Usually.

At night she read. And if that didn't help, she switched on the wireless.

It was all over the news: while the Afrikaners celebrated the Van Riebeeck Festival, the nonwhites were launching an organized campaign. The Defiance Campaign, they called it.

On Saturday, April 5, Van Riebeeck's landing at the Cape in the *Drommedaris*, of which a forty-foot replica had been specially built, was reenacted on the seafront in Table Bay.

"Heavens, Pérsomi, did they build the ship?" her ma asked, astounded by the photo in the paper.

The Black, Coloured, and Indian people spoke of protest action against unfair laws and apartheid in the post offices and railways. They organized mass meetings, marches, and demonstrations. They deliberately ignored pass laws and curfews. They openly used the white section of the post offices and railway stations. Thousands were arrested.

"I'm very worried about the situation," said Oom Polla.

"Oom Polla has had it I'm telling you he's had it," sighed Aunt Duifie.

On Sunday, April 6, dedication services were held country-wide, at which Van Riebeeck's prayer was read in Old Dutch and in Afrikaans.

At the Witwatersrand, rebellious masses resisted the forced removals of Sophiatown residents to Soweto. Black women burned their passes.

In Cape Town, wreaths were laid at the statues of Jan and Maria van Riebeeck. Brass bands performed in the stadium. A mass choir sang "Wilhelmus van Nassouwe."

At the Cape Town station, dozens of nonwhites got out of a carriage clearly marked Whites Only. They were arrested on the spot.

"Heavens, Pérsomi!" her ma said anxiously.

"It's far away, Ma, don't worry," said Pérsomi.

No need to worry, we're very far away. The war won't affect us, Meester had said a long time ago.

In Johannesburg's Alexandra township, thousands took part in a bus boycott. "A good thing they're fit from walking to work all these years," De Wet said drily as he folded the newspaper.

"The nonwhite resistance movements have exhausted the option of peaceful petitions," wrote *The Star.*

"The Nationalists have reached the end of their tether with the troublemakers," wrote *Die Transvaler.*

"Violence will be met with violence," said Minister of Justice, Charles Swart.

And Albert Luthuli said, "The year 1952 is a turning point in our history."

"In my history as well," Pérsomi said bitterly.

A few weeks later, the Indian leader Dadoo was branded a Communist. He was relieved of his position in the Joint Planning Council. "Is he a Communist, Yusuf?" Pérsomi asked when she ran into Yusuf at his father's store.

"How should I know, Pérsomi?" he replied. "Communism is

against the law, but I don't know what his personal convictions are. I just know he's a brilliant man."

Some nights she grew angry: at Mr. Fourie, who had known and yet watched them struggle day after day; at Boelie, who had crossed the line—and who seemed so effortlessly to have left the line behind him and moved on.

In winter the nights were so much longer. And the days so much grayer.

One day De Wet said, "You know, Pérsomi, Christine and I thought at one stage that something was developing between you and Boelie."

"We're just good friends, De Wet."

"Still?" he asked skeptically.

She shook her head slowly. "No, I suppose not. We had a serious difference of opinion."

"So serious that both of you have clearly lost weight?"

She shrugged. "Serious," she said.

"I still think there was more than friendship between you," he kept prodding.

"No, there was nothing more. Boelie has always been like an older brother to me, especially after Gerbrand left. Like you were . . . still are."

He smiled indulgently and nodded. "You're right. You know, you're like a sister to me."

The case she represented was complicated, full of tangled legal concepts. It was a case of *Fide Curiosum*, where a grandson was faced with a hundred-year embargo placed on the farm he inherited from his grandfather thirty years earlier. There were complicated family feuds and complex promises and misunderstandings and emotions—and the land could not be sold. It was the family's only asset, and the line of petitioners kept growing longer.

She was tired as she walked back to the office from the courthouse. Though it was early September, it was hot and dry.

When she pushed open the office door, Ms. Steyn wasn't in her usual spot at reception. Pérsomi went through to the small kitchen to fetch a glass of cold water.

In the passage a wave of excitement struck her.

"Have you heard, Pérsomi? There's going to be a wedding!" one of the typists bubbled.

The second typist interrupted her. "Ms. Steyn says it'll be the wedding of the century, like this town has never seen," she said.

"Ms. Steyn says money will be no object," the first typist took over again, "Mr. De Vos will want nothing but the best for his only daughter."

"Is . . . Annabel getting married?" Pérsomi asked. Her mouth was suddenly bone-dry.

"Yes, to Boelie Fourie. It's just . . . perfect!" sighed the typist, her earlier indignation wiped out by the prospect of a fairytale wedding.

"They're the perfect couple," sighed the second typist. "She's so beautiful and so mod. And he's so rich, and so handsome!" Her eyes were dreamy. Gone were all the vengeful thoughts about the boss's daughter and her royal demeanor.

Pérsomi turned and walked out.

Her fingers found the key in her handbag. Her hands trembled as she inserted it in the ignition. Bucket coughed, then headed down the street of its own accord, turned onto the main road, continued in the direction of the railway line.

Boelie, who had pleaded with her to think again only six months before? He was . . . getting married?

She crossed the railway line, unsure where she was going.

She didn't think she'd ever be okay again. Because on this warm spring afternoon she could not turn to Boelie with the scorching pain inside her.

She could no longer go to her mountain either. Her mountain was on Boelie's farm. Her mountain was no longer her mountain.

The sun was shining. The veld lay motionless in the hazy heat. The only sound was the screeching of cicadas.

She pulled to the side of the road. Her throat was tight. Tears welled up and spilled out of her eyes. The veld began to swim.

There was no anger left, no self-contempt, maybe not even any pain.

Only an indescribable loneliness.

For the first time in her life she cried in broad daylight.

🌿

The De Vos and De Vos law offices became Annabel's wedding headquarters. Her mother did nothing. Her father paid for everything. Arrangements were made at breakneck speed.

Pérsomi ate and slept and bathed and read the papers and listened to the news on the wireless. She worked from early morning late into the night. She worked all through her lunch hour. The lump in her stomach remained rock hard.

"Don't tell me you've been working every lunch hour?" Reinier asked one lunchtime, sticking his head around her door.

The wedding gown was ordered from France, specially designed for the bride's big day. "It must cost a fortune," one of the typists sighed.

Pérsomi kept working, her head down.

The two typists spent an entire day addressing the invitations. The lettering was gold. "You can smell the money," Ms. Steyn said with satisfaction. They sealed the envelopes and put a stamp on each. "Yuck, my tongue is sticking to my teeth," one said.

Court work often took Pérsomi out of the office. A mercy. Her preparation was faultless, her logic impeccable, her evidence unshakable. But not even the intensity of the arguments could distract her. And nothing could make the rock inside her crumble.

Loads of flowers were ordered. The butcher had to sterilize his fridges to keep the flowers fresh. "The bushveld must be the hottest, dustiest place in the world," said Annabel. She would know. She had traveled the world.

One afternoon Pérsomi ran into Boelie in the passage. "Hello, Pérsomi," he said stiffly.

"Good afternoon, Boelie." After the initial shock it was anger that surfaced.

For a moment their eyes met, then he said, "Is De Wet here?"

"I'm sure he's in his office," she answered. She turned and walked into her own office, closing the door behind her.

For a long time she sat without moving, trembling at first. Then she just sat, stunned.

The pain had broken through, more searing than ever.

❧

"You can't stay away from the wedding," Reinier told her. He looked very serious. "You have to go."

"I don't feel like it," she protested. "I don't like weddings and funerals."

Despite the earnest expression in his eyes, he smiled. "You can't mention weddings and funerals in the same breath. Besides, not feeling like it is no excuse. The daughter and brother of your two colleagues, De Wet and my dad, are getting married. Come with me. We'll cheer each other up."

"Reinier, you don't understand," she said, dispirited.

"I do," he said softly. "I know you were a little in love with Boelie, and it's not easy to go to his wedding. But he and Annabel were always meant for each other."

She nodded. What was the use of arguing?

"I'm in the same boat," he said. "Irene . . ." He shrugged. "She's bringing her English boyfriend to the wedding."

"Don't tell me you're still carrying a torch for Irene?" she asked, surprised.

He gave an embarrassed smile. "You see, I really do understand. And I'd love you to go with me, because Annabel is my sister. There's no way I can avoid this. We'll have a good time. What do you say?"

She went to Mr. Ismail's store to buy a dress and shoes. Feeling reckless, she spent almost half her salary on her outfit.

🌿

The church was filled with flowers. The pulpit was dwarfed by pyramids of bouquets. Every pew along the aisle sported a bunch of flowers. More flowers cascaded from the balconies.

She and Reinier sat down in the third pew from the front, in the section reserved for the bride's family.

Boelie was already there, seated in the first pew. He sat motionless, staring at the pulpit cloth straight ahead. God With Us, said the words, embroidered in gold thread.

Across the aisle, in the section reserved for the groom's relatives, sat Irene and her English boyfriend, along with De Wet and Christine and Klara and Antonio. None of their children were present. The invitation had expressly said *no children*.

The church was bursting at the seams. Everyone who was anyone in the town and district had been invited.

Just before the bells began to peal, Mr. Fourie and Aunt Lulu entered with Reinier's mother and took their seats.

Pérsomi steeled herself.

The organ began to play. Everyone stood. Everyone turned to the aisle.

Pérsomi watched with unseeing eyes.

She saw the bride: radiant, breathtakingly beautiful.

She saw the bride's father: strangely emotional.

She avoided looking at the groom.

They took their vows before God and the congregation—*Till death us do part.*

❧

The hotel was decked out in festive array. The town had never seen the likes of it. "Even the caterers are from Joburg," someone whispered. "Just look at the starters!"

"I hear there are more than five hundred guests," a second guest added. "It must have cost a fortune."

Somewhere, someday, Boelie had said, "Give me a good old farm wedding anytime . . ."

They shared a table with Reinier's uncle and his family from Johannesburg. The conversation failed to flow. At the next table sat the Fouries: De Wet and Christine, Irene and her boyfriend, Klara and Antonio, as well as Dr. Lettie Louw and Antonio's brother, Marco. They were having fun even before the proposal of the toasts.

Pérsomi wanted to kick off her shoes and run. Instead she smiled at everyone. She made conversation with one of Reinier's cousins.

"What do you think of him?" Reinier asked after the starter.

She took a critical look at Irene's boyfriend—tall, dark, athletically built, clearly super fit. "A washed-out Tommy," she said.

His laughter was spontaneous. "You'll stick to me through thick and thin, won't you?"

They toasted the health of the bridegroom's parents. "Drink up, there's more where this came from," Reinier said.

They toasted the bride's parents. The bride's mother clearly had nothing but grape juice in her glass.

"Drink," said Reinier and motioned to the waiter to open a second bottle of champagne.

De Wet proposed a toast to the bride and groom. He gave a brilliant speech. The guests laughed heartily and at the right moments they wiped away a tear. Christine sat looking at him with a soft smile on her lips, her eyes radiant with admiration.

Pérsomi felt the champagne warm her from the inside. She felt her face relax, a reckless abandon take hold of her.

Antonio and his brother serenaded the bridal couple, their rich tenor voices filling the hotel with heavenly notes.

"Goodness, those two Italians can sing!" said Reinier. "Wait, I'll order something stronger, or we won't make it through the night."

It was the groom's turn to make a speech. Pérsomi and Reinier joined in the fun. The groom was no longer Boelie—he was a rooster dressed like a penguin.

The bridal couple cut the towering wedding cake with great aplomb. Pérsomi clung to Reinier's arm.

She was vaguely aware of the bride and groom opening the dance floor. Reinier held her in his arms, and they twirled round and round, stopping only to down another glass.

"So this is the wedding of the century," Pérsomi said cynically.

"Just goes to show, doesn't it?" Reinier laughed and raised his glass. "To us!"

"Watch out, you're spilling liquor all over my new dress," she protested, clumsily dabbing at the wet spot.

She clung to him. Or perhaps he clung to her. For hours, it seemed. How long did a wedding last?

Suddenly, out of nowhere, Boelie stood in front of them, in front of her. She saw his mouth speak, saw his lips move. She heard his voice, harsh with fury. "Good heavens, Reinier, stop making a scene! Just take her home! Take her home at once. See that she gets to bed. And you get to bed too!"

The words burned into her befuddled brain. Boelie's glowing black eyes burned into her memory.

When she woke, her head was threatening to explode. She held it with both hands and sat up slowly.

Her shoes lay next to the bed, where she had kicked them off. She was still wearing her silk stockings and her new dress.

She closed her eyes, drew a deep breath, carefully pushed back her hair.

Slowly the previous night's events came back, began to take shape.

What had she done?

Early Monday morning she walked to the office, hoping the exercise might calm her. She left early, wanting to be first to arrive. She would have to face the people who had witnessed the humiliation of her excess. Mr. De Vos. De Wet. Eventually Boelie. Everyone who remembered that she was still just Pérsomi, the bywoner child from the house on the ridge.

She put her handbag and briefcase in her office. When she turned, Mr. De Vos was in the doorway. She put her hand over her startled heart.

"Can we talk?" he asked, then led the way to his office.

She followed, numb with shock. He would fire her for sure.

He closed his door. "Sit," he said, indicating the chair in front of his desk.

Wordlessly she obeyed. She hadn't been prepared for this, but she should probably have expected it.

He crossed to the window and looked out over the small courtyard.

"Sir, I'm truly sorry," she stammered. "If you want, I'll go away, somewhere else, find a job elsewhere."

He turned slowly. He shook his head. "You don't have to go away." His voice sounded strange. His eyes looked strange, too, she noticed. He had taken off his thick glasses. His dark eyes blinked in the light. There were dark circles under his eyes.

She sat quietly, waiting.

"I suppose I could say a lot of things about Saturday night, Pérsomi, but I'm not going to. We all have a night like that sometime." He was pacing up and down, occasionally stopping to look through the window.

"Sir?"

"I'm going to ask only one thing of you." He had stopped at the window again. For a moment he looked at her, then he averted his eyes.

"Sir?"

"It's . . . that you stay away from Reinier, Pérsomi. Completely."

His words hit her in the pit of her stomach. "Reinier?" she asked. Reinier, whom she had phoned the day before, with whom she'd had a long talk, with whom she could partly share her grief about Boelie? Reinier, who had consoled her about their scandalous behavior? Reinier, who had laughed at the truth? *"We were both a little sad, Pérsomi, and then we got a little drunk, that's all."*

"Reinier?" she said again, shaking her head in disbelief.

Mr. De Vos sat down at his desk and faced her. He looked at her, his hands motionless on the desktop. "I've been worried about your friendship for a while now," he said. "For years, actually. But now it has reached a stage where I have to speak out. I have no other option."

Her shock and confusion changed into irrational anger. "Because I misbehaved on Saturday night?" she asked. "Or because I'm a bywoner child without breeding?"

Mr. De Vos looked her in the eye. "No, Pérsomi," he said, "because I'm your father."

PART III

FIFTEEN

THAT SAME AFTERNOON SHE HANDED IN HER RESIGNATION.

"I understand how you feel, Pérsomi, but I don't accept your resignation. You're staying," Mr. De Vos said firmly. "You and De Wet are a rare combination in the same firm. Together you will be a formidable team in the future. And . . . er . . ." He ran his hand over his bald head, avoiding her eyes, fumbling with his papers. "This is your legacy. On merit, I might add."

She thought about it long and hard. She had no one to talk to.

She withdrew her resignation. Mr. De Vos drew up a document that transferred his share in De Vos and De Vos to Pérsomi Pieterse in the event of his retirement.

She did not thank him. She would be angry with the egocentric man forever.

Right from the start she was angry with her ma, who had caused the misunderstanding with her clumsy handling of the situation. But Pérsomi couldn't remain angry. Her ma was a simple soul who had stuck to the terms of her promise to the best of her ability.

Pérsomi was angry with herself. She should have gathered more information.

She was angry with Boelie, who had lost no time in welcoming someone else into his heart. And when little Nelius was born only seven months after the extravagant wedding, the ground fell out from under her feet once again.

If she stayed in the town, it slowly dawned on her, she would be unable to avoid Boelie and his family. He drove along the streets, he used the post office and bank and shops, he attended church. He was married to her boss's daughter. He was her partner's brother and neighbor. No matter how she withdrew, he would always be a part of her inner circle.

Acceptance came to her slowly. I'm not someone to hide, she told herself over and over, and lifted her chin. I can't turn my back on this opportunity that has fallen into my lap, on this thriving practice that is my rightful inheritance.

Her grandfather had begun and built this successful law office. She stared at his portrait in the hallway. A seed of pride began to grow. The knowledge that she came from a real family sprouted in her.

Two years after her ma had cried out, "What if you marry your own brother?" Pérsomi could finally face life again.

❧

Gerbrand was in standard three. He was doing well at school and on Saturdays he was captain of his rugby team. Pérsomi spent most Saturdays beside the field with De Wet and Christine, and once or twice Boelie came to watch. Next year Annetjie would also spend her afternoons with Jemima, followed two years later by Lulani. At Christmas, Sissie and Hannapat came to visit. Mercifully Piet no longer came. Oom Polla was still living with his phthisis and the rotund Aunt Duifie. Under the enthusiastic hands of Aunt Duifie, her ma's hair underwent a regular change in style.

On Sundays Pérsomi and her ma often drove out to Oom

Freddie le Roux's farm. Her ma spent the day with Auntie Sis and Oom Attie, while Pérsomi visited De Wet and Christine. She got to know her nieces and nephew well, and grew to love each of them individually. When Gerbrand asked, she spoke to him about his father. *My-daddy-who's-dead,* Gerbrand called him. But most of the time the boy was in the veld while his two little sisters tagged along behind Pérsomi, wanting to comb or plait her long hair. She and Christine became firm friends.

Braam began to call again. "I want to apply for a post at the high school, Pérsomi. What do you think?" he asked in May.

"If it's a promotion, you should definitely go for it," she answered cautiously. She didn't want to encourage him—not so soon, in any event.

"It is," he said, "and it would be nice to live here, near you."

When he didn't get the appointment, she was secretly relieved. "There will be other jobs," she tried to comfort him.

"Yes, but not here," he said.

On May 29, 1953, Sir Edmund Hillary became the first person to reach the peak of Mount Everest. "I used to be a very good mountaineer back in the day," Oom Polla wheezed. "I used to jog up the Magaliesbergs. Before breakfast, mind you. But Mount Everest is high. I never tried a mountain that high."

"Of course, Oom Polla," said Pérsomi and slipped off to her room with a pile of documents.

It took hours of research and reading to keep track of the proliferating laws of the new government's apartheid policy.

In 1953 the Reservation of Separate Amenities Act came into being, restricting each racial group to the use of its own public amenities.

"It's not the whole truth, Pérsomi," said Yusuf Ismail. "There are only separate amenities for whites. Everyone who is not white"—he left a deliberate pause between *not* and *white*—"is lumped together. The Indians and natives stand in the same line at the back door of the post office or bank. In rural areas they have no movie theatres to go to. They travel together by train, not separately, in third class. Just look around you."

Dr. Verwoerd had the Bantu Education Bill passed, and all black schools were placed under government control, their study material adapted to meet the needs of the Bantu.

"Needs determined by whites, Pérsomi," said Yusuf Ismail. "To honor the Bantu's tribal heritage, but, in reality, to keep them from advancing."

❧

"I hear Braam is beating a path to your door?" Reinier said as they shared lunch.

"He came to visit last weekend," she protested. "Where did you hear he was beating a path to my door?"

"Aunt Duifie, in the post office. She just wanted to tip me off. She probably thought he was poaching on my territory."

Pérsomi wondered what Reinier would say if he knew she was his half sister. Aloud she said, "Did you tell her not to stick her nose in other people's affairs?"

He gave her an amused look. "What do you think?"

Smiling, she shook her head. "No, you're much too kind," she replied.

"Your sandwiches are getting better by the day. Pass me another one," he said. "So does the Braam thing mean I no longer have a movie partner?"

"Weekends when he's not here, I'm game for a movie, as long as it's not a Western or a war movie, or one of those spy stories or that stupid Laurel-and-Hardy stuff or—"

"What's left?" he interrupted, laughing.

"Romances, musicals, historical dramas . . ."

He gave a loud groan. "I'm going to start looking for a new movie partner without delay."

"If she's female, she'll like the same things I do," Pérsomi said. "Do you want to share the last sandwich?"

She began to feel again: real feelings, more than just anger and sadness.

"My parents are moving to Margate," De Wet mentioned one teatime.

"Margate?" she said, trying to imagine the farm without the elder Fouries. "Why Margate?"

"I suppose they want to spend their last days at the seaside," he said offhandedly.

"But the farm!"

De Wet was quiet for a long time. "My father and Boelie can't live on the same farm, Pérsomi."

She nodded. "Yes, I know there has been conflict."

"It's more than conflict," he said, "especially with Annabel also there."

Pérsomi wondered whether Boelie had someone to talk to. Annabel, of course. She ignored the jealous pang that suddenly rose to the surface from a place deep inside.

"De Wet invited us to the Le Roux farm for New Year's Eve," Braam told her shortly before Christmas. "What do you say: shall we welcome 1954 with a good old shindig in the barn?"

Boelie and Annabel would be there, maybe with the baby. Could she face them?

"We can do something else," said Braam when he noticed her hesitation.

She couldn't keep running away. She wasn't a child anymore. "No, let's go, it'll be fun," she said firmly.

She imagined every possible scenario, preparing herself mentally as she had done before track meetings so many years before. I'll win this race, she thought as she was washing her hair. I'm strong enough, she told herself as she put on her new dress. I look good, she decided as she studied herself in the full-length mirror.

Pérsomi decided to enjoy the evening.

A campfire was burning high when they arrived on the farm. There was a lamb on the spit, and soon the men would begin to rake hot coals under it.

De Wet came walking toward them, his hand outstretched. "Hello, Braam, Pérsomi, how lovely to see you." He turned to Pérsomi. "You look beautiful, colleague. What do you think, Braam?"

"She sweeps me off my feet every time I see her," Braam said honestly, sounding almost too serious.

"Thanks, you two," Pérsomi laughed, embarrassed. "Look, there's Christine."

"It's self-service tonight," De Wet said when Christine had welcomed them. "Braam, the drinks are over there." He turned. "Oh, look, Boelie and Annabel have arrived."

Pérsomi turned, bracing herself as she had rehearsed at home. She saw him approach, a spring in his step. She took in the strong figure, the thick, dark hair combed back tonight.

Beside him was his beautiful wife, elegant in her wide calf-length skirt and snug top, a wide belt round her slender waist. She wore her dark hair on her shoulders, the ends cheekily flicked up. Her calves were perfectly shaped, her ankles slim, the nails of her fingers and toes painted crimson. There was a barely visible swing in her hips as she approached. She had perfected the art.

"Come, brother, get yourselves drinks," De Wet said.

"Hello, you two," Christine beamed.

"Don't you look sweet," said Annabel. She leaned forward and gave Christine a peck on the cheek. Christine looked somewhat taken aback.

De Wet put his arm around his pretty wife's shoulders. "She might be a mother, but she still looks sixteen, doesn't she?" he said. "Look, there's Lettie."

"How wonderful! Christine, Lettie, and I—almost the old four again," Annabel smiled. "Only Klara is missing. Look, Braam's here as well." She was in control of the entire conversation. "We should spend more time together! It's just like the old days."

Then she turned to Pérsomi. "Oh, you're here as well, Pérsomi? How are you faring at my dad's office?"

"Good evening, Annabel," Pérsomi said calmly, her eyes level with Annabel's. She was the only woman present who was tall enough.

Annabel looked away first, striking up a conversation with Lettie. Pérsomi turned to Braam. "I'm going to the kitchen to see if I can lend Christine a hand," she said.

He smiled and squeezed her arm. "Don't stay away too long," he said.

The kitchen looked as if a hurricane had passed through it. "It's a bit of a mess in here. I want to make a salad, and I still have to give the girls their supper," Christine apologized helplessly.

"Carry on with the kids, I'll finish up here," Pérsomi suggested.

Two or three others also came to lend a hand, and in a flash everything was running smoothly. "I'll never be a good housewife," Christine complained when she returned to the kitchen half an hour later.

"You don't have to be one," said Pérsomi, linking her arm with Christine's. "You're a wonderful wife and mother, and that's what's most important. Let's join the guests."

The men were gathered around the fire, watching De Wet at the spit. The women sat to one side, talking. Lettie waved at Christine, motioning at two empty chairs beside her.

"You sit, I want to check on what Gerbrand's doing," said Christine.

Pérsomi sat down, but Lettie and Annabel were talking about their children, and she couldn't join in. After a while she stopped listening, yet she couldn't help overhearing scraps of the conversation. "You're lucky to have joined your dad's practice, Lettie. You'll be able to carry on working after the birth of your children," said Annabel. "I really miss my work. I don't find changing diapers and bottle-feeding every four hours very stimulating. If it wasn't for Maggie, I don't know what I'd do. She's very good with the baby."

She didn't hear Lettie's soft reply. Actually she didn't want to hear any more. She got up and joined Braam, who was sitting on a log, watching the lamb roasting over the coals. "Oh, here you are," he said and motioned for her to sit.

"Gosh, it smells lovely, doesn't it?" She smiled and sat down, stretching her long legs.

When she looked up, she noticed Boelie sitting directly opposite her, frowning slightly, watching her.

For a moment their eyes met. Then he looked away.

She felt the familiar tenderness. For this, she hadn't been prepared.

After more than two years, the pain was no less intense.

She didn't understand it. She led a full life, almost too full, she sometimes thought. Besides her job, which kept her busy and which she truly enjoyed, she'd joined a club at church and made friends with other young women, though most girls her age were married. She had wonderful friends in De Wet and Christine, a very special friend in Braam, and Reinier was still her very best friend. Yet deep inside she remained unfulfilled. There was a bottomless vacuum, a loneliness that never left her.

After supper someone put dance music on the gramophone De Wet had placed on a table beside the threshing floor. "We'll dance out here," he'd said earlier, "it's much too hot in the barn."

"Come, guys, let's raise the roof!" someone cried merrily. "Let's dance till daybreak!"

"The stars, not the roof!" someone else said, laughing.

The merriment increased by the hour.

As the night progressed, an unpleasant realisation grew inside Pérsomi. She wasn't being fair to Braam. She'd never love him the way she once loved Boelie.

She danced with Braam again and again. She danced with De Wet and Reinier and Antonio's brother, Marco. She danced with the new bank clerk in town and with almost all the neighbors, even Oom Freddie.

Boelie never asked her to dance. As it should be, she knew.

Later she danced to dull the ache in her heart.

In April Annabel stormed into the reception area and headed straight for her father's office. "Your father isn't here, Annabel!" Ms. Steyn called after her.

She turned. "Well, is De Wet here?" she asked, opening the door to De Wet's office. One of the typists peered inquisitively down the passage.

"No, no, De Wet isn't here either, only Pérsomi," said Ms. Steyn.

Annabel burst into tears. "Drieka, bring some tea," Ms. Steyn called down the passage. She took Annabel by the arm and led her into De Wet's office.

Later Drieka came out of the office, her eyes wide. "She's just come from the doctor. She's pregnant again, and she's very angry. She doesn't want another baby. Gosh, you won't believe how Ms. Steyn is comforting her."

Will the pain never stop? Pérsomi wondered.

At the end of September Boelie and Annabel's daughter was safely delivered in the hospital for whites. "Auntie Annabel doesn't want the baby, I heard her tell my mom," Annetjie told Jemima and Aunt Duifie.

"Heavens, Pérsomi, the baby doesn't even have a name yet!" her ma told Pérsomi late that afternoon. Aunt Duifie nodded so energetically that her plump figure bobbed up and down.

"Don't encourage Annetjie to tell tales," Pérsomi warned them. "What if she repeats it at school?"

"No, no, we told her not to say so," Jemima protested, her hand going to her new hairdo.

But that night sleep evaded her again. What was Boelie going through? What kind of life was waiting for the nameless little girl?

And the next Sunday at church, when Boelie sat down alone

again, she didn't look away, like every other Sunday. She looked at the back of his head four pews ahead and to the left, at the dark curls that touched the collar of the white shirt, at the dark jacket that fit so neatly across the broad shoulders. She didn't wonder where Annabel was. She thought of nothing—she just kept looking.

The Star reported comprehensively on the Congress of the People, held at Kliptown in June 1955. The young guard in the ANC and their leaders Nelson Mandela, Walter Sisulu, and Oliver Tambo were given a lot of prominence.

A Program of Action was adopted, meant to pave the way to equal rights. The Freedom Charter, as it was called, was drafted and adopted.

Pérsomi studied the published document and read various commentaries. She sat reading the paper late into the evening, understanding that some people were skeptical and defensive. But looking at the document objectively, she found it quite fair. It proposed a democratically elected government with equal rights for all, equality in front of the law, security, education, and housing for everyone, peace and friendship.

But the Afrikaans newspapers paid hardly any attention to the Congress of the People. And when she and Braam went to the movies Saturday night, there was no news on the reel about the ANC conference.

In July a bus boycott in Evaton resulted in serious tension and violence. Thousands of people gathered at the police station for protection, and thousands fled to other townships.

"The situation in the country is worsening," Pérsomi said to Mr. De Vos and De Wet Monday morning at their weekly meeting. "I'm worried. Where's it all going to end?"

"There's no need to worry. These are just interim problems caused by a small group of Communist radicals. The majority are good, loyal natives who want to live in peace and go to work every day."

Mr. De Vos agreed. "The sooner the police arrest the ringleaders and troublemakers the sooner these riots will be suppressed. It's the innocent women and children who suffer." He cleared his throat. "Before we begin with routine matters, there's something I have to tell you."

Pérsomi looked up quickly from the minutes book, where she had just written the date.

Mr. De Vos ran his hand over his bald head. "I resigned from the town council on Friday evening," he said gravely.

"Oh?" said De Wet. Pérsomi wondered if he had feared something more serious, such as his retirement.

"Yes," said Mr. De Vos and began to fidget with his papers. "Things could . . . become difficult."

De Wet leaned back in his chair until it was balanced on two legs.

"Difficult?" he asked.

"Dr. Verwoerd's policy of separate development is forcing town and city councils to develop separate residential and business premises," he said.

"Our township is well outside the town limits," De Wet said.

"But the Indians live in the heart of town," Mr. De Vos said somberly.

Pérsomi's hand flew to her face. "Don't tell me the council wants to relocate Mr. Ismail's people?" She turned to face Mr. De Vos. "Is that what they want to do?"

"They don't have much choice. The law is the law," he replied. "The council plans to create new amenities in an area about four miles out of town: a fully serviced residential area, a school, sport facilities, business premises—all the infrastructure will be ready before the people are asked to move."

"Four miles out of . . . It's a no-man's land! You can't do it!" she cried. "Mr. Ismail is part of our community!"

Mr. De Vos looked at her. "That's why I resigned, Pérsomi."

"But why didn't you stay and fight?" she asked.

Mr. De Vos sighed. "This thing has come a long way," he said. "It's not something that suddenly came up on Friday night. The council is divided about the matter, but in the end apartheid is a legal requirement."

A helpless feeling gripped Pérsomi. "How do the majority of the councillors feel?" she asked.

"The majority are in favor of cleaning up the Indian area. It's in the center of town, on the main route. Whether we want to admit it or not, those stores are an eyesore. They're run down and dirty, with unsavory characters lazing about on the verandas. It's not the impression we want to leave with travelers to our town."

"Those are *people* you want to move!" Pérsomi said, leaning forward in her chair. "People who have lived there for generations. They're taxpayers too. They pay their municipal levies and service fees and everything."

"Yes, Pérsomi," said Mr. De Vos.

"What are your feelings about it?" Pérsomi asked.

"I think that's his personal affair," De Wet said. "The fact that he resigned—"

"I asked Mr. De Vos."

Mr. De Vos held up both hands. "In principle I agree with you, Pérsomi," he nodded. "I believe many people agree with you in their hearts, because we know the Ismails, as you rightly say. But with the bigger picture in mind, I think relocation is inevitable."

"What bigger picture?" she asked crossly.

"The apartheid policy," he replied without looking up.

"There's Grand Apartheid, which is the overarching objective of separate development, and there's Petty Apartheid, of which this is an example, which doesn't advance people, but cuts their throats," she said firmly. "How can Mr. Ismail run a store on an empty plain four miles out of town? Who's going to buy there? How must Yusuf Ismail's sick patients get to him? Are they expected to travel four miles on foot in the scorching bushveld sun?"

"I just wanted to tell you I resigned from the town council," said Mr. De Vos, rearranging his papers. "Let's continue with the agenda."

"And I believe—"

"That's enough, thank you," Mr. De Vos said firmly. "De Wet, how are you getting on with the Grobbelaar case?"

The countrywide riots in the townships dragged on. Women in black sashes and bright headscarves prevented passengers from getting on buses. A photo in *Die Transvaler* showed a woman throwing herself in front of a bus to stop it from leaving. The riots went on for weeks. In September a bus was burned, and bus services were terminated.

"They're marching again," said De Wet at teatime and folded the newspaper. "I'm telling you, that's how they keep fit."

"Goodness, De Wet," Pérsomi said, annoyed, "these people walk miles every day to get to work."

By 1956 the negotiations to purchase the land earmarked for the new Indian development at Modderkuil had begun.

One day in early March Mr. De Vos fell ill. He was bent double with pain. Old Dr. Louw and Lettie were both busy and the sister at the hospital didn't know when they would be available.

"Shall I ask Yusuf Ismail to come and take a look?" Pérsomi asked her father.

"He's an Indian!" Ms. Steyn protested.

"Phone him," De Wet said immediately. "I fear it could be a heart attack."

But it wasn't a heart attack. It was cancer, the tests revealed when they came back a week later. Mr. De Vos was admitted to a hospital in Pretoria for surgery.

De Wet and Pérsomi were alone at the office when a call came through a week later: Gerbrand had fallen from the roof of the school during recess. His arm was broken, and De Wet was needed at the hospital at once.

"Go," Pérsomi said. "Let me know how he is."

So it was that Pérsomi was the only lawyer in the office when Boelie walked in just after eleven, furious. "Where's De Wet?" he raged.

"At the hospital. Gerbrand broke his arm. And Mr. De Vos is—"

"Yes, I know he's in Pretoria," said Boelie, pacing the room impatiently.

"Come through, Boelie, Ms. Steyn will arrange for coffee," said Pérsomi. She led the way to her office and took a deep breath before she faced him. "Sit down. Is there anything I can help you with?"

"No, I'll stand. I'm too pissed off to sit," he said. "And don't be so bloody professional!"

"Fine," she said and sat down behind her desk. "Why are you so pissed off?"

"Don't swear," he said.

The years fell away between them.

She gave a slow smile. "I won't. I almost forgot," she said. "Why are you so angry?"

"Crazy coolie with his fancy car ran into my bull. Dead as a bloody doornail." He sat down on the edge of the chair.

"Your bull?"

"The young bull I bought at the Rand Easter Show last year. Paid almost three thousand pounds for him, hasn't even covered a single cow, and now . . ." He flew up again and paced the floor of her small office.

"Boelie, steady now," she said. "We'll find a solution."

He took a deep breath and looked through the window. "What happened? To Gerbrand, I mean?"

"Apparently the standard sixes were kicking a rugby ball during recess. It landed on the roof and Gerbrand clambered up the downpipe to fetch it."

"And the pipe broke?" he asked.

"Yes, when he reached the second floor."

He sat back down. "He could have broken his neck," he said.

"Fortunately it was only his arm. Now tell me about the bull."

"Bloody Joburg—"

"Boelie, stop swearing and tell me exactly what happened."

Surprised, he looked at her for a moment, then leaned back slightly in his chair. "Okay."

Ms. Steyn entered with coffee on a tray. "Thank you," said Pérsomi and added three spoons of sugar and a dash of milk to Boelie's cup. She drank hers black and bitter.

"One of those rich Indians from Joburg in a fancy car knocked down my bull this morning and killed it," said Boelie. He looked slightly calmer as he stirred his coffee. "Now he wants to hold me responsible for the damage to his new car."

"Okay," said Pérsomi, taking out her notebook. "Where did the accident happen?"

"On the gravel road, about half a mile after he'd turned off the tarred road."

"The road to Oom Dennis's farm?"

"That's right. It goes past one of my paddocks."

"It's a provincial road?" asked Pérsomi.

"A district road, yes," Boelie replied.

"Why was your bull in the road?"

"I don't know! He must have broken through the fence or something. The question is, what was the Indian doing there—he had no business to be there!"

"Forget about the fact that the driver was Indian, Boelie, it's irrelevant," she said calmly. "It's a public road and anyone is free to use it. If your bull was in the middle of the road . . ."

Boelie flew up from his chair. "He was next to the road, not in the bloody middle of the road!"

"Boelie, sit!" she said. "We're trying to reach a solution here, but if you don't cooperate, we won't get anywhere."

He crossed to the window again and looked out. "It's not just the Indian who's upset me. Or my bull," he said.

"What else is there?" she asked. She kept her voice calm, though her heart was pounding. His bulk filled her office, his dark eyes were . . . She curbed her thoughts.

He turned to look at her. "You," he said.

She drew a sharp breath. "Then maybe you should wait until tomorrow and talk to De Wet," she said.

He was quiet for a moment, his dark eyes fixed on her. Then he shook his head slightly. "The bull was next to the road. I suspect the car came round the bend too fast, and hit the bull. Or the Indian might have got a fright and lost control of the car around the bend. The skid marks are visible right up to where the dead bull lies."

"And the car?" she asked.

"The front is bashed in. The bright pink back end stands beside the road."

"Was anyone hurt?"

"Apparently the driver, but not seriously. Someone took him to Yusuf Ismail, who took him to the police station and told him to lay a charge against me for damages!"

"Yusuf said that?" she asked, surprised.

"That weasel, yes! Just because the man is Indian and I'm white. He mustn't think—"

"Are you sure Yusuf took him, Boelie?"

"Sergeant Jansen phoned me. He took down the complaint. Can you believe—"

"Wait, Boelie, let's think," she interrupted. "You suffered the loss of your bull, let's say it comes to three thousand pounds. The driver suffered damage to his car. What do you think the replacement value will be?"

"I don't have a clue. Two thousand pounds, at most, I suppose," he said. "De Wet will know better."

"Fine, we'll say two thousand for now. Your bull was beside the road, where he shouldn't have been. Most likely the driver took the corner too fast on the gravel road, but it's going to be hard to prove. He probably lost control of his car, killed your bull, and in the process damaged his car."

Suddenly she looked up. "Boelie, where's the bull now?"

"I told Linksom and the others to start cutting it up and carting it off. In this heat—"

"Did you call the police out to the scene of the accident? Did they see the skid marks, see where the bull was hit?"

"No," he said, "but they have my word."

"Your word won't stand up in court. I suggest you take them

out to the scene. Personally, if possible, before rain or other traffic erases the evidence."

"What do you want to do, Pérsomi?" he asked.

"Lay a charge against him immediately for damages. Do you still have the invoice for the bull?"

"Everything, yes."

"Okay, then we'll claim damages of four thousand pounds— the bull is a little older now, yes?"

He gave a slight smile. "A bull doesn't appreciate that much in value," he said.

"Well, we'll risk it. Remember, he's going to add his personal injuries and trauma to the amount he claims. Go to the police station, Boelie. Now."

When he was almost at the door, he turned. "How are you, Pers?" he asked.

His question caught her off-guard. She was completely disarmed. She nodded slowly. "Fine, Boelie. And you?"

"Fine," he said. He didn't leave, but lingered at the door.

"Tell me about the kids." She clung to the scrap of conversation between them.

He turned to face her. "Nelius is three, a stocky little man. And Lientjie is eight months. The apple of her daddy's eye."

"I'm glad, Boelie."

He returned to her desk and sat down. "Why did you end our relationship, Pérsomi?"

Her mouth fell open. "I . . . I told you—"

"Don't come with that you're-like-a-brother-to-me story again! Today I want the truth."

His face was dark, his eyes pitch black, pinning her down in the narrow boundaries of the truth.

"I believed you were my brother."

"Your . . . brother? Are you crazy?"

"Don't speak to me like that, Boelie."

He was still on the attack. "How could you have believed that? Surely you didn't think . . ." She saw him track her own logic. "My father? Heavens, Pérsomi!"

"Why else would he have allowed us to stay on the farm, even after Gerbrand and Piet and Lewies had left? There were many other things, too, Boelie." It sounded as if she were pleading, and she didn't want to plead.

He got up, placed his hat on his head. "And because you believed this nonsense, you . . . trampled on everything between us, on everything that might have been. Do you realize what you did?"

She sat motionless, dismayed. She had no defense.

At the door he turned. "When did you find out I'm not your brother?" he asked.

"Shortly after your wedding."

Slowly he shook his head. Then he walked out and closed the door behind him. He didn't say good-bye.

❧

On December 5, 1956, 156 leading activists were arrested. "It's a hotbed of Communism," said De Wet at lunchtime. "A good thing they've been arrested. It will probably turn into a treason trial."

That same afternoon, Ms. Steyn put a jug of water with ice cubes on a plastic cloth in the middle of the boardroom table. She put three water glasses on one side of the table and three on the other. The chairs faced each other. "Nothing good can come of this meeting," she mumbled, glaring at Pérsomi.

"Don't forget the peppermints," Pérsomi said and returned to her office.

At exactly three o'clock Mr. Ismail, his eldest son, Abram Ismail, and his eldest grandson, Dr. Yusuf Ismail, arrived. Ms. Steyn's back was stiff as she led the way to the boardroom. She didn't offer them tea.

The three lawyers shook hands all around, then sat down, facing them. Mr. Ismail had specifically asked for all three to be present.

Mr. Ismail began to speak. They had come about the forced removals, he said. They were due to be moved from the place where they had lived for nearly seventy years to a barren plot of land. There were a few things they wanted to discuss with the lawyers.

"The mosque must stay where it is," Mr. Ismail began. "It's built on holy ground. No one can move it."

"Yes, we know. The mosque will stay," Mr. De Vos agreed. "The law respects your religion. That's what freedom of religion means in this country."

"But our homes will be four miles from our mosque?" Mr. Ismail shook his head. "How does that work, Mr. De Vos?"

"It's the law, Mr. Ismail," said Mr. De Vos, fumbling with the pile of papers in front of him.

"And what does the move entail?" asked Mr. Ismail.

"The council will provide serviced plots. You may build your homes to suit your requirements, within municipal regulations, of course," Mr. De Vos explained.

"And our existing homes?" asked Mr. Ismail.

"The council will give you market-related compensation for your homes."

"Mr. De Vos, look at our homes. They're old. My father built the house I live in, and we simply added on. Do you really think, Mr. De Vos, that we'll be able to build new houses with the money the council pays us?"

There was no fault to his arguments, Pérsomi thought.

"Yes, that is a problem," Mr. De Vos admitted.

"But it's not our biggest problem," Mr. Ismail said seriously. He looked at each of them in turn. "I want you, Mr. De Vos, to tell the council that we are willing to move to the new Indian area they are planning outside the town, but only on certain conditions."

"I am no longer a member of the council, Mr. Ismail. I resigned more than a year ago."

"I want you to go to them as my lawyer. I'll pay you well."

Mr. De Vos began to shake his head. "Mr. Ismail—"

"Listen to our proposal before you decide."

"Fine," Mr. De Vos agreed reluctantly.

Mr. Ismail unfolded a folio-sized page and laid it on the table. Pérsomi recognized Yusuf's neat handwriting. She looked at him, but his eyes were fixed on Mr. De Vos.

"We'll move," began Mr. Ismail, "but then we want full ownership. We want a school for our children of the same standard as the white schools, not a building with a concrete floor and a tin roof like the township schools. We want more than market value for our houses, or we won't be able to build new homes."

"Mr. Ismail, I don't know—"

"But most importantly, Mr. De Vos, we refuse to move our businesses out of town. Tell the council we'll move, but we want to keep our stores and businesses in town."

"We can try to negotiate about the other things," Mr. De Vos said, shaking his head, "though I fear we won't have much success. But to keep the businesses in town? I don't know about that."

"It's the only way we can survive. You do understand that, don't you, Mr. De Vos? Would your business survive four miles out of town if there was another lawyer in town—even though you might be cheaper?"

"You don't understand, Mr. Ismail," Mr. De Vos began. He looked down at his papers. "The law—"

"No, *you* don't understand," said Mr. Ismail. "Or don't you want to help us?"

Mr. De Vos looked up quickly. "Heavens, Ismail, of course I understand. But the law is the law, we can't get past it."

"There's always a loophole, Mr. De Vos."

"Even if we manage to find a loophole, you must understand my situation." Mr. De Vos looked at each of the men. Calmly they stared back at him. "We are in one of the strongest National Party constituencies in the country. The people of this town and district have voted the lawmakers into parliament. I earn my bread and butter among these people."

"So do I, Mr. De Vos, so do I."

Slowly Mr. De Vos shook his head. "Find someone from the city to take the case," he suggested wearily. "They're cleverer."

"Mr. De Vos," Mr. Ismail said seriously, "you're a very clever man. You know our people, you've known us from childhood. You came to my store with your mother when you were still in diapers. Your father was the first lawyer in this town, and my father had the first store. This case isn't just about book learning, it's a matter of the heart."

The small boardroom fell silent. Only the fan churned the heavy air. Mr. Ismail waited quietly: humble, serious. His son looked worried and slightly despondent. His head was lowered. Yusuf Ismail sat with a closed face, his cold, almost hostile eyes fixed on Mr. De Vos. Not once had he looked in Pérsomi's direction.

Mr. De Vos shook his head. "I can't, Ismail, my business won't survive."

Mr. Ismail leaned forward slightly. He spoke softly, as if he were addressing Mr. De Vos alone. "Mr. De Vos, you and I both know I have come through for you in the past. I might even have saved your business."

Pérsomi turned her head quickly and looked at the big man beside her, knowing what Mr. Ismail referred to.

But Mr. De Vos kept shaking his head. He turned to De Wet on his left. "De Wet?" he said, looking for support.

"I really can't. Mr. Ismail, I'm sorry. It's official National Party policy. My brother, Boelie, is the chairman of the local NP branch. Until four years ago my father-in-law was a member of the Provincial Council. I can't do it without causing a serious rift in my family."

Mr. Ismail took a deep breath. His pale-brown wrinkled hands were folded on the table, almost in an attitude of prayer. "Mr. De Vos, please," he said.

There was silence in the boardroom. Then Pérsomi said, "If I may, Mr. De Vos, Mr. Ismail . . . I'm willing to take the case."

SIXTEEN

CHRISTMAS CAME AND WENT, AS ALWAYS. EVERYONE GATH-
ered in Auntie Sis's upgraded house. "Good people, De Wet and
Christine," said Auntie Sis, "good kids."

Hannapat had married in haste. Her husband lay under his
car, trying to find an oil leak. The baby was on Hannapat's lap.
Sissie had a boyfriend, a widower with four children. He seemed
a good man and Sissie looked happier than ever before.

Pérsomi celebrated the New Year with De Wet and Christine,
and everyone wished each other a prosperous year—as always.

Yet no two years are ever the same. In January 1957, the
Putco bus company increased the fare from the Bantu township Alexandra to the Johannesburg city center by a penny.
Fifteen thousand people walked the ten miles to the city, singing freedom songs like, "Asina mali"—we have no money, and
"Asikwelwa"—we won't ride. The news was full of the bus boy-
cotts in Sophiatown and in the townships surrounding Pretoria.

"I see they're marching again," De Wet said at teatime.

"Oh, stop it, De Wet!" Pérsomi snapped. She turned her back on
him and went to her office. But he followed, his teacup in his hand.

"Can we talk?" he asked.

She motioned at one of the chairs and sat down behind her
desk. "About the bus boycott or the Faber case?"

"About the Ismail case."

"Oh?" She moved her empty cup to the edge of her desk.

"Why do you insist on taking it, Pérsomi?"

"Why not?"

"You have everything to lose and nothing to gain!"

"Is that what you really think?" she asked.

"Yes," De Wet said earnestly. "You can't win. The forced removals are backed by the Group Areas Act. You're not going to change that."

"There are ways of getting around the law," she said.

"Did you become a lawyer to find ways around the law or to help maintain an orderly society that functions within the law?"

"I became a lawyer to help people get justice," she said. "I believe in this case the council is using the law for their own selfish goals, namely to clear up the so-called Indian slum. I believe they could—"

"I'm sure you've thought of solutions, but you should also think of your future in this town. I'm afraid you're going to brand yourself a revolutionary, a Communist."

"I couldn't live with myself if I didn't fight for what I believe is right, De Wet."

When she looked up, Mr. De Vos was standing in the doorway. For a moment she thought she saw a glimmer of pride in his eyes. Then he turned and went back to his own office.

🌿

Pérsomi's first meeting with the Ismails took place in Feburary.

Just after three, Mr. Ismail and Abram stepped into the boardroom. Outside was the shrill sound of cicadas. Inside, the ice in the water jug melted within minutes.

"Is Yusuf coming?" Pérsomi asked, taking a seat at the head of the table.

"No," said Mr. Ismail. He said nothing more, and she didn't ask. Abram's dark head, topped by a fez, was slightly lowered. He had a habit of peering at people almost timidly from under his dense eyebrows. His shoulders seemed to sag under an invisible burden. They sat facing each other.

Pérsomi said, "I think we should start by asking the council to grant you permission to remain in your present homes, and for the services to be upgraded as soon as possible, before they begin spending money on the development at Modderkuil."

"It won't work. They want us out," Abram said despondently.

"We'll draw up a petition," said Pérsomi. "If it doesn't work, we'll talk to the councillors face-to-face. I know not all the councillors support the removals."

"The land we live on," Mr. Ismail said slowly, "was given to my father in 1884 by Paul Kruger himself, just after he became president. I still have the deed. My father supplied the president's people with food and blankets during the war against the Sekukuni in 1879. The land was his compensation."

"That's interesting information," said Pérsomi. "I don't know whether we should use it now or keep it for later. I'll discuss it with Mr. De Vos."

"And if the Boers still want us gone after that?" asked Abram.

"Then we'll suggest that you move your homes but let your businesses remain in town."

Abram nodded gravely. "And better prices for our homes?"

"We'll try everything, yes," answered Pérsomi. "Can I go ahead and draft the petition?"

The two men nodded. "Yes," said Mr. Ismail, "let's start there, that's good."

"And you'll inform the other families?"

"I will, yes. Thank you, Miss Pérsomi, I feel better now."

She watched the two men walk down the street, back to their

friendly, cluttered stores. Their white robes fluttered gently in the warm westerly wind; their long white trousers flapped just above their sandals. They were fighting for survival, she knew. Because their complexions were dark, their religion considered heathen, their traditions unfamiliar.

Had she been foolish to take on this battle? Was she giving them false hope? What would happen if she lost the case, if the Indians were moved out of town lock, stock, and barrel, homes, stores, school, and all?

"Why did you do it, Pérsomi?" Boelie asked for the second time in two months.

"I won't discuss it again, Boelie."

"You've never discussed it with me."

She looked at him, astounded. "What more do you want me to say? I'm sorry, I was mistaken, there's nothing I can do about it now."

"Why couldn't they have gone to someone in the city?"

She frowned and shook her head. "Boelie, are we talking about the Ismails?"

"Yes, what else?" His expression softened. "Did you think . . . I mean . . . ?"

"Forget it," she said.

His dark eyes bored into her own. He frowned, then nodded and said, "Fine. I see you're acting as their lawyer."

She was prepared; she had been for weeks. "See or hear?"

"See. Gustav Jooste showed me the petition, the one you drafted that was signed by all the Indian heads of families."

"The petition was addressed to the town council," she said. "Why did they show it to you, Boelie?"

"I'm chairman of the National Party in the district. It's in that capacity that I saw the petition. I'd hoped to avoid this confrontation," he said quietly.

She shook her head. "Then I suggest you resign as chairman of the National Party."

"Is it likely?" he said.

"No, Boelie, you can't help it, it's part of who you are. I know that."

"I believe in the government. I believe in their policy, Pérsomi."

"I know."

"I wish I could talk to you about it."

"I know that policy inside and out, Boelie. I've scrutinized each new law. I'm informed. I'm not going into this blindly. I know you're also fully informed. And both of us know it's one thing we'll never agree on."

He nodded slowly and got to his feet. "Then . . . I'll say good-bye."

"Just like you, Boelie, I can't help it either," she said.

He nodded. "I know, Pérsomi," he said. "I know."

He had been in her office for no more than five minutes. When he left, loneliness closed in around her again.

In mid-April a letter arrived. The council had decided that the Indian community would be relocated to Modderkuil as soon as possible. The council would honor its commitment to create the necessary amenities, to provide residential plots . . .

Pérsomi stopped reading. Slowly she folded the letter. She didn't know what she felt. Anger? Helplessness? Disappointment? Dismay?

She closed her eyes and pressed her fingertips to her temples.

When she looked up, Reinier stood in the doorway. She felt an unexpected joy, a kind of relief. He always came at the right time. He was still her best friend.

"I brought fish and chips," he said, slapping the greasy parcel down on her desk.

"Reinier, no!" she tried to stop him. "My desk!"

"Sorry," he said, wiping the greasy patch with the back of his hand and making it worse. "That's no good, we'll have to clean afterward." When he unwrapped the parcel, the entire office smelled of hot French fries and vinegar. "Have some."

Smiling, she shook her head. "I really couldn't eat fish and chips right now, but I'm glad you're here."

"Bad news?" he mumbled past the fries in his mouth.

"Sit," she said, pointing at a chair. "The town council rejected our petition. They're continuing with the development at Modderkuil."

He nodded and popped a piece of fish into his mouth. "You've been expecting it, Pérsomi," he said.

She shrugged. "I was hoping we could compromise. Now we'll have to go on to Plan B."

"Hmm, will you speak to your clients?" he asked, looking around the office. "You don't happen to have a napkin, do you?"

She got up and handed him a dishcloth. He wiped his hands. "I'll go and see them, yes. But tell me, did you enjoy the weekend with the math teacher?"

"Mathilda? Goodness, no, I'm on the run," he said. "Take a chip, won't you? No use letting it go to waste."

"No thanks, really," she protested, "too greasy. Why do you want to run? I thought you went to meet her parents."

"Long story," he said. He took his time wrapping up the remaining fish and chips. Then he looked up. "Pérsomi?"

"Yes?" Why did he sound so serious? Did something unpleasant happen at work?

Silence.

"You were saying?" she asked again.

"I . . ." He made a lame gesture with his hands. "I think you know who your father is."

She felt herself grow cold. But she managed a nonchalant shrug. "It doesn't matter anymore," she said convincingly.

"Because you know," he said.

"Reinier, let it go."

"I might have to confront him," he trumped her.

"Leave it," she said firmly. "People will get hurt. Why don't you tell me instead why you want to run from Marietha."

"Mathilda. You're changing the subject."

"I won't discuss it, Reinier, and that's final."

In the bushveld there are no sudden cold spells. Almost imperceptibly the leaves turn coppery and red and gold. You know summer is over when the days get shorter, the trees and grass wither, and the mosquitoes vanish. The children start to wear shoes to school, the boys kick rugby balls, and the girls put on black jumpers and long black stockings.

One Friday afternoon in May, Pérsomi sipped her tea and watched as Boelie's pickup pulled up and he got out, lost in thought. She turned from the window and sat back down behind her desk. He greeted her offhandedly as he walked past her open door. He went straight through to Mr. De Vos's office.

Nearly an hour later there was a gentle knock on her door. After all the years she still felt warm inside whenever he was near. But only for a moment. Then she regained her composure.

"May I come in, Pérsomi? There's something I want to tell you," he said.

She smiled. "Of course, Boelie. Please sit. I've just finished my work for the week."

"It's nice when one can say that," he said. "A farmer's work is never done." He sat down awkwardly and placed his hat on the edge of her desk.

"How can I help?" she asked.

He cleared his throat. "I just wanted to say . . ." He gave her a long, hard look. "I want you to go on with your life, Pérsomi."

Surprised, she shook her head. "I thought that was what I was doing," she said.

"That didn't come out right." He pushed his fingers through his hair. "But you know what I mean."

She gave a slight frown. "I really don't, Boelie."

He cleared his throat again. "What happened to Braam?"

"He . . . we . . . oh, Boelie!" She made a helpless gesture with her hand. "It . . . wouldn't have worked," she said feebly.

"What I mean, Pérsomi, is . . ." He hesitated a moment, shifting uncomfortably in his seat. "Don't wait for me. No matter how serious the rift between Annabel and me, or how impossible my own situation has become, I'll never get a divorce."

"I know that, Boelie. You're a man of principle, steady as a rock. It's one of the reasons why I love you."

He looked at her, his dark eyes gentle. "It's the first time you've ever said those words," he said.

She felt herself flush. "Is it? I'm sorry, I shouldn't have said it. It just . . . slipped out."

He averted his eyes. "You'll never know what it means to me."

"I shouldn't have . . ." She shrugged. "I'm sorry."

After a long silence he said, "Annabel was offered an excellent opportunity. It's what I came to discuss with her father. And . . . with you, actually."

"Annabel?"

"It's a senior position at SAPA," said Boelie.

"In Joburg?"

"In London."

"London! Surely she's not considering it, Boelie!"

He pushed his fingers through his hair again, nodded slowly. "Yes, she is."

"Boelie!" She couldn't hide her dismay. "That's im—" She bit back the words. "How do you feel about it, Boelie?"

He took a deep breath. "At this point it might be best—for all of us."

"But . . . the children! They're so young!"

"I won't be the first father to raise his kids alone for a while," he said. "It's not permanent. They've offered her a two-year contract. She needs to get away. I think her present lifestyle is smothering her."

Pérsomi kept shaking her head. Nelius had just turned four, Lientjie was only two. How could their mother leave them? "Do you really believe it's best?" she asked.

He nodded quietly. His elbows were on the desk between them. His big hands were folded, the fingers entwined, his chin rested on his thumbs.

She looked away. She had no right to think of the children. It was none of her business. She had to remain objective.

"Boelie, how can two people who loved each other enough to pledge their word before God grow apart so quickly?"

"In our case," he said slowly, lowering his hands onto the desk, "we would probably never have married if it hadn't been . . ." He searched for the right words, then shrugged. "Well, if the situation hadn't forced us. I always knew De Wet was her first choice, not me, just as she knew she wasn't my first choice. It wasn't a very good foundation to build on."

She felt every word inside her, felt them pass through her.

"But . . . I could never get divorced. Even if she leaves, she's still my wife."

"I know, Boelie."

"That's . . . why I came to talk to you. Don't get the wrong idea, I don't think you . . ." There was another awkward silence.

"I understand, Boelie."

"That's why I want you to carry on, Pérsomi. You should get married, lead a normal life."

She gave him a slow smile. "Is my life not normal?"

He refused to be distracted. "You know what I mean."

"Yes, Boelie, I know. And I understand that you want me to be happy."

"You do understand." For the first time he smiled. "Like you always do."

When she came home late that afternoon, thankful that it was Friday and the weekend lay ahead, her ma, Aunt Duifie, and Oom Polla were in the sitting room. They often sat there, listening to the serials on Springbok Radio. But the minute she walked in, she sensed she had walked into a lion's den.

"Pérsomi!" her ma's shrill cry summoned her.

As usual, Oom Polla and Aunt Duifie were sitting on the sofa. Her ma was on the chair with its brand-new, garish cover. Pérsomi sank into the deep easy chair and stretched her legs in front of her.

Oom Polla came straight to the point. "I hear you're going to represent the Asians in court?"

"That's right, Oom Polla."

Jemima's hands flew to her face. "Oh heavens, in court?"

"Yes, Ma, that's where I work, every week."

"It's not a good thing I told Oom Polla here it's not good he must speak," wheezed Aunt Duifie.

"Pérsomi, my girl, like Aunt Duifie here says, it's not a good thing," Oom Polla said, and coughed. "I know politics, if anyone knows politics—"

"People are talking, they're talking everywhere—at the hairdresser's and everywhere!" Aunt Duifie interrupted.

"Oom Polla, Aunt Duifie, it's my job, and it's what I'm going to do. If people want to talk, let them. At least I've given them something to talk about."

"But heavens, Pérsomi, the Indians? *Must* you do it?" her ma asked.

"No, Ma, I choose to do it, because I believe the removal of Mr. Ismail and his family and the other Indian families is wrong." Pérsomi felt her patience wearing thin, her anger mounting. The afternoon was taking its toll. "Next time people talk," she said, "ask them why they don't come and talk to me."

"That's what I said straight talking it's the only way but people will never do it they're too scared of you," said Aunt Duifie, bobbing her head.

"If they're too spineless to say things to my face, there's nothing we can do about it," said Pérsomi and got to her feet. "I'm going to the drive-in tonight. I want to take a bath."

"With a boyfriend?" her ma asked as she turned to go.

No, Ma, with my loyal friend Reinier, she wanted to say, but she held her tongue.

It was just the beginning. The following Tuesday evening there was a knock on the door. When she opened, the minister, Pieter Hanekom, stood on the doorstep.

She noticed the chief elder behind him, awkward in a black suit and tie. She immediately guessed the purpose of the visit. She had noticed the sidelong glances in church on Sunday.

"Dominee Pieter, Oom Daan, please come inside," she said, opening the door wider.

The minister placed his Bible on the coffee table. They had tea. Her ma didn't say a word. In awe of the company, she sat stiffly in her chair. When they'd had their tea, Pérsomi said: "I think Oom Daan du Plesssis and Dominee Hanekom have come to speak to me about my representing the Indian families in court, Ma." She looked at the elder. "Am I right, Oom Daan?"

The elder flushed and shifted uncomfortably in his seat. His thick forefinger tugged at the tie that was strangling him. "Well, if you want to put it that way."

"It would be best to talk alone. Would you like to go to bed, Ma?" Pérsomi suggested.

"Oh heavens," said her ma, getting up.

"See you in the morning. Sleep tight," Pérsomi said reassuringly.

When her ma had left, Oom Daan cleared his throat. "Pérsomi," he said in a solemn voice, "the honorable church council thought it our duty to conduct a conversation with you about certain rumors that have come to our ears."

Oom Daan could be very long-winded. She waited for him to continue.

"We've heard you want to help the Asians resist their relocation to Modderkuil."

"That's right, Oom Daan."

Oom Daan sat back smugly. He had done his duty, now the young minister could take over. Here it comes, thought Pérsomi. Because Oom Daan was one thing, but Pieter Hanekom was more than just words.

Pieter leaned forward slightly, his elbows on his knees, his long fingers entwined.

He has lovely eyes, Pérsomi thought briefly, deep blue, flecked with gray.

He gave her an earnest look, then jumped right in, going way back in history, crossing Blood River, traveling barefoot across the Drakensberg, passing along the way the burning farmsteads and the concentration camps . . .

He had a beautiful voice and was clever with words. But she had no need of a history lesson. "Pieter," she interrupted, "get to the point."

He gave her an amused smile, then nodded. The point, as she had expected, was that the church supported the policy of separate development because it had its roots in the Scriptures.

"By defending the Indians in their suit against the town council you are undermining the entire foundation of goverment policy," he argued. "How can you justify that?"

"We have a Christian government, Pieter," she said. "How do you justify supporting laws that are utterly un-Christian, such as the Group Areas Act?"

He shook his head slightly. "We have a Christian government, quite right, and it stands to reason they wouldn't make laws that are in breach of biblical values. The government introduced these laws because the Bible clearly preaches separation between nations."

"Where in the Bible does it propagate the segregation of people?" she asked, frowning.

"Remember the Tower of Babel, where God Himself instituted segregation by dividing the people into different language groups, thereby causing them to move into separate areas? Read Genesis 11, Pérsomi, and you'll see that God Himself is the Great Separator. He wants people of different languages and cultures to people the earth."

"I also believe that people should honor their language and culture," she said, "but why can't it happen while they are neighbors, so mutual contact can take place? Why should they be moved four miles out of town?"

Pieter reached for his Bible. His long fingers carefully turned the delicate pages. "In Acts 17, verse 26, the apostle Paul says in his sermon at the Areopagus: 'And (He) hath made of one blood all nations of men for to dwell on all the face of the earth, and hath determined the times before appointed, and the bounds of their habitation.' Paul tells the Greeks in no uncertain terms that God ordained a permanent dwelling place for each nation."

"That sermon, as I understand it, is not about a division between nations, but about Paul explaining that the 'unknown God' is the God who created everything, and not a God who resides in temples. In any case, Paul refers to dwelling places in verse 26. Does he also mention the various nations' places of business?"

Pieter thought for a moment, a guarded expression in his eyes. "You're known as a clever lawyer, Pérsomi." He drew a deep breath. "But we shouldn't try to outsmart God. Like the various nations in St. Paul's sermon, the various racial groups in South Africa should each be given their own residential area so they can uphold their respective languages, cultures, and traditions."

"And what about the justice God demands from us, Pieter?" she asked calmly. "Tell me you honestly believe we can swear before God we're being fair to the Indian families, and especially the traders, if we move them four miles out of town."

"The Asians in our town are Muslims. Heathens, Pérsomi," Pieter said earnestly. "Our church has tried to persuade them, but their hearts remain hard. We can no longer allow Satan to dwell in the heart of our town. We can no longer support the children of Satan with our money."

"So it's not because of their skin color that the council is relocating them, but because of their religion?" asked Pérsomi.

"Pérsomi, I don't serve on the council and I don't know what their motives are. But to me the removal is justifiable on religious grounds, yes."

"I see. And what about Mr. Cohen then?" she asked, referring to a Jewish businessman. "Or is his religion close enough to ours? He regards Abraham, Isaac, and Jacob as his ancestors, after all, while Mr. Ismail's religion acknowledges only Father Abraham—the Muslims are the descendants of Ishmael, aren't they, of Hagar, the concubine? Or will we eventually relocate Mr. Cohen and his tailor's shop as well, because of his religion? Followed by the Perreiras, because they represent the Roman threat? And what about Mr. Angelo, the café owner? I hear in their church—"

"Pérsomi, wait," Pieter threw up his hands. "I see your point, but . . ."

"And what about the Great Commandment, Pieter? Love thy neighbor? Do you really think the town council's action against Mr. Ismail and his people speaks of neighborly love? Didn't Jesus Himself teach us to love our neighbors as ourselves? Would we have moved one of our own Afrikaner traders four miles out of town and told him, build a store on this bare earth and sell your goods to . . . who?"

"In the long run I do believe we are acting out of love, Pérsomi. We Afrikaners want our own residential areas, am I right?"

"I believe most Afrikaners do, yes."

"Well, from a Christian viewpoint we also want to grant all the different races their own areas, where they can live and prosper. It may not seem like a charitable action to you now, but think of the future: in ten years' time, won't the Indian community be much happier in their own area, among their own people?"

"Let's say you're right, Pieter, which, by the way, I don't believe you are, but let's leave it there. Let's say you're right. How are the traders supposed to survive? Who will buy their wares—the other Indian traders? The majority of their customers are the whites and natives of the town and surrounding areas, not their own people."

Pieter shook his head. "I'm here to inform you of the official view of the church—a view I totally support. If you can't accept that, Pérsomi, then I don't know."

She leaned forward in her chair. Her voice sounded cold to her own ears. "If I carry on with the case, Pieter, are you and the church council going to deny me the sacraments?"

He drew a slow breath. "Pérsomi, let's not say things we might later regret."

"I do sometimes regret things I've said or done, Pieter. But more often I've regretted things I didn't say or do."

The minister and the elder left late that evening, their mission unaccomplished. But I didn't accomplish anything either, Pérsomi thought when sleep evaded her yet again. They still believe they're right.

In the early hours doubt set in: Am I doing the right thing? What if . . .

And when Gerbrand sat down in the deck chair beside her the following Sunday after lunch and asked, "Pérsomi, are you a Communist?" she realized with a shock how far-reaching the consequences of her decision were.

"Who said so?" she asked.

"Some kids at school."

"Because I'm acting on behalf of Mr. Ismail?"

"They say you're a coolie lover," he muttered, not looking at her.

"Don't ever use that word again, Gerbrand," Pérsomi said.

A frown creased his forehead. "What word?"

"Coolie. They're Indians. It's like swearing at them if you call them coolies."

"Oh," he said.

"Do you know what this thing is about, Gerbrand?"

"Yes," he answered and dug with his bare toes into a groove in the red cement porch. "Pa explained it to me."

"Maybe you should explain it to the other kids then," she proposed.

He turned to her, his freckled face very serious. "They wouldn't listen," he said, "so I beat them up."

She drew a sharp breath. "Gerbrand! Don't ever do that! Violence doesn't solve anything."

"Well, they stopped talking about you," he said defensively. "I just wanted to ask if you're a Communist."

"Not everyone who doesn't agree with the government is a Communist, Gerbrand. I believe that the relocation of Mr. Ismail's store is wrong, so I'm willing to help them. I'm definitely not a Communist."

"I'm glad," he said, getting to his feet. "I put nine partridge eggs under old Bettie, and she hatched them all, she's my ma's best hen. The chicks are really pretty, would you like to see, Pérsomi?"

Pérsomi wrote to the town council early in June, inviting them to a dinner hosted by the Indian community, "during which they hope to have a friendly discussion about the proposed relocation to Modderkuil."

"Miss Pérsomi, you must help us," said Mrs. Ravat, wringing her puffy hands. "We want to give the Boers a smart dinner."

"I suggest you serve them traditional Indian fare," said

Pérsomi, "only with less curry and peppers, or the councillors' mouths will be on fire and they won't be able to say a word."

The Indian women laughed shyly. "Do you really think we should make our own food?" she asked.

Two weeks before the dinner Pérsomi went in search of Yusuf at his surgery. She hadn't seen him for a long time, except in passing, and she hadn't spoken to him in a while. He seemed surprised to see her and greeted her rather stiffly. "Aren't you afraid to come here?" he asked.

"Afraid?" she asked. "Of course not. Why?"

He shrugged. "What brings you here?"

"Well, I want to know how you are," she stalled.

"Fine, but I can't offer you tea. I have to get to the hospital," he said, gathering his instruments. "How can I help you?"

She hesitated a moment. She had hoped for time to create a more congenial atmosphere. "Yusuf, I think you should attend the dinner. Actually, I think you should be the spokesperson for the Indian community."

"My grandpa is the leader of our community, Pérsomi."

"We can let your grandpa speak as well, but he's a simple man who speaks from his heart. You have a university degree. You can deliver an academic argument. Together you'll make a good team."

He shook his head. "I want nothing to do with those people," he said. "They can do as they please with me, I can fight my own battles. But my grandpa and the others . . . Heavens, Pérsomi, they're old people. If they hurt my grandpa I couldn't handle it."

"That's why you should join me in the fight, Yusuf," she said. "I know there's dissension in the council. If we put our case well enough, we might be able to swing two or three councillors' votes in our favor. That may be enough to save at least your stores and your surgery."

He shut his doctor's case. "We know how these people think,

Pérsomi. And accommodating the needs of a few local Indian families is definitely not high on their list of priorities."

"We can't just give up and lie down, Yusuf," she said.

He picked up his case. "I'll think about it," he said vaguely.

"Thanks, Yusuf." She headed for the door.

When she reached the door, he said, "Pérsomi?"

She turned. "Yes, Yusuf?"

"Don't come here again."

She gave him a baffled look. "Why not?"

There was a grim expression around his mouth. "I have enough problems already. I don't want to be arrested for immorality as well."

❦

The men transported the tables and arranged them in a straight line down the middle of the town hall. Around the tables they put twelve council chairs—the same ones that were used for the movies on a Saturday night.

The women, dressed in their customary long black frocks and wide trousers, covered the tables with snow-white tablecloths. They brought brand-new crockery from their stores, unpacked boxes of shiny new cutlery, set the tables exactly the way Pérsomi had shown them.

Only the councillors would be sitting down to eat. Whites and Asians could not dine together. It was unheard of. Besides, Asians were not allowed to attend social functions in the town hall.

"But two of you can address them, after dinner," Pérsomi had said. "I obtained special permission from the magistrate."

Behind the scenes the tension was tangible. Everything had to be perfect.

But the dishes piled with the delicious food were returned to a back room—temporarily serving as a kitchen—still half full.

"The people aren't eating," said Mrs. Ravat worriedly. "There's nothing wrong with the food, is there?"

"The food is delicious," Pérsomi assured her. "I suppose they're just not very hungry."

Her voice was cheerful and there was a smile on her face, but her unease was growing.

After dinner Mr. Ismail addressed the diners. He spoke from his heart, as Pérsomi had known he would. He began by referring to the Honorable President Kruger who had given them the land seventy years ago. He spoke about his papa, whom some of the councillors had known. He took them through the Boer War and the Rebellion, when they had kept their stores open for the Boers, through the drought and depression of '33, when maize flour and sugar and coffee were supplied "on the book"—at a time when the storekeepers themselves often didn't know how they were going to put food on their tables the following day.

"But we folk here in this part of the bushveld have always looked after each other," he said.

A few councillors nodded, a few studied the tablecloth, while others turned their deadpan gazes to the back wall.

Mr. Ismail mentioned the councillors' children, whom he had seen grow up, by name. He ended with a plea that the council review their decision to relocate the Indians. "For humane reasons, because we are storekeepers. Just as a farmer can't plough and sow in the desert, we won't survive without customers on that barren plain," he concluded.

That went well, Pérsomi thought as Mr. Ismail left the hall through a side door.

Yusuf Ismail entered, dressed in a stylish suit—unlike his grandfather, who had been in traditional Muslim attire. He treated the company to an academic, politically loaded tirade. As he spoke, his underlying anger was apparent, as was his scorn for the system that made his grandfather beg for what was rightfully his.

Pérsomi closed her eyes. Yusuf was destroying everything his grandfather had so carefully built up. By the time he came to a few workable suggestions, he had already cut his own throat.

※

The first Sunday after Annabel left for London, Boelie attended church. Pérsomi felt awkward and uncertain. He sat three rows in front of her. Quietly she studied the back of his head, which was bowed in prayer for a long time before he raised it to gaze at the pulpit.

A strange thing happened. She felt her loneliness lift. She felt a strange affinity. Not just with Boelie but with the entire congregation. A feeling of great peace washed over her, so that when Dominee Pieter took his place on the pulpit and delivered a message of hope and love, she could calmly listen to the sermon.

After the service, with Nelius and Lientjie by his side, Boelie said, "All the best for the new year, Pérsomi. I know this is an . . . important year for you."

"Thanks, Boelie, the same to you," she said, smiling. "I hope the rains fill your dam."

He gave a slight smile and nodded. The little family headed for his pickup, parked under a thorn tree. She noticed for the first time that his hair was turning gray.

A few Sundays later, Lientjie was standing beside her, and Pérsomi spontaneously put out her hand. Instantly the bony fingers found hers. "Are you cold?" asked Pérsomi.

The child looked up at her with big brown eyes. "No," she said.

The council upheld its decision to relocate the Indian community to Modderkuil.

One hot morning in March four of the Indian family heads were waiting for Pérsomi at the back door when she arrived at the office. "Come in," she said, unlocking the door. "We'll go through to the boardroom."

Mr. Ismail came straight to the point. "The police came to our homes and our stores yesterday. They gave each of us a document to sign."

"Did you sign?" she asked.

He nodded. "The police told us we must."

"What did the document say?" she asked.

"That the relocation will take place in accordance with the law that has proclaimed our area a white neighborhood. We have to sell—everything. The government will pay us only what the appraiser decides."

"Okay," she said, "it means they want to fight."

"Miss Pérsomi, what do we do now?"

"Those who want to can try to sell their homes and stores," she said calmly, though she felt anger growing inside her. "The rest of you, including those who would like to sell but can't find a buyer, carry on living peacefully in your homes and continue with your businesses."

"And what next, Miss Pérsomi?" one of the older men asked.

"In the meantime we'll keep trying to find a way. Just don't give your properties away for a song. Remember, if you do move, wherever you go, you must have enough money to start over."

After they were gone, she went down the hall and tapped on Mr. De Vos's door.

He looked up. He had lost a lot of weight. His complexion was gray.

"Come in, Pérsomi," he said, arranging the papers before him into a neat pile. "Can I help you?"

She recounted the latest developments. "I told them not to let their properties go too cheaply," she concluded, "or they'll have no money to start over somewhere else."

"Good advice," he said.

"What do you propose I should do next?" she asked.

"What do you think?"

"I think I should prepare an application to prevent the council from going ahead with the eviction, and get a court order that will allow the Indian families to continue living in town and carry on with their businesses until the matter is settled in court."

"That's right. What next?"

"I apply to the court to have the town council's decision declared invalid."

He nodded. "You must realize the council has the law on their side," he said. "You said Mr. Ismail and the others are prepared to move?"

"As long as their new homes are subsidized, yes."

"Then it might be time to apply for a special permit for the Indians to retain their businesses in town and continue plying their trade," he suggested.

"Yes, you're right, I'll consider it," she said. "When I've drafted the document, will you look at it for me?"

He nodded. "I will."

At the door she turned. "Mr. De Vos, how are you?"

He regarded her impersonally for a moment. "Well," he said, "quite well."

❧

The day before Boelie's fortieth birthday, Pérsomi and Reinier arrived at Christine and De Wet's home just after Klara, Antonio, and their children had arrived from Pretoria. It was a happy reunion, the grown-ups laughing and talking, the children ecstatic to see their cousins again.

When Boelie drove up none the wiser at one—Christine had phoned to ask that he bring the kids over to play—the sincere surprise on his face was rewarding for everyone. "I can't believe you came all the way from Pretoria for my birthday," he told Klara, shaking his head.

"Well, you *are* officially old tomorrow." She laughed happily.

He looked around, still shaking his head. "Are you also part of this plot?" he asked Pérsomi.

"It was actually Christine's idea," she said as neutrally as possible. "You're surprised, aren't you?"

He nodded. "Very," he said.

Just before three another car pulled up and, to the delight of everyone, Irene got out. "Irene!" Klara cried. "Christine, you didn't say Irene was coming too!"

"I didn't even know!" De Wet said, astounded. "Irene, how did you get here?"

"Took leave and drove," she answered happily, "I'm staying for a week. Pérsomi, are you here too?" Pérsomi got a kiss as well. "And Reinier! Oh, lovely!" She linked her arm with his and looked around, laughing. "Only Christine knew I was coming. It was our secret surprise."

"Well," said De Wet, "let's find something to drink. Then we men must start making the fires."

Long before the other party guests began to arrive, Pérsomi, Christine, Klara, and Irene had everything ready. They had worked all afternoon, catching up with one another's news. "Goodness, it's been a long time since we girls were last together like this," Christine exclaimed.

More like never, Pérsomi thought.

When the children crowded noisily around the kitchen table to eat. Lientjie wasn't with them.

"She must be playing on her own again," said Christine. "The others are too old for her."

"I'll find her," Pérsomi offered.

She found the child on the floor of Lulani's room, playing with a doll. The child's thin legs were tucked underneath her, the straight dark hair was in need of a haircut, the little face was serious.

"Lientjie? Are you hungry?" she asked softly.

The dark eyes looked up into hers, and the head nodded.

Pérsomi held out her hand. "Come, there's supper in the kitchen," she said.

The child got up and reached out, the small hand almost disappearing in hers. "Are you going to give me my supper?"

Pérsomi smiled down at her. "Yes, I will."

It turned into a special evening. The guests sat around the fire long after the meat was done. The men brought out chairs and piled huge logs on the flames. The children played around the grown-ups, the little ones falling asleep in their moms' laps, or between their feet. "I'll fetch a few blankets, it's getting chilly," said Christine.

"Get your guitar, Antonio, let's sing," Irene suggested.

The Fouries could certainly sing. And with Antonio there, one melody after another rose up with the smoke into the cloudless, starry sky.

When Pérsomi looked down, Lientjie was standing close to her, holding her doll. Pérsomi held out her arm. Timidly the little girl approached. "Cold?" Pérsomi asked.

The child gave a slight nod.

Pérsomi lifted her onto her lap and wrapped her coat around the child. "Now you'll be warm," she whispered.

After a while the small figure relaxed. Her breathing became regular.

A strange sensation washed over Pérsomi, a great tenderness toward this child. She held Lientjie more tightly, and the little girl gave a soft sigh. Lost in thought, Pérsomi stroked the straight, wispy hair.

The week after the party Mr. De Vos suffered a serious setback.

"I have to go for more intensive treatment," he said when he was discharged from the local hospital. It was dead quiet in the small boardroom. The staff sat motionless, listening. Mr. De Vos had lost even more weight, and his once ruddy complexion was gray. The hand wrapped around the water glass was bony and pale.

"I'll be at the Pretoria General Hospital for at least a month, according to the specialist." He took another careful sip of water. Ms. Steyn drew a handkerchief from her bosom.

"I have therefore decided to retire," he continued with great effort. "From the first of May Pérsomi will take my place as full partner in the firm De Vos and De Vos."

Ms. Steyn gave a soft gasp and covered her nose and mouth with the handkerchief.

No one else moved.

Then De Wet got up quietly. In his resonant voice he thanked Mr. De Vos for the years they had worked together. "I could never have found a better mentor," he said sincerely. He turned to face the old man. "Oom Bartel, all of us will miss you, but I in particular am going to miss you terribly. We wish you a speedy recovery because, even though you're officially retiring, we'll still be calling on you for support and advice."

Mr. De Vos nodded. "Thank you," he said when De Wet sat down.

Pérsomi got up slowly.

"It's an indescribable privilege to be made a partner in the firm of De Vos and De Vos," she said cautiously. She turned to the old man at the head of the table. "Mr. De Vos, I'll do my best to honor this excellent firm that you and your father established. I pray for your return to good health."

Mr. De Vos looked at her and nodded. He understood.

Then De Wet helped him to his car and drove him home.

The court application to stop the Indian families from being evicted, which Pérsomi had asked him to look at, was left lying among the other documents on his table.

🌿

Pérsomi woke with a start and sat up in bed. Dawn was just breaking. Someone was hammering on the back door. "Miss Pérsomi! Miss Pérsomi!" The voice sounded like a frightened child's.

Pérsomi threw her dressing gown over her shoulders and rushed to the door on bare feet. "I'm coming!" she shouted as she ran.

At the door was an Indian boy of about twelve, in his night-clothes. She thought he might be one of Mr. Ravat's grandchildren. "The police!" he cried. "The police are going to come this morning and throw our things out of our homes! My grandpa says—"

"I'll be right there!" she said. "Go back. I'll get dressed and come straightaway."

She got dressed as quickly as possible. "No, Ma, I don't want coffee," she said over her shoulder as she hurried to her car.

It was a cool autumn morning. The first trees were just shedding their leaves. The swallows were getting ready to fly north. But Pérsomi didn't notice any of those things as she drove to the ill-fated neighborhood at the center of town.

When she got out, some of the older Indian men were in the street. "Miss Pérsomi, we had a phone call early this morning," Mr. Ismail said anxiously. "The man didn't say his name, just that the police were coming to throw us out."

"Surely the time we were granted can't be over," Pérsomi said, pressing her hands to her face. "I'll . . ." Suddenly she was unable to think clearly. What had she done, telling them to ignore the eviction notice?

De Wet approached. She didn't know where he had come from, she only knew he was there.

She pointed helplessly at the row of Indian stores. "De Wet, the waiting period can't possibly be over! I didn't expect them to crack down so soon. They said they'd grant the people sufficient time to sell their properties. What shall I do?"

"Good morning, Pérsomi," De Wet said calmly. "A reasonable period is a relative concept. But your information is correct, apparently the police are going to act today. I'm glad they're not here yet. And you know exactly what to do."

Pérsomi pressed her hands to her face. "I . . . must lodge an urgent application for an interim interdict against the town council, preventing them from evicting the families until a ruling has been made," she said in a daze. As she wiped the loose strands of hair from her face, she felt her mind open up and her confidence return. "I must ask that any criminal proceedings instituted against the applicants be suspended, pending a settlement of the dispute."

De Wet gave her an encouraging smile. "Go. First reassure your clients."

Pérsomi hurried to where the men were anxiously waiting.

"I'm going to the magistrate's court to get an interdict that will stop the police from acting," she said calmly. "Go back to your homes and stores."

They nodded earnestly. "Thank you, Miss Pérsomi," they said.

When she rejoined De Wet, she asked, "How did you get here?" They began to walk to their cars. "I mean, how did you know?"

"It was Gerbrand," said De Wet. "The father of one of his classmates said something, and the child taunted Gerbrand. He said something like: 'The Indians are going to be thrown out tomorrow, then we'll see what your aunt will do.' Gerbrand only realized the meaning this morning and came to wake me up."

"I'm very glad to see you. Thanks, De Wet."

"Listen, Pérsomi, if you need my help, I'll go with you to the magistrate's court. If not, I'm going back to the farm to shave and get dressed."

She noticed now that he was unshaven and was dressed in shorts and an open-necked shirt, obviously put on in haste. "I'll manage, thanks. I . . . For a while I was shocked senseless, I'm sorry. Please go."

"Sure?"

"Very sure."

"Well good luck. I'll see you later."

Pérsomi glanced at her watch. She didn't have time to go home and dress more appropriately. She had to do the paperwork. She got into her car and drove to the office, where she sat down behind a typewriter and typed the application as quickly as her two fingers allowed.

❧

Pérsomi knew the magistrate well. She had been appearing before him for years. "This is an urgent application," she said as he looked over her papers. "The police are planning to evict the Indians from their homes and stores today."

He looked up from the documents. "Pérsomi, this has to do with the Group Areas Act. Because of the controversy surrounding the act and the sensitivity of this particular case, I'd rather handle the application in an open court."

She sighed softly. "How soon can that happen?"

He thought for a moment. "I'll see you in half an hour."

"Thanks," said Pérsomi. She hurried out to fetch her gown.

On her way back, she felt the car list sideways, but there was no time to pay it any heed.

Minutes later Pérsomi walked into the same courtroom where, so many years before, she had decided to become a lawyer in order to see that justice was done.

She presented the motivation for requesting an interim interdict: the applicants were the heads of a number of Indian families. They had a *prima facie* right not to be relocated, she maintained. They had been given an unreasonably short period in which to sell their properties. Besides, who were they supposed to sell to? Word in town was that the council planned to demolish the buildings in favor of new business premises.

"Your Honor, if the police forcefully evict the Indian families," she argued, "the applicants will suffer irreparable damages."

She went on to say that the applicants had a very good chance of winning their action against the town council. They were building a strong case.

"And finally, Your Honor," she concluded, "there is at this

point no alternative remedy for the immediate problem, except that the court grant an interdict that will prohibit the police from forcefully evicting the applicants and their families from their homes and businesses today."

She tossed her hair back and looked the magistrate in the eye.

He looked back at her pensively. "You have confidence in your case, Miss Pieterse?" he asked.

"Yes, Your Honor, I do, or I wouldn't be standing here."

He studied the document in front of him, then looked up. "I'll grant the order, though I'm not doing so without reservation," he said hesitantly. "When the matter appears before the court, it will be heard by a different magistrate. I plan to recuse myself, on the grounds that I know the parties too well."

Pérsomi nodded, waiting.

She saw a movement from the corner of her eye. Boelie had gotten up at the back of the courtroom. He was pale and his face wore a strange, tight-lipped expression. She couldn't fathom what he was doing there.

When she stepped out of the courtroom, there was no sign of him. But there was no time to give it any more thought. She hurried to her car, unlocked it, put her briefcase and gown on the back seat, and reached for the door on the driver's side.

She froze. The front tire was completely flat. The car was leaning to the side. She looked around helplessly. The street was deserted.

Pérsomi bent down, removed her high-heeled shoes and began to sprint, the court order in her hand.

It's liberating, she realized as she raced to the town center, the wind in her loose hair, the pavement under her bare feet. She ran until the tension left her body.

When she turned the last corner before the Indian neighborhood, she stopped and stared in dismay at the scene that greeted her.

There seemed to be an army of police vehicles and men in blue. Clearly reinforcements had been called in from neighboring towns. Bulky men were throwing items out of houses, without any regard for their possible value.

The entire Indian community was in the street, trying to salvage their possessions, running to and fro, pleading. Some of the older women stood looking on in dismay as their belongings were tossed into the street.

Pérsomi broke into a run again, heading for the commanding officer. "Stop! Stop at once!" she said at the top of her voice. "You're breaking their things, stop! I have a court order prohibiting this action." She waved the document in the air.

Two policemen grabbed her from behind and held her arms. "Let me go at once!" she said, trying to free herself.

But they held on.

More and more cars stopped, more and more townspeople came to see the commotion. They stood at the fringes. One man approached to take photos with his Brownie.

The commanding officer took the document but didn't look at it. "My men are just doing their job, Miss Pieterse, and we won't stand for any obstruction."

"For Pete's sake, just read the document in your hand!" she said, beside herself with anger. "And let go of my arms, you're hurting me!"

Still they held on.

When she looked up, Boelie was beside her, his face white.

"Let go of Miss Pieterse," he said stiffly. "She's the legal representative of the Indian community. She has a court order to temporarily halt the eviction process."

The commanding officer gave Boelie a surprised look.

"Are you taking the Asians' side now?" the officer asked, astounded.

"I'm merely suggesting you read the document in your hand," said Boelie. He was still pale. He turned to the two young constables. "And you two, let go of the lady's arms this minute."

They let her go and stepped back.

The officer studied the document, then reluctantly called a halt to the eviction.

Somewhat deflated, the uniformed men got into the waiting vehicles and returned to their stations.

The Indians gathered up their possessions and carried them back inside.

The townspeople turned and slowly walked away.

"Come, I'll take you home," said Boelie. "Where are your shoes?"

He changed her tire, then drove the car back to her home and knocked on her door. She had calmed down.

"Thank you, Boelie," she said, for both his intervention and the repair. "Would you like some coffee?"

He closed the door and sat down in her kitchen, facing her. She prepared for him to take another shot at convincing her to give up the case.

"I know who your father is," Boelie said. His dark eyes burned into hers.

"Boelie," she began to protest.

"I can't believe I never saw the family likeness between you and Annabel, the two women I know best in the entire world."

She held up both hands. "Boelie," she said.

"In court this morning, watching you in action, the way you move your head and hands, it struck me like a bucket of icy water."

"It really doesn't matter anymore," she pleaded. "It's water under the bridge."

"It matters to me, Pérsomi," he said slowly. "I have lain awake so many nights, wondering how I could have fallen for her. Now I understand. And I understand so much more than that."

SEVENTEEN

"ACTUALLY, WE'RE MEANT FOR EACH OTHER, WE'VE ALWAYS been," Reinier said one chilly winter's morning. "I really wish you'd get to know her properly, Pérsomi."

"I've known her all my life," said Pérsomi. "I know you're making a mistake."

"You know the image she holds up to the world," Reinier said earnestly. "There are things in her past that have forced her to build walls around herself."

"Oh, please, Reinier!" Pérsomi snapped. "Irene is a youngest child who grew up as a spoiled brat in a wealthy home. How hard could it have been?"

"Irene was the pesky little sister who spent her days, without success, trying to equal the achievements of her brothers and sister," he said calmly, "and the other little girl who lived on the same farm."

Pérsomi gave him a hostile look. "The bywoner child," she said.

He looked squarely back at her. "The illegitimate child of a man who refused to accept his responsibilities," he said.

"Don't."

"Well, then don't give me that bywoner nonsense."

She closed her eyes and pushed her fingers through her hair. "Reinier, what are we doing?"

"Arguing like two stupid teenagers," he said.

"Let's stop."

"Fine," he said. "I'm going to Pietermaritzburg for a week. Irene and I must talk about things that can't be discussed on the phone. But I want you to know, Pérsomi, that I'm very serious about Irene. You know when the other person is right for you— for marriage, I mean."

"Are you really that serious, Reinier? Marriage serious?"

"Yes, Pérsomi, I am."

Early one morning Pérsomi arrived at the office to find a delegation of Indian leaders waiting for her under the bare jacaranda trees behind the building. "Is something wrong?" she asked anxiously as she got out of her car.

"No, Miss Pérsomi, everything is good," said Mr. Ismail.

"Would you like to come inside?" she asked, heading for the back door.

"No, Miss Pérsomi, we can talk here," Mr. Ismail answered. "Miss Pérsomi, we've decided to move. Mr. Japie de Villiers showed us the plans for the new town. The houses are nicer and the school will also be better."

She frowned. "Are you sure it's what you want to do?" she asked. "Or did Japie de Villiers talk you into it?"

"The mayor explained everything to us," said Mr. Ravat. "The houses will be bigger, with enough space for gardens. And the compensation isn't bad."

Pérsomi thought of the crowded circumstances they lived in at present, the patched-up houses squeezed in between the stores, the narrow streets and alleyways. There were no gardens where the children could play. "Fine," she said hesitantly. "Won't you come inside?"

"No, thank you, Miss Pérsomi," said Mr. Ismail. "But Miss Pérsomi, we're going to keep our businesses in town."

"I see." She thought for a moment. "Did you discuss that with Mr. De Villiers?"

They all shook their heads. "No," Mr. Ismail spoke up again, "we're telling you now."

"If you decide to move your places of residence but not your businesses, you're still contravening the law. Sooner or later you're going to clash with the police," she said. "Did you give the matter careful thought?"

"We did, Miss Pérsomi, and we can't move our businesses," said Mr. Ismail.

"Okay," Pérsomi nodded. After a moment's pause, she said, "In that case our next step is to apply for a special permit to allow you to operate your businesses from their present premises. Section 14 of the Group Areas Act makes provision for the issuing of special permits. I'll make sure of all the legal aspects. Give me a week, then we'll talk again."

"Thank you, Miss Pérsomi," the bearded men chorused. They walked down the street on their way back to their stores, striking in their long white robes, each head neatly crowned with a fez.

When she entered the office, Ms. Steyn was already there. "Why do those Indians have to gather in our parking area?" she complained. "It isn't good for the image of De Vos and De Vos."

🌿

"We ought to look in on Oom Bartel," said De Wet one teatime early in August. "He's not doing well. I think he could do with our support."

Pérsomi frowned. She had been so busy preparing for the

hearing that she'd given hardly a thought to anything else. "Is he in the hospital?" she asked.

"No, he's at home, but he's mostly in bed."

He was trying to tell her that *she* should go and see Mr. De Vos. That much was clear to Pérsomi. Of course, De Wet didn't really understand. She had never been in Reinier's home before. How could she simply show up and say, "Good morning, Mr. De Vos, how are you this morning?"

She put it off for another day or two. But on Friday morning she took her briefcase and drove to the big house in Voortrekker Street.

A black woman in a neat uniform opened the heavy front door. "Mr. De Vos is on the sun porch," she said and led the way across the shiny floors and thick carpets, through the house where Reinier and Annabel had grown up.

The covered porch was warm. Mr. De Vos lay back against a sofa, with pillows behind his back and a blanket over his legs. His face looked gaunt.

The porch smelled of medicine and black tea.

"Will you bring us a tray of tea?" Mr. De Vos asked the woman. She nodded and left.

Pérsomi sat down awkwardly on a chair facing him. "How are you?"

"Not bad, under the circumstances. I'm mostly free from pain."

Silence.

"How are things at the office?" he asked.

"Fine. Very busy, but that's good." What else could she say? "Rudolf Naudé starts next Monday. The young lawyer we appointed."

"Yes. That's good," he said.

Silence.

The woman brought in the tea. Pérsomi got up. "Shall I pour?" she asked.

"Help yourself, I've just had some." Mr. De Vos motioned with his hands. They were nothing but skin and bone.

Pérsomi sipped her tea.

"How are you faring with your preparation for the Ismail case?"

"I think it's going well." She put her empty cup back on the tray. "There are a few things I'd like to discuss with you, if you feel up to it."

"I'd like to hear your arguments."

He listened with his eyes shut as she read him parts of her argument. Sometimes he interrupted to suggest a different word or phrase. Sometimes he asked a question.

After a while the uniformed woman entered again. "Time for your medication," she said apologetically.

Pérsomi realized she'd been there for more than an hour. "I'm sorry, I shouldn't have tired you out. It was most inconsiderate," she said.

He shook his head. "No, it's good you came," he said. But he looked exhausted.

She drove home not knowing what she felt. Resentment, maybe, and sadness. She supposed deep down she had been hoping for him to apologize, to give her a reason to put her anger behind her.

But to see him like that?

❧

It was a lazy Sunday afternoon in spring. Somewhere in the house the wireless was playing soft, sad music.

They were lying in two deck chairs on Christine and De

Wet's porch, their legs in the sun. Gerbrand had taken Nelius along to the veld, Lientjie was playing with the two little girls in their bedroom, and De Wet and Christine were enjoying their Sunday afternoon nap.

The old Le Roux farmyard had fallen into a languid sleep. Only the wireless played ceaseless music, in lonely minor tones.

"Boelie?"

"Hmm?"

"Are you asleep?"

"Hmm."

"Then why are you saying 'hmm'?"

He gave a slight smile and lazily opened his eyes. "Yes?" he asked.

"Boelie, are you lonely sometimes?"

He turned his head and studied her. Then he said, "No, Pérsomi, not really. Alone, yes, but not lonely. I know . . . I know you're there."

Her hand reached for his. He lay watching her, the expression in his dark eyes gentle. Almost imperceptibly he shook his head.

She smiled and nodded. They both understood.

Alone, yes. Not lonely.

❦

"Reinier and Irene are getting married this afternoon," Pérsomi told her ma on Thursday.

"Irene . . . Fourie?" her ma asked, confused. "And Reinier . . ."

"Mr. De Vos's son, Reinier, is going to marry Mr. Fourie's daughter Irene."

"Heavens, Pérsomi, I know who Irene is, I'm not stupid," her ma said irritably.

"I just thought I'd tell you," said Pérsomi.

"But it's Thursday afternoon. Why would they get married on a Thursday afternoon?"

"Mr. De Vos is very ill, Ma, I've told you. He's in the hospital. They were planning to get married in two months' time but he might not have made it to the wedding."

"Is he so ill?" her ma asked, distressed.

"Yes, Ma, I told you."

Pérsomi recalled the day under the wild fig tree, surrounded by the smell of overripe fruit and the chirping of the bushveld parrots. "Yes, Ma, he's very ill," she said more gently. "The wedding will take place in the hospital, at his bedside."

"Heavens, Pérsomi, I didn't realize it was that serious."

Pérsomi wasn't keen to go and had tried her best to get out of it. She had objected to Reinier. "The only people present will be your parents and your brothers and sisters!"

"That's exactly why you belong there," he had said seriously. "Pérsomi, I know everything. My dad told me and . . . yes, I'm glad I know. You are . . . someone to be proud of."

Tears came to her eyes.

He smiled. "*I* want you there. We've come a long way, Pérsomi."

So she dressed carefully to celebrate the wedding at the hospital with the two families.

Outside the hospital she saw Mr. Fourie and Aunt Lulu for the first time in years. They looked well—healthy, happy. "Pérsomi!" Aunt Lulu said happily, drawing her close. "Goodness, you're lovelier than ever!"

Pérsomi laughed, embarrassed. "It's good to see you," she said.

"De Wet tells us how well you're doing. We're incredibly proud of you," Aunt Lulu said heartily. "And Christine says you're a wonderful friend."

"Yes, De Wet and Christine are very kind to me."

"Oh, look, here's Klara," Aunt Lulu said and huried away to meet her daughter.

Pérsomi fetched the hastily made bouquets from her car and set off for the ward. A few nurses came to help with the flowers. Earlier they had moved Mr. De Vos to a bigger ward, strategically positioned the bed, and brought in extra chairs for the guests.

Mr. De Vos was propped up against the pillows, dressed and shaven. Beside his bed stood the oxygen tanks, the tube in his arm confining him to his bed. His glasses looked too big for his face and his complexion was gray, but he was cheerful. "I see they put you to work as well, Pérsomi," he said.

She placed flowers on the windowsill and the table. When he saw her looking around, searching for another suitable spot, he said, "Why don't you put them on the nightstand beside my bed? We can put the medicine away for now."

Dominee Pieter entered, carrying a wooden lectern and his books. "Hello, Pérsomi, how nice to see you again. Shall I put my things over here?" he asked as if she were in charge.

Aunt Lulu came in, with De Wet and Christine and Klara and Antonio. "Where shall we sit, Pérsomi?" they asked.

Then Reinier entered with his mother, a thin, bewildered figure in a navy-blue dress. He put her chair next to the bed and greeted everyone. He was the only one with a flower in his buttonhole.

Just before the bride entered, Boelie came in with Annabel on his arm. She floated in, elegant and beautiful and exquisitely groomed. She greeted everyone effusively. "To think my little brother and Boelie's little sister are getting married! Isn't it wonderful?" She hung on Boelie's arm, snuggled up to him and stroked his neck.

She didn't fool anyone.

Mr. Fourie came in with Irene on his arm, radiant as only a

bride can be. Reinier looked happier than Pérsomi had ever seen him. Maybe, just maybe, he would find happiness.

The application for the special permit was denied. The Indian traders had to vacate their places of business as well as their homes. Two weeks later, when Pérsomi saw Mr. Ismail and Mr. Moosa waiting in the parking area behind the office, their shoulders slumped, their faces anxious, she guessed they had been sued to appear in court.

"Good morning, Mr. Ismail, Mr. Moosa." She took her briefcase and handbag from her car.

"Good morning, Miss Pérsomi," they chorused.

"Let's go inside."

"No, right here is fine, Miss Pérsomi," Mr. Ismail said. "We've just come to tell you, the police brought this." He held out a document.

"Is it a summons for you to appear in court?" she asked, unfolding the document.

"Yes, Miss Pérsomi, we have to sign, all of us," said Mr. Moosa.

"We have to be in court two weeks from Tuesday," Mr. Ismail added.

Pérsomi folded the document again. "Who has been summoned?" she asked.

"The two of us, and Isaac Ravat and my grandson Yusuf," Mr. Ismail answered.

"Fine, we'll go to court," said Pérsomi, heading for the back door. "I've finished my preparation for the hearing, but I want to discuss my arguments with you to make sure we're on the same page."

"Right, Miss Pérsomi."

She unlocked the back door. "Are you sure you won't come in?" she asked.

"No, we're fine, Miss Pérsomi, we must get to our stores," Mr. Ismail assured her.

"Mr. Ismail, it's very important that Yusuf is present when we discuss the hearing. I realize he's busy but he still hasn't spoken to me. Ask him when he can attend a meeting, then phone Ms. Steyn for an appointment. It must be this week, okay?"

"Okay, Miss Pérsomi," they said, nodding. "Thank you, Miss Pérsomi."

De Wet knocked on Pérsomi's office door one morning when he returned from the hospital.

"Mr. De Vos is very weak. He told me he'd like to see you. I suggest you go as soon as possible. I think he might want to . . . Well, I don't know." It wasn't often that De Wet was at a loss for words. "He's looking for forgiveness, Pérsomi. Go at once, please. Be kind."

"You . . . know?" she asked cautiously.

He shrugged. "I suspected it for years. When he made you partner, I knew for sure."

She turned and picked up her handbag. "Do you think . . . Annabel knows?"

"Yes, she's known for years. When you were still a student, she once made a remark that I didn't understand at the time. But yes, she definitely knows."

She didn't ask what Annabel had said. It wasn't important.

Pérsomi drove to the hospital in silence.

The man in the white hospital bed was hardly recognizable.

Reinier and his mother were there.

"Pa, here's Pérsomi," Reinier said, getting to his feet. He took his mother's elbow and said, "Let's go for coffee. We'll be back in about twenty minutes."

Pérsomi approached uncertainly. "Good morning, Mr. De Vos." Her voice sounded strange to her own ears.

He stirred slightly, gave a slight nod.

She waited. He lay motionless. Was he asleep? "De Wet says you want to see me."

"I asked you to come . . ." His voice was no more than a hoarse whisper. With difficulty he opened his eyes. His bony hand moved slightly.

She did not take his hand.

". . . I wanted to say . . . I'm proud of you . . . that you're my . . . daughter."

The words hit her much harder than she could have expected.

"I . . ." He seemed too exhausted to continue.

Pérsomi felt trapped. How could she forgive him if he never apologized for what he did to her and her ma?

"I appreciate the help you've given me over the years," she said, "and especially . . . my share in De Vos and De Vos."

Her words seemed to have a calming effect on him.

She reached out and gently laid her hand on his. "Mr. De Vos, can I give my ma a message from you?"

He lay motionless for so long that she thought he hadn't heard. Then he mumbled, "Tell your ma . . . she made a wonderful success of raising you."

She licked her dry lips. "Is that all?" she asked.

His eyelids fluttered slightly, closed again. "Yes, that's all," he whispered.

Slowly she withdrew her hand and left the room.

"I told you Mr. De Vos was very ill, didn't I?" she asked her ma that evening. They were in the sitting room, having coffee.

Her ma nervously touched her hair. "Yes?"

"Ma, he died late this afternoon."

Her ma's hands flew to her face. "Oh heavens, Pérsomi."

"It had to come, Ma. And it's for the best. He was in a lot of pain toward the end."

Her ma looked at her with dull eyes as she wrung a gray handkerchief in her hands.

"He told me to tell you . . . that you made a wonderful success of raising me," she said.

Her ma closed her eyes and sat motionless for a long time. Then she opened her eyes and asked, "Is that all he said?"

Pérsomi hesitated. She looked at her ma's anxious face. "He was very weak, Ma." She swallowed. "He might have wanted to say more, but he was too weak."

Her ma nodded slowly. "He loved me a lot," she said. "He really loved me a lot."

It was a big funeral, and the church was packed. Pérsomi sat with the office staff.

At exactly three o'clock the bells began to peal, loud enough for the entire town to hear. Then the family entered. Reinier and Annabel flanked their mother, followed by Irene and Boelie. Irene was holding Nelius's hand. Boelie had Lientjie in his arms. They took their seats in the first pew.

Dominee Pieter spoke, the congregation sang, and the eulogies followed. Then the long procession drove slowly to the cemetery, a traffic officer on his motorbike up ahead, followed by the black hearse and the cars with their bright headlights. The

Indian community lined up in front of their stores in a show of silent respect, as they always did when there was a funeral in town.

The coffin was slowly lowered into the open grave. Boelie's arm was around Annabel's shoulders as she sobbed against his chest. Pérsomi turned away.

Then she felt a small, cold hand in hers. Her heart contracted and she bent down. "Lientjie, go to your daddy," she told the little girl softly.

"I want to hold your hand," the child said.

"I want to hold your hand, too," Pérsomi said, "but you must go to Daddy now. Put your hand in his, and he'll pick you up. Will you do that for me?"

The child looked at her with big brown eyes. "Okay," she said.

Pérsomi took in the skinny legs in the oversize navy-blue dress. The child walked to her father. Pérsomi saw Boelie's expression soften as he looked down, picked up the little girl, and hugged her to his chest.

She turned and walked through the cemetery gate to her car.

❧

The Tuesday of the hearing arrived clear and cloudless. "Think of me today, Ma, it's the hearing," Pérsomi said at breakfast.

"Oh, I didn't know," her ma said. "We're out of maize flour. You must buy some this afternoon."

"Okay, Ma," said Pérsomi.

"And hair dye, Aunt Duifie must touch up my roots."

"Okay," said Pérsomi. "I'm going now."

The magistrate's court was a large building built of gray cement blocks, with bulky pillars in front and two weather-beaten flagpoles overhead. The Union flag hung limply from one, pale and faded in the scorching bushveld sun. The second flagpole was empty—the Union Jack was no longer hoisted.

Slowly Pérsomi walked up the wide, worn stone steps. There was a knot in her stomach.

"If Jakobus Lourens is the prosecutor, you have a problem," De Wet had told her the day before. "His research will be faultless, which isn't a bad thing. But he plays dirty."

I must relax, she told herself. I'm not afraid of Jakobus Lourens. But she was emotionally involved in the case.

Mr. Ismail, Mr. Ravat, Mr. Moosa, and Yusuf were waiting in the narrow passage for nonwhites. "Everything okay?" she asked.

"We're ready," Mr. Ismail answered quietly. Yusuf nodded. He looked pale and tense. A muscle jumped in his cheek.

"Well, let's go in." She smiled and fell into step beside Yusuf. "I think we'll finish in one day, Yusuf. I know you're in a hurry to get back to your surgery."

"If I still have a surgery after today," he said.

"It's going to be fine," she assured him despite the tension she felt building inside her.

When they walked through the big doors of the courtroom, the men in their snow-white robes stopped somewhat uncertainly. "Here, you sit over here," Pérsomi said, indicating the place where Lewies Pieterse had sat almost twenty years before. She put her briefcase on the table and hastened to the restroom to wash her hands.

"Good morning, Miss Pieterse," a voice said behind her in the passage.

She closed her eyes for a moment. Dear Lord, give me strength. Calmly she turned. "Good morning, Mr. Lourens."

Jakobus Lourens was a big man with a rugged complexion and a large, reddish nose. He had a booming voice, emanating from his enormous chest. "A *pro Deo* legal aid case, Miss Pieterse?" he asked congenially.

"No, Mr. Lourens."

He raised his eyebrows. "You're not telling me you're serious with this case, are you?" he asked, nudging Pérsomi's arm in a familiar gesture.

She gave him an icy stare. "Are you insinuating, Mr. Lourens, that I took the case for financial reasons only?"

"Get off your high horse, doll. I'm as fond of a joke as the next man, but we'll see who laughs last."

Pérsomi turned and led the way into the courtroom, her shoulders straight.

The room was filled to capacity, the atmosphere loaded with anticipation.

An unfamiliar magistrate from Pretoria entered. His gray hair contrasted sharply with his black gown. The spectators fell silent. The defendants stood. The clerk of the court read the charge sheet—the defendants were being charged with contravening the Group Areas Act.

"How does the first defendant plead?" asked the magistrate.

"Not guilty, Your Honor," said Mr. Ismail.

"How does the second defendant plead?" asked the magistrate.

"Not guilty, Your Honor," said Mr. Moosa.

"Not guilty, Your Honor," echoed Mr. Ravat and Dr. Yusuf Ismail.

"The state may proceed with its case," said the magistrate, leaning back.

Jakobus Lourens eyed Pérsomi, a derisive smile on his lips. Then he got to his feet. "It is my intention to prove to the court that the four defendants deliberately contravened the law, Your Honor."

"You may begin, Mr. Lourens," said the magistrate, looking slightly impatient.

"The Group Areas Act of 1950 is very clear: if an area has been rezoned for use by a particular racial group and the authorities have created the necessary facilities to relocate any other racial group living in the area, the law compels the other racial group to move. If they refuse to move, it is a criminal offense, and the state must act accordingly. That, in a nutshell, is what this case is about, Your Honor."

He sniffed and continued, "As a result of the self-evident nature of this case and the fact that it is a plain and simple contravention of a specific act, I won't waste the court's time. I therefore call my only witness, Mr. Carel Thompson."

Carel Thompson was a tall, pasty fellow with sparse hair and horn-rimmed spectacles. He was sworn in and took his place on the witness stand.

"Mr. Thompson," Jakobus Lourens began, "you are employed by the municipality, is that right?"

"Yes, I'm the town clerk," Thompson answered, clearing his throat.

"Do you know the defendants present in this court?"

"Yes, they are the Indian shopkeepers who do business in the main street," he answered, "and the Indian doctor. They can no longer operate their businesses from there."

"Can you tell the court why not?" Jakobus Lourens sounded bored.

"Their stores are in a white area. They are nonwhite."

"You would therefore say they are acting in contravention of the stipulations of the Group Areas Act?"

"Yes," said the town clerk, "and they refuse to move their businesses to the area at Modderkuil that has been zoned for Indians."

"And the necessary facilities have been created for them at Modderkuil?"

"The town council has met all the legal requirements, yes."

The prosecutor gave a satisfied nod and turned his gaze on the four defendants. "I see," he said. Then he turned back to the town clerk. "Mr. Thompson, are you aware that the defendants present here in court today applied for a special permit to continue to ply their trade in the area?"

"Yes, I know they did. The town council denied their request."

"Why?"

"The town council didn't think a special permit was necessary," the clerk answered. "Another area has been allocated to them from where they can operate their businesses."

"And did they, after the permit was denied, still refuse to move?" the prosecutor asked.

"They did."

The prosecutor turned to the magistrate. "No further questions, Your Honor."

"Miss Pieterse?" the magistrate asked.

"Thank you, Your Honor." Pérsomi got up and turned to the man on the witness stand. "Mr. Thompson, you're an experienced town clerk, are you not?" she asked.

"I have filled the position for years, yes."

"And I understand you have a thorough knowledge of the legal aspects pertaining to your position?"

"I know the laws that pertain to my job, yes," the town clerk said.

"That's what I was told," Pérsomi said, nodding. "Mr. Thompson, would you agree that the present Indian business district in our town is a segregated area of about six acres, where the Indian community's places of trade and their mosque are confined to one specific area?"

"In the white town center, yes," the town clerk replied.

"Are you aware that the stands on which they are currently trading were given to them in 1884 by President Paul Kruger in lieu of payment for goods supplied by them during the war against the Sekukuni in 1879?"

"Yes, I know this."

"Do you know that their right to the land was upheld in 1908, in terms of the Townships Amendment Act, number 34 of the Transvaal Colony, which allowed Indians to reside and trade in a preallocated area?" asked Pérsomi.

"I don't have knowledge of archaic laws," the town clerk answered.

"Then allow me to enlighten you," Pérsomi said calmly. "The trading licenses of the defendants were reconfirmed by the local government—in other words the town council at the time—in compliance with the Transvaal Dealers Control Ordinance 11 of 1925. Furthermore, the Transvaal Asiatic Land Tenure Amendment Act 35 of 1932, directly applicable to the defendants present in court, makes provision not only for statutory segregation, but allows the Indians legally to reside in the specified areas. Do you agree, Mr. Thompson?"

"I can't express an opinion on laws I don't know," the town clerk protested.

"Then it's a good thing the prosecutor and the honorable magistrate know the laws," said Pérsomi. "They will know that the Feetham Commission allocated certain areas to the Asians in 1937, which, admittedly, did not include the area where the defendants have their businesses at present. But in 1941 certain Asians in the Transvaal with old, established businesses in areas outside those earmarked in 1937 were exempted from the law. The defendants fall in this category."

Jakobus Lourens got to his feet. "Your Honor," he said, sounding somewhat bored, "I really think the counsel for the defense is wasting the court's time, quoting laws dating from the ark. We are here to review the Group Areas Act, not to listen to a history lesson."

The magistrate gave him an impassive look. "Miss Pieterse, is this line of questioning leading anywhere?" he asked.

"Yes, Your Honor. My submission, Your Honor *and* Mr. Thompson, is that for more than seventy years the defendants have been legally plying their trade in a segregated and restricted area, namely the premises they currently occupy. From the very beginning there has been no logical reason to relocate them."

She stopped for a moment to take a sip of water. "But that's not all, Your Honor," she said and picked up a hefty document. "This is a copy of the Group Areas Act. It states, among other things, that if a local government wants to move a racial group from a specific area they must"—she put on her spectacles and read from the document—"provide *suitable living conditions.*" She removed her spectacles and turned her gaze on the town clerk. "You are aware of this requirement?"

"Of course I am," the town clerk said, sounding annoyed.

"And you think the town council has met this requirement?" asked Pérsomi.

"Definitely, yes," came the confident answer. "The new Indian area at Modderkuil has been provided with good roads, an adequate school building, and sporting facilities. And the stands are bigger than the ones they had. That is why many Indian families have accepted the compensation offered to them and moved. The feedback we're getting is that the people are happy there."

"Yes, that's the feedback I got as well," Pérsomi said, nodding affably, "I was very glad to hear it."

She looked down at the document in her hand. The town clerk leaned back, pleased.

Pérsomi looked up. "Mr. Thompson, do you think the

amenities established by the council also guarantee *suitable economic conditions*? That the council has also provided suitable conditions under which the Indians can ply their trades?"

The town clerk frowned slightly. "I . . . don't understand."

There was silence in the courtroom. The magistrate was leaning slightly forward. "Explain the question, Miss Pieterse," he said.

Pérsomi picked up a second document from the table and turned to the magistrate. "This survey shows there are eight Indian families, which include thirty-seven working men, Your Honor. Four of them are teachers at the local school, one is a doctor, one is a tailor, two are builders, and one is a spiritual leader. The remaining twenty-eight Indian working men in our town are traders in the six existing stores—five general dealers and one hardware store.

"That means," she continued, "that a large majority of the people who have to relocate are traders dependent on the revenue from their stores. Do you agree, Mr. Thompson?"

"I didn't see the survey," he said cautiously.

She handed the document over and said, "Providing premises for stores and even buildings in the Modderkuil area is not enough. There must be buyers for their goods. It's the most important aspect, after all. Don't you agree that it's only logical that the traders cannot move their businesses to the new residential area before a community has settled there and the necessity has arisen for maybe one general dealer? Definitely not five. Don't you agree, Mr. Thompson?"

She continued without waiting for a reply. "Suitable living conditions within the bigger picture, Mr. Thompson, implies that people must be able to make an economically viable living in the area under discussion. Suitable living conditions should therefore include sufficient trading potential and the prospect of drawing customers to the area in the same numbers as before the relocation." She turned to the magistrate. "Without that, Your Honor, the town council has not fulfilled the socioeconomic requirements as stipulated by the law. No further questions."

"Mr. Lourens?" said the magistrate.

"Nothing further, Your Honor. The state closes the case for the prosecution," said the prosecutor without getting up.

"There will be a recess of fifteen minutes, whereafter the defense will state its case," said the magistrate.

"Miss Pérsomi, you are very smart," said Mr. Ismail as the men stood in the passage, drinking cold tea from a bottle.

Even Yusuf appeared more relaxed. "You're doing well, Pérsomi," he said. "I really don't know where you get all those arguments from."

"The worst is still to come," she warned. "Jakobus Lourens is experienced and shrewd. But fortunately the magistrate also has years of experience. We'll have to see what happens."

❧

Back in the courtroom, Pérsomi called Aletta Johanna Louw as the first witness for the defense. Lettie looked pale and there were fine beads of sweat on her nose. She adjusted her thick spectacles and hesitantly took her place on the witness stand.

"Dr. Louw, how do you know the defendants?" Pérsomi began, smiling reassuringly.

"I've known Mr. Ismail, Mr. Ravat, and Mr. Moosa all my life as storekeepers, just like everyone in town does. I've always regarded them as friendly, polite gentlemen, willing to help where they can. And . . . they are generous. They treat others with respect."

"And Dr. Yusuf Ismail?" asked Pérsomi.

"Dr. Yusuf Ismail and I studied at the same university, Wits in Johannesburg. He completed his studies six years after me. I know he was a brilliant student."

"And have you ever worked with him professionally, here in town?"

"I've assisted him during operations on several occasions, and he has done the same for me," Lettie answered. She was speaking softly, looking only at Pérsomi.

"And during the infantile paralysis epidemic four years ago?" Pérsomi asked gently.

Lettie swallowed. It was hard to talk about it. "During the infant . . ." She licked her lips. "During the epidemic Yusuf was . . . an absolute tower of strength. He worked day and night, and . . . took over when I couldn't carry on. As a colleague, I have the highest regard for him."

Pérsomi smiled encouragingly. "Dr. Louw," she asked, "what do you think would be the consequences if Dr. Yusuf Ismail had to move his surgery from the town center to Modderkuil?"

They had rehearsed the answer thoroughly. Lettie spoke a little louder than before. "I truly believe it would be a catastrophe, especially for his patients," she said. "There is no transport to Modderkuil. The patients would have to walk."

"They could go to the district surgeon in town, or to the non-white hospital," Pérsomi suggested.

"The district surgeon is available for consultations three mornings a week," said Lettie. "The rest of the time he deals with routine health matters. He can't see even a quarter of the patients waiting in long lines out in the sun."

She had forgotten about Yusuf's work at the nonwhite hospital, Pérsomi realized. "And how do you think Dr. Ismail's work at the hospital would be affected if he had to relocate?" she asked.

For a moment Lettie looked startled, but she soon composed herself. "He . . . Modderkuil and the township are at opposite ends of the town," she replied. "If Dr. Ismail had to relocate, he'd be about eight miles from the nonwhite hospital. It's a long way to travel there and back two or three times a day. In an emergency it could be the difference between life and death. And . . . Dr. Ismail does wonderful work at the hospital."

Pérsomi smiled. "That is all, Dr. Louw," she said and sat down.

Jakobus Lourens slowly got to his feet. There was an amused expression on his face. He stood looking at Lettie for a while. Sizing her up.

"*Doctor* Louw," he sneered. His body language was clear. *Why don't you and your lawyer friend go home—it's the proper place for a woman,* he seemed to be saying.

"That's right," said Lettie uncertainly.

"So, you say you know Dr. Yusuf Ismail personally?"

"I know him professionally, yes." Lettie licked her dry lips.

"I see. You knew him at university?"

"Not really. I was an intern when he was a first-year student. I lent him some of my books while he was studying."

"I see." Jakobus Lourens seemed to be examining the papers in his hand. Then he raised his eyes and asked, "Are you aware that Dr. Yusuf Ismail was involved with Communist activities at the university?"

Pérsomi got to her feet. "Objection, Your Honor! Speculation. It was never proved in a court of law that he was involved with Communist activities."

"Do you have any proof that Dr. Ismail was involved with such activities?" the magistrate asked Jakobus Lourens.

"His close friend, Benny Sischy, was found guilty of distributing Communist propaganda, and sentenced," Jakobus Lourens said somewhat brusquely. "It was mentioned in court that Yusuf Ismail participated in marches and demonstrations in favor of Communism and that he had close ties with the Reverend Michael Scott. We all know what that means, Your Honor."

"Was it proved in court?" the magistrate asked again.

"There wasn't sufficient evidence to find him guilty."

"Objection sustained," the magistrate said tersely.

Jakobus Lourens raised his bushy eyebrows. His expression clearly implied that everybody knew it was just a technical point.

The seed had been planted.

Jakobus Lourens turned back to Lettie. "Did you know, Dr. Louw, that this Dr. Yusuf Ismail, this Mohammedan of irreproachable character, while he was a student, was in a relationship with a white Jewish girl?"

Pérsomi felt herself grow ice-cold. She knew Jakobus Lourens's facts were seldom wrong.

"Objection!" she said loudly.

"I . . . didn't know," Lettie said, startled. Her eyes behind the thick lenses were as big as saucers.

"Do you know that the relationship was so serious that her father, also a well-known medical doctor in Johannesburg, was forced to get a court order to keep Yusuf Ismail away from his daughter?" the prosecutor continued.

Pérsomi jumped to her feet. "Your Honor, the prosecutor is completely out of order. The question is inappropriate and completely irrelevant to today's proceedings!"

But Jakobus Lourens ignored her. "Do you realize, Dr. Louw, that in the present dispensation he would have been charged under the Immorality Act?"

"Your Honor, I strongly object," Pérsomi said loudly. "The Immorality Act has absolutely nothing to do with this case. Dr. Louw was referring to Dr. Ismail's work as a medical practitioner in this town. His student days and his private life are completely irrelevant. Her evidence solely concerns his professional services."

"It appears he's willing to provide other services as well," the prosecutor scoffed.

Pérsomi heard someone snort behind her. Lettie visibly paled.

"That, Your Honor, is a despicable insinuation," Pérsomi said furiously. "I ask that you call the prosecutor to order. I demand that the remark be immediately withdrawn!"

"Withdrawn," said Jakobus Lourens with a nonchalant shrug of his shoulders. "No further questions, Your Honor."

"You will conduct yourself in a professional manner in my courtroom, Mr. Lourens, or I will rule you out of order. Is that clear?" said the magistrate.

"It is clear, Your Honor," said Jakobus Lourens, smiling serenely.

Just before Pérsomi sat down she saw Mr. Ismail's face. In a matter of minutes he seemed to have aged. His grandson, his pride and joy—a Communist? And even worse, his eldest grandson, bearer of the family name after his older brother had fallen on the battlefield, involved with a *Jewish* girl?

❦

The purple jacaranda blossoms lay in a thick carpet at their feet. The smell of the bruised flowers wafted up from under their sandals. Everyone was there: the heads of the families, the younger men, the women with their children pressed against them. Only Yusuf Ismail was absent. He had stepped out the minute the court was adjourned for the lunch hour.

The group was quiet. Dismayed. Even the children were quiet.

The minutes ticked past.

At last the clock in the church steeple struck two.

"We have a very good chance," Pérsomi said again before they went back inside.

But based on his knowledge of the law and his experience, the magistrate decided differently.

EIGHTEEN

"How could they do it?" Yusuf asked later that same afternoon when they were alone in Pérsomi's office, each holding a mug of tea. Though it wasn't cold outside, they had wrapped their hands around the mugs in search of warmth.

"I don't know," Pérsomi replied, "but they did. They've done it in the past, they'll certainly do it again in the future."

Yusuf closed his eyes and took a deep breath. "I'm going away, Pérsomi," he said.

She was gripped by a helpless grief. "To where? Joburg?"

He shook his head. "I can't stay in this country any longer. I'm leaving. I won't raise my children here. I'm going somewhere else, to a better place. England, probably, or maybe Australia."

It was as she had feared. "And . . . your family, Yusuf?" she asked, dismayed.

"My father is going to Pretoria. He decided a while ago that if the special permit wasn't granted he would open a new store there. He has a cousin in Laudium and he thinks he can make a living there."

"And your grandfather?"

"My grandparents are too old to move. They're staying here."

"Alone?" she asked, dismayed.

"The Ravats and the Moosas are staying. They're going to try

374

to make a living at Modderkuil," Yusuf replied, "though most of their sons have also decided to move on."

"We can still appeal. And we can appoint an advocate who—"

"We can't appeal, Pérsomi. We simply don't have the money."

She nodded quietly. Sadness filled her entire body.

When he had finished his tea, he got up. "I'll be on my way," he said.

At the door he turned. "In the end it wasn't the town council or the government who hurt my grandfather today—more than he had ever been hurt before, including when my eldest brother died. It was me. I think that's what saddens me most, Pérsomi."

Long after he was gone she remained in her chair, remembering that afternoon a lifetime ago, when two prospective students had cheerfully toasted each other with tea in tin mugs. "To us," Yusuf had said. "To Counselor Pérsomi and Doctor Yusuf!"

For two years the Indian stores stood abandoned, the houses huddled lifelessly around the shops. The alleys between the houses were deserted except for a few stray cats, and weeds flourished in the cracked surfaces of the narrow streets. Children no longer played outside, nor did women chat at the washing lines. At dusk no voices called out to one another, no delicious smells filled the air, no lights shone behind the windows of the dead houses and streets.

On Fridays life returned to the sacred ground of the freshly painted mosque for an hour or two. Hollow footsteps echoed through the deserted streets, respectful male voices rose in a murmuring chant. Then silence fell again.

When the town woke up on August 13, 1961, bulldozers were thundering down the streets. Children ran out to stand at garden gates, and housewives pushed white lace curtains aside to take a peek. Dogs barked at the terrifying yellow monsters in the streets.

Pérsomi put on her tailored suit and fixed her hair in a chignon. Though the windows and doors were all tightly closed, the roar of the vehicles filled the townhouse.

"The bulldozers are here. Aunt Duifie and I are going to watch," said her ma.

"Yes, Ma," said Pérsomi.

The noise followed her to work and into her office. The muted drone, the mounting revolutions of the engines, the dim noise of collapsing structures cut right through her, threatening to suffocate her.

Brown dust sifted down on everything.

She worked ceaselessly, but the noise ripped through everything, entered her being.

"Maybe it would be better if you go and take a look, Pérsomi," De Wet said at lunchtime. "Maybe it will make it real, bring some closure."

"I . . . don't want to see it."

"I still think you should go."

But she went back to her office and closed the door behind her. Brown dust was beginning to coat the white walls of the office.

Just after three she got up and left the building. She did not get into her car. She wasn't planning to go anywhere. But the town center drew her like a magnet. She found herself hurrying down the street.

She saw the commotion from a distance. The crowd of onlookers had dispersed, the buzz had died down, and the townspeople had gone to wash the dust from their clothing, their faces and hands. "It will take days to clean up our houses," Pérsomi heard someone say.

"And the town!" another agreed. "But it's a good thing they're cleaning up that slum."

Pérsomi slowed down. The face of the main street had changed. On one side the bakery and the butchery and the service station and the corner café remained. On the other side, she could see nothing but rubble where curved pillars and wide verandas and little stores full of magical wares had stood for decades.

Heavy trucks were idling in the streets. Diggers pushed their arms deep into the rubble, scooping up broken bricks, pieces of plaster, and bent sheets of metal, then dumping them securely onto a waiting truck bed.

When the load was full, the truck pulled away slowly and the next one took its place. The community's life was carted away piece by piece to the garbage dump.

The ache of grief filled Pérsomi.

She crossed the street to where the rubble lay in piles. A rope prevented the public from coming any closer.

From a distance she gazed at the skeletons of buildings, their roofs torn off, their windows broken. The bulldozers were still growling and roaring, digging and pushing, their gigantic jaws extended, uprooting and flattening everything in their way. A pink wall gave way, twisted windowframes bent like hairpins under the violence. Another wall, covered in blue-and-yellow wallpaper, remained stubbornly upright, a gaping tunnel through it like an open wound.

After a while she discovered that Boelie was standing beside her. "I didn't want to come," she said, "but I had to."

"De Wet told me, yes," he said and put his hand on her shoulder.

They didn't speak again. He stayed by her side.

Finally, the five-room schoolhouse yielded under the wheels of the bulldozers and caterpillars. It was the last building to remain standing.

Except the mosque.

Brown dust stained the whitewashed wall around the church.

Boelie stroked her hair and said, "Come, Pers, I'll take you home."

NINETEEN

On January 10, 1968, Jacobus Johannes Fouché was inaugurated as the second State President of the Republic of South Africa. In the United States, President Lyndon B. Johnson's government was wavering. The war in Vietnam was taking its toll. Robert Kennedy announced that he was planning to run as presidential candidate, in honor of his late brother.

In March a massive gold embargo was launched against South Africa. The world wanted to force its biggest supplier of gold to abolish the apartheid policy.

"This gold boycott could deal our economy a severe blow," De Wet remarked at the dinner table on Sunday.

"The Outspan boycott will hit you and me a lot harder, brother," Boelie said. "People are protesting in the streets of London, Paris, and Madrid against South African oranges. Where are we going to find a market for our produce this year?"

In April the foremost civil rights leader in America, Martin Luther King Jr., was assassinated. "This murder will have wide repercussions," De Wet said at teatime. And two months later, when Robert Kennedy met with the same fate, he said: "The year 1968 is going to be a watershed, worldwide."

Lientjie was invited to her first evening party. "I'm so excited, Pérsomi," she said on Sunday. "We're going to dance, and everything! I must wear the right clothes!"

"Why don't you wear the green dress your mom brought from England last time she was here on a visit?"

"Pérsomi! I hate green, you know that. Besides, I hate that dress. My dad said he'd give me money for a new dress."

"Your dad spoils you," Pérsomi said lazily from her deck chair.

"My dad is super strict!" Lientjie protested. "Pérsomi, don't fall asleep, I want to talk to you. Do you know why I've got to look nice?"

Pérsomi gave a slow smile. "I won't sleep, I promise. And I know why you want to look nice—for the new minister's son."

Lientjie drew a sharp breath. "How did you know?"

"I noticed the way the handsome young lad was looking at you this morning," Pérsomi answered, enjoying the Sunday afternoon languor.

Lientjie's cheeks flamed. "He's taller than me, did you see?" Lientjie chattered on. "Pérsomi, open your eyes. If you close your eyes, you're going to fall asleep, I know. Pérsomi, will you come with me to look for a dress? You're so chic, I want to look like you."

Pérsomi opened her eyes lazily and smiled at the girl. "I'd love to go with you. It would be nice."

"And I want to do something special with my hair."

"Your hair is special anyway."

"Yes, but . . . I want to cut my hair, wear it like my mom's. She's very pretty. Do you think we could cut my hair?"

"You'll have to discuss it with your dad."

"But Pérsomi, if you tell him we must cut my hair, he'll agree. When I ask him for something, he always says, 'What does Pérsomi say?' Will you ask him?"

"No, love," Pérsomi said firmly, "you'll have to ask him yourself. Your dad loves long hair."

There was a moment's silence, then Lientjie asked, "Pérsomi, are you asleep?"

"No-o, not really."

"Have you ever been in love?"

Pérsomi opened her eyes. "Yes, head over heels."

"Can you remember what it felt like?"

Pérsomi closed her eyes again and smiled. "Yes, Lientjie, I remember."

"It's . . . very nice, isn't it?"

"Very, very nice," Pérsomi agreed. "But being in love means you could get hurt, sometimes badly."

Lientjie sighed. "I know." After a while she asked, "Will you tell me one day? About the boy who hurt you?"

Boy? "He didn't hurt me, Lientjie. The situation hurt us both. But it was long ago. It's over now. I don't talk about it anymore. I'm happy with my present life."

In the late afternoon, just before she left, Boelie said: "I'm glad Lientjie's got you. She's such a reserved child, you're the only one she really talks to."

"She's lovely, Boelie," said Pérsomi with a smile.

His dark eyes became very gentle. "She's not the only one," he said and closed her car door.

The year 1968 turned out to be a good one for De Vos and De Vos. The tin mine outside the town made plans to expand, new contracts came through, a new residential area went up. The provincial hospital added a wing, a second primary school opened, and even the Indian area at Modderkuil showed unexpected growth.

Good rains fell in the bushveld. The cattle in the grassy valleys and scrubland grew plump. In the fields, brand-new John Deere and Massey Ferguson and Fordson tractors plowed deep furrows in the red earth. The citrus farmers formed a closed corporation and built their own juice factory.

When the farmers prosper, so do the lawyers and speculators, the storekeepers and the business owners. And the architects.

"I'll have to take in a partner," Reinier said one Sunday. "I want to come over tomorrow to discuss it with you, if it's okay, De Wet."

"I wish Antonio could go in with you," said Christine dreamily, "then Klara could also come and live here."

"Wishful thinking, Chrissie." Reinier smiled. "Antonio has a thriving practice in the city. He'd never give it up."

"But Klara did say they would like to return here one day," Christine said. "Maybe they'll come. I'm really looking forward to Christmas, when everyone will be here again."

Pérsomi looked up into Boelie's eyes, just for a moment, then she looked away. But she knew that Boelie understood. "Everyone here" meant different things to different people.

Once or twice Lewies Pieterse approached Pérsomi for money, but lately he had been keeping his distance. No one knew where Piet was. Sissie, still happily married to her widower, worked in the kitchen of a Western Transvaal boarding school. They lived too far away to come for Christmas this year.

Only Hannapat, her handy husband, and their four children would make the long trip to the bushveld. Then Hannapat and their ma would sit in the front room, chatting for hours. Pérsomi would keep busy trying to fill the tummies of the four lively kids, and the handy husband would fix everything around the house that needed fixing.

"There you are! It should see you through till next Christmas," he would say before he left.

Her ma would say, "Hannapat has clever children."

And Pérsomi would say, "Yes, Ma."

Early one Saturday morning in December 1968 there was a knock on the front door.

Pérsomi had just come out of the bath and wrapped a towel around her wet hair. She hurried down the passage and opened the door.

Boelie stood on the doorstep, his dark eyes fixed on her, the shadow of a smile on his lips. His hair was more gray than she remembered, but he was still well built, tall, proud.

"Good morning, Pérsomi."

His voice still thrilled her.

"Good morning, this is a surprise," she said evenly. "Come in, how about some coffee?"

"No, thanks," he said. "I want you to come with me."

"Now?" she asked, puzzled, and looked past him to where his car was parked in the street.

"Yes, now," he said.

She looked down at her short summer frock and bare feet. "Like this?"

"You look lovely, Pérsomi. Just put shoes on, bare feet won't do, and take that . . . er . . . towel-turban thing off your head."

She began to laugh. "Boelie, my hair is sopping wet. I'm not wearing makeup. And my—"

"Come," he ordered.

In a daze, she went to her room. When she unwrapped the towel from her head, her wet hair tumbled down on her shoulders. At the mirror she pressed her hands to her flushed cheeks.

Then the shock hit her. She raced back to the porch on bare feet. "Boelie, did something happen to Lientjie? Or Nelius? Who's in the hospital?"

He gave her a reassuring smile. "Nothing's wrong, Pérsomi. We just have a . . . surprise for you, I hope. Wear walking shoes, you hear?"

Walking shoes? She put on shorts and a cool blouse. She couldn't very well wear walking shoes with a summer frock. With a ribbon she tied her wet hair into a ponytail and returned to the front porch. "I'll be back in a while, Ma," she called toward her ma's bedroom door.

Boelie opened the car door and she got in.

"It must be a big surprise," she said. "You're looking so pleased."

He smiled down at her and closed the door.

"Are we going to the farm?" she asked as they drove through the town.

"What do you think?"

"To De Wet's place?"

"Stop being so nosy, Pérsomi," he said. "Wait and see."

On their way to the farm they chatted as usual, at ease in each other's company. She asked about the kids and his parents and how the new Bonsmara cattle he had bought were doing. He heard about the labor problems at the new tin mine and the planned new development at the hot springs outside the town.

They crossed the Pontenilo and he turned in at his farm gate instead of continuing to De Wet's farm.

"Boelie?" she asked.

He smiled but did not say anything as he drove past the farm-house and stopped in the barn. "Come," he said again.

She felt strangely ill at ease as she got out of the car. She had not been in Boelie's home since he and Annabel moved in. Even the slaughtering had taken place at De Wet's house on the Le Roux farm.

Boelie opened the trunk and took out a backpack.

"Where are we going?"

He motioned for her to follow and began to walk along the footpath to the mountain. She followed, but stopped after a while. "Tell me, where are you going?"

"We're going for a walk," he said over his shoulder.

She didn't budge. "Where are the kids?"

He stopped and turned. "Relax, Pérsomi, everything is fine. Just come." He turned and continued along the footpath.

She followed him as the going got harder. She watched his calf muscles contract and relax, his muscular shoulders and arms, toughened by hours of physical labor. His skin was bronzed from daily exposure to the African sun.

She was hurting herself, she realized. She looked away.

They were out of the scrubland now, surrounded by rocks and ledges, where grass and wild plum trees struggled to get a grip on the soil. "Can we rest?" she asked.

He stopped for a moment. "Tired?" he asked.

"Not really."

"We're nearly there," he said and carried on walking.

The kids must be waiting at the top, she guessed. Maybe De Wet and Christine would be there as well.

They passed the baboon cliffs. She looked down and saw the waterfall and the old wild fig by the pool.

Suddenly she felt inexplicably vulnerable, almost sad. She stopped. "I . . . don't want to go to the cave, Boelie."

He turned. He was standing on a rock about two feet above her. His expression was serious, his voice soothing. "We must go to the cave, Pérsomi," he said and held out his hand.

She hesitated a moment, then took his hand. He pulled her up until she was standing beside him. "Would you like to rest for a while?" he asked.

She shook her head. "No, I'm fine," she said.

He let go of her hand and they walked on in silence. The sun blazed down on their heads, shoulders, and arms. "This had better be a good surprise," she said.

At the cave, no one was there. Pérsomi looked around in vain.

"There's no one," he said, sitting down on the stone floor in the mouth of the cave. He placed the backpack beside him. "Sit down, won't you?" he said.

She didn't sit. She stood, waiting for him to explain.

He calmly gazed at the landscape below: at his farm, the barren ridge on the other side of the Pontenilo, and the road winding its way toward the town.

"Who else did you mean when you said *we*?" she asked.

"I had to say it, or you wouldn't have come."

"I didn't want to come to the cave again, Boelie. Why did you bring me here?"

"I had to," he said. "Sit, please."

She shook her head and sighed. Then she sank down beside him.

"I hope there's food in that backpack," she said, trying to lighten the atmosphere. "I'm famished. And parched."

"Plenty," he said and drew the backpack closer.

But he did not open it. Instead, he put his hand into a side pocket and took out a document. Without a word he held it out to her.

Frowning slightly, she took the document, unfolded it carefully, and glanced at its contents.

Application for the Dissolution of the Marriage Between Annabel Fourie (Nee De Vos) and Cornelius Johannes Fourie . . .

Shock jolted through her. She looked up. His dark eyes were regarding her seriously.

Divorce? The word flashed through her confused mind. "Who requested it?"

He kept looking at her. "Annabel. From England."

She glanced down at the document, looked up at him again. She felt a kind of practiced professionalism take over. "Divorce is divorce, Boelie, no matter who requested it."

"Adultery is not only against the seventh commandment, Pérsomi. It is also the only biblical grounds for divorce."

She drew a deep breath. "There's another man?"

He nodded. "She met someone, yes. Through her work."

"After . . . all these years?"

"No, Pérsomi. Long ago. But his wife had the money. She died about six months ago."

Her hand flew to her face. "You knew? All the time?"

"Yes, Pérsomi."

Her brain seemed to have frozen. The open mouth of the cave was swallowing her. She got up and walked away.

She looked down at the document in her hand.

She registered the date. The divorce was made final the previous Monday.

"Pérsomi?" his voice got through to her.

She turned. He was standing five yards away.

"I love you," he said for the first time in nearly seventeen years.

She stood transfixed.

He opened his arms. "Come to me."

Something deep inside her began to thaw—the ramparts built over years began to crumble.

He smiled, his dark eyes infinitely gentle.

She kept staring at him. Her mind could not think clearly, but her heart beat warmly.

She felt herself break open, begin to fly. "I love you, too, Boelie."

He reached for her and untied the ribbon round her ponytail. He pulled his fingers through her long, cascading hair. "Pérsomi, will you marry me?"

She reached out and stroked his rough cheek. Her heart sang.

Her head was nodding and nodding. "Yes, Boelie," she said, "yes."

He clasped her to his solid body. After a lifetime she once more felt his wild heartbeat against her own heart. She felt the strength of the man she loved and knew she would never be alone again.

DISCUSSION QUESTIONS

1. The novel contains three basic storylines. The first deals with Pérsomi's personal life—she's the child of a poor white *bywoner*, or sharecropper. How does Pérsomi's background define her perception of herself, and how does her upbringing inform her decisions about how to invest her life?

2. The second storyline deals with the Apartheid laws. Based on what you learned from this story, how was Apartheid-era South Africa similar to or different from the Jim Crow American South?

3. The third storyline is the romance between Pérsomi and Boelie. Did you find the progression of their relationship compelling or frustrating? Did you feel, by the end of the novel, that Pérsomi and Boelie could truly forgive the past and overcome their political differences and have a happy life together?

4. Discuss Pérsomi and Boelie's very different understandings about how the teachings of the Bible should inform their attitudes toward Apartheid.

5. Who are the male figures who play significant roles in Pérsomi's life, and which part do they each play?

6. Who are the key female figures who play a life-shaping role in Pérsomi's story? How does Pérsomi manage to overcome the lack of strong female role models in her life?

7. Pérsomi's mother tolerates behavior from her husband that is extremely difficult for us to accept. Why does she not take stronger steps to protect her family?

8. Pérsomi never experiences the ravages of WWII first hand, but the war has a huge impact on her life. Discuss the way that the war shapes Pérsomi's destiny and her perceptions of the world around her.

9. Pérsomi rises above her circumstances and pursues an education and uses that education in support of a deeply held political belief that puts her into conflict with those closest to her. What is it about Pérsomi's character and/or experience that allows her to become the idealist that she is? Why do some people rise above their circumstances while others become a product or a victim of their circumstances?

10. Define and discuss Pérsomi's core beliefs and defining values and how they inform her choices and decisions.

11. Can the fact that Pérsomi was kept in the dark about the identity of her biological father be considered a deciding factor in her life? If yes, how so?

12. What was your reaction to the outcome of Pérsomi's legal efforts to protect the Indian population from being forced to leave their homes?

ACKNOWLEDGMENTS

THANKS TO EVERYONE WHO COMES TO ME WITH A STORY—
all my historic novels are based on true stories people have
told me.

Thanks to Oom Leon van Deventer and Mr. Ravat, both
from Nylstroom, who lived through the relocation of the Indian
traders from the town during the Group Areas Act and gave me
incredibly valuable firsthand information and insights.

Thanks to Dr. Nico Smith, who granted me a few interviews shortly before his death in June 2010. He was the minister
at Louis Trichardt during the late 1950s and experienced the
forced removal of the Indian community. And to my mom, Alida
Moerdyk, who clearly recalled the Centenary celebrations, the
Second World War, and the relocations, and could tell me anec-
dotes and answers that are not in books.

Thanks to Johannes de Villiers for fascinating information
on spiritualism and superstition among Afrikaners in the first
half of the previous century, and for the books and articles he
recommended.

A special thanks to friend Daan Nortier of Bloemfontein
and my son Wikus, who helped me with the apartheid laws
dealing specifically with the Indian community and with court
proceedings.

Thanks to Jan-Jan, Madeleine, and Suzette for advice with

the manuscript. Thank you very much, Elize, for excellent ideas during the writing process and for the language editing you are always willing to do for me.

Thanks to my husband, Jan, who keeps loving his wife who writes.

Most of all, thanks to my heavenly Father, who gave me a childhood that allows me to keep myself occupied in my retirement years, and who still fills my imagination with stories.

SOURCES

Bizos, George. *No One to Blame? In Pursuit of Justice in South Africa.* Cape Town: David Philip Publishers, 1998.

Botha, D. P. *Die opkoms van ons Derde Stand.* Cape Town: Human & Rousseau, 1960.

Coetzee, Abel. *Die Afrikaanse Volksgeloof.* Amsterdam: N. V. Swerts & Zertlinger Boekhandel & Uitgeversmij, 1938.

Du Plessis, I. D. *Goëlery.* Cape Town: Nasionale Pers, 1941.

Grobler, Jackie. *Ontdek die Voortrekkermonument.* Pretoria: Grourie Entrepreneurs, 1999.

Grosskopf, J. F. W. *Plattelandsverarming en Plaasverlating.* Stellenbosch, 1932.

Hall, Walter, and William Davis. *The Course of Europe Since Waterloo.* New York: Appleton-Century-Crofts Inc., 1951.

Keene, John, ed. *South Africa in World War II.* Cape Town: Human & Rousseau, 1995.

Leipoldt, C. Louis. *The Bushveld Doctor.* London: Jonathan Cape Ltd., 1937; Cape Town: Human & Rousseau, 1980.

Orpen, Neil. *Cape Town Rifles—The Dukes 1856–1984.* Self-published, 1984.

Reddy, E. S. "Defiance Campaign in South Africa, Recalled," *Asian Times*, 26 June 1987.

Strydom, Hans. *For Volk and Führer: Robey Leibbrandt & Operation Weissdorn.* Jonathan Ball Publishers, 1983.

Terblanche, H. O. *John Vorster—OB-Generaal en Afrikanervegter.* Cum Books, 1983.

Van Wyk, At. *Vyf dae*. Tafelberg, 1985.

Vermeulen, Irma. *Man en Monument—die lewe en werk van Gerard Moerdijk*. J. L. Van Schaik, 1999.

Verslag van die Carnegie-kommissie, Deel I, Ekonomiese verslag. Stellenbosch: Pro Ecclesia Printers, 1932.

ABOUT THE AUTHOR

 INTERNATIONAL BESTSELLING AUTHOR Irma Joubert lives and works in South Africa and writes in her native Afrikaans. A teacher for thirty-five years, Irma began to write after her retirement. She is the author of eight novels and is a fixture on bestseller lists in both South Africa and the Netherlands. Irma and her husband Jan have been married for forty-five years, and they have three sons and a daughter, two daughters-in-law, a son-in-law, and three grandchildren. Another one of her novels, *The Girl from the Train*, has also been translated into English.

ENJOY AN EXCERPT FROM
IRMA JOUBERT'S
THE GIRL FROM THE TRAIN

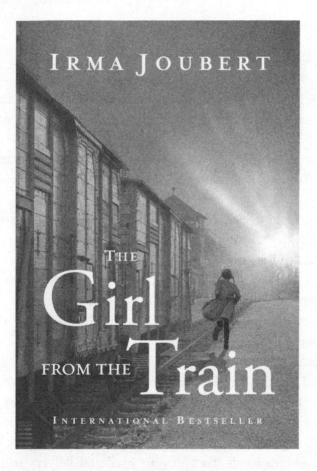

1

SOUTHERN POLAND, APRIL 1944

"LET GO!" HER GRANDMOTHER SAID.

She held on for dear life. The metal edge bit into her fingers. Her frantic feet searched for a foothold in the air. The dragon swayed dangerously from side to side.

"Gretl, let go!" Her grandmother's shrill voice cut through the huffing noise of the dragon. "We're nearly at the top, you must let go *now!*"

The child looked down. The ground was a long way below. Strewn with sharp stones, it sloped down into a deep gully.

Her arms were aching.

Her fingers were losing their grip.

Then her grandmother pried her fingers loose.

Gretl hit the ground. Shock jolted through her skinny little body.

She fell, slid, rolled down the embankment, stones grazing her face and legs. She clenched her jaw to stop herself from screaming.

At the bottom she slid to a stop. For a moment she lay panting, her heart pounding in her ears. It was so loud that she was afraid the guards might hear.

"Roll into a ball. Tuck in your head and lie very still," her grandmother had told her. "And don't move until Elza comes to find you."

She rolled into a ball. The earth trembled. Beside her, around her, she felt sand and stones shifting. She kept her head down. Above her the long dragon was still groaning and puffing up the hill, spitting smoke and pumping steam. She could smell its rancid breath, but she didn't look.

It was at the top now. She heard it panting, the iron wheels *clickety-clacking* faster and faster on the track.

She was very thirsty.

It was dead quiet.

Slowly she opened her eyes to the pitch-black night. There were no stars.

"What if we're afraid?" Elza had asked.

"Then you think about other things," Oma had said.

Mutti had just cried, without tears, because she had no more water in her body for tears. *I'm not afraid*, Gretl thought. *I escaped from the dragon. First Elza, then me. I'm brave. So is Elza.*

Carefully, painfully, she rolled onto her back and straightened her legs. They were still working, but her knee burned.

At the next uphill, Mutti and Oma would jump out as well. Then they would all go back to Oma's little house at the edge of the forest. *Not* to the ghetto.

There was sand in her mouth. No saliva. If only she could have just a sip of water.

Gingerly she rubbed her smarting knee. It felt sticky and clammy.

The water had run out yesterday, before the sun was even up. At the station the grown-ups put their arms through the railings of the cars and pleaded for water. But the guards with their rifles made sure that no one gave them any. The dogs with the teeth and the drooling jaws barked endlessly. And drank sloppily from large bowls.

The train had filled its belly with water.

"Don't look, think about other things," Oma had said. Oma's face looked strange, blistered by the sun. She had lost her hat.

Her voice had been strange as well. Dry.

Later Mutti stopped crying. Just sat.

It was hard to think about other things.

Gretl wasn't afraid of the dark. "Darkness is your best friend," Oma had said. "Get as far away from the railroad as possible while it's still dark. And hide during the day."

But now there were no stars at all, and the moon appeared only briefly from behind the clouds. Now and again there was a flash of lightning.

She wasn't afraid of lightning. Maybe it would rain soon. Then she would roll onto her back, open her mouth, and let the rain fill her up until she overflowed.

She had to think about other things.

Oma had a little house at the edge of the forest. Like Hansel and Gretel's, but without the witch. In the forest they picked berries. She knew there was no wolf, but she always stayed close to Mutti or Elza just the same.

Maybe she should sit up and softly call Elza's name. The guards and their dogs were gone, over the hill. She no longer heard the *choo-choo* and *clickety-clack*. Elza would never find her in this blackness.

She sat up slowly. Her head ached a little. She peered into the curtain of fog that surrounded her, trying hard to focus. She could see nothing.

"Elza?" Her voice was thin.

She took a deep breath. "Elza!" Much better. "Elza! El-zaa-a!"

Not even a cricket replied.

Jakób Kowalski moved the heavy bag to his other shoulder. Flashes of lightning played sporadically among the dense clouds. It was their only source of light. The terrain was reasonably even underfoot, but as soon as they started the descent toward the river they would need to see where they were going. He ran his fingers through his black hair and screwed up his eyes.

"I can barely see a thing," said Zygmund behind him. At odd intervals his voice still cracked. He was barely fifteen.

"And the rain is going to catch us," Andrei complained. "Why do we have to do it tonight?"

"The coded message said the troop train will pass here just before daybreak, on its way back to Germany." Jakób felt his patience wearing thin. The Home Army had given him two adolescents to help with this dangerous mission. "We must plant the bombs under the bridge before then."

"And you're sure there are no guards on the bridge?" asked Andrei.

"I'm not sure of anything," Jakób replied brusquely, "except that we've got to blow up the bridge tonight."

In silence they progressed slowly under the weight of their cargo through the tall grass and bushes. When the moon appeared for a moment from behind the clouds, Jakób said, "Let's go down here."

"Will we have to swim downstream?" Andrei asked. "Or clamber over the rocks?"

"It's going to be hard with the bags," said Zygmund.

"Are you in or are you out?" Jakób asked, exasperated. "If you're in, shut your traps."

They struggled down the steep slope, slipping in places, clinging to their dangerous load. The clouds seemed to be lifting somewhat, and once or twice the moon showed its face.

Dislodged stones rolled down the slope, splashing into the water.

The final trek to the bridge took them more than half an hour. The water rushed past, glimmering in the faint moonlight. They tried to stay at the water's edge, but the pebbles were round and smooth and the bank was steep. The heavy bags dragged at their shoulders. The darkness provided good cover, but it also made the going tough. After every few steps Jakób stopped to listen, trying to figure out where they were. Then the clouds lit up faintly in the distance, there was a crash of thunder, and Jakób saw the bridge about ten yards ahead.

We're here, he motioned.

The other two showed him a thumbs-up.

At the bridge, Jakób placed their bags at the foot of the second column. Zygmund took off his boots, then his coat. Jakób tied two ropes around his waist. *I'm going up,* Zyg motioned, and he began to climb.

His progress was painfully slow. He found an occasional foothold on the crossbars of the smooth, steel column, but for the most part he had to hoist his wiry body up by his own strength. Fortunately the clouds seemed to be receding. Jakób stared upward, tension tightening between his shoulder blades, but all he could see was an occasional vague movement. Next to him Andrei stood waiting to catch the ropes. It was dead quiet.

After what seemed like an eternity, they saw both ends of one rope dangling in front of them, swinging beside the steel column. They attached the first bag to one end, then Jakób and Andrei pulled on the opposite end while Zyg worked at the top, all three of them lifting the shells together, inch by inch, careful not to let the bag swing.

After the bag with its hazardous contents arrived safely at the top, they transported the second load, a landmine acquired after the

Home Army regaled a Russian battalion with homemade vodka, then relieved them of an entire consignment of light weaponry.

The third load was more difficult. It was an unexploded two-hundred-pound bomb left behind when the Nazis had passed through Poland in 1940. The slightest jolt might set it off. It took all Jakób's and Andrei's strength to hoist the bag.

When it was at the top, Jakób said, "Hold it steady. I'll tie the rope to the base of the column."

"Okay, but hurry," Andrei answered, panting.

When the rope was firmly secured, Zyg sent down the second rope for Jakób to climb. He removed his shoes and tested it before he began his ascent. He hauled his lithe body up the rough cord without too much difficulty, his muscles honed since boyhood by farm labor, his hands toughened over the past three years at the steelworks. A moment later he sat on the crossbar next to Zygmund.

Zyg clung to the bag containing the bomb. Together they found a good position for it under the track. It was a pity they had to sacrifice the sturdy bag, but removing the heavy bomb was too dangerous. Next they planted the landmine, took a final look around to make sure everything was ready, and began their careful descent.

The return journey was a lot easier. They were rid of their heavy load, and the clouds that had been obscuring the moon were dispersing. The two boys were frantic to get away, as if they had only just realized the adventure was real.

Jakób looked at the sky. In less than an hour, he reckoned, the moon would set. It would be about another three hours before daybreak.

Zygmund said, "I hear a train."

"Impossible," said Jakób.

"It's a train," Zygmund insisted.

They turned and looked downriver in the direction of the

bridge, which was no more than two hundred yards from their present position.

Then Jakób heard it as well. "Find shelter!" he shouted. "Behind this rock! Quick!"

They scurried over the loose stones, then threw themselves down behind a low, flat rock. "Will this be enough cover?" asked Zygmund.

"It'll have to do," said Jakób.

He saw a light drilling a tunnel through the darkness and felt shock shoot through his body. "The train is coming from the wrong direction!" he exclaimed. "It can't be the—"

A brilliant flash lit up the sky, the horizon exploded with an incredible boom, and a blinding light shot upward, as if an enormous thunderstorm had been let loose over the bridge.

"God help us!" said Andrei, covering his head with both hands.

There were the sounds of steel ripping apart, of people screaming.

A second blast followed, louder than the first. Zygmund drew his head into the shell of his body. "Mother Mary!" he sobbed.

Andrei cursed and crossed his broad chest twice.

"That was the boiler exploding," said Jakób.

But where had this train come from? From the wrong side? On its way to . . .

In a flash he knew. Nausea pushed up in his throat, bitter as gall. "Come," he said. "Let's go."

The story continues in Irma Joubert's *The Girl From the Train* . . .